Spark of Sorcery

The Firestone Academy
Book 2

Hannah Haze

Foreword

This book is a 'why choose' paranormal romance with one female main character and more than one potential love interest. This story is based in a dystopian world where the powerful prey on the weak and where much inequality and unfairness exists. There is physical and verbal bullying of the female main character in this story (although not by the love interests) as well as steamy scenes. For more detailed content warnings, please visit my website.

If you spot any typos in this book, please drop me a line so I can make it right: hannahhazewrites@gmail.com (Or just drop me an email anyway. I love to chat!).

The Realm

Prologue

Briony

Fresh earth hits the top of the plain wooden coffin, dissolving into the sheets of rain and forming a thick sludge that sticks to the surface.

To one side of me stands my father, silent, swaying slightly in his old winter coat. Beyond him is the priest. He's wrapped up warm but his face is just as hard and worn as my father's, and though he says the words he's meant to, they're said with no feeling and compassion.

What's another girl dead after all? One from Slate? One without a mother? One less mouth to feed, one less soul to worry over. It's not like anyone expected her to go off to the academy and return to anywhere but this wasteland of a Quarter.

No one believed that. No one but her and me.

I stare down at the rapidly disappearing coffin and try to

imagine her laid out down there, in the cold, in the mud, all alone.

How could this have happened? It seems so unfair – so damned unfair – to lose a mother first and then a sister – a sister who had been more of a parent to me than my own father.

I have the urge to leap down into that hole with her, to scrape back the thick, sticky muck with my hands, and pry open the lid.

She'd blink up at me and grin, her nose crinkling.

"Only joking, Briony!"

I'd grab her by the hand, tug her right out of that ugly box and run with her, run with her far far away.

Like I should have done when she was alive.

But she isn't. She's gone. Taken from me. And when I can't take it any longer, when the sight of my precious sister swamped by all that mud has acid sloshing in my stomach, burning in my throat, I turn and run away alone.

No Amelia by my side – even if I think I hear her voice in the wind rushing through the towering branches of the yew trees overhead.

That's how it will be from now on. Just me.

Apart from the wind, no one calls after me. Nobody tells me to stop. I wonder if they even notice me gone.

I run away from the old stone church and its circle of graves, down the hill, away from the town and out to the woods, plunging into the darkness of the undergrowth, running and running, not caring at the way the branches scratch at my face or scrape against my legs, ripping the only pair of stockings I own.

I just keep running. There's no point in stopping. There is nothing to stop for, and I don't want to go back there. Without Amelia, there is no home.

Soon I know I'm lost deep in the forest, the sky gray with the incoming night, the wildlife out here stirring awake – a screech, a howl, a far off bark.

I stop.

Do I want to die? Is that why I came all this way? To fall down a ravine and break my neck or meet one of the old grizzlies and have my innards mauled?

"Do you want to join me, Briony?" she calls far above me as she rushes through the trees.

My face is wet with tears; they roll down my cheeks, run off my chin and drip onto my coat, lost among all the raindrops.

I shake my head.

I'm not ready to go yet, I call back, *not until...*

Not until I've made them pay for what they did to her. For taking her from me. She gave me everything. This is the least I can do for her.

It's as I say these words to myself – or do I whisper them out loud? – that I first feel it. A force outside my body, pulling me along, as if I am a piece of old metal and it is a magnet.

At first, I pull back against it, peering down at my feet and wondering if I am losing my mind.

But then I think, what the heck? I've lost everything now. My sister to the academy, my father to the bottom of a liquor bottle. Neither is coming back.

I let the force pull me. At first, it's weak, my feet moving slowly, but then the force grows stronger and stronger, pulling me along more quickly until I'm running through the forest again, this time leaping over scrubs, and ducking under branches.

I'm even more lost. This isn't a part of the forest I know, one I've ever seen. It's wetter here and greener, vines spinning up the trees and moss covering the stones and sticks on the forest floor. The dying light glows an emerald-green and when I lift my hand to my face, even my skin is tinged with it. The air is heavy, too, with moisture, the chill less permeating in this carpet of lush greenery and sweat trickles down my spine.

Then I see it – a small pond beneath the trees. The light has almost gone now and the waters are black like tar. It's impossible to see how deep it sits, but across its surface rest bright white lily pads – the kind of which I've not seen before.

The force beckons me onward.

"Uh uh," I say out loud. "I'm not wading into that."

My imagination is running wild. Perhaps I have gone mad? Chasing feelings through the forest with dusk falling. But I'm not mad enough to plunge into unknown waters. I'd freeze to death. Or perhaps I'd be pulled down to my grave, drowned without anyone ever knowing.

No, thank you.

The force doesn't take no for an answer, it continues to pull. I dig my heels into the mud and cling to an overhead branch to stop myself from being dragged forward.

But then, just as quickly as it started, it stops. I stumble backward into the undergrowth. When I pick myself up, the pond glows a deep orange in front of me. It lasts but for a fraction of a second before it plunges into darkness again. However, it's long enough for me to have seen what lies on its bottom.

A small black stone, the size of a large goose egg.

I don't know how, but I know it is that egg that has pulled me here.

But why? What does it want me to do?

Rolling up my sleeves, I kneel down by the side of the

pond, the wet and the mud penetrating through my stockings, and lean over the water. The depths are too dark for me to make the egg out now, but I guess where it was and plunge my arms down into the water. It's icy and I gasp, the cold permeating right the way up into my chest.

I swim my hands through the water, searching for the egg beneath the surface. Finally, when I think I can no longer bear the cold water any longer, the back of my left fingers hit something hard and solid. I feel at it with my fingers and my palms.

The egg.

Gripping it carefully, I pull at it. The mud has sucked it tight, but with more effort, I yank it free and it comes bobbing up towards the surface, floating right in front of me. It is blacker than the water, so black it has no marking or coloring at all.

I cradle it carefully and bring it out onto dry land, admiring the smooth polish of its surface. It's warm to touch, like freshly baked bread, and it smells like the forest and the pond.

It's beautiful. A giant precious jewel.

I could take it to old Jeb in the market. They say he'll buy just about anything hidden under the table. I'm sure this would fetch a fair few pennies – perhaps enough to feed us for weeks, even months.

But even as I think it, the stone warm and smooth between my palms, I know I won't.

The stone asked me to find it and I will keep it safe.

Chapter One

B eaufort

"You're handling this all wrong," Thorne growls at my retreating back.

I pause and spin around. He stands at the bottom of Briony's tower, straight-backed, chin raised, like a soldier lining up for inspection.

Dray hovers in the space between us, eyes flicking from me to Thorne and back again.

"What am I handling incorrectly, Brother?" I snap.

"The girl," he says.

I almost laugh out loud. Is he serious? He's hardly spoken two words to her. Has refused to spend any time with her. And now he's going to lecture me on 'handling' her correctly?

"Oh yeah," I say. "And how exactly should I be 'handling' her?"

"You should have insisted on healing her injuries," Dray says, shifting from one foot to the other and peering up towards the top of the old rickety tower.

"I was asking Thorne," I growl.

Thorne's dark gaze meets mine, unrelenting and unperturbed.

I run my hand through my hair in frustration.

"You saw what she's like," I say. "Unreasonable, temperamental, damn bratty. She's a fucking nightmare." A fucking delicious nightmare I never want to wake up from.

"You should have told her the truth from the start."

"It wouldn't have made any difference. She doesn't trust us. She doesn't trust shadow weavers at all. She would have thought I was lying."

Thorne doesn't respond, just keeps on staring at me.

I won't admit he's right. The truth is, I don't know if she would have believed me or not. If I'd been truthful from the start, would everything have run a lot more smoothly? With Briony Damn Storm who knows.

"Are you coming?" I say to them both. "We need to find out what the hell happened to her and why."

"What do you mean?" Dray says, scratching at his cheek.

"She was in that maze for far too long and you saw the way she looked. They're meant to fish them out when they're struggling. It's a fucking rule – no one gets hurt in the first official trial. It's like a warm up – a baby beginner's one. It definitely felt simple." I kick at a loose stone with my foot, sending it hurtling across the pathway. "Something happened. And I want to know who is responsible."

Dray scratches his cheek some more, thinking this over. Then he grins. "Sounds like fun. I'm in."

We both look to our bond brother. "You coming?" I ask

him stiffly. That remark about the girl has stung me more deeply than he realizes.

He shakes his head. "I'm going to stay here, ensure she's safe."

Anguish flickers across Dray's face as he swings his gaze between us again, torn between his instincts to stay and protect the girl and go rip out the throat of whoever hurt her.

"Thorne has it covered," I say. "Let's go ask some questions."

I march away and soon Dray is bouncing along beside me.

"Who are you thinking? Where do you want to start? Can we go tear Kratos' nuts off?"

"Too many questions." I wince. I'm trying to think this through in my head. The only ones who could have tampered with the trial – if that is what happened – are the teachers themselves. Possibly one or two of the officials from the Empress's court. Both of those seem unlikely. Why would they be concerned with manipulating the trial of some girl from Slate Quarter?

Unless someone knows she means more to us than just a thrall and is using her as a way to punch through to us.

We have enemies. Inside the court. Inside Onyx Quarter. Inside the realm. Plenty of enemies. There are the other shifter packs, for starters. Dray has had run-ins with most of them. There are the other powerful shadow weaver families jostling for dominion, who may be taking the chance to swipe at a band of formidable brothers. And then there are the Hardies.

The Hardies are petty and stupid enough to do this, but that's the problem – they are too stupid. They wouldn't know how to begin to manipulate the trial.

The shifters like their revenge to be served hot and bluntly. If they wanted to strike at us, they'd come charging full pelt. They wouldn't choose this devious route.

Which leaves one of the powerful families. While they might not be able to manipulate the trials directly, they may have connections and they certainly have money and influence. Bribery may even have been involved.

"Let's go see the Titan twins," I say. "They help set up the trials, don't they? Maybe they know something."

The head and deputy-head have rooms in the same building as the Great Hall. The rest of the teachers are consigned to a tower at the back of the academy where I suppose they can't be disturbed by students. There's a gated courtyard out front with a large sign instructing students to stay away.

Dray tuts at the sign and leaps straight over the metal fence. I open the gate and walk straight through.

We walk up the little path and find a sign listing the various rooms and their occupants. The Titan twins share a room that takes up the entirety of the first floor.

The front door to the tower is unlocked and we pass straight through, heading for the Titan twins' door.

"Sounds like they're having some kind of party in there," I say.

Dray cocks his head to one side. "It sounds more like a fucking orgy than a party."

"Who the hell would want to sleep with those two?" I shake my head and knock my fist on the door.

Nothing happens. The rhythmic thudding and the revolting grunts and groans from the other side of the door continue. I bang again, this time harder and louder.

The noise stops. There is some whispering. What sounds like a female voice giggles.

Then one of the twins calls out. "Go away. We're busy."

"We'll give you thirty seconds. Should be long enough to finish what you were, erm, doing," Dray says, with a wicked grin.

"Who the hell is that?" one of the twins asks angrily.

"Beaufort Lincoln and Dray Eros," I say. "We want to talk now."

There's some muttering from inside and then one of the twins opens the door, a towel that was once white wrapped tightly around his waist and not leaving a lot to the imagination. His body is covered in sweat and his face purple.

I have to force myself not to gag. Seriously, how are these dudes getting laid?

"What is it?" he says, obviously annoyed but trying his best to suppress it. Any other students, he'd probably be ripping them a new asshole, but he knows to keep on our good side.

"The trial today," I say, "anything unusual happen?"

"Can this not wait until tomorrow?" he grunts as his twin joins him. He's wrapped in a black silk dressing gown that gives off mega sleaze vibes.

"No," I say simply.

The two twins look at each other, before the one in the towel says, "No."

He goes to close the door, but Dray jams his foot in the way. "You sure about that?" he says, with his usual charming smile. "I know there were a lot of kids that went through the trial together. Everything was normal, nothing out of the ordinary for any of them."

The one in the towel scratches the top of his head, the other looks about, as if trying to remember.

"I don't think–"

"Because we could jog your memories, if you'd find that

helpful," Dray purrs, his shadow magic weaving from his fingertips.

Mine unwinds to join his and lingers right in front of the twins.

"Do you think something unusual happened?" the one in the towel asks us, looking confused. I can't tell if it's genuine – whether they are in fact as stupid as the Hardies – or whether this is a ruse.

I give them the benefit of the doubt.

"The girl from Slate — the one who went last," I say, attempting to jog his memory.

"Ahhh," the one in the dressing gown says, "the last student to go. Yeah, that was strange." He nods, looking at his twin.

"Strange how?" his brother asks.

"That was why I was late. She took fucking ages to come out of the trial. Probably was in there for two hours."

Two hours. The time limit for the trial was one. All students, whether they were near the end or a million miles from it, should have been whisked out of the maze as soon as that one hour marker was hit.

"Did that happen to any of the other students?"

He scratches his head like his twin did earlier, the gesture identical.

"Nah."

"You know why she was in there so long? Why it happened?" Dray asks.

He shakes his head.

"Did you report it? To Madame Bardin, to one of the officials?"

He shuffles on his feet uncomfortably. "Not yet."

I take a step closer to him. "But you will, won't you?"

"Sure," he says.

"Do things go wrong like this often with the trials?" Dray asks next.

They look at each other and shrug.

Yeah, I think they are as dumb as they look.

"Hector, honey," a female voice squeaks from somewhere behind them. Is that the potion mistress' voice? Fuck me! "You done yet? We're waiting."

"Anything else?" the first twin asks, his hand now tight on the door.

"No," I say. "But if you hear anything, you be sure to tell us."

They both nod obediently, then slam the door in our faces.

"What do you think?" I ask Dray. With his nose, he can sniff out a lie a mile away.

"I don't think they know what's going on," he says carefully, "but if they find out, they won't be telling us."

Which means their loyalty lies somewhere else. With who? I glare at the door. If it's someone at the academy, it won't be any of the kids from Iron, Granite, or Slate.

"I think it's time we show our faces at the shadow weaver party," I tell my bond brother.

Chapter Two

T horne

I linger in the shadows at the base of her tower like some forlorn story-tale prince waiting for the princess to take pity on him and lower her hair. Except – though they may call us the princes – I am not one. And the princess in this story does not know I even exist.

Rain pours from the sky, soaking through my clothes until my skin is sopping wet. Water runs into my eyes and into my mouth. The sting of it is brutally cold. But I don't shiver.

Up above and through the curtain of rain, I see the weak light of her window, flickering every so often as she passes by. However, the distance is too great and the window too narrow for me to peer inside, to watch her like I yearn to do. I know she is in there, though. Hurting, suffering, in pain. I swear I can feel it in my aching bones.

The image of her battered body flickers in front of my face and the shadows roar inside my blood. They want to burst free and rampage through the academy, burning everyone and everything to the ground. They demand to be set loose. To make them all suffer like she has. They are bloodthirsty for revenge and retribution.

I bunch my hands into tight fists and wrestle them down.

That isn't going to help the girl. It will only make things worse.

But the image of her won't leave me alone. She needs to be healed. Damn Beaufort and his stupid arrogance. Damn Dray and his stupid antics.

And damn me.

She doesn't trust us enough to let us heal her. She'd rather suffer instead. And there isn't one single thing I can do about it. I can't even drag her to the commoner's clinic and insist she be seen to.

I'm useless. All I can do is stand here and watch over her. The rain falls heavily on my head and slides down my face.

My gloves feel especially tight tonight, my skin itchy against the leather and damp with warm perspiration. I have the sudden urge to strip them right off my hands and live with the consequences. To let my shadows do their worst after all.

I have an urge to find her. To let my magic ...

I close my eyes. A million voices shout and scream inside my skull and her bright green eyes burn back at me.

The sound of footsteps slapping on the wet cobblestones sucks me back into the present.

It's her. Huddled in a pathetic winter coat, picking her way through the puddles.

What is she doing? Seeking out treatment? Coming to find us to be healed? Making her way to the clinic?

But she turns the wrong way, heads in the opposite direction.

I follow at a safe distance, hugging the darkness, watching as she pulls the coat more tightly around her tiny frame.

The thin leather of her boots does not protect her feet, instead they soak up the water, turning a dirty gray and damp marks the back of her coat.

She turns right, right again, left and then she's at the tallest tower of the academy, the one reserved for teaching. Tonight its windows are dark, the classrooms empty, no one is learning today. Nonetheless, she pushes against the door with her shoulder, groaning as she does, and steps inside. What the hell is she doing?

I can't follow after her. I'd have to get too close to her. She'd know I was there.

Instead, I remain out of sight, watching as the doorway swallows her inside.

And then I'm left standing and staring at the doorway as more rain cascades down on my head. Even to me, the walls and the door of this tower are impenetrable. I can't hear what's happening inside. I can't see and I can't feel either.

Instead, I'm left outside and alone as always, waiting, my bitter imagination my sole companion.

Chapter Three

F ox

I push uneaten steak around my plate, candle light flickering across the table and the hum of human voices loud in my ears, pressing against the inside of my skull.

I can't tolerate all the inane chatter and excited conversation. Not when my mind is focused elsewhere. Not when I fear she'll read exactly where it is focused.

I glance up from my plate and across the long table, meeting her steely gaze immediately. She glares at me and maybe if I had a heart, it would be leaping into my throat. Maybe I'd even be afraid. There's a mania in her eyes tonight, even more wild and cruel than usual. She lost her hold on me long ago, but to think some other has it now, it would drive her to distraction. It would make her even more dangerous than she already is.

I push my chair away from the table, the legs scraping

along the floor like fingernails down a black board. Nobody seems to notice but her. They are all tucking into their food, filling their bellies and knocking back the free-flowing wine.

She lowers her glass and watches me walk across the Great Hall, through the shadows and to the door. I know she is still watching me as I slip through the doorway.

The heavy clouds that have hung above the academy all day have finally split open and water pours from the sky, running down the towers and through the cobbled pathways. I pull the hood of my cloak over my head and stride through the rain, water splashing against my ankles and into my face, leaving the banquet behind me in the Great Hall.

Despite the cold and the wet, there are students out on the pathways, lounging in doorways, hanging from windows. They don't see me and I pass through the shadows and down into the cellars, finding the sanctuary of my own room. Dark and cold. Empty and soulless. More like a prison cell than the room of a professor. But it suits me. I am cold and dark, empty and soulless, after all.

At least, I thought I was. The girl has stirred sensations inside me I thought were long dead. Like she's knocked the smallest chink in the walls of this cell and the tiniest drop of light has slithered through.

I snap off my cloak, sling it across the back of a chair and sink low onto the single bed that occupies my room. I rest my hands on my head.

She's safe. There were no casualties in today's trials. I made sure of that. I took responsibility for hooking the kids that needed saving out of the maze myself, and she was not among them. Somehow that slip of a girl made it the full sixty minutes. The corner of my mouth tugs up into a smile. I jolt – it's such an unusual sensation. I used to smile like that – I used to smirk like an asshole – all the fucking time. Now those muscles feel tired and weak.

I toe off my boots and my socks, tug off the tie from around my neck and shrug off my shirt. Then I roll down onto the hard mattress and close my eyes. I won't sleep – I never do – but I can think. I need to think. If Veronica knows, then Briony is not safe, and I need to find a way to protect her.

As if my very thoughts have dragged her to me, my peace is disturbed by the whisper of her scent in the air – so faint at first, I think I'm imagining it. But then there is the hammering of a fist on my door – insistent and urgent.

My eyelids flick open and I inhale, everything in my cold body tingling with life.

Her.

Definitely her.

I wait to see if she'll leave, but the hammering becomes more urgent still, and I stride across my room, through my classroom and fling back the door.

She's soaked through, her eyelashes stuck together in clumps, her wet hair plastered to her head. She's shaking from the cold, her arms buried under her thin winter jacket. Cuts slice across her face and bruises mark her cheek, her brow, her chin.

She opens her mouth, takes a step forward, and then her eyes alight on my half-dressed state. She halts.

All that glorious blood rushes right the way up into her cheeks, making that bruise all the darker and she averts her eyes to my face.

"I need to talk to you," she says, pushing her way inside the classroom.

"Miss Storm," I say, keeping my fist coiled tight around the door handle, anchoring myself where I am, "I think we may have misunderstood each other. While I insist you attend each and every one of my lessons and you attend them on time every time, I do not wish to see you outside of lessons."

"I just told you," she says, wiping the water away from her face with her sleeve, "I need to talk to you."

"And this couldn't wait until—"

"No," she says, her gaze flicking momentarily down to my chest before returning to my face. She swallows.

Of course, the sensible thing to do would be to send her away. The sensible and the safe thing. But my damn curiosity – or is it the way the damn girl looks, water sliding down her face, like a far more appetizing dish than the one served up in the Great Hall tonight – won't let me.

I close the door carefully and walk past her into my room, and poke with my magic at the ancient fireplace, one that hasn't seen a fire lick its hearth in years and years.

"Take your jacket off and go dry by the fire," I tell her as I stride towards my wardrobe and pluck out a clean shirt. She hesitates by the entranceway to my room, then does as I say, and I watch as she turns her back to me and carefully removes her jacket, keeping it clutched to her stomach in front of her. Underneath, she's still wearing the gray tracksuit uniform of the academy except it's now shredded to pieces.

I frown.

"What happened?" I say, leaving my shirt hanging open across my chest and stepping back towards her.

"You said ..." She pauses. The warmth from the fire lifts the water from her skin in visible puffs of air and the firelight plays across her flesh. "You said Madame Bardin couldn't be trusted. That she was dangerous. Why did you say that?"

"Did something happen?" I ask her, thinking of the madame's eyes across the Great Hall this evening. Full of malice.

"You know," she says, peering into the flames and not at me, "you always answer every single one of my questions with one of your own."

"Do I?"

She snorts and glances over her shoulder at me. The fire illuminates her face, bathing it in mellow light, catching in the strands of her hair and turning them into gold. She looks otherworldly. Her eyes are like emeralds in the darkness.

I want to tell her. I want to tell her everything. About how I came to be here, why, what it all means. How I feel about her, how I'm losing my mind over her, how obsessive and out-of-control I'm falling.

But I can't. I can't let her see me for what I really am. She would despise me, fear me, loathe me. There would be no more moments like this – no matter how fleeting and desperate they are. Because I am that addicted. Unable to resist even the most meagre of encounters.

She reads the silence on my face.

"She attacked me. In the maze, she attacked me."

I frown. "What?"

"Madame Bardin attacked me in the maze."

"That isn't possible," I say.

I was watching, keeping my eye on all students straying close to danger, and hooking them out when that danger came too near. Briony never came close to being in danger. Not once.

And yet as I look at her, past the rain and the fire, and really look at her, I see I'm wrong. All those scrapes and bruises, all those injuries. They didn't come from nothing. She must have been in danger.

Then why the hell did I not feel it?

I feel a darkness fall across my face, one she must read.

"She manufactured it, manipulated things somehow, didn't she?" she says. "I was told I'd been in the maze for two hours."

"Two hours," I repeat, my voice catching in my throat.

How did Veronica do it? How the hell did she do it?

And why? She knew I would find out. Is that why? A provocation? A warning shot?

"She seemed to be under the impression I was keeping secrets from her and she tried to force those secrets from me with violence."

A deep growl rumbles in my chest as heat pours through my soul. "How?"

A shiver transcends down her spine and she senses the danger, even if she doesn't register it.

"With lightning."

My eyes flick across her face. Those aren't bruises. They are burn marks.

"I will kill her," I whisper.

"Why?" she says. "Why are you going to kill her?"

I scowl at her. "You know why."

She tilts her head to one side. "Do I?"

The sound of her heart pounds against my ear drums, and the rush of her blood all around her body is like the fierce rapids of a river. Even the whisper of her breath is like a yell in the silence of my room.

Behind her, the fire cracks. She waits for me to speak and when I don't, she turns her head to stare back into the flames.

"Wouldn't it be better if we just reported her?" she says, her voice full of sarcasm. "I mean, I know this academy is fucked up, but surely even teachers aren't allowed to torture students."

"Veronica can do whatever the hell she likes," I mutter.

"But surely the Head–"

"I've worked here for years now, Briony, and I've not met him once. We all know it's Madame Bardin who runs the school."

She shakes her head in disgust. "If the Empress knew–"

"And how exactly would she find out? And even by some miracle, you were to get a message to the Court, whom do you think the Empress would believe? Some girl from Slate or the woman she has placed her trust in running the academy?"

"I know," she snaps. "I'm not stupid, Professor. I know how the system works. I know it doesn't give a shit about someone like me. That doesn't mean that I have to be happy about it. Happy that any moment she could come for me again."

"I won't let that happen," I whisper, and the earnestness in my tone has her turning her face back towards mine. "I won't let her hurt you again."

"I don't see how you can promise that. You said it yourself – she's untouchable."

Which is correct. Veronica is untouchable if you're prepared to stick to the rules, if you aren't prepared to risk your own position and your own life. But I know in that cold heart of mine, I'd be prepared to risk both to keep this girl safe.

"Are you hurt, Briony?" I ask her.

She hesitates and then shakes her head. I tut in annoyance and let the shadows stream from my fingers towards her.

"You don't have to ..." she begins but the words are lost

to a sigh, her eyelids drooping closed as my magic connects with her skin and steals away all the pain and brings it into me instead. I feel the burn of electricity, the stab of it through my body and my muscles, I smell burning in my nose. But it isn't the only hurt; sharp thorns slash at my skin and a monster, its fangs drooling with foam, chases me through the maze.

I let the pain ravish my body, not moving, not making a sound, simply watching as the pain leaves her face, the creases on her brow melting away, the hardness of her jaw softening.

"Better," I say softly, when the marks on her face are gone.

Her eyes flicker open and for a moment she seems alarmed to find me right in front of her. "Y-y-y-yes." She swallows. "Thank you. You didn't need to ... That wasn't why I ..."

"I'm sorry I wasn't there to stop it, but I won't let her hurt you again," I say. "I swear it."

"It wasn't you then," she mutters, confused. I frown. What does she mean? "And if it wasn't ... then ... I don't know if I can trust you, Fox."

"Professor," I correct, because her saying my name sounds far too personal, far too intimate in this room, the firelight falling over both of us, her scent vivid in my nose and in my mouth.

"Professor," she says. "Perhaps coming here was a mistake."

She spins around to face me and I step right up to her and take her arm in my hand. My skin against hers makes her gasp, her eyes widening and falling to the place where our flesh meets.

"What is it?" I ask her.

"Your skin, it's so cold. Like ice." Her shocked gaze skims back up to my face.

I take a risk. "Some shadow weavers are. It's just the way it is."

A little crease forms between her brows, but she appears to accept my explanation, and is it my imagination or does she shuffle just a little closer towards me?

"My sister trusted the wrong people at this academy," she says, her bright green eyes searching mine. "I don't want to make the same mistake."

"You can't trust anyone in this place, Briony."

"I don't think that's true. I think I can trust my friends – Fly and Clare."

"And yet here you are, late at night in my room, and not theirs."

"Because I don't want to endanger them."

"But you're happy to endanger me?" I snipe.

"I don't think anything could endanger you, could it? You seem pretty invincible to me."

"If you're trying to flatter me–"

"I'm right, this was a–" She tries to shake off my hold and walk past me, but I grip onto her all the tighter.

"Tell me."

She halts, inhales, then exhales with frustration.

"I think we both have secrets, Professor, and unless we're both prepared to divulge them, I don't think we can ever be friends."

Chapter Four

D^{ray}

"I'm beginning to suspect that while people are nodding obediently to our faces, they're ignoring our fucking commands behind our backs," I say, my gaze flicking around the Onyx common room, my left leg jiggling, my jaw working as I chew on gum.

The trial is over. Nearly every shadow weaver, but a handful, fucking aced it. Obviously not as fast or with as much style as I did, but as suspected we performed better as a collective than any of the commoner kids from the other Quarters. It's made the kids here tonight high! It's not their fault. They've been told all their lives how wonderful they are. Now they've proved it. They're dancing on the tables, firing magic around the room, hooking up, and snorting lines of dust.

Usually I'd be right in the thick of it, shirt off, balancing some girl on my shoulders, licking powder off another's chest, and howling up at the ceiling.

Tonight, I'm stewing in the corner with Beaufort, observing. Every one of my wolfish senses is alert and finely tuned.

"What makes you say that?" Beaufort asks, dragging his own gaze away from the spectacle and back towards me.

"Despite making it clear she's ours," I say, rocking back on my heels and then forward again, "despite Thorne's little temper tantrum, she's still walking around like she's a punchbag and not a human person."

"Agreed," Beaufort says, leaning against the wall, and drumming his fingers against the plaster, "the question is, which of the idiots gathered here tonight do you think was responsible for what happened to her in the maze?"

I sweep my gaze across the collection of fuckwits – sweaty and disheveled, grinding against one another, pawing at each other.

"None of them," I say.

"Yeah, agreed," Beaufort mutters with irritation, "but then who was?"

I fix him with a hard cold stare. "If she was talking to us, we'd know. If you'd told her the tru–"

"She's not ready for that," he snaps back.

You'd think we'd all be as high as the rest of them tonight. We're not. We're irritated. Moody. Brewing for a fight.

"If she knew the tru–"

"Maybe she'd be in even more danger," Beaufort says lowly so that only the two of us hear.

"What makes you say that?" I ask, my body suddenly deadly still, my ears practically pitched as if I'm standing here in wolf form and not human. "Have you seen some-thing more?" I whisper, barely moving my lips.

Beaufort shakes his head.

"Then what–"

"The argument."

"You said it was just a stupid disagreement," I say.

"Because I thought it was," he drags his hand down his face, "but the more I think about it, about what she told me, the more I think, maybe it wasn't."

"What the hell are you talking about, dickhead?" I mutter in irritation. "Stop talking in fucking riddles and tell me."

"It could be nothing..."

My body convulses, flicking for the briefest of moments between my two forms. "Fucking tell me before I rip you limb from limb."

"Fine." He stares right ahead. "She had a sister. An older sister who died at the academy."

"How?"

"Accident apparently. But Briony doesn't believe it. The way she talks about her sister, it's as if she was special or something."

"Everyone talks about their sister that way," I mutter.

"You might talk about your sister that way, pervert," Beaufort snaps, "but I–"

"Go to hell," I snap right back. "I don't have a sister and you know what I mean."

"What if Briony is right?" Beaufort continues, scratching at his cheek. "I don't know, man. The name, Storm, I feel like I heard it somewhere else before."

"How? When?"

"I don't remember. In fact, I'm not sure if I'm just imagining it." He growls in frustration. "But what if someone killed her sister and now they're going after Briony too?"

"It doesn't make any sense, though, Beau. Why would anyone waste their time trying to kill a couple of girls from Slate?" I say. "It's not like she has any powers. You said so yourself. Those scars. No shadow weaver could withstand that kind of torture without their magic breaking through."

"Yeah," Beaufort says, nodding his head. "Yeah, you're right. Much more likely to be one of those cunts thinking they've grown too powerful to listen to what we have to say. Trying to get at us, through her."

"Then let's fucking remind them," I say, bouncing forward, my shadows all too ready to inflict some serious damage on all these dickwads.

"No," Beaufort says, catching me by the arm. "That didn't work last time. They're operating behind our backs."

"If she just wore the damn collar," I say, scowling at Beaufort.

If he just kept his mouth focused on satisfying her pussy instead of spouting fucking nonsense and ending up entangled in arguments with her, things would probably be a lot more different to how they are. In fact, I'm pretty damn certain she'd be lying in my bed right now – she'd probably be coming on the end of my tongue right this second.

"You don't think I've told her that over and over again."

"You need to go say you're sorry. Make it up with her. Girls love that shit. Get down on your knees, beg for forgiveness and before you know it, she'll be riding your cock again."

Beaufort grunts. He doesn't do apologies, it's not in his nature, plus he's never had to. Guys in his position never do.

"You could go now," I prompt. "Night isn't over. It's

clear we're not going to solve this mystery tonight and besides, our best lead is the girl herself anyway."

"It's too late," he mutters.

"Then in the morning?" His body tenses. I cock my head. "You're heading home?"

"Yeah." He rakes his hand through his head. "I've been told."

"Got my Ma bitching at me to come home too," I say. I didn't mind the idea yesterday. The thought of heading home for the night, eating home-cooked meals, sleeping in my own bed, hanging with my brothers, sounded pretty tempting. Tonight, it's the last thing I want to do.

I guess Beau feels the same way because he says, "Leaving Briony here at the academy after what just happened, is risky."

"You think she'd come with one of us?" I say, and by one of us – I mean me.

Beau shakes his head. "Anyway, it could be just as dangerous. We don't know who's using her to get to us and if they suspect the truth ..."

I chew this over, munching on the gum in my mouth that's starting to lose its flavor.

"Thorne will be here," I say at last, "we'll make sure he's watching her."

Chapter Five

B^{riony}

It wasn't Fox.

Whoever – or whatever – it was that saved me in the maze, it wasn't the professor.

I race back up the stairs, berating myself as I go, the stone still clutched in my hands, buried under my jacket.

What the hell was I thinking? Of course, it wasn't Fox Tudor who saved me. Why the hell would he? Just because he offered me advice about Madame Bardin does not mean … does not mean … what was I even considering it did mean? That the man cared about me? Had feelings for me?

How stupid could one person be? Whatever Fox Tudor once was, Professor Tudor is cold and hard and apathetic. He'd no more care for me than he would care to cut off his own foot from his leg.

No, it wasn't Fox who saved me in that maze, and, there-fore, it isn't him I can trust with this secret.

Which leaves the question? Who the hell was it?

I race back along the pathways. The rain batters around me, the cobbled stones slippery and wet. Twice I slip, clutching the stone tightly to my body as I regain my footing.

Finally, I make it back to the safety of my tower and my room.

I sit down on my bed and stare down at the stone, tracing my fingertips along the fissures forming on its surface.

What can it mean? And why did it happen now?

I turn the stone over again and again in my hands. Apart from those cracks there are no other differences. The weight is the same, the heat it penetrates no greater and no lesser, and the surface is still smooth.

"Was it you?" I ask the stone. "Was it you who saved me?"

"Saved you from what?"

I jerk, immediately stuffing the stone under my pillow, then I spin around and find Fly standing in my doorway.

"We've been searching for you everywhere," he says, coming to sit beside me on the bed. Like me, he's still wearing his gray tracksuit and, like mine, it has seen better days. "You know the Princes have been looking for you too."

"Yeah, they found me," I say.

"They did?" He looks surprised. "Those shitheads. They could have told us. Do you know Clare is actually searching for you in the library as we speak?" He leans in closer. "That place gives me the creeps, so I offered to come check your room again. I was not expecting to find you here." He tilts his head to one side. "You weren't here an hour ago. Were you at the clinic after all?"

He frowns because, if I was at the clinic, they have done a very good job of fixing me up. Much better than usual. I'm no longer covered in scrapes, bruises and burn marks. I bet I look unscratched. Unlike most of the other students probably receiving pathetic patching up at the clinic.

As if reading my thoughts, Fly says, "There are quite a few casualties in the clinic. It's pretty full tonight. That ... thing!"

"You came up against it too?"

Fly shivers. "I managed to beat it away with a heavy branch I found. How about you?"

"I outran it – lost it in the maze."

"You outran it?" he says, then shakes his head. "Cupcake, you're fast but not that fast. That thing moved like a rabid hunting dog."

It was fast; I remember it gaining on me quickly, I remember thinking it was going to catch me. And then it had stopped. I assumed I outran it but maybe I didn't. Does that mean I was helped more than once?

Fly shudders again, this time so hard the bed wobbles, and I glance towards my pillow hoping the stone is secure under there.

It's not that I don't want to tell Fly about it. I've been half tempted for weeks. But that run-in with Madame Bardin has reminded me how dangerous this academy can be. Fly and Clare have been kind to me – heck, they've even seemed to enjoy hanging out with me. Like I told Fox, I don't want to endanger my friends.

That's also why I won't be telling him about what happened in that maze. The less he knows the safer he'll be.

"So if not at the clinic or playing make-up with the Princes, where the hell have you been?"

I stare at him, my mind struggling to grasp a suitable explanation. In the end, I decide to go for a half truth.

"Something went funny with the trial. I was in there for two hours instead of one."

"What?" he says, incomprehension and shock spreading across his face. "Like a malfunction? But how is that even possible?"

I shrug. "I guess I got lucky."

"Seriously lucky, Cupcake," Fly wraps me in a hug. "You could have been killed."

"But I wasn't. Unfortunately for you, you can't lose me that easily."

"Thank goodness," he says, "you're growing on me."

He ends the hug and holds me arms' length away from him, examining my face. "Those shitheads healed you, huh? At least they can do something right."

"It wasn't them. We're still not really on speaking terms."

"They're the Princes! If they wanted to speak with you, then, sorry Cupcake, but even you yourself couldn't stop them."

I shrug a second time. "Let's not think about them now. Tell me, is Clare okay? Did she make it through without being hurt?"

"A few scrapes and bruises like me. Nothing too serious. Apparently she got seriously close to finishing the maze."

"That's my girl." I grin.

Twenty minutes later we're sitting in Clare's room again, passing the open bottle of liquor between us and singing along to one of Clare's records – I'm starting to remember the lyrics.

"Pleeeaaaase!" Fly begs as he swigs back the bottle. "It looks really terrible."

"Jeez thanks," I say, lifting my hand to my head. I've seen my reflection now. My face and body may be healed, but I have lost a clump of my hair and have gained a scorch mark to my scalp.

"I can fix it for you," he says, bouncing up and down on his knees, "can hide that bit." He motions to my bald patch.

"I don't know," I say, staring down into the bottle.

"I promise it won't hurt."

"It's not that I'm worried about it hurting," I begin.

"Great!" Fly says, clapping his hands together and bouncing right up onto his feet, taking me with him and pushing me down into Clare's desk chair. He swings me around and starts to pluck pins from my head.

"Hey!" I moan. "That does hurt."

"No pain, no gain," he sings.

"But you said it wouldn't hurt."

"It won't. You're being a wimp."

I glare up at him but he simply smiles and loosens my hair down over my shoulders.

"Wow," Clare says, coming to stand beside Fly. "Your hair's really pretty, Briony. Why don't you wear it down like that more often."

"I don't like it," I tell her.

"You don't?" she says. "But it's gorgeous."

"It draws attention to me. Attention I don't want."

And it reminds me of her. She had the same hair and she always wore it down. It turned heads wherever we went. If she'd just stayed hidden, tried to shrink away in the shadows like I've always tried to do, maybe she'd still be with us.

"No offense, Cupcake," Fly says, combing his fingers

through my hair and attempting to untangle the knots, "you've already brought quite a lot of attention to yourself. I don't think your hair will make a lot of difference. So why don't you let me style it down?" I shake my head. "Can I at least do an interesting braid – one that will cover the," he lowers his voice to a whisper, "unfortunate patch."

"Sure," I say. I do have some pride, and though I may not care so much about my hair, I'd rather avoid all the snide remarks and stupid jokes when people spot I now have parts of my hair missing.

Clare perches on her desk and I watch her eyes follow Fly as he skips around my head, tugging and twisting pieces of hair.

"How did you lose that clump anyway?" Clare asks after a while. "It looks like it was burned right off your head. I didn't come across any fire."

"I didn't come across any tornados," I point out.

"I thought it was going to shoot me right out into space. If Professor Tudor hadn't sucked me off, I guess I'd be floating somewhere out by the moon right about now," she mutters.

Fly snorts and we both peer at him. "Okay, okay, I have the sense of humor of a twelve-year-old, but she did just say Professor Tudor sucked her off." Clare blinks. "We talked about this, remember?"

"Ewww," Clare says, although in the next second the disgust morphs into something more dream-like, "although …"

"Seriously?!" Fly says, almost dropping the pieces of hair in his hands. "The man scares me to death."

"Well, that too, but he's also very strong and very muscular and when he wrapped his arms around me–"

"He did what?!" I shriek, my voice sounding unnaturally high.

Why should I care who Professor Fox wraps his arms around – even if he wraps them around Madame Bardin?

"Well he had to in order to rescue me from the maze," she says matter-of-factly.

"He rescued you?" I say, wondering if that high-pitch note in my voice is jealousy.

I have three of the academy's hottest men chasing me – okay, I don't want anything to do with them but that is hardly the point. Why the hell would I begrudge Clare this? She is intelligent, pretty and kind. Why wouldn't a cold-hearted soulless man like Fox Tudor want her?

"Briony," Fly says, tugging on my hair, "that was his job. To fish any students in danger out of the maze."

"Oh," I say, the jealousy fading as quickly as it had risen, replaced with something just as bitter.

Because if Professor Tudor was meant to rescue students from the maze, then why the hell didn't he rescue me?

Chapter Six

F^{ox}

Rain still cascades from the sky as I fly along the cobbled pathways back in the direction of the Great Hall. Its windows still glow from within but when I crash through the doors, I find only servants remaining, clearing the remnants of this evening's dinner. They look up at me in alarm and I suspect I look wild. I *feel* fucking wild.

I sweep straight back out of the hall, up the staircase and along the corridor, stopping right outside her room. Inside, she'll be entertaining – maybe an old lover, maybe a new, maybe someone she hopes to seduce.

I don't give a shit.

I shoot my magic against the heavy door and it flies right off its hinges and crashes into the room.

Through the gap in the now open doorway, I spy her,

leaning against her desk, smoking one of her thin cigarettes. There is no one with her tonight.

"Do you always have to be so damn dramatic?" she says, sucking on her cigarette and rolling her kohl-rimmed eyes. This evening she's wearing a red velvet dress that clings to her body like blood, matching the color of her lips and her nails.

Lifting my hands, I stride into her room. I haven't been here in years. I've avoided it at all costs. It gives me the creeps – and this from a man who sleeps in a fucking dungeon.

"What the hell did you do?" I bark.

She removes the cigarette from her mouth, rocking it between her fingers and flicking ash into the glass ashtray behind her.

"Plenty, I'm sure. You'll need to be more precise, Fox."

"You doctored that trial, manipulated it, kept her locked inside the maze for longer than she should have been."

"And who exactly are we talking about?" Her eyes flash.

There's no point attempting to hide it or to deny it. She attacked the girl in the maze – tortured her. It's clear she's worked it out for herself.

I am more transparent than I thought and it has brought her into danger.

"You know," I growl, scowling at her.

She stubs out her cigarette and pushes off her desk, stepping towards me.

"I'm afraid I don't," she says all innocently. "You are going to have to tell me."

She must feel the rage radiating off my body, she must see how tightly coiled I am, ready to launch at her – to fucking destroy her. But she looks amused rather than afraid, as if I'm nothing but a nuisance child come to bother her.

"What did you do to her?" My magic sparks from my fingertips, shooting across the space and curling around her neck.

She grins, licking her lips.

"One of our favorite games, Fox. Do you remember? We had such fun together. I don't understand why we still couldn't."

"I know what you did." I squeeze. "You don't touch her. Ever again. If you do …"

"And how did you know? Because some silly girl told you?" She laughs, although the shadows around her neck make the sound strangled. "I don't know what she did tell you, but it isn't true."

Her own shadows snake from her fingers and sidle up against mine, stroking and caressing them. It makes me jolt. It makes me sick to the stomach. I can't stand this woman anywhere near me. I can't stand to touch her. I can't stand to be touched by her. And yet I'd do it to destroy her, to keep Briony safe.

As soon as her name enters my mind, I know my mistake.

"Little Briony Storm." Her eyes dance with amusement and triumph radiates across her face as she reads my thoughts. "A confused girl. Her head full of all kinds of delusions. It's not unusual, Fox. It was bound to happen eventually. It happens to us all." She licks her lips again. "At some point, there's always a student who develops an unhealthy interest, an infatuation, a crush. Why, even Cornelius had some love-sick boy follow him around like a lost puppy one year."

"That's not what this is."

"Poor Fox, you don't think it's real do you?"

"She doesn't even notice me."

"And yet, she's come running to you with tales of me," she hisses with a sudden savageness.

"Where the hell else was she meant to go when one of her teachers attacked her?"

"Attacked her?" She scoffs. "Their imaginations are so young and so highly sexualised – they can't help but run wild. I'm sure that's all this is, Fox. This girl has probably never had a man show her any interest before and then you come along – forceful, strong ... commanding – and her little imagination can't control itself. She wants to make you the hero of some strange, twisted fairytale – and well, of course, I'd be a prime candidate for the wicked witch."

She curls her tongue behind her teeth and smiles wickedly.

"You are a fucking witch!" I spit the words in her face, my magic prickling violently against her skin.

It simply makes her shiver, a little moan escaping her throat.

"It's been so long since we did this last, Fox. Remember how good it used to be? Your magic curled around mine, mine around yours. Remember how good it felt? How good I made you feel?"

I tighten my grip on her neck and then slam her back against the desk, the wood cracks behind her, and she slides down to the floor. This time there's nothing sexual about her groan.

"Stay away from her. Stay away from me. Otherwise I will kill you."

"This is all for nothing. You can't have her, Fox. The Princes have already claimed her."

"It makes no difference."

"Although, heaven knows why! There's nothing special about her, Fox. I'd know if there were. She's just a nothing girl from the shitholes of Slate."

"Same place I'm from, you forget, Veronica."

I fire electricity straight into her body, leaving her to writhe on the floor. Just like she did to Briony.

When I stop, her hair stands on end around her head and her lipstick and eyeliner is smudged across her face.

"Maybe I thought you were different," she screeches. "Maybe I thought there was something special about you."

"You were wrong." I step closer to her, bending down so my face is right up close to hers. Her breath smells of sweet tobacco, my stomach turning over again. "I'm warning you!"

Chapter Seven

Briony

I head straight for my hiding place when I return that evening, unwrapping the stone and examining its surface, trying to decide if the fissures have grown any bigger. I don't think they have, but by the time I wake in the morning and check the stone again, I'm sure the long crack down its length has grown half an inch or so.

What can it mean? Why the hell would a stone like this crack? It wasn't dropped or thrown. No one has struck it with a weapon or with magic. No, it's cracked all by itself.

I think back to last night and my almost-confession with Professor Tudor. I've no doubt he'd be able to identify this stone and why it has cracked. Should I have shown him?

But I don't trust him. If I show this stone to anyone, it will be snatched from my hands. I doubt I'd ever see it again and I can't be parted from it – that strange force that dragged me to it on the day of Amelia's burial, lingers in my chest even now.

I stroke my palm over the stone's surface, whispering words of comfort to it, like it can actually hear me.

Then, after enough craziness, I pull on some clothes, and go in search of Fly.

In honor of the completion of the second trial (or non-completion in most people's cases), all students have the next two days free. No lessons, no training, no learning. We are free to do as we please. Not that, as I've already discovered, there is anything to do in this academy – especially as I plan to avoid kite flying for the rest of my time here. In fact, I plan to avoid any form of electrocution for the rest of my life – which probably means avoiding the Smyte twins and Madame Bardin if I can.

When we step out onto the cobbled pathways, we find two things different from usual.

Firstly, last night's storm has cleared and above us hangs the sun, bright and glorious and even slightly warm against our skin.

I close my eyes and let it tickle against my face. The sun was a rarity back in Slate Quarter and I'll take every opportunity I have to lap it up.

Secondly, the entire campus is in a state of chaos.

"What's going on?" I ask Fly as we watch people racing past us towards a crowd gathered further down on the paths. "Did the sunshine turn everyone crazy?"

"The scores must be out," he says. We look at each other for one whole second and then we're following everyone else along the pathways towards the Great Hall. A notice board has been erected alongside the statue of the dragons and a huge crowd of students are gathered around it.

We join the back of the queue, shuffling forward as people file back past us, some with smiles of triumph, others sobbing miserably.

Neither of those potential reactions fill me with reassurance. I nibble on my fingernails, balancing up on my tiptoes every now and again to see if I can make out my name.

Finally, we're buffeted forward and the large sheet of paper with everyone's names printed in a swirling calligraphy greets us. I scan the list, as people push and shove from behind. Unsurprising, the Princes are right at the top with one thousand points a piece in the category of magic and a hell of a lot of points in the categories of physical agility and mental ability as well. Clare's is the first name I spy. She's scored a big fat zero under physical but one hundred and ninety-three points in mental ability. I tut my tongue. Have they met my friend? She's way smarter than the Princes, yet she's scored less than them in that category.

If I didn't already know the system was fixed, I'd know it now.

I spot Fly's name next. He's scored one hundred and nine points in physical and ninety-eight in mental.

"Not bad," I tell him.

He hooks his arm around my shoulder. "Yeah, I'm happy with that. Puts me in with a running chance of making Granite. How about you, Briony?"

"I haven't found my name yet," I say, bending over as I follow the list of names down and down towards the ground. The list continues on for what feels like forever. At last, I find my name. It's right at the very bottom. And my score?

Zero points in all categories.

"That can't be right," Fly mumbles as I turn away from

the board and push my way through the crowd. "Briony!" he calls after me.

When he catches up to me, his face is full of outrage. "It must be a mistake."

"It isn't," I say, calmly. "It's what I expected." I manage a little smile, willing myself not to cry, to not let this upset me.

Stars, I'm freaking disappointed. I thought I did well-ish. I thought I had a chance of some points at least.

But I'm also kicking myself. Because, didn't I know this would happen? Did I really believe it would be any different? That I, Briony Storm from Slate Quarter, would actually earn myself some points? Would actually find my way out of Slate?

Nope, I did not think that. Therefore, this is not unexpected. And I have no cause for disappointment.

"Come on," I say, pulling on Fly's arm. "Let's go find Clare and tell her the good news."

"Good news? This isn't good news." Poor Fly looks genuinely disgusted. He may have been treated unfairly at home. He may be more cynical than most about the system, but he still believes in it. He still trusts it to work. "We should go tell the Princes. I'm sure they'll have something to say about this."

"Let's not involve them." I tug his arm.

He takes a big dramatic sigh, then capitulates to being dragged towards Clare's tower.

The mood and the number of students out on the paths is still crazy. Several of them rushing in the same direction.

"Jeez, what is it with everyone today?" I mumble as several people in a row knock into me.

"Freedom day," Fly says.

"Yeah, but why all the excitement? We have a freedom day every Sunday. It's no big deal."

Fly shakes his head. "This is *freedom* freedom day. You're allowed to leave campus if you want."

"But there's nowhere to go!"

"There is if you have transport. I suspect most of the shadow weavers are going back home."

"And even that requires an audience does it?"

"I'm guessing you've never seen a shadow weaver's set of wheels?" Fly says.

"Nope. Only the mayor owns a vehicle back in Slate Quarter and while some of the boys and girls used to drool over it, I never saw the appeal."

"Well, Cupcake, this is likely to be a little different." He grabs my hand and drags me along after the crowd. "Thrall coming through!" he chimes and people shuffle out of our way.

"I am not ..." I hiss at him but I don't finish my words because my attention is stolen by the sleek, elegant machine parked in the square in front of us. "Shit!" I mutter.

"Told you," he says.

"I've seen pictures of vehicles like this but those seemed so fanciful and peculiar. I didn't really believe they were real."

"My parents have a vehicle," Fly says, absentmindedly. "Nothing like this. Only shadow weavers could afford something like this."

I spin around and grip my friend's shoulders. "Are you going home for the next couple of days?"

"Me?" I nod and he shakes his head in response. "I haven't been invited. Not that I'd want to go if I were," he adds hurriedly. "It would take most of the day to get there and then I'd have to turn around and come straight back."

We watch as the Smyte sisters come sauntering onto the path. They're wearing matching short green dresses with little white sailor hats perched on their red heads. Behind them trails their thrall, his arms full of bags.

"I think it'll only be the shadow weavers going home today."

"Oh," I say, as Henrietta waits for their thrall to open the door to the vehicle and helps her inside.

Fly bumps me with his elbow. "Don't worry. They'll all be back tomorrow in time for the ball."

"Why would I be worried?" I say, watching Henrietta rev the engine of the machine, a cloud of smoke shooting from its exhaust, making the crowd of onlookers splutter. "I'm not going to the ball."

"Don't be silly. Of course, you are," Fly says, as Linette climbs in beside her sister and the thrall is forced to cram into the tiny seats in the back with the luggage. I guess he's going home with them – to Onyx Quarter. Does that mean I would have gone if I was playing nice with the Princes? Just like these sleek machines, I've seen pictures of Onyx Quarter too – they were as surreal looking as the pictures of the vehicles.

"Parties aren't really my thing."

The last door of the vehicle slams shut, and it darts forward, the vehicle heading right towards us and the crowd scattering and screaming. I yank on Fly's arm and push us just clear of the vehicle's path, Henrietta waving and smiling at us through the sparkling windscreen.

"I swear she did that on purpose," I grumble, watching the vehicle career off through the campus.

"Of course she did. She's tried to kill you numerous times. If you just told Thorne Cadieux, she would most definitely stop."

"I can look after myself."

Fly mutters a few choice words under his breath, then takes me by the shoulders and turns me to face him.

"No offense, Cupcake, but have you ever actually been to a party?"

"Yes," I say, insulted.

He looks at me with suspicion. "Describe this party."

I shuffle on my feet. "There were games, some food and some drinks."

"What kind of food and what kind of drink?"

"Does it matter?"

"Cupcake ..."

"Water and some crackers."

"And who exactly was at this party?"

I sigh. "My sister, our dog and my old teddy bear."

"That is not a party." I open my mouth to argue and he slams his hand over my mouth. "If you want to keep being my friend, you have to go to the party. I can't go alone."

"I'm sure Clare will go with you."

"I can't go with just Clare. I need you both there. Besides, you might actually enjoy yourself." His face softens. "Something you are allowed to do."

"I should be investigating more about my sister's death," I mumble.

"There'll be time for that. Ball first." I drop my gaze to the ground and chew on my cheek. "Are you worried about those Princes?"

"No, it's just ... I really don't have anything to wear." I doubt I'll be alone in that. There wasn't exactly the greatest need for ball dresses at home in Slate Quarter. I doubt any of the Slate kids have any clothes worthy enough of a ball. I wonder if they'll all be missing out like me.

"Lucky you have a fairy godmother then, huh,

Cinderella? Those Princes aren't going to know what hit them."

"What does that mean?" I ask.

"You'll see," he says, tapping his forefinger against his nose.

Chapter Eight

Beaufort

I lean back against the seat and adjust the sun visor, shading my eyes from the glaring sun as I weave the vehicle through the academy campus.

I don't want to be heading home today. I want to remain here. Something happened to her in that maze. People have been hurting her. I want to stay here and keep her safe.

But I've procrastinated for as long as I can, turning over Dray's words from last night, working out if I could see Briony before I go, put things right between us, or whether I'd only make matters worse. Concluding she'd probably refuse to see me anyway.

Now duty calls and as much as I'd like to resist that duty, I can't.

Nope, even I, Beaufort fucking Lincoln – one of the

most powerful shadow weavers in the realm – can't refuse a summons home.

I am also no closer to working out who manipulated the trial. I can't keep Briony safe. Haven't I proved that again and again?

So much for my fucking powers.

I thump my fist against the steering wheel and swear under my breath.

The paths are full of students today, crowding around to watch the shadow weavers in their vehicles, staring at us like they've never seen a set of wheels before.

I scoff, letting my gaze sweep over them, not paying them any notice. Until there's one face I am noticing, sweeping past my window. I snap around in my seat.

"Shit!" I yell, hitting the brakes immediately. The vehicle slams to a halt and I'm out and striding her way before the door shuts behind me.

She's so busy chatting to her friend she doesn't sense or hear me, and I'm forced to land my hand on her shoulder to gain her fucking attention.

"What the fuck?!" I growl, as she turns to face me, because that face doesn't look like it did yesterday. No cuts, no scrapes, no bruises. No nothing. Smooth and flawless. "What the *fuck*?!" I repeat.

My shock descends into annoyance. An emotion that mirrors the one on her face. A face that has been healed by magic.

Someone has healed her face with magic and it wasn't us.

"Who did that?" I spit, shunting my chin in her direction, not giving a shit about the crowd that's now turned away from my vehicle and towards us instead.

"Did what?" she says. Her hair's different too, braided

around her head, framing her face, making her eyes even more vivid and bright.

"Healed your face," I say through gritted teeth.

Here I was worried about someone hurting her again. About Dray and I heading home and leaving only Thorne to guard her.

Seems what I should have been worried about was some fucking scumbag groping his hands all over our thrall.

"Was it you?" I snap at her friend.

"Woah," he says, lifting both his hands up in defense. "I'm not a shadow weaver."

I glare back at her. "Then who was it?"

"None of your business."

My blood boils under my skin.

Every time.

She has to make this difficult every time.

Clutching her arm, I pull her along with me, her friend trotting behind us anxiously. At my vehicle, I open the passenger door and throw her inside, slamming the door shut so she can't shuffle out. Then I walk around the car, open the other door. Before she can escape through the driver's side, I sidle into my seat next to her.

"What the hell are you doing?" she yelps. Her friend knocks his knuckles against the glass.

"We're going for a little drive," I say, slamming my foot down on the accelerator and letting the car shoot away, her friend left standing gobsmacked.

Briony spins in her seat, looking back through the rear windscreen.

"You're such an asshole! You could have hurt him!!"

"Always more concerned about that dude than your own protectors."

"Because he is my friend and you are not." She rattles the door handle. "Let me out."

"Not until we've finished this little conversation."

She tugs on the door but finding it hopeless, flops back into the seat and crosses her arms angrily across her chest.

I zoom us through the campus, leaving students to jump out of our path, and then we're crossing the moorland on the single-tracked lane.

I don't know where the hell I'm taking her. I can't take her home. There would be too many questions. Doing this is going to make me late as it is. I should care. I find I don't.

"You can't stay angry at me forever," I tell her, glancing away from the windscreen to peer at her face.

"When you pull stupid stunts like this, I can."

"It's the only way I can get you to talk to me."

"Maybe that's because I don't want to talk to you."

"Maybe you don't have a choice," I say, then regret it almost immediately. She's right. Dray's right. I am an asshole and I don't know how to do this. I sigh. "I want to make things right between us."

She shakes her head. "You said all that stuff. You showed me who you really are, Beaufort Lincoln, and I didn't like what I saw."

We reach the forest, the road cutting under the leafless branches. I swing between two tree trunks and slam on the brakes.

"And what did you see?" I shift around in my seat and stare at her, right into her eyes so she's forced to stare right into mine.

"A man who's only out for himself."

I keep staring right back at her. "Then you don't know me at all." I twist my head back around and look out into the forest. It's dark under the trees, but a few stray rays of sunlight filter through the branches, dust particles spinning trapped in their glare. "Because I want to look after you, Briony. I want to help you." I frown, remembering what brought us under these trees in the first place. "Of course, if you've found some other shadow weaver to lend you–"

"That's not what this was."

"Wasn't it? Then why can't you tell me who it was? Why the secret?"

"You have secrets too, Beaufort. Things you aren't telling me." I nod. I can't deny it. "So why don't we call it quits? I won't tell you and you won't tell me."

"I can't help you, if you don't tell me."

"I don't need your help."

"Really?" I snort. "And how's it going with that little investigation into your sister's death? Found your answers yet?"

She opens her mouth, closes it and then turns her head away from me.

I sigh once more and lean my head back against the headrest. I don't want to fight. I want to be lifting her into my lap, sucking on her throat and making her moan with my fingers. I don't want her hating on me.

People don't hate Beaufort Lincoln. They admire him. They are afraid of him. They don't hate him.

Yet, every wave of energy rolling off her right now says hate.

Could I tell her? I said I would. But would she understand? She comes from Slate, the backend of nowhere. Bland, miserable, pathetic. Not a world of magic. She doesn't know what it's like to bend reality, warp perception, or manipulate the very building blocks of the universe.

Would she look at me and think I was lying? Worse, would she look at me and think I was a freak?

"It was Professor Tudor," she says, "who healed me."

"The teacher?"

She nods. "There's nothing going on. I'm not interested in getting tangled up in relationships. What happened between you and me was a mistake."

"It wasn't," I growl. "It was damn good." Her gaze flicks back to me and the heat in my eyes makes her swallow. "And it's too late. We're already tangled up together." She opens her mouth to argue. I beat her to it. "You're right."

Her brows leap up her forehead in surprise, then plummet back down into a suspicious frown. "About what exactly?"

"Me being an asshole. What I said about your sister – it was–"

"Wrong."

"Cruel. And, despite what you may think about me, I am not cruel. Not to the people I care about anyway."

I scratch my nail along the leather seam on the steering wheel.

"Are you apologizing to me, Beaufort Lincoln?" she asks, puzzled.

"I guess I am."

"Then you know if you mean it you should probably say the words."

"I'm sorry I hurt your feelings."

"And ..." she says, a slight smile playing on her lips.

"And?" I say, shrugging.

"You're sorry for being an asshole?"

"Yes, that too." She tilts her head to one side. "Okay, I'm also sorry for being an asshole."

I give her a smoldering look I know has most girls creaming their panties. She lifts an eyebrow expectantly.

"Anything else?" she prompts.

"Erm ..." I rack my brain. What else have I fucked up? "The stuff about your sister, there may be some merit in your theory given someone manipulated the trial and you were trapped inside for much longer than you should have been."

"So you don't think that was an accident too?" she says, her voice full of sarcasm.

"No, I don't.".

"Hmmm," she says, her eyes flicking away from me as she stares down at the hands in her lap. "Have you seen the scores?"

"I haven't." No point. I know I did well. I know where I'm going to end up. It's my destiny.

"I ..." she swallows, "I scored zero points."

"What?" I say, even though I heard her perfectly well the first time.

"It doesn't matter," she says, the anger rising in her voice again. "I knew I wasn't going to score well. I know they're going to send me back to Slate."

"No, they're not."

She laughs. "Zero points, Beaufort. Zero! Even if I score really well in the next few trials, there is no way I'm making that up."

"There must be some kind of mistake."

"No. This is what happens to people like me. It doesn't matter how good we are, we all end up back in Slate."

"I'll look into it," I tell her. "I'm already looking into who manipulated the trial."

She looks back up at me. "You are?" I nod. "Thank you," she says. "I appreciate that."

Which was not what I was expecting her to say at all. Maybe Dray was right for once after all.

"Thank you?" I venture. "Does that mean I'm forgiven?"

"I'm not sure."

"While you're thinking it over, will you at least come sit on my lap and make out with me?"

She spins her gaze around the interior of the car.

"Have you made out with a lot of girls in this car?"

"A few," I lie. I reach over and take a hold of her hips in my hands, dragging her across to my seat so she's straddling my lap. "None turned me on as much as you do."

She shakes her head in disbelief. "I find that very hard to believe."

"Well, believe it," I growl, scraping my teeth down her throat. Then kissing where I've made the skin red, my fingers sinking into the flesh of her waist, holding her in place, making it clear I won't be letting her go.

She whimpers a little, rubbing herself against my stiffening cock. "I don't know if I forgive you. I don't know if I should."

"You should," I murmur against her skin, sucking on her pulse point. "You should really really forgive me and you should let me make it up to you."

From the corner of my eye I catch the time blinking on the dashboard. I'm already late. Staying behind to mess around with her in my car is going to make me really fucking late.

I'm finding it exceedingly hard to give a shit.

I lift her skirt and slide my hands into her panties, squeezing her ass cheeks before I slide my fingers between her thighs. She's wet and I groan.

Yeah, I'm going to be late – really fucking late.

Her hands bunch into fists in my shirt as I stroke along the seam of her pussy lips, teasing her. Then I part her folds and thrum my thumb against her stiff little nub, kissing up and down her neck. Her legs start to shake and her skin flush. I can feel the heat of it against my lips.

"Ohhh," she moans, her nails digging deep into my chest. "Ohhh."

"See what you were missing, little thrall? See how good I make you feel?"

I nip at her throat and then I capture her mouth with mine, kissing her hard as she comes against my thumb, sliding my fingers inside her pussy, loving how wet and warm and soft she feels, how tightly she squeezes around my fingers as she rides her orgasm.

I pump my fingers in and out of her, the sound sloppy and obscene, forcing a second orgasm from her body, watching transfixed as she bucks and jolts on my lap.

When she's ridden it completely, she collapses against me panting and sated. I brush the stray wisps of hair that have come loose from her braid away from her ear and whisper, "That was just a taster, little thrall, when I come back tomorrow, I'm going to fuck you properly."

She rocks back to look me in the face, another one of those frowns on her face.

"You're not going to fuck me now?" She grinds my fingers on her pussy and my cock twitches in my pants.

There's nothing more that I want to do. Especially as I'll be riding home with a stiff cock and aching balls.

I groan, eyes flicking back to the clock. I should have left an hour ago. I can't delay any longer.

"Tomorrow," I promise. "We're going to be escorting you to the ball."

"Of course," she says, my fingers still inside her because I don't want to remove them, "you do have to ask me first. You never know, someone might already have asked me."

I grin. "And if they have, I will kill them."

The humor doesn't go down well, she frowns even harder and despite my best attempts to keep her where she is, wriggles off my lap.

"It was a joke," I tell her.

"Was it?" she says.

But I don't feel like descending into another argument. I bring my fingers to my mouth and suck at my fingers. The musky sweet flavor dissolves across my tongue.

"Thorne is staying at the academy. If you need anything ..." I tell her, and then I rev the engine up and drive her back to the academy. "We'll pick you up at seven tomorrow," I call as she climbs out of my car, her cheeks still rosy from those orgasms. "Be ready."

Chapter Nine

Briony

"You were gone a long time," Fly says, eyeing me with suspicion when I find him hanging out with Clare in her room later. "Hmmm ... and you have that flush about you."

"What flush about me?" I say. "I don't have a flush about me."

Clare adjusts her glasses and steps in closer to take a better look at me. "You do."

"Can we take it this means Beaufort Lincoln is forgiven?" Fly crows.

I give him the finger. "I don't want to talk about it."

"Urgh," Fly says, throwing himself down on the mattress. "You're the only one getting some and yet you won't share any of the delicious details with us." He lifts his head and peers at me. "Please say you did it in his car."

"We did not do it in his car," Fly drops his head back

down on the bed and groans, "but we did do some stuff," I say to pacify him. "Although, you don't have to beg for scraps of information about my love life. You could have one of your own."

"Right," he says flatly.

"You could," Clare says. "You're really very handsome."

"In a way," I add and Fly returns the finger.

"Plus you're stylish."

"Talking of which," he says, rolling up onto his feet with sudden excitement. "Come and take a look at what your old godmother has for you ..." He leads me towards Clare's closet and opens the door. Hanging on the other side is a pale silver dress with a beaded corset and light floaty skirt. The straps are mere pieces of string but Fly has draped a matching bolero over the hanger.

For a full minute I stand there gobsmacked. I don't think I've ever seen anything so pretty in real life before.

"Where did you get this from?" I ask, running my hand down the delicate gauze material.

"Not everyone in my family despises and detests me," Fly says, lifting the dress down from where it's hanging and feeding the jacket and the delicate shoulder straps off the hanger. "I have one member of my family who actually likes me – my sister-in-law. Don't get me wrong, she only likes me because I make her pretty dresses when she asks me to, but it means she's occasionally willing to do things in return for me. Like sending me this dress so you can borrow it for the ball tomorrow."

I shake my head and take a step away.

"Oh no," he says, wagging his finger at my face, "don't you start all that stupid nonsense. No," he holds his hand to his chest and adopts a high-pitched voice, "I couldn't possibly, it's too beautiful, I'm not worthy."

"I do not sound like that!"

"Try it on," he thrusts it towards me, "I need time to make any adjustments."

"Everyone will stare at me in a dress like this," I protest.

"I gather that's the idea," Clare says.

I turn to my other friend. "Give it to Clare. It would suit her skin tone better."

"Clare already has a dress," Fly says.

"And I am not thrall to the Princes. You need to look the part."

"Exactly," I say, "if I turn up in a dress like this on the arm of Beaufort Lincoln–"

"So he is taking you then?" Fly says, glancing towards Clare with excitement.

"–everyone will hate me more than they already do. They'll think I've grown too big-headed, too conceited."

"Only because they'll be dying of intense jealousy because you'll look stunning and they'll be in no doubt why you have captured the attention of the academy's three hottest dudes."

"I'm not exactly sure–"

"I made this myself, Cupcake," he says, "if you don't wear it, I will be severely insulted, heart broken and dejected, and may never be able to talk to you again."

"Jeez," I say, blowing out my cheeks, "okay."

Despite Fly's complaints that we are all good enough friends to see each other in our underwear now, I usher the both of them out of the room and slip on the fragile dress.

My skin still tingles from Beaufort's touch and the way he had me falling apart on his lap, and although I know I'm asking for trouble, that I'm falling into the trap I said I would avoid the most, I can't help but turn and stare at myself in the mirror, wondering what he'd make of me in this dress.

The girl I find in the mirror has me gasping in shock and for a moment, just a fraction of a moment, my mind is fooled into believing ... until my senses swoop back. It's me. Just me. But for that moment, that fleeting moment, I thought it was her.

I run my hand over the tight corset, imagining Beaufort's hands holding me there, then let them trail down the soft skirt. I don't look like me, like some kid from the Slate Quarter. The usual bruises and marks on my face have been smoothed away by Fox's magic, my hair is braided around my head like a crown for everyone to see, and the dress pinches in my waist and makes me look like I actually own some curves.

"Can we come in?" Clare whispers from behind the door.

"Uh huh," I whisper.

"Wow, Cupcake!" Fly says, clapping his hands together. "You look sensational."

"Like a princess," Clare says, mouth hanging open.

I don't know if it was thinking my sister was here with me in the room, or the stress of everything that's happened over the last twenty-four hours, but a sadness stabs me right in the center of my heart. I sniff and shake my head, tears burn behind my eyes. I don't want to cry, not when my friend has done something nice for me like this.

"What is it?" Fly says, half joking, "is my design and needle work really that bad?"

"It's beautiful, Fly, you know it is. But I can't wear it."

"Why not?" Clare asks. "You can't really be worried about what others think?"

"It feels like a betrayal," I whisper. Every glimmer of

happiness does. Standing here with my friends. Making out with Beaufort in his car. Going to the ball in a dress far too good for me. It's all a betrayal.

"To who?"

"My sister. I shouldn't be worrying about boys, or balls or dresses. I should be out there finding answers. I'm letting her down."

"Cupcake," Fly says, resting his hand on my shoulder. "Your sister sounds like she was a really ..." he searches for the word, "kind girl. It sounds like you both truly cared about and loved each other. Tell me, if the roles were reversed, if it was your sister standing here in front of this mirror, would you begrudge her some fun, some happiness? Stars know, we don't get a lot of it – especially you kids from Slate."

"You really think so?"

"You knew her, not me. What do you think?"

"I think she only ever wanted me to be happy. She was always going out of her way to make me happy – to make me laugh or to make me feel better or to ensure I wasn't afraid."

"Then she'd want you to be enjoying yourself – as much as it's possible to – here."

"But I should be finding the truth. I owe it to her."

"Is there any reason why you can't do both?" Clare asks.

"And you know, the more I think about it," Fly says, straightening the dress a little and pinching in the corset just a tad, "the more I think you've been looking at this all wrong. You want answers about your sister. You suspect shadow weavers may have those answers. And three of the most powerful want to make you theirs. Don't you think that might prove pretty useful?"

"He's right–"

"Obviously!"

"–they might be able to help you, Briony. If you let them."

"Maybe," I mumble.

"Definitely," Fly says, "don't cut off your own nose to spite your face. You're pretty, but not that pretty. You couldn't pull off the no-nose look."

"And," Clare says, ignoring Fly's silliness, "you could also let us help you."

"It's too dangerous."

"Cupcake, just being in the same vicinity as you is dangerous. Today I was nearly run over by Beaufort Lincoln," I cringe apologetically, "the week before I was nearly electrocuted by Henrietta Smyte."

"I think we may be able to help," Clare says.

"How?"

"I'm quite good at researching things."

"Clare, you're very good," Fly laughs. "You worked out the first trial was going to be a maze. You have no idea how much that helped us out! And you earned a zillion points."

Clare blushes and adjusts her glasses. "The next trial isn't for another two months. There's no need to start researching yet, which means I could look into your sister. If you'd let me."

"You really wouldn't mind?"

Clare shakes her head.

"There we have it then," Fly says, clicking his fingers. "Clare will be in charge of library research, I will be in charge of costume design. And you, Cupcake," he bops me on the nose, "will be in charge of seduction."

"Sed–"

"Uh uh," he says, pressing his finger against my lips. "No arguing with the master plan."

Fly insists on spending the rest of his day off making what he terms 'necessary adjustments' to the dress, even though I can see nothing wrong with it. The gown appears near perfect to me.

Clare and I debate going for a walk around the grounds or even into the forest, but seeing as the last time we wandered off like that, I ended up struck by lightning, we decide we may as well start the library studies.

"The last time I tried to find a book in here," I say, "it was as if the library was being deliberately unhelpful, the shelves seemed to be moving around me."

"Ahhh," Clare says, "that's because it is an enchanted library."

"Of course it is," I say flatly, "stars forbid the academy would actually have anything ordinary and useful."

"An enchanted library is useful if you know how to use it."

"Do you have them back in Granite Quarter?" I ask.

"No, but I read about them ..." she giggles, "in the library. Every enchanted library has its own personality – some are more friendly than others, some more secretive, and some down right obstructive."

"This one is definitely obstructive."

"Not if you get on her right side."

"Her?"

"Well, of course, knowledgeable, intelligent, astute – she'd have to be female, don't you think?"

"Definitely," I say, threading my arm through my friend's as we walk up the steps towards the main door.

"Besides, I've been buttering her up. Reading to her. Donating some of my own books to her. Filling her in on all the gossip. I think she likes me. She certainly led me to all the most useful books about past academy trials."

"There aren't many books in the library back in Slate Quarter, but it's a hell of a lot easier to borrow one."

"Shhh," Clare says, "you don't want to upset her."

We walk though into the main entrance and Clare says cheerfully, "Good morning, Library."

Just like before, it's gloomy, crammed and untidy but this afternoon sunlight pours through the high-up windows, making the library appear colorful, friendly even.

Still, I can't help glancing at my friend and wondering if she's a little cuckoo.

"It's a beautiful day outside," Clare continues, "but we prefer to spend our time in here with you reading." The library shelves seem to vibrate with pleasure, the books themselves seeming to hum. "Is there really anything better to do?" she asks.

"Sex?" I suggest.

Several shelves slam together, one coming to shoot right across our path and block our entrance. Clare glares at me.

"Best you keep quiet," she hisses, then addresses all the books again. "Library, I think the two of you may have gotten off to a bad start. Briony here loves books and learning as much as I do, don't you, Briony?" She nudges me in the ribs and I nod exaggeratedly. "And she's befriended me when no one else would. I promise, she really is very lovely."

The shelf slides across the floor slowly but still blocks our path and above our heads the ancient chandelier turns on its chain.

"Now you speak," Clare whispers.

"What should I say?"

"Tell her why you're here." I squirm on my feet. It feels

ridiculous to talk into an empty room. I'm not even sure who or where I should be directing my words to. Clare nudges me again. "Go on."

"Okay." I take a deep breath. "My sister was killed at the academy nine years ago. I want to find out what happened to her."

"And we think there may be some answers, or at least some information, that could help us in the library. If we can find it."

The chandelier twists back the other way, the chain groaning and I get the distinct impression the library is considering me and my request.

"Please," I say, "I owe it to her to discover the truth and I don't know where else to start."

Nothing happens. I glimpse at Clare.

"Maybe this isn't going to work," I say. "The library is a part of the academy and if the academy is keeping secrets maybe the library is too."

The shelf blocking our path, slams backwards and in front of us, the stacks begin to dance, churning and spinning and twisting, so quickly it makes me dizzy.

Then, as quickly as it all starts, it freezes, a path through the stacks laid out in front of us.

"Come on," Clare says, taking my hand in hers and dragging me through the library, right into its depths. It reminds me a lot of the maze we had to fight our way through as part of the last trial, and seeing as I came close to losing my life in that maze – even though Professor Tudor was meant to be keeping that from happening – I don't love the feeling.

"This place gives me the creeps," I whisper into Clare's ear.

"Shhh," she says, pulling me around a bend, a flock of

library books discarded around our feet, and then stops. We've come as far as we can.

The shelves here are especially high, reaching all the way up to the ceiling and blocking out the sunshine up above. Long ladders rest against the shelves, although they don't look at all steady. The shelves themselves are rammed full with huge leather-bound volumes.

"This is it," Clare says, stepping towards the shelves and running her fingers over the spines, "the history of the academy." She pulls one from the shelf, a cloud of dust bellowing up into her face. She wipes a thick layer from the cover and peels open the first page. Even from a pace away I can smell how musty the book is. "I don't think anyone's looked through these in a long, long time."

Sliding the book into place, she runs her finger along the spines of the other books lining the shelf, then tips her head backwards and looks up.

"This isn't what I found last time. That was like an official yearbook."

"They aren't the books I found when we were looking for information about the trials either. These seem more like ledgers, record keeping. See how this one has been filled in by hand." She tilts the book towards me and I see dark ink scrawling across the yellowing page.

"Is it the right year?" I ask her.

She shakes her head and I step forward and help her search among the shelves. Soon it becomes apparent that the year we want is somewhere high on a shelf above us.

"Fiddle sticks," Clare mutters.

"My thoughts exactly," I say, examining the ladders and their missing rungs.

"Do you think it's safe?" she asks.

"Probably not," I say, rolling up my sleeves and stepping up to the one that looks the most secure.

"Here, at least let me hold it steady for you," she insists, taking a grip of the ladder. The thing is so long and spindly looking I'm not sure it will help much, but I let her go ahead, and I start to climb.

"Just like a tree," I call down to her as I ascend up the shelves, passing decade after decade, climbing forward in time as I do, wondering if the books I'm passing contain the details of my ancestors. A great-great-grandfather perhaps, maybe a distant cousin. Were we always bound to Slate Quarter, doomed to spend our days there from the creation of the realm? Did none of them have talents, skills, abilities? Was Amelia the only one who was different?

I'm so consumed with my thoughts, I stop paying attention to my footing, and halfway up the towering bookcase, as I lean all my weight on my left foot, the rung gives way, falling out from the ladder. My foot falls with it, and I plunge, grasping at the rung above me with both my hands and clinging to it for dear life.

Below me, Clare screams, the ladder wobbles, shaking me as it does, and I hear the dislodged rung clatter violently onto the floor.

"Briony!" Clare calls up to me. "Are you okay?"

My palms are damp from the climb and my hands slipping against the rung, but I cling with all my might and swing my feet upwards. The first time I miss, the sole of my shoe sliding hopelessly against the bookshelf. The second time is no better, and my hand slides that much more against the wood.

"Briony!" Clare yelps.

But on the third time I do it, swinging my body into the bookcase and landing my feet on the shelf. I wobble dangerously for one moment, almost tipping right backward, before I right myself and let out a long exhale.

"I'm okay," I call back down to Clare. "Are you? Did that piece of wood hit you?"

"No, just missed me." She mutters some unusual curse words to herself. "Please be careful. I think the Princes might burn me alive if I let anything happen to you."

I wipe the palms of my hands against my pant legs and start climbing again.

This time I'm more careful, testing each rung before I commit to it. Three more prove to be unstable and I have to yank myself past them, reaching up high for the rung above.

Finally, the years become more recent. I pass the year my grandmother was here. The year my parents must have come. I'm so tempted to stop and flick through them. My father never spoke about his time at the academy, although I know he met my mother here. Marion spoke about it all the time, delighting in frightening me with horrific stories. She always swore she lost the top half of her right index finger at the academy as well as her left ear. It was enough to give me nightmares when I was younger, especially after the loss of Amelia.

The highest shelf contains the books from this decade. There are several for each year and I realize the details contained inside must be vast. I shimmy along the shelf, Clare sucking in breath and warning me to be careful from below. I spy my sister's year along the shelf, but not before I pass the year Fox Tudor must have come as a student. For a moment I pause.

Would it tell me his secrets inside? How he came to realize he owned the ability to weave shadows? What happened when it was discovered? How that led to him teaching here at the academy and not going to live with the other shadow weavers in Onyx Quarter? My fingers brush across the spine, and I'm oh so tempted to pull the book out and riffle through the pages.

Something stops me though, and it isn't just my very big need to get down from this dangerously high shelf. To open the book would feel like an invasion of privacy. I know what it's like to have secrets. He hasn't chosen to share this information with me. I don't think it would be right to go sneaking behind his back searching for it – no matter how tempting it may be. Fox Tudor is an enigma – a very hot, very sexy one. For now he'll have to remain one.

I force myself away from that book and along to the right year. There are three volumes for the year my sister attended the academy. And there is no way I am going to be able to carry them down the ladder without breaking my neck.

"I'm going to have to throw the books down," I call to Clare.

"Erm," she says hesitantly, "I don't think Library will like that. You could damage them."

I peer over my shoulder, out towards the library. "Sorry Library, I don't want to hurt these books anymore than you do, but I don't have a choice."

I go to hook the first one off the shelf and throw it to the floor, but before I do, it slides from the shelf itself and, spreading open its pages, takes off like a bird in flight, fluttering out across the library and then spiraling down to land by Clare's feet. The second book does the same, followed lastly by the third.

"You couldn't have done that before I climbed all the way up here," I say.

The shelf wobbles slightly and I take it the library doesn't find my cheek amusing.

I'm about to make my way back along the shelf and down the ladder, when my eye catches the end of the shelf. It's half empty – the books for the future are yet to be written, bound and placed on the shelf alongside its cousins. But right at the very end of the row, sits this year's volume. It is slim compared to the others – we're only four weeks into the academic year after all – but I'm surprised to see a book there at all.

I may have been able to resist the temptation of rifling through Fox Tudor's yearbooks, but I cannot resist the temptation to peer into my own. I shuffle along the shelf towards it.

"What are you doing?" Clare calls. "Aren't you coming down?"

"Just one second," I call back.

I stretch out for the book and slip it into my shirt, then I shuffle back to the ladder and make my careful descent back to the ground. This time there are no near accidents. I know the rungs to avoid and climbing down is quicker work than the ascent.

When I reach the ground, I find Clare sitting cross-legged on the floor, already pouring through the pages.

"Found anything yet?" I ask.

"Huh?" She looks up at me blinking, then shakes her head. "But there's so much information in here – from what was served in the canteen each day to the lessons taught and which pupils attended." She stares up at me, her eyes wide behind her glasses. "It's like a treasure trove, Briony. I think it could give you a day-by-day account of your sister's time at the academy." She gathers the books up in her arms and stands. "I think it could give you answers."

I take one of the books from her hands and flick through

the pages. She's right, the record keeping inside is meticulous and thorough.

"Who wrote these?" I say, because whoever they are, I think I should talk to them.

"I have no idea," Clare says, turning the books in her hands. "There's no author." She looks up at me. "This might sound really strange, but it's almost like they wrote themselves."

Chapter Ten

D^{ray}

I climb out of the vehicle and raise my hand to shield my eyes against the glaring sun. Scents blow towards me on the wind along with familiar howls and short sharp barks.

I grin, swipe off my shades, spit my gum to the ground and start to unbutton my shirt.

Fuck, it's good to be home.

I tip my head backwards and let all that sunlight tickle across my face. Feels awesome.

The academy is entertaining and all – in fact it has some very distracting entertainments – but it isn't the savannah of Onyx Quarter. It isn't home.

I yank off my shirt, toe off my boots and then I'm jogging out into the open space, bypassing the house alto-gether. In less than ten strides I'm already down on four paws thundering across the dry grass in pursuit of those scents and those sounds.

The wind sweeps through my fur, the ground comes up to meet my paws, and I stretch out my limbs, whipping across the land.

I've run to meet the horizon twice by the time I see them, laid out on rocks by the river, basking in the sunshine.

Lazy fucks.

They hear me coming, raising their heads off the rocks to peer out towards me. Then they're up on their paws and bounding towards me. Six great big wolves – not as big as me – but big, nonetheless.

Danders reaches me first and we plow into each other, rolling over and over on the ground before the others catch up, all seven of us tumbling over and over each other. I pin Damson down but then Danders and Dyle knock me off and I'm pinned beneath the three of them, until I nip Damson on the leg and yank Dyle's tail.

Then we're tumbling some more, over and over until I'm dizzy and in the river, splashing about with my brothers until we're soaking wet, our fur stuck flat to our muscular bodies.

Afterwards, we climb back out onto the rocks and I flicker back into human form. My brothers will want to talk. I'm the oldest, the strongest, the biggest, the first to enter the academy. The little freaks are going to have fuck loads of questions.

I lie out on my back, hands tucked behind my head and stare up at the blue sky. It feels like a fucking age since I saw the sky.

The others are as naked as I am. And while they're not as handsome as me – they aren't bad looking. It would be enough to give those virgins at the academy freaking seizures in their pussies.

It seems pussies are exactly what my brothers have on their minds. It's the first question out of Danders mouth. Not surprising he'll be heading to the academy himself next year.

"Is it like they say?" he says, scratching his taut stomach, "girls falling over themselves to grab some shadow weaver cock?"

I laugh. "Yeah, it's something like that."

I snap a stalk of grass and chew it between my teeth.

"Man," Dyle shakes his head. He still has another three years to wait. Not that any of my brothers struggle to get pussy – it's just out here in the savannah it's not as plentiful as seven brothers would like.

"Is it true they'll let you fuck them with their friends?" Dirk asks. As the youngest, he only got his first girlfriend a month ago.

"You saying Shiva doesn't let you fuck her with her best friend?" Deny says, nudging his twin in the ribs and both of them snorting.

"She's fucking killing me, man," Dirk says, dragging his hands down his face. "My balls are so blue I look like a fucking alien."

"She's still not giving it up," Deny asks him.

"Nah, we're taking it *slow*," he says, exaggerating the word so it drags on forever.

"Fuck that, man. If she won't let you fuck her, then get her to suck your cock."

Dirk lifts his head and grins. "Ahh, she does that already."

Deny kicks him. "Then stop complaining. In fact, shut

up altogether. I want to hear about Dray's exploits, not your pathetic hand holding with your girlfriend."

"How many have you fucked?" Damson asks. "We've got a wager going."

"You are sick fucks," I say, staring up at the sun as I chew on the grass.

"Don't be coy," Damson whines. "You know we've been killing ourselves waiting to hear this stuff."

Their impatience is understandable. I've usually spilled my guts by now, reliving every detail and every titbit from whatever trip or campaign or rustle I've just returned from.

Thing is, even if I did have anything to share about my little kitten, I'm not sure I want these bozos pouring over the details. She's too special for that. She's mine. Not something to be shared with these fuckers – even if the sharing is only secondhand.

"Have any let you fuck them in your wolf form?" Deny asks.

"We've got a wager going about that too," his twin adds.

I groan. That's the fantasy – the ultimate fucking fantasy. There aren't so many of us shifters these days. Every year, there are fewer and fewer of us born. It's why our family – with seven strong, healthy boys – has become the most powerful pack in the realm. Problem is, female shifters are becoming even rarer and, while the human girls are willing to let me do all fucking sorts to them, they draw the line at the whole wolf-fuck thing.

"We'll take that as a no," Damson scoffs, disappointed and disgusted with me. Partly my fault. I may have bragged my fucking ass off about all the things I was going to do at the academy.

Plans change. Circumstances change.

I wasn't expecting her.

I remove the stick of grass from my mouth and roll onto my side, propping myself up on my elbow and glaring at my younger brothers.

"Careful," I warn, my tone low and dangerous.

I don't mind messing around with these losers, but let's not forget who's the alpha in this pack.

The younger ones drop their gazes immediately to the ground, showing me their submission and their obedience.

Wonder if I could get the little kitten to be as obedient. Whether she'd drop on her knees for me and do exactly as I say. The thought is positively electric.

Danders, Damson and Dyle are not so willing to submit. They've all grown bigger in the last few months and maybe they are under the illusion that they can beat me in a battle. They couldn't, my wolf is stronger and my magic harder. None of them has ever come close to testing me.

"Are you shitting me, boys?" I cackle. "Sit the fuck down. Mama won't want me whipping your asses on my couple days back. She'll want us acting like one big happy family."

The younger two peer at each other, then drop their gazes. Damson just keeps right on staring at me. One month away from home and he already thinks he rules the place.

I laugh. Maybe Mama wants it all to be peaceful, but it's a hell of a lot more fun when it's not. And how long has it been since I've had the excuse to whip my younger brothers back into place?

I grin.

"Have it your way," I murmur, and then I'm shooting shadow magic at all six of them. It snaps around their necks, crushing their windpipes.

"Dray," Dirk whines, "what the hell did I do?"

The younger five submit to my deadly grip, bodies limp,

eyes downcast, only Damson attempts to struggle against it, grappling with the shadows, firing frantic magic of his own at me. I bounce away as if it's a ball and watch it plummet into the river.

For a moment, his form flickers between human and wolf and he becomes more frantic, kicking out his legs and twisting his body. I only squeeze all the harder.

"Submit, little brothers," I say, from where I'm lying on my side, twisting blades of grass around my fingers.

The five younger ones murmur their surrender and I release them immediately, all of them coughing, spluttering and rubbing at their necks.

Damson growls and I shake my head.

"Okay," I say, lifting him up from the ground and leaving him to hang, thrashing about in the air. The others look up at him and laugh, which makes him all the madder.

But he's running out of oxygen now and in another few seconds, he's gurgling, "Okay, okay, Dray, I fucking submit."

I drop him and he falls to the earth, landing with a grunt.

I jump up to my feet and walk over to where he's groaning on the floor.

I lean over him, cup his jaw in my hand and then smack a fat kiss on his cheek, ruffling his hair.

"Nice try, Bro. Nice try."

The parents are waiting for me out on the veranda when I return an hour later – Dad in his chair, blanket wrapped over his legs, mama leaning against the railing.

"You couldn't come and pay your respects to your father when you arrived?" she hisses into my ear as I bend down to kiss her cheek.

"I'm paying my respects now," I say, bending down to kiss his face too. He pats my cheek.

"You've been missed," he says.

"They've been running around like a pack of wild animals," my mama says, peering out to the land where my brothers are still chasing one another across the grass. "You know they caught a pale stag last week. I had the Empress's guard here asking questions."

"They're just kids," I say, collapsing down into one of the chairs and letting her pour me a glass of home-made lemonade. It could do with something more potent, something with a kick. But alcohol's been banned in our household since the accident – as far as she's concerned anyway.

"They need to grow up," she says with a tut.

"How was the first trial?" my dad asks, cutting straight to the chase as always.

"Piece of piss," I say, knocking back the drink.

"Language." My mama tuts. She's seen me rip out the throats of our enemies and yet she still takes offense at a few curse words. No wonder I'm so fucked up in the head.

"It was easy?" my dad asks.

I shrug. "Easy for me. For others ... I don't know."

"How did you fare in comparison to Cadieux? To Lincoln?"

I lean down and place my glass on the floor. "We haven't been given the points yet," I say. It's only half a lie. They posted them this morning, but I never bothered to go and check. What's the point? I know I aced it. "But if you're asking if they–"

My dad's eyes flare. "Not good enough."

I lift my gaze and smile at him. It's not like he was top of the academy in his day. From what I've heard, his wolf was weedy and pathetic. Yet, somehow he expects more from me.

"Noted, Sir," I say.

He leans away from me. Despite the tough guy act, I scare him. I think I scare them all.

"What's this about some girl?" my mama asks, wheeling my dad's chair around a little so he's not staring into the setting sun.

"What girl?" I ask, my spine stiffening and my hackles rising. It would be dangerous if they knew about the girl. Fuck knows what they'd do with that information. I don't trust them. It was probably the two of them who put the idea in Damson's head to challenge me in the first place.

Then again, I don't trust anyone in this pack. It's just what packs are like. Backstabbing, conniving, treacherous. How'd you think my father ended up in the chair and I took his place as head of the family?

"You found yourself a cute little thrall to keep you happy?"

I lean back in my chair, rubbing my fingers against my chin. "Yeah, yeah we did. Cute enough, nothing special."

"Something you can chew up and spit out," my mama says, eyes twinkling just like mine.

"Yeah," I say, "yeah, something like that."

Chapter Eleven

B riony

"While I understand your need to find out what happened to your sister," Fly says, bouncing his fork up and down in his dinner, "does this mean we are officially geeks now and will be spending all our time with our noses in books?"

"I'm from Granite Quarter. Both my parents are doctors. Being a geek is in my blood," Clare says, taking a mouthful of pasta and turning her page, eyes not leaving her book.

"What's your excuse?" Fly says, kicking me under the table to get my attention. "I didn't think you kids from Slate could read."

"Huh?" I say, peering up from my book and staring blankly at him.

"Is it that interesting?" he says, "or am I way more boring than I realized?"

"You are a bit of a bore," I tell him with a grin, "but there's just so much information in these books. It's going to take us an entire year just to wade our way through them."

"Can't you just skip to the bit ..." Fly trails off, "you know what I mean."

"Got to find that bit first," Clare says, eyes skimming over the text, "time doesn't exactly move fluidly through the books. I just read five pages about a potions lesson that went horribly wrong and then it skimmed by the next two weeks. It's like only the important – or interesting – events have been given in detail."

Fly sighs dramatically and I close my book, then close Clare's.

"We have been at it for several hours. We should take a break."

"I was at an interesting bit!" Clare protests.

"Really?" Fly says, tipping salt into his stew and stirring it around. "Interesting how? Did someone crack the spine of their book?"

Clare looks at him with horror, then shakes her head.

"I was reading up about the second trial that took place in your sister's year. Did you know that someone got caught cheating?"

"No, she never mentioned that. The postal service back in Slate is pretty unreliable. Her letters came sporadically. I think some may have gone missing." Fly and Clare both stare at me. "What?"

"Isn't that sort of suspicious?" Clare says, taking off her glasses and buffing them with the sleeve of her cardigan. An item of clothing Fly has threatened to burn, but she refuses to part with because it's comfy. I understand – I wouldn't mind one for myself. "It's sort of odd your sister's letters never reached you given what happened."

I want to smack myself on the forehead. Hard.

"Yes," I say. "Yes! That is. Why the hell did I never think of that?" For a moment my spirits soar high – this is proof, proof something strange was going on. But then, just as quickly as they soar, my spirits plummet right back down as if they've been shot right out of the sky.

So what?

Knowing some of her letters went missing on their way to me provides me with no more actual information, no more actual insight. It's not like I can summon those letters to me. It's not like I'll find them hidden under a floorboard in my room. Or some mysterious stranger will present them to me. Where ever those letters went, wherever they are, they're long gone now and I can't ever hope to land my hands on them.

The three of us are quiet for a moment, then Fly asks, "So what happened with the cheating?"

Clare flicks open the book to the page she was studying and runs her fingers down the text. "A kid from Onyx Quarter was caught helping another student – a student also from Onyx Quarter."

"Why?" Fly snorts. "Like they don't have enough of an advantage to begin with."

"It doesn't say. And the names of the individuals involved have been omitted. But they were severely punished."

"Huh?" Fly snorts a second time. "Were they forced to eat in the canteen with the rest of us commoners?" He lifts his fork and lets the gloopy stew drip off the prongs.

"No," Clare says, color draining from her face. "It doesn't say what happened to the student who was helped, but the shadow weaver that helped them was banished from the realm."

Fly and I stare at Clare gobsmacked, and I'm certain the color drains right from my face too.

Banished. Not even expelled to one of the lesser Quarters. Or sent for a life of misery in Slate.

Banished from the realm. Which can mean only one thing. Certain death.

"Shit," Fly says, "that's ... I thought the punishment meant you lost your points for that trial – that is ..."

"There must have been more to it," I say. "They wouldn't banish someone from the realm simply for helping a friend."

Clare skims her finger down the page. "That's what it says here. I mean, I guess we have no idea if it's accurate or truthful, but it's so detailed in every other aspect, why make something like that up?"

"To scare us," Fly says, finally giving up on the stew and dropping his fork onto his plate.

"Except nobody reads these books," I say, "and even if they did, this detail is buried among many other events in hundreds and hundreds of pages."

"I think Briony is right. I think the purpose of these books is to record what happens at the academy. All of it."

"I wonder why they helped the other student like that," I say.

"Sex," Fly says. "Sex is always the reason for everything."

"Or love," Clare says, her eyes turning slightly dreamy. "That's so romantic."

"Or it could have been friendship," I say. "If you needed my help, I would risk my neck for you."

"You'd risk banishment?" Clare says, a wobble to her voice.

I shiver. "It wouldn't be my first choice, but yes, yes, I would."

Fly rests his elbow on the table and leans his chin on his hand. "Awww, Cupcake, you're adorable. But no you wouldn't. I wouldn't let you."

"Have you ever heard what it's like out there beyond the realm?" Clare asks. "Have the Princes ever spoken about it?"

I hesitate. Beaufort alluded to it in that argument we had, but he never went into details. "Not really."

"My older brother's been out there once on an assignment," Fly says. "They were sent as backup to some shadow weavers who were disposing of demons attempting to break through the protective barriers."

"And?" Clare says, her eyes wide with horror.

"He wouldn't talk about it."

"Why not?"

"He came back with third-degree burns all down his left arm. Burns the shadow weavers couldn't heal. I take it he didn't want to go over it. He wanted to forget about it."

"Jeez," Clare says.

"If it doesn't tell you why the shadow weaver helped their friend in the trial," I say, pointing back to Clare's book, "does it tell you how they helped the other student? What did they do?"

"I'm not exactly sure. It's written in a long-winded and complicated manner as if the writer is trying to avoid spitting out the truth. But I think," she pushes her glasses up her nose, "they gave them some of their magic."

"What?" Fly says, lowering his voice and leaning forward. "Is that even possible?"

Clare shrugs and lowers her voice in reply. "I've never heard of it before."

"Have you, Briony? Briony?"

I stare down at the table, the blood roaring in my ears.

I'm back in the maze, that wisp of shadow magic dancing before my eyes, protecting me from danger.

Is that what happened? Did a shadow weaver give me their magic?

And if they did, who the hell was it?

Clare takes her volume back to her room with her and I take all the others back to mine.

Fly complains about being ignored in favor of books so I stay up chatting with him a while before retreating back to my room.

I head straight for my closet, pull out the stone and bring it into bed with me, resting it in my lap as I pull the volumes from the library towards me.

The cracks have grown even longer during the day and the stone feels warmer than normal against my skin. I run my palm over its surface and it seems to reverberate.

That's new.

I stare down at the volumes – at the thick ones from my sister's year and the thin one from my own.

I flip open the cover of my own, cautious to see what lies within.

The account starts right when the last train – the one from Slate Quarter – arrived at the station and the last of the students filed out onto the platform. It recounts the Empress's speech and even the words of that asshole shadow weaver who stood on the pile of bags and threatened everyone. Then it goes on to list what happened that night. I skim over all the harrowing details of shadow weavers attacking other students – beating them, frying them, strangling them. It doesn't make easy reading. And Beaufort wondered why the hell I'd be resentful about his kind.

I keep skimming and then, to my utmost surprise, catch a glimpse of my own name. I retreat back up the text and find it again.

My encounter with Beaufort.

I stare at it in shock. I don't know why, everyone else's encounters are included – it's just ours was so fleeting, such a passing nothing event. He didn't hurt me. He barely spoke to me.

And yet, while other altercations are given a line at the most, our encounter is described in detail over one paragraph.

I frown, reading it again and again, reliving it as I do, unable to help but shiver.

There's one sentence in particular that puzzles me, that I don't understand.

The shadow weaver saw and that is why he pursued the girl from Slate Quarter.

What the hell does that mean? Saw what?

Are all our other encounters included in here? Are they included in as much detail? My cheeks burn as I flick through the pages, the stone warm in my lap.

I catch snippets of bits and pieces as I flip the pages. Stanley has been enjoying himself as far as I can see – sleeping with most of the girls from Iron Quarter already. Odessa has been up to all sorts with the Hardies. And it seems I'm also not the only one she's been bullying.

I find my various encounters with Beaufort, even with Dray too, but – thank goodness – the book doesn't go into as much detail as that first encounter. They are more just passing comments.

I'm about to put the book away for the evening, when another idea occurs to me.

I flick right to the back of the book, looking for the account of the maze trial.

Maybe it'll give me information about who helped me in the maze.

I have to wade through a lot of information. Several hundred students went through the trial and it gives at least some details about how each did. I see Thorne Cadieux completed the maze the fastest – Beaufort and Dray not too far behind him. I find details of Clare being whisked away by a tornado, Fly chased by that beast. And then finally I find myself.

I stare at the few words written about my ordeal in the maze. And then I stare some more.

It says I failed.

That's all. Nothing more. Nothing about the brambles retreating. Nothing about Madame Bardin attacking me. Nothing about the wisp of a shadow.

Should I be surprised? The academy has its secrets and its cover-ups. Of course, there'd be no record of a teacher attacking a student.

I shake my head in disgust and run my finger over the deceptive words. As I do I feel the texture of the paper is different here. Holding the book up to the light, I peer in more closely. Something's been altered. The words have been tampered with.

Chapter Twelve

T horne

The raven hops on the ledge, knocking its beak against the pane of glass.

I ignore it, but then it knocks again and again, becoming increasingly frustrated.

"Shoo," I growl at it. "You've got the wrong person."

It halts its jumping, looks at me with its beady black eyes, tilts its head to one side, and then squawks.

The message is clear: it isn't giving up.

I stride to the window, draw back the latch and let the bird fly inside.

"Fine," I mumble. "On your head be it."

The raven, its jet wings spread wide, circles my room twice, before landing alongside my gloves on the chest of drawers and lifting its right leg into the air.

Careful, I untie the note from his leg. It isn't easy. My

gloves are restrictive and this is fiddly work, but using my magic could harm the creature.

As soon as the note is loose, the bird squawks angrily, hops away and then takes off through the window.

Whoever sent me the note wasn't expecting a reply.

I unfurl the note. The writing is Beaufort's, but it's so tiny I can't read it. I stomp up to his study and hold the note beneath the magnifying glass that stands on his desk.

Short and sweet.

Professor Tudor healed her injuries.

To the point. There's no question of who he's referring to or why I'd consider this information of interest.

And now it makes sense. That's where she was headed. Professor Tudor's classroom lies at the base of the teaching tower, down in the old dungeons.

Despite our investigations, we have no further information about what happened to the girl in the maze. What we do know is that Tudor was meant to whisk any students facing danger out of there. So why didn't he help Briony? And why was he the one to fix her injuries?

Is there something going on between the two of them?

I crush the note in my fist. The shadows roar inside me.

I take the note back down to my room and toss it into the fire. It catches alight, shriveling and shrinking into ash. Then I step out into the night.

I've been watching over the girl as best I can. It isn't always possible. There are moments she slips away, moments I cannot be with her, moments I've failed to keep her safe. Were there also moments she was with him?

The night is still and bitterly cold, the stars bright and clear in the sky above the towers.

I take the long roundabout route, avoiding anyone out

tonight, and then sink down into the dungeons. This is where his classroom is. I'm hoping this is where he will be.

I hammer my fist against the door and after several drawn out minutes, it creaks open, Professor Tudor hovering on the other side. He's as tall and broad as I am and maybe the fight would be evenly matched if it were down only to fists, but with magic involved I'm sure I could crush him.

Not that I'm here for that, despite the eagerness of my shadows to unleash carnage.

"Cadieux," the professor says. I've barely seen his face since I've been at the academy. He tends to linger, hidden in the shadows, like he doesn't want to be seen.

Sometimes I've wondered if we share an affliction. But now, as I peer into his ghostly face, I realize we don't.

"It's my day off," the professor says.

"We need to talk."

He's probably surprised to hear that. I'm not known for my talking.

He considers me, then nods and steps inside, leaving the door ajar behind him.

The classroom is even colder than outside, my breath hanging in a pale cloud in front of my face.

"You've come to talk about Briony," he says.

I nod.

He perches on the edge of his desk, folding his arms over his chest, making his biceps strain against the material of his shirt. Deliberate perhaps?

"What is it you wish to discuss?"

"You healed her."

Annoyance forms on his face. "And I guess you're going to tell me that I shouldn't have? That she's your thrall," he spits, "and I shouldn't have touched her. And maybe I wouldn't have had to if you were taking better care of her."

"*You* were meant to remove any students from the maze who were in danger. Why didn't you remove her?"

He glowers at me, then stares down at his shoes. "Something went wrong. I would have if I'd known she was in ..." He halts mid sentence and peers back up at me. "She hasn't told you what happened, has she?"

I take a menacing pace towards him.

"Tell me what *did* happen."

"You think it was me?" he chuckles. "Why the hell would I attack the girl and then heal her afterwards?"

"It's what abusers do," I whisper. Full of remorse after the event. Begging for your forgiveness. Right before they do it all over again.

"I'm here to teach my students, not abuse them," he growls. His magic is cold and prickling against my skin. "She told *me* what happened. *I* know who is responsible and I've dealt with it."

"Who?" I say, taking another pace towards him, my hands clenching inside my gloves, straining against the leather, my shadows hot and raging and menacing.

He draws himself to his full height so we're glaring into each other's eyes, his glowing in the darkness.

"I've told you, I've dealt with it. It won't be happening again. She's safe – at least she is from that direction."

"If you're insinuating–"

"The girl doesn't want to be your thrall," he hisses. "Can you blame her when you've been doing such a terrific job at protecting her?"

He's deliberately trying to provoke me, to draw my attention away from who was responsible.

"Tudor, who was it?"

"It's best you leave this to me. I know you boys think you're indestructible, untouchable – but this is someone you don't want to cross."

"Beaufort is untouchable."

"This person doesn't care." He stares off into the distance. "Sometimes I think they are fucking insane."

"That doesn't make me feel any better about the situation," I growl, wracking my brain to identify who he must be talking about. Not one of the students. There are rumors Henrietta Smyte has inherited her mother's insanity. She used to date Beaufort and the way she likes to drape herself all over him has me believing she would still like to date him. But would she be foolish enough – insane enough – to attack the girl? Possibly, but I don't think she has the powers or the skills to manipulate what happened in the maze.

"This person isn't a problem," the professor says. "They won't be hurting Briony again. You have my word."

I consider him the way he considered me only moments ago. Can I trust him?

There's something hovering in his eyes – something I wonder if he can see in my own.

"I'll be holding you to that word," I tell him.

When I return to my room, I write a short note of my own.

Tudor knows who was responsible for what happened in the trial. He is going to deal with it.

I send the note to Beaufort via raven. An hour later, another bird is knocking at my window.

And we can trust him?

I consider that look in his eyes, the determination in his voice.

Yes, I reply. *We can.*

Chapter Thirteen

B riony

I sleep with my body curled around the stone, my arms clutching it tightly to my chest. All night it radiates heat, vibrating against my body and by morning I swear the cracks have penetrated more deeply into the stone's surface.

Is it broken? Did I break it somehow?

Once again I consider returning to Professor Tudor and showing him my treasure. Or perhaps I could brave the library again, see if it would help me find a book that could identify the stone.

Neither of those options seems appealing. Instead, I sit in bed and flip through that book again. I reread the account of my meeting with Beaufort. Look again at the description of what happened in the maze. It seems all the other students were hooked out of that maze as soon as that beast got too near, or the bramble started to entwine them or any other danger ventured too close for comfort.

Did Madame Bardin manufacture things somehow so that I wasn't saved? Or was it that shadow? Did that shadow interfere somehow?

This book isn't going to answer my question though. However, as I'm flicking through pages again, I realize it might help answer another.

I skim through the pages, hunting for the night Odessa trashed my room. I find a description of my room being destroyed, only I was wrong. It wasn't Odessa at all.

It seems someone else hates me as much as Odessa does. I guess I'm not surprised. Although, if I'd had to place money on this, I'd have guessed Henrietta would have been the one to destroy all my possessions.

Not Linette.

I *am* surprised that a shadow weaver like her didn't find the stone buried in the bottom of my closet. If the stone pulls me towards it – a commoner – I'm certain it would attract the awareness of someone who can wield magic.

I flick through the next few pages. There is other information in between. A fight between two Iron Quarter boys. A description of a new homework club. And details about that day's meal. Then there I am returning to my room and finding it trashed.

And right beneath, the information I was hoping for.

The girl from Slate Quarter lifts the firestone from her bag, relieved to find it was not stolen.

Firestone.

I'd always suspected and then dismissed the possibility. Firestones haven't been found in the realm for hundreds of years and the last ones vanished around the same time.

But here it is in black and white. The stone I found, the

stone that called me to it, is a firestone. I just don't know what the hell that can mean.

I insist we hang out in my room the next day, which my friends definitely do not understand given that I probably have the worst room in the academy. Plus yesterday's sunshine is long gone; today there's an icy wind sweeping through the academy and right through my ceiling, bringing with it the odd flake of snow.

"Do we really have to hang out in here?" Fly asks me for at least the tenth time, poking at the pathetic flames in my very small fireplace.

It is a lot warmer, a lot more comfortable and a lot less vermin-infested in Clare's room, but I'm already going to have to be dragged away from my stone for the evening. I don't want to be parted from it for the entire day. Not now I know just how special it is – even if I don't understand what that can mean and what if anything a firestone can do.

However, I do have someone who might be able to help me – a walking, talking, breathing encyclopedia.

Clare.

In fact, I wouldn't be surprised if she knew more than Professor Tudor and Professor Cornelius combined!

The only problem is how to introduce the topic into our conversation subtly without giving myself away. Subtlety is not exactly my forte.

I spend most of the morning coming up with clever ways to shoehorn it into our conversion, then chickening out. In the end, with the ball approaching, I simply blurt it out.

"Ever wondered where the academy got its name?"

"Nope," Fly says. He has several pins in his mouth. He's insisted on raising the hem of Clare's dress because, and I quote, she is not living in a convent.

"They say the first firestones were found in this location," Clare says.

"Oh," I say as casually as I can, "they never really taught us much about firestones back in Slate Quarter. The lessons were more ... practically focused." I pull a face.

"Yeah, we didn't learn much about it," Fly mumbles around his pins.

I look at Clare hopefully, but she's concentrating on the passage she's reading.

"Clare?" I prompt.

"Oh, sorry," she says, "I'm getting seriously invested in this relationship between two dudes from Iron Quarter. Their relationship is seriously on-again off-again and so much drama."

"We were talking about firestones," I say.

She's still focused on the book. "I don't really know much about them – except there's that statue outside the Great Hall."

"There is?"

Fly laughs. "You can't really miss it. Big, ugly bronze thing with those three ugly dragons." He stabs a needle into Clare's dress. "Honestly, I don't understand the obsession with dragons. They are so flipping ugly."

"What's it got to do with firestones?" I ask.

"Briony," Fly says, clearly doubting my intelligence, "that giant oval thing in the middle of the statue – that's a firestone."

I'm about to open my mouth and ask more questions but my words are cut off by the roar of an engine. It's so loud I swear the floor vibrates beneath us. Fly goes to investigate out the window, although how he can see anything out of those long narrow slits, I've no idea.

"Yep," he calls. "The shadow weavers are back."

"Oh yay," I say flatly.

"You're not fooling anyone, girlie," he calls back, still staring out the window, "we haven't forgotten that flush yesterday."

"I bet they'll be seriously disappointed with their audience today." Surely, no one's stupid enough to hang around outside just to ogle some stupid vehicles when it's this frigging cold.

"There's still quite a crowd out there." He swings back around. "Right, if the shadow weavers are back then that definitely means it's time to put those books away and start getting ready. You girls go get showered. I'm nearly done with this stitching."

I shiver at the thought. "There's no way I'm showering today," I say. "I don't want to catch pneumonia."

"You won't and if you did, I'm sure Beaufort would cure you."

"Still, I'd rather not freeze my tits off."

"Briony," Fly says, striding towards me and taking ahold of both my shoulders. "I love you. You're a truly wonderful human being. But you stink and your hair needs washing."

"I do not stink," I say, lowering my chin and attempting to sniff myself. "I took a shower yesterday."

"Cupcake," he says gently, "in Slate Quarter it may be acceptable to bathe once a fortnight but everywhere else we wash daily."

"Asshole," I tell him.

"Who only has your best interests at heart. All our interests at heart. I'm determined we're all going to get laid tonight."

"Oh, I don't think that's likely," Clare says, fiddling with her glasses.

"With the adjustments I've made to this dress, it's *highly* likely. Now get moving both of you." We stand there staring at him. "Go!"

The shower is far colder than I dreaded. Around me I can hear others squealing, gasping and even screaming in agony.

I wash as quickly as is humanly possible, scrubbing my hair with some shampoo Fly has lent me, and then go stand in front of my pathetic fire, hoping to warm up.

I think of the raging fires in the Princes' tower. How warm and toasty it is even in the bathrooms. I think of that deep hot bath.

Maybe being their thrall wouldn't be all bad. Well, clearly it wouldn't. Beaufort has the ability to turn my body to fire. He drags orgasms from me that must be magical.

I sigh, thinking about that and then I snap the hell out of it and concentrate on rubbing my body dry with the flimsy towel.

Twenty minutes later, my body may be dry (although still freaking freezing) but my hair is damp. Fly knocks on the door and enters.

"I've come to do your makeup."

"Makeup?" I say, peering at him from a funny angle as I dangle my hair in front of the fire.

He points a finger at me as if it were a dagger. "Don't even think about arguing. Everyone needs makeup. Even the most stunningly beautiful of human beings."

"Are you going to wear some then?" I ask.

He steps in closer and flutters his eyelashes at me. Over his eyelids he's dusted something sparkly and his eyelashes are coated in a dark paint that make them look thicker and longer than usual. "Already am, Cupcake."

"You can do that to me too?" I ask.

"We're going to do a little more than this to you, Cupcake." He takes my face in his hands and angles it upright. "You don't have naturally defined cheekbones like I do and your lips are a tad on the thin side."

"Jeez, thanks," I say.

"No worries. This is what makeup was invented for. Now where is your makeup bag?"

I stare at him with an amused look.

"You really think we have luxuries like makeup back in Slate Quarter?" I say, a little annoyed at my friend. "You know once we went without bread for two whole days."

He cringes. "Shit, Cupcake. You're so ... stoic about this bullshit, I sometimes just forget. Let me go get mine."

He halts by the door. "Do you think Clare has no makeup too?"

I shrug and continue to rub at my hair.

Another five minutes later, he has me sitting on the bed, bottles and tubes and little cases spread across the mattress.

"It's not the best stuff," Fly mutters, smudging something pink over my cheeks. "It's all the bits and pieces my sister-in-law didn't want anymore. Smuggled of course, because ..." He shrugs. "Tip your head back and don't blink." I tip my chin up, but as soon as he comes towards me with a short black stick, I flinch. "It's mascara," he explains. "Hold still or I'll poke your eye out."

"Gosh, that sounds reassuring! Do I want to lose an eye in the pursuit of beauty?"

"Yes," he says, "the dress is stunning. You can't let it down with drab hair and makeup."

"Will you do my hair in braids again for me?" I ask,

trying my best not to tear up as he combs black liquid across my eyelashes with a tiny comb.

"Uh uh, we're going to do something more elegant this time."

I sit quietly, attempting to imagine what on earth that can mean as he brushes colored powder across my eyelids and paints my lips a pinky-red color.

"There," he says. "Not bad. Go take a look."

I walk to the mirror and peer at the reflection.

"Wow," I say, tipping my face one way and then another. "I look like a shadow weaver."

"They just look better than us because they can afford better cosmetics and face creams," he says.

"And can probably use their magic to remove pimples," I point out.

"That too." He bends down and rummages in the bag he brought with him. "Now, for your hair."

He pulls out another implement – something that again looks suspiciously like an instrument of torture.

"What the hell is that?" I yelp.

"Curling irons." He walks over to the fire and places them carefully alongside.

"Are you going to brand me on the ass?"

"No, I'm going to curl your hair."

"With something you're heating in the fire?!" He nods. "No way. I've already lost parts of my hair."

"You won't lose any more. I will be careful."

I shake my head.

He nods his.

We glare at each other.

The fire crackles. I can smell the irons warming.

We stare some more.

I'm the first to blink.

"Fine. But if any more of my hair is burned off, this will be the end of our short but sweet friendship."

"Understood," he says, lifting the irons out of the fire with the rubber handle. He touches it lightly with his hand and then, instructing me to take my seat on the bed again, gets to work on my hair.

"I think," he says with a grin on his face, as he arranges my hair in waves of curls, "even Cinderella's fairy Godmother didn't achieve such an amazing outcome."

Chapter Fourteen

Briony

The tower clock chimes at seven o'clock and I am suddenly a bag of nerves, probably feeling a lot like Cinderella did herself.

I take one last glance at myself in the warped mirror. I have to admit, Fly has worked some kind of miracle. I don't look like myself at all. It makes me uncomfortable – this isn't me, is it? Some glamorous woman hanging on the arm of powerful men? For the last few years it's been just me looking out for myself, scraping by to survive. Will others look at me and think I'm one big fat fraud? Will they resent me even more for it?

I straighten my shoulders and lift my chin.

Do I care what they think? No, no I don't. After all the girl from Slate has a damn firestone hidden in her room!

With one last straighten of my skirt, I walk towards the

door. Fly has returned to his own room, and I promised to go knock for him.

However, I get no further than my own doorway, because there, standing on the other side of the door when I draw it open, is Dray Eros, leaning against the wall and chewing gum.

A huge grin stretches across his face as his eyes meander down my form. Slowly. Very slowly.

"Fuck me, Kitten," he says, removing the gum from his mouth and pressing it into the wall, "you look good enough to eat."

"Jeez," I say, nearly jumping right out of my skin. "You scared me."

"What? Me?" He grins. "The big bad wolf?"

"What are you doing here?" I ask, closing the door behind me, before I realize this leaves the two of us trapped together on the narrow strip of landing.

"Come to collect you. That was the deal, right?"

"Were you going to knock, or were you just going to wait there all day?"

"Depends if I got impatient or not. Come on, the others are waiting." He goes to take ahold of my elbow and I move it straight out of his reach.

"Erm, no. I'm going with my friends – not with you."

He groans like I've just said something really dull. "Not this bullshit again. Can't you and Beaufort just kiss and make up already? It's getting boring."

"We did … sort of …" I say, crinkling my brow and trying to decipher what exactly did happen yesterday.

"Sort of?" he says with a smirk.

"It's complicated with him. Every time I think we can get along, he shows me who he really is."

"You didn't know already?"

"Oh, because he's so popular and so wonderful, I'd have to know who he was."

"No, because he's an asshole and it's clear all the way from outer space. Look," he bends down low so our gazes are level, "he messed up. You never mess up before?"

"Did he tell you what he said to me?" I ask, scowling right into Dray Eros's ridiculously mesmerizing eyes.

"Uh uh, but, come on, he can tell me now." He grabs my hand and this time I don't get the chance to dodge it, nor am I strong enough to pull my hand from his tight grip. Unless I want to scream and shout and make a scene, I'm left with no choice but to trot along after him as he pulls me along.

It's as I do that I take in for the first time what he's wearing. Not the academy uniform or his usual favored outfit – sweatpants and a T-shirt. Tonight he's dressed in a well-fitted dark suit. Okay, so he isn't wearing a tie and his shirt is undone all the way to his sternum, but he still looks the smartest I've ever seen him, especially with his long platinum hair combed loose.

I guess his nose really does have super powers or something because as I'm checking him out, he peers over his shoulder at me and grins. I don't need superpowers myself to know what that look means.

My cheeks warm.

"Where exactly are we going?" I ask.

"There are drinks in the shadow weaver common room before the ball starts."

"Uh uh," I say, shaking my head wildly. "There is no way in hell I'm going to that."

"Rather go back to my room and mess around instead?" he growls.

The way he looks tonight, I hate to admit, but that offer is tempting.

I bite on my lip. What the hell is wrong with me?

Okay, so protectors share their thralls and, though Thorne is clearly unhappy about that prospect, Beaufort and Dray have both made it very clear that they want me. That they both want me. But isn't it still crazy that maybe, just maybe, I want them both as well? Because, aren't I only meant to want one person at a time? Isn't it a little bit greedy that I'd happily take both of them?

Dray chuckles and pulls me in close to his body, wrapping his arms tightly around my waist and peering down into my face.

"I can see you're considering that offer, Kitten." He leans down and whispers in my ear: "I can smell you are too." He nips at my earlobe. "But good things come to little kittens who wait. I'm going to have you dripping wet by the time I take you home to bed tonight."

I swallow. Dray Eros has a very dirty mouth and I wish it didn't have such a potent effect on me. Unfortunately, with that damn nose of his, he knows exactly how potent he is.

He nibbles his teeth down my throat, then back up to my ear and whispers, "Come on. I want to show you off at this party. Every other dude – and every other girl – is going to be fucking sick with envy."

He's pulling me along again before I can voice any more objections. His pace is swift and excitable and I have to trot along to keep up, relieved the heels Fly found me were too big and I'm in flats instead.

We weave along the campus pathways, brimming with other students this evening – some already dressed up, others dashing from one tower to another with arms full of dress or bags of makeup. Everyone we pass stops and stares as Dray pulls me along. They're not even subtle about it and as usual I can hear them whispering, wondering who the girl Dray is with is.

Do I really look that different or are the students here extremely unobservant?

Outside a tall glamorous-looking tower, my heart once again leaps into my throat.

"Do we have to go to this party?" I ask, peering up to the top of the tower. The top floor is made of glass and multi-colored lights flash from within and the pound of music wafts our way. It's like nothing I've seen before.

"Yep," Dray says. His grip on my arm has loosened but his grin is just as wicked. "I wanna show those other losers how fucking amazing you look. Rub their noses in it."

"I don't think that is going to do me any favors," I mutter.

"What do you mean by that?" he asks, suddenly serious.

"Nothing," I mutter.

"You did," he says, eyes boring into me. I glare right back at him but he's a hell of a lot scarier than I am and in the end I have no choice but to concede.

"Everyone in this academy already hates me."

"We don't," Dray says, grinning. I think of Thorne. I don't think Dray is right about that.

"You guys are largely responsible for that. They don't think I should be your thrall." Because I'm not good enough – not pretty enough, or popular enough, not even that skilled at anything.

"We don't give a shit what those losers think. And they're wrong," Dray says.

"Doesn't matter. They still hate me."

"Who cares," he says, snaking his arm around my waist.

I care because the hate directed at me from the other students has often been physical. Black eyes, broken noses and strained ankles are all testaments of that. If I mention that now though, there will be a lot of follow-up questions. He'll want to know who has hurt me. I don't fancy being dragged down that path again.

"Can't we just go to the ball?" I try one last time.

"Come on," Dray says, "it'll be fun. I promise."

I let him lead me inside the tower, because, really, what choice do I have? It's grand – like I imagine the interior of a posh hotel in Onyx Quarter must be like – all mahogany woods and dark velvets. There is no staircase leading up to the top of the tower where I assume the common room and this party is. Instead, there's an elevator. I've never been inside one – not even the ones back in the mines in Slate Quarter. Although, I'm sure the mine elevators don't have polished mirror walls, gold buttons and twinkly music. The box lifts us up into the air and I gasp as my stomach fails to keep up with the rest of my body.

"All right?" Dray asks.

"Uh huh," I say, laying my palm over my stomach. "I've never been inside one of these before."

"We've got four inside the mansion back home," he says, matter-of-factly without a trace of a boast.

"Did you go back home for the break?" I ask, suddenly curious. "To your family?"

He examines my face with amusement. "You heard about my brothers, huh?"

I shake my head. "Brothers."

"Yeah, there's seven of us." My eyebrows shoot up my forehead. "But don't get excited, little Kitten," he leans in and whispers in my ear. "I'm the most handsome, the strongest and the best."

Somehow I don't doubt it. "That wasn't what I was–"

"Fuck! That reminds me!

He steps to the side and slams his fist against the array of golden buttons. The elevator comes to a juddering halt, jolting me forward and into his waiting arms.

"I got something for you." He reaches into his pocket and pulls something out. "To match your eyes."

"I'm not wearing a col–" I begin.

"Relax, Kitten."

He opens his fist and a delicate golden chain falls through the air and catches. At the end is a bright green gem the shape of a teardrop and the size of a galleon. It bounces on the end of the chain.

"I figured you'd need something pretty to wear." I watch mesmerized as it swings from side to side, wondering if it possesses magical, or maybe even hypnotic, properties.

He snaps open the clasp and then he reaches around my throat and fastens it at the back of my neck.

"W-w-where did you get it?" I ask, trying to keep a hold of my thoughts as he slides his hands under my loose hair, his fingers warm on the back of my neck, and frees my locks from the chain, letting the cool necklace settle against my skin.

"My mom," he answers, his gaze fixed on the crystal that now hangs against my chest.

"Your mom let you give this to me?" I say, surprised. Does that mean his mom knows about me? Does that mean she approves? I can't see that she would. A girl from Slate.

Dray strokes his fingers over my shoulder, along my clavicle and positions the crystal at the apex of my cleavage.

"Not exactly," he says, his eyes flashing darker. He sweeps his fingers along the soft skin of my chest.

"Huh?" I say, finding it even harder to focus on our conversation and not the feel of his fingers, of his magic, against my flesh, warming my skin, making it tingle with awareness, my body turning to liquid. I'm surprised I'm not a puddle on the floor.

"I wanted it for you," he growls, leaning down to nuzzle at my throat, "so I took it."

My eyes start to drift shut and I've definitely lost all track of his words. But then, without warning, the lift creaks and shoots upward again.

Not that it deters Dray, he's still scraping his teeth up and down my throat, inhaling my scent, as the elevator rises quickly – I can hear the passing floors rushing past us – and then it slows and comes to a halt, the doors drawing open and two large shadow weavers waiting right there, the party in full flow behind them.

Beaufort and Thorne.

Like Dray, they are dressed up tonight in expensive-looking suits. Beaufort's a midnight blue that makes his silver eyes all the more dazzling and Thorne a jet black. Beaufort has tied his hair back showing off his chiseled features and Thorne's gaze seems even more penetrating than usual.

If they chose to seduce me tonight, I think I'd need super powers in order to resist.

"Dray," Beaufort growls, and with a petulant groan, the shifter lifts his mouth from my throat and turns to face his friends. "Where the hell have you been?" Beaufort says.

"I got distracted," he says, shrugging his shoulders and then stepping aside so the other two see me properly for the first time.

"Fuuuuck," Beaufort says, his eyes swimming all over me. "You look so damn beautiful, Briony."

"You don't have to sound so surprised," I mutter, because I don't exactly know what else to say. I'm not used to people offering me compliments. Especially about the way I look.

"I'm not," he says, meeting my eyes. "I saw it from the moment I first laid eyes on you."

That sounds like bullshit to me. I had a black and swollen eye and had just spent eight hours on a train.

Although I do remember how good he looked, even in the half-dust, even in the darkness.

Thorne doesn't say a thing, just stares at me unblinking. I can't tell if, like the others, he thinks I look great, or he disapproves.

"Come on," Dray says, hand on the small of my back, guiding me out of the elevator.

It's probably my imagination but I swear, as I step into the common room with the three Princes by my side, the party music cuts off and every single person in that room turns to stare at us.

Chapter Fifteen

D^{ray}

I love making a fucking entrance and tonight we are making a hell of a one.

Our thrall looks stunning – like whip your breath right away and leave you with a hard-on so stiff it's painful to walk stunning. I can't stop looking at her, can't stop touching her. And I really, really want to fucking lick her because as always her scent is like wolf-fucking-nip!

As the elevator doors draw back, everyone in that Onyx common room spins our way and I just grin.

Yeah, eat shit, dickwads. You think we picked the wrong thrall? You have no fucking idea. Because our thrall is the most beautiful woman in this room. In the entire academy. Probably in the realm.

"Hey shitheads," I call out. "I thought there was meant

to be a party happening here tonight. But I guess you were waiting for me, were you?"

I pull the little kitten right into the center of the room, the crowd parting to let us through, their mouths hanging so far open, they're practically hitting the floor. I twirl her under my arm and drag her close. Then I lift my right arm above my head and click my fingers. The music starts. I twirl her around again.

"Stop fucking drooling over our thrall, you perverts," I yell my eyes not leaving hers, "unless you want the three of us to rearrange your faces. And let's face it, you're all ugly enough as it is."

Slowly, continuing to steal glances our way, the other shadow weavers, a few thralls among them, start dancing, drinking and talking again. I can see the Smyte sisters in the corner with their thrall. If looks could kill, I'd be bleeding from every orifice.

"Hold on tight, little Kitten," I whisper into her ear. "We're going for a little journey."

"What–" she starts, her brow crinkling, but then I'm twirling her around and around again, leading her right across the floor towards the place where the Smyte sisters are hovering like a pair of hags.

Seriously, what the hell did Beaufort ever see in Henrietta? Okay, she's hot and unhinged, which can be fun, but the girl is way too high maintenance – and not in the good way. Besides, I've heard them fucking. The girl is a bad lay.

"Hey ladies," I say, as they scowl at me. "I believe you've met Briony before."

"Yeah," Briony says coolly in a way that has my wolf sitting up and taking notice. "We've met."

"How lovely you look, Briony," Henrietta says,

smacking a brittle smile across her lips. "What a pretty little dress. Where on earth did you find it?"

I'm guessing this is some girly shit, a disguised insult – although fuck me if I understand how that works.

"It looks good enough to rip off," I growl, "and that is all that matters." I lean down and nibble my kitten's throat, the little thing wilting against me despite the audience. I can literally feel the sisters seething at us. I have a feeling Henrietta saw herself with more than just Beaufort. I think she hoped she'd be all of ours. I peer up at them. "Enjoy your evening, ladies," I say with a wink, and then I spin our girl away, back towards the other side of the room where Thorne's lurking.

"I think we made our point," I say, "wanna go to this ball?"

"Go?" Beaufort says, appearing from behind us. He's carrying four glasses of champagne in his hands. "I just got us drinks."

I take one from him and knock it straight back.

Thorne shakes his head so I take his too and finish it off.

I tilt my head towards the remaining two.

"You having one, Kitten?"

"What is it?" she says, peering at it with suspicion.

"Champagne." I take the glass from Beaufort and offer it up to her. "You ever had champagne before?"

She cocks an eyebrow at me. "What do you think?"

"It's meant to taste like the wolf's bollocks. Personally I think it tastes like sweet grape juice."

"The wolf's bollocks?"

"It's a turn of phrase among us shifters."

"It's because they all think their balls taste like the best shit on this earth," Beaufort mutters.

"I wouldn't know," I tell her. "That's not really my thing, but from what the girls tell me ..." I wink.

"Jeez," she says, rolling her eyes and knocking back the champagne. She wasn't expecting the bubbles, and she wrinkles up her nose and blinks rapidly.

"Easy," Beaufort says, taking a sip of his and then resting it down on the nearest table.

She glares at him and before the two of them can start arguing again, I weave my arm around her waist and lead her back to the elevator.

"Come on, let's get to that ball. We made our point."

"And what point exactly were we trying to make?" she queries as the others follow us in and I hit the button for the first floor.

Trapped inside this tin can, her scent is contained and amplified and smells so fucking awesome my fingers are twitching to slam her against the nearest wall and devour her.

But there's no way Beaufort would allow it, even if he did have her over his desk himself.

"Just wanted to remind them all that you're ours and under our protection," Beaufort says, "seeing as you won't tell us what happened in the maze or who's been hurting you."

"And you refuse to wear our collar," Thorne mumbles, staring straight ahead at the metal doors.

Rather than argue, like this little kitten is prone to do, tonight she simply nods.

The ball – if you can really call it that – is held in the Great Hall. An old decrepit building with none of the modern conveniences most ballrooms back in Onyx Quarter have. No grand chandeliers, no full-piece band, no ornamental lighting show. It's pretty basic, although some effort has been made with glowing orbs floating up near the ceiling and a table laid out with some basic food the commoners are crowded around.

The little kitten tips back her head though, her eyes go wide and her mouth forms an oh shape. She's impressed – possibly even wowed.

I shake my head. "If you think this is impressive, you'll be blown off your feet when you see Beaufort's place."

She looks at me with curiosity, opening her mouth to ask me a question, but I'm bored with talking.

"Wanna dance again, Kitten?" I ask her, already leading her to the dance floor, ignoring Beaufort's complaints that it's his turn.

There are more people dancing here than there were back in the common room and it gives me the excuse to press her body right against mine, lean down and nibble on her throat, breathing in mouthful after mouthful of her delectable scent.

I would die a happy wolf with my nose pressed in the crook where her neck meets her shoulder, where her scent is vivid and intense. It makes my head spin. Makes me wild. Makes the wolf howl inside me. I hold her close and grind against her.

"People are watching," she hisses, although she isn't pulling away, isn't telling me no. In fact, her scent is screaming yes fucking please.

"Let them watch. Half of them will be fucking before the night is out."

I growl lowly and grind some more.

This time she tuts and to my delight tugs on my hair. Wonder if the kitten would do that in bed? "Don't you know how to behave?"

"Kitten, where the fuck is the fun in behaving? Besides,

if you wanted me to behave, you shouldn't have worn this dress. All my wolf wants to do is tear it to pieces with his teeth."

She stops tugging and, as I nibble with more force down her throat, she sighs and buries her fingers in my hair.

"Beaufort's giving us the evil eye," she murmurs.

I spin her around so she's no longer facing his way. While I'm willing to share and all – a condition of our brothers' bond, one of those things we have to live with – I don't want the little thing thinking of him when she's in my arms. Not right now, anyway.

As if she can read my thoughts, she yanks on my hair more forcefully, forcing my head up so I'm staring into her face.

"How does this work exactly? The sharing thing? I mean, you three could have anybody you wanted in this academy. Why would you want to share? Why would you want to share me?"

"Sweetheart," I say, "there can be a lot of fun sharing. Just imagine it." I lean down and whisper right into her ear: "Three men pleasuring you together, pleasuring you at the same time." She's silent but I don't miss the shiver she tries to suppress. I'm hardly surprised. I bet everybody has that fantasy, even if they never admit it. "You thought fucking Beau was intense – imagine fucking all three of us at once."

"You've done that before?" she asks, a little astonished.

"Nah," I say, "but we want to. We want to have you together."

"Thorne doesn't want me," she mutters, but I note she's not arguing about the concept, the idea of it.

And fuck, that turns me on. I'm so hard, I feel like my balls are about to explode. Who am I kidding? They've been like this for days. Probably weeks now. That comes from the lack of fucking around. Usually I'd have a different girl visiting my bed every night – my brothers weren't wrong about that. Heck, they wouldn't even need to be visiting my bed.

But since this little thrall walked into our lives – black eye and a little grubby looking – I've been fucking hooked. No other girl is doing it for me. Which is fucked up when you're a wolf-shifter with a fuck load of wild oats to sow.

"Maybe not in that way," I say, "but don't take it personally. He's not into anyone in that way. Doesn't mean he doesn't want you as ours."

She gazes over at my quiet bond brother and bites her lip.

"Hmmmm, I like it when you do that, Kitten."

Her eyes flick back to mine. "Do what?"

"Bite your lip like that." I pull her right up close against my stiff cock and lean down to her ear again. "Your lips are sinful. All I can think about is them wrapped around my cock."

One thing about my kitten I've noticed, she can't get enough of my dirty mouth. Hell, wait till my dirty mouth is fixated on her pussy, then she really won't be able to get enough!

My words make her wet. I can smell that sweet musky aroma of hers, permeating the air.

It makes my head spin and my balls ache even harder.

I lick around the shell of her ear and she whimpers a little.

"Your scent is sinful too, little Kitten. You smell just like a wet mate ought to."

"Mate–" she begins to say, not finishing her words because I've had enough. The dance floor is filling up. Too many people pushing and jostling around us. Not enough room, not enough space to do what I want to do to her.

Hooking my arm firmly around her waist, I guide her through the crowd of people – way more wasted than they were an hour ago – and towards the far side of the hall, into the shadows.

We pass one couple making out against one of the stone pillars, a girl sobbing on the floor being comforted by her friend, and a boy with a tie wrapped around his head, vomiting into a bowl he's pinched from the food table.

We walk further into the shadows, where the glowing lights don't penetrate and we're hidden from prying eyes.

"Where are we going?" she asks.

"Somewhere private, little Kitten."

Except we don't make it any further because blocking our path, arms crossed, scowl on his face, is Professor Tudor.

Chapter Sixteen

B riony

"Turn around and walk back the way you've come," Fox growls, scowling at Dray so hard I'm surprised the shadow weaver doesn't spin us around on the spot.

Of course, this is Dray Eros and he never ever does what I expect.

"Hey Prof.," he says, slinging his arm up around my shoulder and grinning. "I know lurking around in the shadows is your favorite past-time but seriously, man, don't you have better things to do?"

"I'm here to guard against any students who think this is a suitable place to get up to mischief. This is a sacred hall. Not to be desecrated."

"Desecrated?" Dray snorts. "This isn't a fucking temple. And have you seen what they're doing out there?" He points out towards the well-lit dance floor where the music has turned sultry and most of the dancers are necking.

Fox ignores him and directs his withering gaze on me. "I'm also here to ensure students who have drunk too much don't do anything they might regret."

It's clear what he's implying and I lift my chin in defiance, even as my cheeks flame.

"Oh, she isn't going to regret anything, Prof. I can promise you that."

Fox whips his gaze back around and they stare each other down.

I shift my weight from one foot to another, feeling mighty uncomfortable. Fox is a teacher. He probably has a duty to be here ensuring student welfare. But this feels personal and I don't appreciate him interfering in my love life. I definitely don't appreciate him suggesting I don't know what I'm doing.

Okay, so maybe I don't. Dray is making me feel things I don't quite understand – is making me feel things I'm finding it hard to resist.

"We should–" I start, twisting in Dray's embrace.

"No, we shouldn't," he says, his grasp on me tightening, "if the professor wants to stand there and watch us make out, little thrall, he's more than welcome. It might even be fun." He chuckles. "Hell, he may even learn a thing or two."

"From you, Eros," Fox sniffs, "I very much doubt it." His eyes flick to mine. "And she's not your thrall."

"Just because she's not wearing our collar, doesn't mean she's not ours," Dray says possessively.

"To be clear," I say, "I don't *belong* to anyone."

But neither of them are listening. They're too busy eyeballing each other.

"Seems the professor is a pervert." Dray finally laughs. "Is that the real reason you like lingering around in the shadows? So you can spy on young women? I mean, it's wild. Probably illegal or something. I wonder what Madame Bardin would make of that."

I'm pretty sure the Madame's behavior isn't exactly appropriate, but Dray's words seem to make Fox uncomfortable.

He scrubs his hands through his hair.

Dray laughs. "This is definitely how rumors start, don't you think, Prof.?"

"I can't believe you're wasting your time with this loser," he sneers at me. Like I've personally affronted him, then storms away, back towards the hub of the party.

"Were you threatening him?" I say, with a frown.

Dray shrugs dismissively. "Not exactly. I think the professor has a massive hard on for you, Kitten. I think he'd love to stay and watch me make you come."

"That was really shitty," I say, wriggling out of his grasp.

"He was being shitty," he says, his face falling. "We're just having some fun. Don't we deserve it after what we've been through with that trial?"

I'm not sure Dray went through anything with that trial. Not like the rest of us anyway.

However, he adopts his best puppy dog eyes – the ones that remind me of his wolf, that have me softening despite myself – and reaches out to take my hand.

"Besides," he says, "I'm dying here, kitten. You have no idea what it's like to have the nose of a wolf. All I can smell is your deliciously wet pussy and it's driving ... me ... insane!"

He yanks me towards him and then his mouth is on my

throat again and he's nibbling it in that way that whips away all my reasonable thoughts and processing abilities. It wouldn't matter to me if Professor Fox was standing right here watching us, I wouldn't be able to stop Dray. I wouldn't want to.

I reach up and comb my fingers through the long platinum strands of his hair – just as soft as the fur of his wolf – and he snakes his hands around my waist and down to squeeze my ass.

"I want to devour you, little mate," he groans against my skin.

Mate. That word again.

Dray calls me all sorts of things. Some of which make no sense at all. But the way he says that one word, with meaning, makes me think it has some. Only, what?

He lifts his head and looks me right in the eye, mischief, as always, dancing in his.

Then, he walks me backwards, further and further into the shadows, until my back hits the cool stone of the hall wall.

Then he kisses me.

Dray Eros is chaotic so I shouldn't be surprised to find his kisses are chaotic too. Soft, sensual, slow one moment, hard and frantic and breath-stealing the next. I can hardly keep up, hardly adapt to one feeling before he's evoking the next from me.

Something swoops low in my belly and I shiver with desire as I kiss him back, tasting mint and champagne on his tongue.

Fox is right. Making out in public like this – even if we are hidden in the shadows – is pretty shameless. I don't care though. Half the academy seems to be doing exactly the same thing and most are doing it a lot more publicly. Fly's comment about people getting knocked up obviously wasn't an exaggeration.

Besides, there's something thrilling about kissing Dray Eros in the shadows of the hall, his erection pressing against my belly, his hands gliding all over my body –- kneading my breasts, squeezing my ass, gripping my waist, lifting the hem of my dress.

"Need to know if you really are as wet as you smell, Kitten," he pants.

I'm sure I am in fact wetter. I'm sure I've never been this wet before.

I writhe against the wall, as he strokes a hand up my leg, stroking his knuckles against the inside of my thigh and growling like his wolf when he hits the gusset of my panties. They're wet and he must feel it through the thin material.

"Fuck," he groans, slipping his fingers inside my panties and stroking along the seam of my pussy's lips next.

"All swollen too. What a good little kitten you are. Going to mewl for me now?"

I let out a sound which probably is pretty close to one as he slips a finger between my folds and rings my hole, plunging that finger knuckle-deep inside me as I brace my hands against his chest.

"And tight," he says.

He reaches up higher inside me, finding that spot Beaufort discovered before.

It has ecstasy swooping in my belly and my fingers tightening in his jacket.

"There, huh?" he says. "That's the spot you like. Want me to make you come?"

I squeeze around his finger because I'm struggling to get my words out, all my attention focused on what he's doing to me instead.

"I'll take that as a yes." He chuckles, and leans in to kiss me again, massaging that spot as he does. I'm incapable of kissing him back, I'm too busy trying not to cry out; the sensations he's wringing from my body delicious.

He nips at my bottom lip playfully, then kisses along my jawline to the sensitive point below my ear. Here his lips leave a trail of kisses down my neck, along my clavicle and down to the swell of my breast, to where the gemstone rests against my skin. He kisses the curves of my breasts too, through the material of the dress, and then drops lower still, over my ribcage and my belly, until he's sinking down on his knees.

"Need to taste that pussy, need to taste my mate's pussy."

He lifts my skirt and then he's disappearing beneath it.

"Dray!" I call out, because if what we were doing before was obscene then this is ...

All my thoughts melt away as he yanks my panties to one side and his mouth meets my clit.

"Oh ... stars!" I cry out, my head falling back against the wall.

He growls a second time, even more wolf-like than before and it vibrates against me, sending more delicious sensations spiraling through my body. My legs falter and I scrape my hands along the wall, trying to find purchase.

"Hang on to me," he says, his voice muffled beneath my dress, "I'm about to take you on one hell of a ride, Kitten."

He isn't lying. He flicks his tongue hard against my clit and for a second my vision whitens. It's like being struck by lightning – only this time in a much (a much much much) more satisfying way.

His shadows crackle with excitement in the air around me, tingling against my skin and he licks and flicks at my clit, until my pussy is clenching in waves around his fingers and I'm clinging on to him just to stay upright. Then he's sliding those fingers from me, an action that has me whimpering because it felt so good to be full like that, loved like that, and in a moment his mouth is there too, showing me just how much a pussy can be loved.

If what I did to Beaufort that night in his room – when I sucked him in my mouth and he came down my throat – was half as good as what Dray is doing to me now, then Fly was correct. I could reduce the Princes to mere putty in my hands. Because I would easily beg for this. It feels intimate and dirty, rough and gentle, sensual and filthy all at once. He laps at me, licks at me, freaking slurps at me, thrusting his tongue right up inside me. He damn well feasts on me and I come so hard, my entire body shudders and jolts against the wall and I cry out even louder.

As I do my eyes flick open and I peer out across the cavernous hall, my gaze colliding with someone else's. Someone stood far away, lurking in the shadows too, watching me as Dray eats me out, watching as I come against his mouth.

Fox?

Is he a pervert after all? Unable to help but watch this play out?

But the eyes don't glow like the professor's do. They are dark and penetrating. Soulless and yet so intense.

Thorne.

It's Thorne watching me. And it's not the usual indifference bordering on hate. Tonight his eyes are full of pain, with lust and with longing.

A longing I feel right in my core.

He holds my gaze as I come apart a second time, powerless against Dray's lavish attention.

Thorne watches as my body shudders with ecstasy and my skin flushes hot, his eyes swimming all over my face as if he's soaking up every detail, committing it to memory.

And I know.

In that moment, I know.

It was Thorne that helped me in the maze.

Chapter Seventeen

B riony

Dray staggers to his feet, that usual grin spread across his face along with a lot of my mess. His entire body shakes like a dog's, and then he licks at his lips and wipes at his chin with his sleeve.

He shakes again.

"Woah, Kitten! That was ..." His eyes roll around in their sockets. "I feel like I just snorted ten tons of elixir dust."

I close my eyes and catch my breath. My head is still spinning from what he did to my body and what I think I just discovered.

"A pussy never tasted so good."

I open my eyes and look at him.

"You've eaten a lot of pussies?" I ask.

His smile turns wicked, and he grabs my hand and tugs

me towards him again. Up close, I can smell myself on his skin and it isn't ... unpleasant. It has my core spinning again. He may be a powerful shadow weaver – deadly, dangerous – but I reduced him to his knees and made a mess of his face.

"Are you jealous, Kitten?"

I shake my head. Then tilt it. "When was the last pussy you ate?"

"Other than the delicious one I just ate?" he says. I nod. "Hmmm, probably ... about ... a month ago. Night before I left for the academy."

That piece of news has me frowning. Funny, but I don't like to think of that mouth on anyone else. Am I becoming possessive? I frown even harder.

"Hey," he says, "be fair! I haven't eaten any other pussies since we picked you out as our thrall." Now he frowns. His voice becomes possessive – dangerous like it sometimes does. "When was the last time someone licked you out, Kitten?"

"They haven't," I say. "I've never done that before."

"You mean Beaufort didn't ..."

I shake my head.

"Motherfucker, what the fuck was he thinking?"

I bite my lip. "I don't have any complaints. Not about the time we spent together in that way anyhow. It's just a shame that whenever he opens his mouth, he says something obnoxious."

"Maybe it would be better if his mouth was locked to your pussy, then," Dray teases. "How about we go back to our tower right now and I'll lick out your back hole while he licks out your pussy."

"My back hole!" I gasp.

I'm not naïve like Clare. I know people do things like

that but I'd never given it thought myself. I have no idea if I'd like that. If I'd want to try it.

"You like the sound–"

"Hang on," I say, realizing once again the man has distracted me with his bouncing thoughts. "You really haven't been down on another girl since you've been at the academy?" He shakes his head. I lift an eyebrow. "But they've been down on you?" He shakes his head again. "But you've slept with some?"

"Nope."

"Fingered them?"

"Nope."

"Let them jack you off?"

"Kitten. Why do you think I've been going half-crazed? I've practically been celibate waiting for you to let me touch you."

"Seriously?" I say with suspicion. Dray Eros is crazy. He's also a massive flirt. Hell, I've seen him flirt with Madame Bardin. I've seen girls draping themselves all over him and he hasn't exactly been batting them away.

"Okay," he confesses and my stomach drops. For a minute, I believed him. "I've done a bit of, you know, dirty dancing. Got up and personal. Let them grind their fat asses against me. I'm only human." He laughs. "Half human. But that's it. Nothing more. Not even any making out."

"Oh," I say, astounded. "Why?"

"I told you. Your scent is driving me wild." He leans in and growls in my ear: "It's all I can think about. Do you know how many times I've jerked off with your scent in my nose?"

"It really smells that good?"

"Best damn thing I've ever smelled." He winks at me

and then for about the millionth time this evening he's pulling me along behind him.

"Where have you been?" Beaufort asks, when we find him at the edge of the dance floor talking to a couple of shadow weavers. He takes in my flushed cheeks and Dray's disheveled hair. "Actually, forget it. I don't want to know."

"He does," Dray whispers in my ear, "don't believe him. He's a dirty fucking bastard and is dying to hear every sordid detail. In fact ..." He pushes me gently in Beaufort's direction. "I thought you might want to dance with our thrall," he says more loudly.

"Actually," I say, "I'm going to find my friends and dance with them."

Beaufort looks unhappy about that idea but I scurry off before he can stop me. I need a chance to catch my breath. Being with these men is dizzying and terrifying, intoxicating and disorientating all at once. Plus I need a chance to sit with the information I've just gained.

I spy Fly dancing with some guy in the center of the dance floor. He waves at me, then shakes his head as I start towards him, making it clear he doesn't want me to interrupt. I spin around and find Clare lingering by the food table instead. Her dress isn't quite as glamorous as mine, although it's still pretty, and I feel a twinge of guilt for not offering her this one instead. Especially when she's been kind enough to gift me some of her clothes.

Her face lights up when she sees me.

"Did Fly ditch you for some dude?" I say, realizing I've done exactly the same thing.

"It's fine," she says. "I want him to have fun. He doesn't need to babysit me."

"Are you not having fun?"

She has a half-eaten piece of soggy quiche in one hand and a napkin in the other.

"Lots of fun," she says not very convincingly.

"Have you done any dancing?"

"Some with Fly until that boy from Granite made a move on him. Have you seen? He's very cute."

"And rude for cutting you out of the dancing."

"You can't blame him. Everyone seems excessively horny tonight." I rub at my neck, feeling a bruise where Dray sucked on it. Definitely horny.

"Well, we can dance," I tell her, grabbing her elbow.

"Won't the Princes miss you?"

"That's probably a good thing. I don't want them to think I'm going to be chained to their sides just because ..." I trail off.

"Oh," Clare says, with a knowing smile.

For such a meek and serious person, Clare turns out to be quite the outrageous dancer. She throws her entire body into each move, making bold and frankly bizarre shapes with her body – her arms raised above her head one minute and shimmering extended by her sides the next. Has she had one too many glasses of the sickly smelling punch? Or is this her usual dancing style?

I don't care. I love it. I've always felt self conscious dancing. Of course, I never used to. Me and Amelia would sing and dance all day if we had the food in our bellies to allow it. But Muriel put paid to any of that. She didn't like music or singing or any outward signs of happiness at all. She wanted everyone to be as miserable as she was.

Dancing with Clare is freeing. I don't care what people think of me. I've given up trying to be invisible. They're all whispering and gossiping about me anyway. May as well give them something pretty innocent to gossip about. After all, I'd rather they were talking about my slightly insane dance moves than my very scandalous dalliance with Dray at the back of the hall. Hopefully, no one but Thorne spotted that.

I look for him now as I spin madly round and round with Clare becoming dizzier and dizzier as I do. But I don't spy him, although I do see Beaufort (looking disapproving) and Dray (clearly amused).

It gives me an idea.

"Has anyone asked you to dance yet?" I shout above the music.

Clare shakes her head. Her glasses are all fogged up from the humidity in the hall so I can't tell if she's disappointed by that. I've a feeling she is though.

"Come on then."

I link my arm through hers and lead her to where those two shadow weavers were watching us.

"It's rude to stare," I tell them.

"Just keeping an eye on you, Kitten. You have a tendency to end up in trouble."

"Well, it would be politer if you danced with us. Especially as my friend has no partner to dance with."

They both stare at me and then Dray jumps forward eagerly.

"I'll dance with you," he tells my friend.

I wouldn't usually consider Clare and Dray's energy to be on the same level but tonight I think they might be evenly matched.

Dray yanks her into a ballroom grip and starts tangoing her dramatically across the dance floor, people leaping out of their way. I giggle, my cheeks pulling up into a smile.

Am I actually having fun?

"Has your friend been taking drugs?" Beaufort grunts beside me.

I groan. "No, has yours?"

He leans down to whisper in my ear: "From what I understand he's been getting high on your pussy."

"I wouldn't exactly describe it like that," I mutter.

"Then you don't understand much about wolves," he says. We watch our two friends as Dray lowers Clare right over backwards and she lifts her leg up into the air. "So you want to dance?" His arm brushes against mine and even through the fabric of his suit, I feel the heat of his body and the tingle of his magic. Why, even when this man has said something to annoy me, do I find myself unable to resist him?

But resist him I force myself to do. Besides, it's kind of pleasant standing by his side and not arguing with him for once.

"Uh uh," I say, "I'm enjoying just watching the dancing."

"You call that dancing?"

I giggle. "Yes, I like it." I turn my head to look up at his face. Even in profile his face is stunning. Chiseled and perfect. It probably isn't so crazy that everyone in this academy hates me. He's so good looking. Everyone wants to be with him. And they resent me because I'm with him instead. "How was your visit home?" I ask him.

I watch as his shoulders stiffen and a discomfort passes across his face, which is definitely not the reaction I was expecting. Dray said Beaufort lived in a place a million times more amazing even than the Great Hall. Why would going home elicit that response? Then I remember that he wasn't exactly eager to leave the academy the day before yesterday.

These Princes already know so much about me – more than anyone else ever has. They know where I come from. They know about the scars on my body. They know my sister was killed at the academy. I've opened myself up to them in a way I haven't even done with Fly and Clare.

Yet, what do I really know about them in return – beyond the obvious? Beyond what everyone has told me? And why have I never thought to ask?

"Fine," he says tightly. He turns his head and meets my gaze. Am I imagining things or is there a sad flint to his silvery eyes? "Why? Did you miss me?"

I snort. "Don't flatter yourself."

He holds my gaze in his silver ones and then slowly reverts his attention back to the dance floor.

"I did a little investigating while I was home, tried to see if I could discover who manipulated that trial, why you scored no points."

"Did you find anything?" I ask, an unease brewing in my stomach. I haven't told him what happened in that maze. He doesn't know it was Madam Bardin who attacked me. I don't know why I'm holding back that information. Is it because I fear what she'll do to me if I tell on her? Or – and this can't be right can it? – am I doing it to protect him? Beaufort Lincoln seems to believe he's untouchable and indestructible. But Madame Bardin is deputy-head and obviously has no problem attacking pupils.

"The situation, as I understand it, has been dealt with," he says, with a self-assurance and confidence I'd usually find annoyingly arrogant; tonight though it turns that unease in my belly into something warmer. "But you come to me immediately, if you find it hasn't."

Like him, I lift my gaze, peering out across the dance floor, watching my friend, searching for Fly, Thorne and the professor. Instead, finding the Madame – as if thinking about her earlier has drawn my gaze right her way.

She stands on the other side of the dance floor, bathed in the mellow light of one of the crystal orbs floating overhead. She wears a black slinky dress that falls down her body, clinging to every curve and gathering in a wave of silk by her feet. Her dark hair is gathered up elegantly and piled on top of her head and her eyes aren't hidden behind glasses tonight, they glow a dark chestnut brown. Around her neck is a chain of sparkling diamonds, more pinned in her ears.

She's surrounded by a ring of young men, all gazing at her enthralled as she holds court, laughing at their comments, reaching out to touch their arms, or rest her fingers on her chest.

It really doesn't look like anyone has 'dealt' with her and she certainly doesn't look like a woman concerned that at any moment one of her students may be about to make a serious complaint and allegation against her.

As if she's heard the thoughts in my head, she rotates her head slowly and meets my gaze, glowering at me over the distance. I half expect her to lift her hand and shoot lightning in my direction. She doesn't. Instead, she simply smiles. A smile with no warmth and no amity. A cold smile which comes with a threat. One I understand clearly. She's not done with me.

I lift my chin, and force myself to smile back, even if my legs are shaking with the memory of the pain and agony she inflicted on my body.

I don't care. I won't let myself be afraid of her.

Eventually, she snaps her attention away from me, back to her court of admirers and my attention is diverted by Dray lifting Clare up into the air and spinning her around so quickly, people go hurtling backwards to avoid being injured by their dance moves.

"Beaufort," I say, "what do you know about firestones?"

I didn't find an awful lot out from my friend. There's the library but I'm not convinced she'll be as friendly without my bookworm friend by my side. Fly says the Princes are a resource I should use so I may as well try.

I'm guessing Beaufort wasn't expecting this conversational topic, because he twists his head around to look at me with a confused frown.

"Firestones?"

"Yes, we weren't taught a lot about them back in Slate, and I guess I'm just curious. I mean, the academy is named after them. There's that statue outside ..."

He smiles at me like I'm cute or something and I roll my eyes.

"Haven't you been listening in Professor Cornelius's Class? He's covered this."

"Really? It's so hard to follow what he's saying."

"What do you want to know?"

"For starters, what are they?"

"Magical rocks that existed hundreds of years ago. Or so people say. Some believe it's where we shadow weavers obtained our powers."

"You don't believe that?" I ask.

"Magic rocks?" he says, with a cynical look. "Yet no one can quite describe what they did. It's like fairies and goblins. Kids' tales."

"I'm guessing you don't believe in dragons either, then?"

"No dragons definitely existed. They used to be a useful weapon against the demons. That was until they died out."

"Why did they die out?"

"That, sweetheart, is the million galleon question."

Chapter Eighteen

B riony

By the end of the night, Fly and the redhead have disappeared altogether and the Princes are talking about taking me back to their tower. Dray clearly wants to make good on his promises from earlier in the evening. But I put my foot down, and no amount of flirtation, disapproving glares or outright threats are going to change my mind. I'm walking my now exceedingly tipsy friend back to her room and then retiring to my own bed. Alone.

Beaufort might not believe in magic rocks but I've had one tugging at my gut all night. I'm desperate to return and check it.

"Okay," Beaufort finally concedes, "but I'm walking with you."

"It's not necessary."

Dray rolls his eyes at me – in clear imitation of my usual response to his crazy remarks. "It is when you look the way you look tonight, and most of the academy are wasted out of their minds."

I tsk at him but I don't argue when Beaufort walks along with Clare and I through the maze of the academy. Dray may actually be right. There are students staggering around. Some being pretty rowdy. We pass three different brawls, a pretty aggressive lovers' tiff and a standoff over what looks like a bottle of alcohol.

All the joviality and downright horniness from early has dissolved into violence and I don't exactly feel like being on the end of that.

I also have a strong suspicion that, while Madame Bardin may be untouchable at the academy, she wouldn't dare attack me with one of the Princes around.

Beaufort waits outside the door like an actual gentle-man, while I help Clare out of her dress, force her to drink a large amount of water and tuck her into bed.

"Can I help you out of your dress and into your bed tonight, sweetheart?" Beaufort asks as I close the door quietly behind me, already hearing Clare's drink-induced snores.

"I'm quite capable of doing it myself, thank you," I say, although with more flirtation and less snark than I usually would, taking a leaf out of Madame's book. She may be a mega bitch who tried to kill me – at least I think she would have if left to her own devices – but she does have the sultry seductress act down to a fine art.

He takes my hand in his, threading his fingers through mine and rubbing the pad of his thumb along my knuckles as we walk towards my tower.

"Last chance," he says, when we reach the door to my

room. "I'd be more than happy to help you out of this dress." He smiles at me and the man really is damn charming when he wants to be. It makes it exceedingly difficult to say no.

"Another time."

He slides his hand around the back of my neck, cupping my head in his large paw.

"I'm going to hold you to that promise, little thrall."

Then he kisses me. It's tender, gentle, slow. It's designed to tease me and let me know exactly what I'm turning down.

But it's more than that. All our kisses before have been fueled by anger and lust, want and longing. This kiss isn't like that. There's more intimacy to it, more emotion. It's a kiss that could fool me into believing he actually cares for me.

"Good night," I tell him, pulling away before I'm unable to resist him at all.

"Good night, Briony," he tells me.

In my room, I lean against my closed door, shutting my eyes and catching my breath. When my head stops spinning and my knees are no longer close to buckling, I stride quickly to my cupboard and pull out the stone.

There are no new cracks but it's as warm as ever and vibrating gently in my palms. I strip off the dress and climb into my pajamas, and then snuggle into my bed with the stone and my notebook. It's full of all the notes I've been keeping about my sister – scribbles mostly. I've added bits and pieces we've learned from the library books. Nothing is obviously related but I've made a note of anything unusual or out of the ordinary.

I don't add any notes about my sister tonight though. Instead I turn the notebook over and open it from the back page.

I write down every bit of information I know about the Princes and everything I've discovered about firestones.

It's a start, but I intend to add more.

Chapter Nineteen

Fox

I'm meant to be supervising events in the Great Hall, ensuring things don't get out of control and the precious building and its ancient artifacts smashed or graffitied. But expecting me to stand around and watch as that mutt mauls my girl – no fucking way.

My life – if you can call this a life – is shitty enough. I don't need to make it any worse.

I storm out of the hall, crashing into students, pushing my way through bystanders, growling and yelling at anyone who so much as blinks my way.

The Titan twins are patrolling the campus this evening. I should go swap with one of them. Send them into the hall and roam the pathways instead.

But I'm in no mood to answer their questions, no mood for conversation at all.

Instead, I need to find a way to calm this passion crashing through my body. Because all I want to do – all I can focus on stopping myself from doing – is to swoop back into the hall, steal her right from Dray Eros's grubby little paws and whisk her away somewhere dark and alone.

The image of it plays out in my mind as I hurtle down the stone steps to the dungeon and slam open my door.

How she'd wilt in my arms, how she'd beg for mercy, how she'd succumb, melting into pleasure.

How good she would smell and how good she would taste as I forced her to come again and again.

I crumple to the floor, my hands as fists against the cold ground.

This is not who I am. I am not a monster.

"I will not succumb to it!" I yell out into the silence. "I will not succumb to her."

But even as the words leave my lips I doubt their sincerity.

If she were here now, standing alone in this empty room, where no one could hear her, would I be able to stop myself?

Because these urges, these needs, the incessant hunger-pangs in my empty stomach, only grow stronger each and every day.

I thump the ground, disgusted by my own weakness, and watch as the stone fissures and cracks. I hit it again and again until I'm breathless and the stone is a mess of shattered pieces.

Then I rock back, panting, leaning back against the door. I shrug off my jacket, then loosen my tie and unbutton the top fastening of my dress shirt.

I peer straight ahead, through the gloom of my classroom. My night vision is so much more astute than it once was. I see the carved detail of the benches, Thursday's lesson still marked out on the board, chalk dust on the floor.

And I see her. Of course I do.

Perched on the bench. The two qualities that define her best, fighting to gain dominance – curiosity and cynicism. I see the shape of her and I smell her scent.

I groan like a man starving to death imagining a feast laid out in front of him, knowing it isn't real, that if he reaches for it, his hand will swim through nothing but air.

But the ghost I see, the ghost my mind creates, is so vivid.

She turns to look at me, a flirtatious smile playing out across her lips. She crooks a finger, beckons me closer, parting her thighs, tipping back her head, offering up her neck.

I groan again.

I'm stiff, so fucking stiff.

I stare down at my crotch.

My own fucking erection was something that used to greet me every morning without fail. A cock that hardened at the merest hint of invitation. A reliable cock. A greedy one. A sated cock too.

It's been a long time since my cock has stirred. Even longer since it was sated.

I'm no fool, it's more that I feel for her than just a hunger.

I want her in all the ways it's possible to have a woman.

I unbutton the fly of my pants with a hurried eagerness and a bitter shame.

I wrap my hand around my neglected cock and stroke down the shaft, then up.

I groan, slumping back against the door.

The ghost watches me just as eagerly, tongue sliding over her bottom lip.

"I want to fuck you," I tell the ghost. "I want to fuck you long and hard and slow until you're screaming my name. Mine!"

"Yes," she purrs and the sound of her voice makes my cock twitch in my fist.

It's been a long, long time and the temptation before my eyes – imaginary as it is – is too great. Half a dozen fucking strokes of my cock and I'm groaning out her name, stomach moaning, the blood pounding in my ear. With the ghost of her watching on, I come.

But even that is different. Different than it was before.

Chapter Twenty

Briony

The mysterious head of the academy most definitely is a masochist because the day after the ball is not a day off as would be entirely reasonable. Nope, it's back to lessons and first up, physical training.

"This is seriously sick," Fly yawns as the Gruesome Twosome announce with obvious glee that it's circuit again today.

Most people seem to be in agreement with Fly. Several of the shadow weavers are wearing shades today despite having access to that anti-hangover draught Dray gave me. Nearly everyone else is either looking pale, green or like they haven't slept in a week.

I'm taking it Fly may be one of the latter. He didn't answer when I knocked for him this morning and I figured he either didn't make it back to his own bed last night or else he had company. Either way, he only just made it to the start of class in time and is looking a lot more ... crumpled than usual.

Clare did make it to breakfast, not that she actually managed to eat anything.

I think I might be the only student in the academy who isn't nursing a hangover. It makes me feel pretty smug, especially when I spy Odessa dry-retching into her fist and being accompanied by the tall toothless girl. The Smyte twins are also not looking as glamorous as usual – both are massaging their temples – although Henrietta still manages to find the energy to scowl across at me.

I consider giving a cheery wave but I probably shouldn't provoke her. I've had enough encounters with lightning to last me a lifetime.

There must be gods out there somewhere after all. It certainly feels like some kind of revenge. Last time we underwent a session of circuits with the two Titan twins, I was the one dying in agony and suffering massively. Today, it's everyone else. There is a lot of moaning and groaning and several cases of vomiting. Most people are covered in a sheen of sickly sweat and the odor isn't exactly pleasant.

Still, I milk it for all it's worth, pleased I can actually do more sit-ups, press-ups and burpees than most of the other students.

Except for the Princes of course. I think they could each lose a limb and several pints of blood and would still make every single exercise known to man look like a piece of cake.

Between different rounds I manage to quiz Fly.

"So how was your evening?" I say, with a knowing look that is totally borrowed from his play book. Is it evil that it's fun to tease him about this for once?

"Lovely, thank you," he says, trying to pat down the unruly curls on the crown of his head.

"Lovely," I say, "is that what the kids are calling it these days?"

"I don't know what you're talking about," he says.

"So nothing you want to tell me about? No details you want to share?"

He peers at me through narrowed eyes. "You never want to share details with me!"

"But I always do in the end," I point out. "Also, something tells me you're dying to spill the beans."

He smiles. "As I said, I had a very pleasant evening with the redhead from group three."

"So I saw. And what did that pleasant evening involve?!" I witnessed them sucking each other's faces off but I assume there is more.

But I'm forced to wait for my answer because twin one blows his whistle and we have to start star-jumping.

"We enjoyed each other's company," he says, bouncing on the spot.

"I saw that in the hall and then you disappeared."

"He took me back to his room."

I squeal which draws a warning growl from twin two. I don't speak again until we're rotating to the next set of exercises.

"So what happened back in his room?"

"We talked, we drank, we listened to some music ... we... enjoyed each other's bodies," he says in a lowered voice. "And then it was morning."

"So are you a thing now?" I say with a little less enthusiasm. It's hypocritical and unfair of me, but I don't love the idea of Fly getting a boyfriend. I've seen how that goes. Bye

bye to all the friends. "Are you going to see each other again?"

"Stars, no," Fly says in obvious outrage. "That was a strictly onetime-only thing. I am not ready to be tied down."

I place my hands on my hips and stare at him. "And yet I should be tied down to the Princes?"

"You're different, Cupcake," he says, bopping me on the nose, "you can't handle sleeping around."

"Who says I can't?"

"I'm getting to understand how that little brain of yours works. Even though bond brothers share their mates, I bet you've still been stewing over sleeping with more than one of the Princes."

Mate?

That word again.

"What do you mean–" I start to ask, but the whistle blows again.

If I hope to quiz Fly and Clare about it at lunch time, I'm sorely disappointed. Both skip lunch and use the break to catch up on some sleep. In fact, the commoner's canteen is three-quarters empty and I sit on my own in a corner, enjoying a very large helping of lunch.

Despite how ill she was looking this morning, Odessa and her posse make it to lunch too. They sit in the center of the canteen being unnecessarily loud, clearly trying to attract everyone's attention.

I try my best to drown them out – I don't want to listen to Odessa's annoying drawl – but it's almost impossible to.

"Kratos says he's going to buy me a totally new wardrobe."

"Really?" one of her adoring fans says, staring at her like she is the sun and moon combined.

"He's already been more than generous." She flutters

her fingers in front of the circle of onlookers' faces, three rings sparkling under the lights.

"Is that a–"

"Diamond?" Odessa asks. "Yes."

I guess my eyes have strayed that way, because she glances over at me and for the briefest of seconds our eyes lock, before I snap my gaze back down to my food.

"I think they must be really into me." She raises her voice even louder. "Unlike some people. I mean, have you noticed how some thralls don't have any gifts at all? How they're still wearing the same scummy clothes they arrived in?"

I assume she's referring to me, even if that statement isn't strictly true. After all, all my original clothes were destroyed.

I ignore her, pretending to be thoroughly fascinated by my boiled potatoes and pretending not to hear. I know her type. She thrives on attention. And denying it her, will be like cutting off her oxygen.

"They must not care about her much. Wouldn't they want her wearing something more ... respectable?"

"She had a nice dress at the ball," some brave soul pipes up. "Did you see it? She looked really pretty then."

"That!" Odessa cackles, the sound brittle. "The color didn't suit her at all. Washed her out. *I* thought she looked positively sickly." No one is brave enough to contradict Odessa a second time. "I heard her friend patched that dress together from rags and off cuts – if you got up close, you'd have seen the appalling stitching and the crooked hemline. It was a complete mess. I would have been embarrassed to have been seen in it."

That's it! I can take all the insults about me personally on the chin. It's nothing I haven't heard from Muriel a thousand million times before. Those types of comments no longer cut so deep.

But criticizing my friend? Implying that his work is bad when it was anything but? I won't let that stand, especially as that kind of comment will be the gospel truth within hours and no one will actually remember how stunning my dress was.

I throw my cutlery down on my plate, pick it up and pace towards the table. Odessa is no longer looking my way, so she doesn't see me coming, but several of her friends do, their eyes drawing wide in astonishment as I approach their table. I smash my plate down right beside Odessa, making her leap in her seat, and lean down to glare in her eyes.

"The hemline was straighter than a ruler, the stitching immaculate and the color perfect. The Princes couldn't keep their hands off me and *your* protectors spent more time looking at me than they did at you."

At first, she's simply astounded, gaping at me with her mouth open in a not very Odessa-like manner (she's usually all coy smiles and fluttered eyelashes), but soon enough her face is turning ugly.

"Excuse me, but I don't remember asking you to join us and we definitely aren't interested in hearing what you have to say."

I remember the night Beaufort came home with his knuckles grazed and his lip split and told me he'd sorted the Odessa problem for me. I was concerned he'd hurt her. Now, hearing the way she's speaking right to my face, seeing the disdain in her eyes, I know he didn't hurt her. He also, most definitely, did not fix the Odessa problem. She may not have attempted to murder me again recently, but the look in her eyes tells me she'd still like to see me dead – she just hasn't had a chance recently.

I wish I'd had that realization three seconds earlier. Maybe then I'd have seen what was going to happen next. Odessa lifts her right hand and jabs her knife hard into mine. I cry out as the blade slices straight through my skin.

The others around the table gasp in horror, several leaping up from the table. The toothless friend grins in admiration.

Odessa ignores them all, pressing the knife more firmly into my hand and leaning in closer to me.

"Don't ever dare speak to me again, scum," she spits.

The pain in my hand brings tears to my eyes and blood seeps from the wound, sliding down my hand and onto the table.

I'm done with this bitch though. If I'm going to endure all this bullshit with the Princes, it may as well be for something – something like knowing I can come back at this bitch without suffering the consequences.

I swing my other arm forward and punch her right in the throat.

Once again, she's more than a little astonished; choking and grappling at her throat as tears glide down her face, taking most of her makeup with them. Is that my imagination or is Odessa's smooth skin not as flawless as it seems under that layer of foundation?

Yanking the knife from my hand which, I won't pretend, hurts like hell, I toss it on the table.

"Don't *you* ever dare speak shit about my friend again."

Back in my room five minutes later, the stone in my lap as I tie a bandage around my hand, all the adrenaline slips away, and I start shaking so hard, I'm forced to curl up in a ball and hug my knees.

What the hell was I thinking? She could have launched that knife at my throat not my hand and the Princes, for all their promises of protection, wouldn't have been able to do a thing to stop it, all the way over in their snooty dining room.

I'm being unfair. If I wore the damn collar, I would be safe – according to them anyway. Then again, Odessa's own collar didn't seem to stop me from punching her in the throat. Which, now I think about it, is strange, isn't it?

I roll onto my back on the floor, my body still trembling and hold both my hands in front of my face – the bandaged one and the one I punched her with. The punching hand is uninjured.

How was I able to hit her?

Chapter Twenty-One

Briony

Both Fly and Clare make it to dinner that evening, although Clare is still too queasy to eat and Fly yawns so much I'm surprised his jaw doesn't dislocate.

"Why do you seem perfectly fine today, Cupcake? Aren't you suffering at all?"

"Nope," I say, stuffing a mouthful of creamy pasta into my mouth. Something which makes Clare cringe.

"How can you eat that?" she hisses.

"Because I didn't drink as much as you," I tell Clare, "and I didn't spend my entire night getting down and dirty with some redhead," I tell Fly.

"No, but you did spend all night getting down and dirty with the Princes."

"Nope," I say, chewing my mouthful.

"Nope?" Clare repeats.

"I put you to bed," I say to her. "Then Beaufort walked me back to my room. We shared a pretty PG-kiss," (sort of), "and afterwards I went to bed alone."

"Why?" Fly says. "I spent a lot of time and effort making you look drop dead gorgeous and it worked. They couldn't keep their eyes off you. You could have been seriously ravished last night, Cupcake."

"Well," I say haughtily, "I didn't want to be."

Fly mutters some choice words under his breath and yawns some more.

"You put me to bed?" Clare says. "I don't remember that!"

"Do you remember much of last night?" Fly asks.

"Bits and pieces. I remember dancing with Dray Eros," her cheeks flame, "and then I remember having so many requests to dance I was having to actually turn men down."

"Shit," Fly says, "good for you. You did look amazing."

"Not as amazing as Briony," she mumbles, adjusting her glasses.

"Bullshit," Fly and I say together.

She smiles at us shyly. "Well, anyway, obviously I didn't look good enough to tempt the one person I was hoping to tempt." She sighs dramatically, pushing her plate away.

Fly and I look at each other, then back at Clare.

"Who?" we say, again in unison.

"Oh, just this boy." She glances across the canteen but it's unclear who she's peering at. "I sit next to him in my history class. He's really sweet. I thought he'd ask me to dance for sure."

"He was probably too scared to due to all the demand," I say.

"And Dray Eros is pretty damn intimidating," Fly points out.

I shrug. "He's a puppy dog."

"He's a wolf," Fly clarifies, "and he's rumored to have killed half a shifter clan."

I stare at Fly. "Seriously?"

"I mean, it's a rumor, but that's what they say."

I think of the scar on his shoulder. I remember what he said about ending the shifter who had bitten him. I didn't take him seriously. Maybe I should have.

"Why didn't you tell me this?"

"Dray Eros and his family are famous across the realm. How do you not know this stuff?"

I stab a piece of pasta with my fork. "News like that doesn't make its way out to Slate Quarter." I lift the pasta to my mouth, then lower it. "It's clear. There's lots I don't know about those three men. Especially Thorne. I need to talk to him."

"Then why don't you?"

"He's ... hard to pin down."

"I bet!" Fly grins.

"Can't you just talk to him when you're at their tower?" Clare asks.

"He tends to avoid me. Usually he shuts himself away in his room."

"You could catch him out on the field in the morning," she suggests next.

"Huh?"

"Thorne, he's out on the field every morning training. I can see him from my window." Her cheeks burn again, and she lowers her voice. "He trains without a shirt. I bet most of the girls in the academy are enjoying that show every morning."

"It's a nice way to wake up to the day," Fly adds.

"You knew about this too?"

"He's very big and very hard to miss."

"I can't see the field from my window," I growl. "What time?"

"He's usually out there before seven," Clare tells me.

I nod. Seems I have an early morning appointment booked with Thorne Cadieux.

The morning is clear but bitterly cold, fine strips of cloud is stretched across the sky and the paths are covered in a fine layer of white crystals that crunch under my boots. My breath hangs in a thick cloud of fog in front of my face and when I reach the field, I find it completely white, the distant trees crystallized as well.

It hasn't stopped Thorne though. As Clare predicted, he's already there, standing out on the far side, his arms braced like they were the last time I caught him training like this.

Today, however, he is wearing a shirt (am I a teeny bit disappointed by that?) as well as his usual gloves, a pair of sweatpants and sneakers.

A stream of dense shadows flows from his outstretched hands and streak across the field and his face is contorted in concentration, his eyes fixed on some distant target.

I glance that way, but I can't see what he's aiming at and I turn my attention back to those shadows.

They are nothing like that wisp that flirted close to my face the day of the trial. The wisp, that, as delicate as it looked, was enough to protect me from Madame Bardin's attack.

I try to look for traces of similarities. Anything that suggests they are the same. Is the shade the same? The density? The way the shadows shimmer in the weak morning light? But I can't truly convince myself I see anything at all that connects the two.

Did I imagine what I saw in the hall the night of the ball? Did I get this wrong?

But I'm sure I'm right. I'm sure I saw it in his eyes.

I wait a few minutes, blowing on my cold fingers and stamping my feet. The uniform with the short skirt and silly socks was a bad idea. I should have layered up in pants and sweatshirts.

It's clear he's too engrossed in his training to have noticed me, so I pluck up the courage to cup my hands around my mouth and call out his name.

He doesn't appear to hear me. His face just as focused as the shadows stream forward and he braces his body with the effort.

I take a deep inhale.

"Thorne Cadieux!" I yell at the top of my voice, suddenly realizing that if Thorne has a little audience every morning, they'll see me out here too. Well, tough. I don't know how else I can get him alone to talk.

That's if he will talk to me.

This time his head jerks around my way and his dark eyes land on me. He frowns and drops his arms immediately, the shadows retreating back to his hands.

I hesitate, and then step forward onto the icy grass. When I'm a few feet from him, I call out.

"Can we talk?" He stares at me, face blank. Is he seriously going to give me the silent treatment, *again*? "I know it was you."

He jolts. It's minimal and quick but I spot it and I conclude that means he knows what I'm talking about.

His eyes dart to the distant campus and then he steps closer.

"I don't know what you mean," he says.

"You do," I say, then looking over my shoulder to determine no one has joined us out here on the field, I step closer to him and lower my voice.

"I know it was you that helped me in the trial. I know it was your magic that protected me."

I stare right into his face. His own gaze falls to the ground.

"I don't know what you're talking about," he mutters.

Despite his denial, despite my doubts only minutes ago, everything about his persona and his reaction tells me that I am correct.

"You do. I know it was you." I step closer still, so I'm right in front of him, and he takes an immediate step away from me. "Why did you do it?"

He lifts his gaze and I see that flash in his usually soulless eyes, a glimpse of what I saw the night of the ball. Pain, longing, anger.

"Don't lie to me, Thorne Cadieux," I whisper.

He opens his mouth as if to deny it again and then closes it without saying a word.

"Why did you do it?" I repeat.

His face contorts as if he's battling his thoughts, determining what is the best thing to do.

"Please!" I say. "Please just tell me the truth! I'm not going to tell anyone. I'm not going to get you into trouble."

He opens his eyes and something tells me that wasn't his concern.

"I know you wouldn't," he says.

I nod. "Then why?"

"Because you're our thrall," he says. "It's our duty to protect you."

I shake my head. I don't buy that for a minute. Dray and Beaufort didn't protect me. From the cast on the Smyte twins' thrall's arm, I don't think they protected him either. And Odessa's been bragging about how the handsome Professor Tudor rescued her from the trial.

He didn't have to protect me, but he did anyway.

"Do you know what they do to people who help others in the trials?" I whisper so quietly I hardly hear my own voice. He stares at me. "You don't even like me. Why would you risk that ... for me?"

"Because you are our thr–"

"That isn't the reason," I snap.

He takes the smallest, most minute step towards me. "Beaufort still hasn't told you."

"For star's sake, told me what?"

"You're more than just a thrall to us, Briony." The way he says my name makes butterflies in my stomach flutter about. "You're our mate."

That word again.

"I don't know what that means," I say in frustration.

Behind us the clock tower bell clangs and there are other students out on the path, their voices carrying over the distance, some passing along the path that skims the field.

Thorne looks out towards them.

"Ask Beaufort," he says with annoyance, and then he strides away, being careful to leave a wide berth around me.

"Thorne," I call after him. "Wait."

He stops and peers over his shoulder at me.

"Thank you," I say. "Thank you for helping me."

"I'd do anything for you," he says, and then he's walking

away again, leaving me utterly gobsmacked and thoroughly confused.

Chapter Twenty-Two

B riony

Mate – what the hell does that mean?

Despite what everybody at the academy seems to believe, us Slate kids did receive some sort of education. I'm not dumb. I can read. I can write. I even know my twelve times table.

I understand the definition of the word mate. Partner – more specifically a sexual partner. Is that what everyone is referring to? Maybe some thralls don't sleep with their protectors – they're too busy cutting their toenails for them or changing their sheets. Maybe only thralls who satisfy their protectors in other ways earn this title. It's just, the way they are all talking about it makes me think there is another different, alternative meaning I'm not party to. Just like firestones, another thing I don't understand.

I could ask my friends. I could even ask Beaufort

himself. But I'm fed up with being the ignorant one. Knowledge is power and right now everyone else appears to be in a much more powerful position than me. I want to be better armed.

Later that evening, I make my way to the library, hoping with every bone in my body that there are no romantic rendezvous happening in there tonight. Also hoping the library doesn't still hate my guts.

The building is dark when I arrive and silent as I step inside. I peer into the gloom and take a deep inhale.

"Good evening, Library," I announce, feeling just as silly as last time talking into an empty room. "I know it's late and I'm very sorry to disturb you, but I was hoping you might be able to help me."

Above me the grand chandelier flickers on and bathes the library in a warm, welcoming light. I take that as a good sign and continue.

"I need to find out about mates." The chandelier spins on its chain and the books vibrate on the shelves. The library is listening to me. "You see, I'm sort of in this relationship with these guys." I tuck loose hair behind my ear and shift from one foot to the next. "They picked me out as their thrall, but now it seems there is more to it than I first thought. They keep referring to me as their mate and I really need to understand what the hell that means."

The chandelier flickers on and off above my head and I have the distinct suspicion that the library is going to turf me out. Maybe my request wasn't intellectual enough.

But then a book comes hurtling over the shelves. It lands with a thump on the polished floor and skids across it, crashing right into my toes.

I stare down at it dumbfounded, as the cover flops open and the pages flip over, halting suddenly. I wait a moment and when nothing more happens, I crouch down and cautiously scoop the book up into my arms.

At the top of the page is a title embossed in gold.

Fated mates.

I drop down onto my backside, legs crossed and settle the book into my lap. Then I get to reading, devouring everything I can find on the topic in this book.

When I'm done my mind is spinning. It's answered a lot of questions and given me a whole heap more.

Fated mates – couples, throuples and even quadruples brought together and bound together by destiny. Their connection intense, irresistible and often unbreakable.

Do the princes truly believe I am their mate? Do they feel such a connection?

Do I?

My head spins even more because maybe I do. Maybe this is the force that has been pushing me towards them even when I've hated, feared and mistrusted them.

I lay my hand on my heart and try to breathe, forcing myself to think straight.

The book says there are signs that prove people are fated mates. As far as I know, as far as I'm concerned, none of those signs apply to us. Sure, they turn me on, sure I find it hard to resist them, but that could be because they've done a very good job at seducing a lonely girl. They could simply be messing with my head.

I blow my air from my lungs, puffing away all the confusion.

They don't know about the firestone in my possession. To them, I am nothing more than a commoner girl from Slate. Which reminds me...

As I'm here, and the library is in a cooperative mood, there's more I need to find out about.

"Thank you, Library," I say. "That was just the book I needed. It was extremely illuminating. I am now much better informed." The lights flicker in a manner I take means the library is pleased with that little compliment. "Now, do you think you could help me with another topic? I'd be really grateful."

The chandelier above me spins and the shelves seems to vibrate with excitement. The library seems to like helping me after all.

"I need to learn about firestones."

Like before the shelves start to spin, books flutter up to the ceiling, then descend back down to the shelves again. I get the impression this request is a harder one to answer. However, after a few more minutes, I have a pile of different books by my feet. One looks like a children's fairytale book, one an encyclopedia and the others are volumes on historical events.

I flick through each in turn and soon I understand why my second request was more difficult. There's no definitive answer like there was about fated mates. The historical accounts disagree as to what firestones were, what they could do and if they ever existed in the first place.

I may have a better understanding of fated mates – even if the entire thing seems incredible to me. But firestones? I'm no clearer at all.

Chapter Twenty-Three

B riony

Thorne Cadieux claims he'd do anything for me. It seems I might need to put that to the test sooner than I expected.

Because Wednesday comes around again before I know it, leaving me with a big dilemma. The stone, little by little, continues to crack. I'm sure any moment now it's going to split and whatever is inside – if there is anything inside at all – is going to be revealed. I don't want to miss it.

Lessons I can't skip. It'll only end in detentions that'll mean more time away from my room. But an evening with the Princes? Surely that can be negotiated. Especially if I ask Thorne.

I don't fancy another altercation out on the field with half the academy watching and the man is impossible to track down. So, reluctantly leaving the stone behind, I make my way to the tower as usual, and when Dray answers the door with a cocky smile on his face, I announce:

"I need to talk to Thorne. Alone."

Dray's grin falls from his face and he gives me those puppy-dog eyes. "That's it. Not even a hello. And after I introduced you to cunnilingus and took you to heaven and back."

"A little presumptuous," I point out.

"Are you denying I took you to heaven?"

I bite my lip and shake my head.

"Good," he says, placated. "Come here and let me inhale that scent of yours. Then I'll go get the Grump for you."

"He's not a grump," I say automatically.

"Ahh," the left side of Dray's mouth lifts in a half-smile, "it's like that, huh?"

He winks, pulls me towards him, buries his face in the crook of my neck, inhales deeply, then his body stiffens and before I know it, my hand is gripped in his and he's unwinding the bandage.

"Want to tell me about this?" he growls.

"Just an accident," I mutter, trying to pull my hand away.

"An accident with a knife," he says, examining the wound that is slowly healing.

I shrug. "I was cutting an apple."

"Aren't you right-handed?"

"Not when it comes to slicing apples."

"Hmmm," he says, stroking his fingertips against the wound, shadows racing across my skin and knitting together the damaged flesh, warm tingles racing up my arm. When my hand is completely healed, he meets my eyes with his chaotic ones. "You're a stubborn little kitten, aren't you?"

I don't even get a chance to reply, he's already skipping away.

I'm left in the hallway feeling like I was just sucked up into a tornado.

A few minutes later, Thorne comes striding down the stairs and into the hallway. I wasn't sure if he would agree to see me, but after that confession out there on the field, things have changed, shifted. I can tell by the way he meets my eyes as he comes towards me. Although, he still stops his obligatory pace away from me as if the air I'm breathing might be toxic.

"It's Beaufort you need to talk to—"

I'm aware of that. The conversation we had and the things I learned in the library have been pressing on my mind, but right now the stone is more urgent.

"I can't come tonight."

He blinks. "Aren't you here?"

"Yes, I know, but I have to get back to my room."

"And you had to tell me this because ..."

"I want you to come with me, back to my room."

"No," he says.

I peer up into his face, trying to read him.

"You said you'd do anything for me," I whisper.

Beaufort would have frowned if I'd caught him in a trap of his own making like this. Dray would chuckle. Thorne's face remains completely blank. He is impossible to read.

"This isn't what I meant."

"What did you mean?" I ask, tipping my head to one side.

He swallows and I think he is considering his next words. "That if you ever needed me, I would be there to help."

"Well, I need your help now."

"What with?"

I peer around him. I suspect Dray is lingering in the background somewhere, listening in on this conversation.

"I can't explain it. I have to show you."

He shakes his head.

"Fuck, Thorne, dude," Dray yells from somewhere – my suspicions proven correct, "she wants to show you something. What the hell are you waiting for?"

Now emotion finally registers on his face: displeasure. He frowns and shucks his chin my way, I hurry through the door and he follows after me.

"It's not like Dray is making out," I clarify, blushing.

"I know," he mumbles, "Dray is an idiot."

We walk in silence back to my room, him following several paces behind me. It's the same up the staircase. If his presence wasn't so dominating, his magic heavy in the air, I'd have to keep checking he was still there.

On the landing, he waits while I unlock the door and follows me in. His gaze skips around my plain room once we're inside and I tuck my keys away and chew on my cheek.

Am I doing the right thing? I haven't trusted anyone with this secret. Not even my own dad. Not even Fly.

But I don't know what is happening to the stone. I don't know what will happen if it splits. If it is a firestone as I suspect, then is this bad?

Thorne risked banishment to help me in the maze. Banishment means death. Which means he risked his life for me. If I can't trust him, I don't believe there is anyone in the realm I can trust.

"I appreciate you coming," I say.

"Is this about who attacked you in the maze?" he asks.

"You must know who it was," I say. "Your magic was right there."

"No," he explains, "once I sever it from me like that, it acts independently." He rubs at his head. "It's difficult to explain. It's still a part of me, it still acts in my interests, but it isn't a part of me as well. I don't know what happened to you in the maze. But I'd like to know."

I consider telling him. But what would it achieve? He and the others would go after Madame Bardin – I've no doubt about that. And she'd know it was one of them that helped me – I suspect she has her suspicions as it is. And then what? Thorne would be banished, banished because of me. And no matter how powerful he may be, he wouldn't last five minutes out there unprotected against the demons and the monsters.

"I can't tell you. I don't want anything bad to happen to you."

"Nothing will happen to me."

I smile at him. "We both know that's not true. You protected me, let me protect you in return."

He looks at me and something like astonishment shines in those dark eyes. After a moment, he nods, rather reluctantly.

"There's something I want to show you. Something I'm trusting you to keep a secret. Do you promise you will?"

"If that's what you want," he says, lingering by the door.

I rock backward and forward on my toes. "In the maze, your shadow made my attacker promise not to harm me again."

"A sacred promise," he says.

"What does it do?"

"Such a promise is extremely hard to break and, if it is broken, there are consequences."

"Consequences?"

"Fate doesn't look kindly on a person who breaks a sacred promise."

"Will you make one of those promises for me now?" I ask him, a little nervously.

"Briony," he scoffs – and the way he says my name makes my insides melt just like before, "fate has already looked down on me with scorn. It would be no consequence for me if I chose to break a sacred promise."

I inhale and exhale. Looked on him with scorn? Is he joking? He's a shadow weaver. One of the most powerful in the academy. Bonded to two of the most powerful shadow weavers in the realm. Fate has clearly blessed him.

"I'd still feel better if you did it anyway."

"Fine," he says.

He closes his eyes and his mouth moves, speaking words silently. I notice for the first time how sensual his lips look, how soft.

A thin slither of shadow dances from his fingertips, and now I see that it is so similar to the one in the maze. It hovers in the space between us and he opens his eyes.

"Briony Storm," he says, and I hold my breath, my heart thumping, "I promise to keep this a secret."

"Thank you," I say and the shadow inches towards me, close enough to touch. I reach out, but it jumps away, then shoots back to his hands.

I can't meet his eyes after that. I feel like I just did something wrong.

"Let me fetch it," I tell him.

I turn away and hurry to my cupboard, pulling out the blanket and my bag and then reaching inside and carefully lifting the stone. I quickly skim its surface. The cracks are more numerous and deeper and the thing vibrates in my palms.

With another inhale, I spin around and step towards Thorne.

His eyes linger on my face and then drop to the stone in my arms.

He studies it silently for several long, drawn-out seconds.

"Is that what I think it is?" he says finally.

"What do you think it is?" I ask him, taking another step forward.

"Can I see it?" he asks.

I walk closer to him and for once, with the door blocking his escape, he can't back away. I hold out the stone to him.

He examines my hands, then carefully and cautiously, he places his hands on the stone and takes it from me, as if he doesn't want our hands to touch.

He turns it over in his hands.

"A firestone," he says, eyes still locked on it.

"That's what I thought too."

"Where did you get it from?"

I chew on my cheek. Will he believe me?

"I found it about nine years ago–"

"Nine years ago?" he says, unbelieving. "You've had it all that time?"

"Yes, that long. But found it isn't quite right." I screw up my temples trying to find the words to explain.

"You took it," he says.

"No!" I scowl at him. "Stars, what is wrong with you men? Just because I'm from Slate, does not make me a thief!"

"I'm sorry," he says, "you're right."

"Hmph," I sulk.

"Please explain what you meant?"

"It's hard to explain. It's like it called me to it."

"What do you mean?"

I rest my right hand against my stomach. "It tugged at me. I could feel it pulling right in the center of my stomach. It tugged me into the forest that lies at the edge of our Quarter, all the way in, and then I found it at the bottom of a lake." I shake my head. "It sounds crazy. No wonder you think I stole it."

"I believe you," he says.

My gaze leaps back to his. "You do?"

"It's a firestone. They're magical."

"Do you ... do you know what they do?"

He hesitates, then shakes his head. "Have you shown it to anyone else?"

"No, never. You're the first one."

His eyebrows lift the tiniest fraction.

"The thing is," I say, "it started pulling me towards it again the night of the trial, and when I got back to my room, I found it was starting to crack."

"It wasn't like that before?"

"No, its surface was completely smooth before," I say. "Now I think it's cracking open and I don't know why."

"We should take it to the Head. He'll know exactly what it is and why it's cracking."

I shake my head violently. "Uh, no. They'd take it away from me."

"We don't know for sure what it is. Or what it can do. It could be dangerous. It would be safer to–"

"–it called me, Thorne. It wanted me to find it."

"That doesn't mean it wants you to keep it."

"It's still pulling me now! It wants you to hand it back."

He nods like that isn't crazy and rests it on the floor between us. I pick it up.

"The cracks are growing bigger and more prominent by the hour," I say. "I think it's going to crack open completely any moment now. That's why I need to be here with it in my own room tonight."

"I understand."

"So you're not going to force me back to your tower? Or go off telling everyone about this?"

"I gave you my word," he says stiffly.

"Right," I say, "good."

We stare at each other.

"And you're not going to try and convince me to hand it in?"

"I've given you my opinion. If you choose not to follow my advice, I accept your decision.

"Good," I repeat, a little surprised. Beaufort and I would be having a mega argument about it by now. But Thorne respects my opinion and my decision.

We stare at each other some more.

"You can go then," I say, "there's no need to stay."

"I'm not going anywhere."

"But–"

"Like I said, it could be dangerous. I'm staying here to be sure."

I glance towards my very narrow, very single bed.

"Oh," I say.

"I'll sleep on the floor," he says quickly.

"You can't sleep on the floor!"

"I can."

"I don't have any spare bedding or…"

He weaves his hand in the air and a thin mattress with blankets appears alongside the small space beside my bed.

"I didn't know you could do that."

He blinks. Things are different but they're still really awkward.

I walk to my bed and rest the stone down on my pillow.

"I don't even have any food or drink to offer you," I mumble. "Can you magic those up too?"

"No," he says. "Food and drink are essential factors of life. Weavers can not conjure them."

"That doesn't exactly make any sense to me, but a lot of things in this world don't." I flop down to sit on the edge of my bed with a sigh. "Like why the stupid Quarters and the stupid academy and the stupid system exist in the first place."

"They exist because they protect us."

"Tell that to the people living back in Slate Quarter," I mumble.

"You would have things differently, then, I suppose?"

"Yes," I say emphatically, "people would be free to decide where they lived and how they lived."

"Sounds like a recipe for chaos to me."

"It sounds like people would be free to choose their own fate."

"Fate is a complex force," he mutters. "None of us can be free of it."

A creature scuttles in the thatch above our heads and we both look up.

"This room is a shithole."

"It's about a million times better than home," I tell him.

"I find it hard to believe."

"Three regular meals a day." I smile and pat my belly. "It's heaven." I pat the mattress next to me. "You don't have to spend the entire evening standing, you know. You can sit."

"I'm fine."

"I'm not going to bite. I mean you are hot, of course, but I think I can control myself." Alarm sparks in his eyes. "Oh, come on, like you don't know about the little fan club that watches you train every morning. I bet you love giving them that little show."

"What?" he says, sounding genuinely confused.

"Look, I think I can control myself. I'm not some nymphomaniac. I promise not to launch myself across the bed at you," I tease.

"I'm fine," he replies.

"Do I smell?" I lift up the neckline of my shirt and sniff. I'm pretty sure I smell okay. Nothing like Odessa, who probably owns bottles upon bottles of perfume gifted to her by her numerous admirers. But I don't smell bad.

"I think Dray has made it clear that you smell good."

"Do you think I smell good?" I ask. Am I fishing for compliments? Possibly. Thorne says he'd do anything for me and yet he's never expressed any sort of admiration for me at all. In fact, all his body language has ever suggested is that he loathes me.

He doesn't answer.

"You really confuse me," I say, tracing the lines on the stone with my forefinger.

"You wouldn't be alone."

"Thorne Cadieux," I say in frustration, "why do you say you'd do anything for me when you clearly don't like me? In fact, I suspect you despise me. Is it to do with this mate thing?" I shake my head. "Is it out of obligation or–"

"I like you."

"You do?" I say, those butterflies fluttering again. I don't understand how these men do this to me. Why that simple confession has the blood stirring in my veins.

He stares at me.

I let out a little grunt of frustration and pull the blanket from the bed, wrapping it around my shoulders as cool air penetrates through the rafters.

"You're cold," he states.

"Always." I sigh. "You know there's snow on the ground half the year back in Slate Quarter. It's hard to feel warm. I was hoping the academy would be a little better, and then I ended up in this room." I'm waffling but it's better than sitting in awkward silence for the evening.

Thorne, to my surprise, moves from his spot at the door and strides towards the small fireplace. He hunches over his knees, examining it for a few minutes, then clicks his fingers. A fire roars into life, bright red flames dancing in place and a heat permeating through the room immediately.

"Hmmm," I murmur, "that is nice." I close my eyes and let the heat play across my face.

When I open my eyes again, he's peering over his shoulder at me.

"I have an idea," he says, "bring the stone here."

Almost immediately I understand. The fire. The stone. Of course. Why hadn't I thought of that before? If it really is a firestone, maybe fire is somehow important to it.

I climb off the bed with the stone in my hands and approach the fire, as I do Thorne steps away. I shake my head and kneel down in front of the fire. This close the heat is intense and I can hear the flames hissing and crackling as they twist through the air.

"Do you think I should put it in the fire?" I ask him.

"I don't know. Let's try in front to begin with."

I rest the stone before the hearth and immediately it starts to glow a dark orange.

"Oh my gosh," I gasp with excitement. "Can you see that?"

"Yes," he says, bending a little closer. "Is it cracking some more?"

"Yes," I say, "yes, it is."

I tip my head back to meet his gaze and find his face mere inches from mine. The closest we've ever been.

"Oh," I murmur, feeling his magic tickle against my skin, seeing the dark colors of his eyes, seeing the wetness of his lips. My stomach spins.

His eyes flick from the stone to mine and his pupils blossom wide, swallowing up what little color there was so I'm peering into nothing but darkness.

I want him to kiss me. I want to kiss him. I don't know why, what power is propelling me to want this, whether we truly are mates and fate is dragging me towards him, but deep inside me I know I can't have it. Thorne Cadieux doesn't want it and I know what it's like to be forced into things. I won't be that person.

I won't touch him unless he wants me to.

"Do you not like to be touched, is that it?" I whisper.

There was a small boy like that who lived a few houses down from us. He couldn't stand to be touched. Even by his own mother. He'd howl and scream, kicking and biting. Is Thorne wired the same way?

He stands up straight, but his eyes don't leave mine.

"I ... I don't know," he says. "I haven't been touched for a long, long time."

"Can I ..." I hesitate. Am I doing the right thing? "Can I touch you?"

He slams shut his eyes and his magic spikes violently, so violently it's like a shock against my skin and I fall away from him.

"Shit," he says, his hands suddenly pulling at his short hair, "shit, shit. I'm sorry."

He tugs on his hair, his eyes screwed shut, his shoulders heaving.

"Thorne?"

He lifts a hand as if asking for a moment. Then gradually his breathing becomes more even, his hands fall away from his face, he stands rigid once more and opens his eyes.

"It's too dangerous," he says.

"What is?" I say.

"I can't touch you." His chest rises and falls. "I can't touch anyone because it's too dangerous."

"Too dangerous? What does that mean?"

"I would hurt them, maim them." He stares right at me. "Possibly kill them."

My gaze falls to his hands. "The gloves," I say, finally understanding. "It's why you always wear the gloves."

"It helps," he explains.

"But," I swivel round on the floor, "can *I* touch *you*?"

That flash in his eyes again. I understand what it means now. He's wrestling to maintain his control. "No," he says simply. "No, you can't."

"Oh," I say, disappointment spiraling through my stomach. I hadn't realized just how much I did want to touch him until that choice was taken away. "Well," I say grumpily, "that isn't very fair."

His mouth twitches. "No, but it's what I deserve." I think he's going to say more, but then his attention is distracted by the stone. His eyes grow wide.

I swing my gaze that way too, just in time to see the stone breaking apart before the fire.

Chapter Twenty-Four

B eaufort

I click my fingers and the desk lamp switches on as I uncurl the tiny note and position it under the magnifying glass. I scan my gaze over the text, decoding the message in my head, then slump back in my chair, swinging it from side to side as I tap my fingers against the arms.

There's been a major infraction through the magical barriers to the East of the realm. The Empress wants some of the most elite and most powerful shadow weavers from the academy to be sent to help drive the dark forces back and repair the damage. She sees it as a good training opportunity.

I scoff. They've been finding these suitable training exercises ever since Dray turned eighteen and the bond between the three of us formed and it became clear just how damn powerful we would be. Reading between the lines, the 'infraction' must be a major breach of our defenses.

Technically we shouldn't be allowed to face any kind of potentially life-threatening missions until we have graduated from Firestone. But they've been breaking those rules when it comes to us for years now.

I crumple the small note in my fist and toss it towards the fire in the corner of the room. It catches in the flames immediately and is ash in a matter of seconds.

I never used to have a problem with this situation. Missions, while dangerous, are what I live for. The adrenaline, the thrill make me feel more alive than anything ever has done.

Anything has done until Briony.

I scrub my hand through my hair.

This is my duty. There is no refusal. I go willingly or I go reluctantly. It makes no difference. Go I will.

And yet, things have changed. I don't want to leave the academy and I don't want to leave her. Partly, because the girl has a propensity for winding up in danger and ultimately hurt. It's more than that though. According to that note, we'll be away for at least four weeks.

I groan. That sounds like a lifetime.

It's pathetic, stupid, ridiculous, but the idea pains me right in the center of my gut.

I stare down at it now.

I laugh.

Who are you kidding, Lincoln?

That isn't your gut paining at the idea of this separation, it's your damned heart.

You care for the girl.

And it's more than the sex. It's more than the way her snarky words and bratty looks turn you on.

It's more than that flash of a vision. It's more than what the future holds.

She's wormed her way under your skin, infected your blood and infiltrated your heart.

I raise my gaze and lose it in the flickering flames of the fire.

Am I falling for her?

Chapter Twenty-Five

Thorne

The glowing stone splits open and something organic, leathery, and slimy slithers out onto the hearth.

Briony squeals and scuttles backwards across the floor.

"What is that?" she cries.

"A creature of some sort," I answer, examining it more closely. The thing is covered in a thick slime similar to the yolk of an egg and it's difficult to make it out as it wriggles beneath the translucent goo.

"Is it alive?" Briony asks, venturing a little closer.

It appears so. The creature struggles in the goo, twisting and turning its sinewy body until finally a small head breaks through. It takes a lungful of air and then it squawks.

"Is it a bird?"

It has a pointed beak so the guess is reasonable and I can

make out a pair of wings folded in the slime. But I don't think it's a bird. Or a griffin.

"A dragon."

"A dragon?" She laughs. "That's impossible."

"A rock calling you towards it sounds impossible, don't you think?"

She tuts and leans over the creature. "Do you think it's dangerous?"

I snort. The little thing is small enough to fit in the palm of my hand. "I don't think so."

The creature squawks again and blinks open a large pair of eyes. Its irises are bright gold, dazzlingly so, as it blinks right up at Briony.

"Aww, it's so cute," she coos. She scurries away and comes back with a threadbare towel, scooping the small creature up into her arms.

"Hello, mister," she says, wiping the goo from its body. "Were you hiding inside all that time?"

With the goo gone, it's easier to make out the creature's body. It has four stubby legs with black talons at the end of each toe. Its body is long and tucked against its back are the pair of wings – made from paper-thin skin and not littered with feathers. Down the center of its back runs a prominent spine and its skin is covered in coppery green scales that sparkle in the firelight.

It is a dragon. There is nothing else it could be.

The little thing curls up in Briony's hands, snuggling into her stomach and squawks some more.

"We need to take it to the Headmaster. A message needs to be sent to the Empress and–"

"He needs feeding."

"After we've–"

"Newborn babies need food."

"It's not a baby."

"He is," she says, scowling at me and hugging the thing protectively.

"You don't even know if it is a he," I mumble.

"Milk. That's what we should feed it. Do you have any back in your tower?"

I pause before answering that question because I see where this is going.

"Yes, but, Briony–"

"Look, Thorne," she says, "you could be right and taking him to the Head is the right thing to do–"

"I am and it is."

"But we don't know that for sure and until we do, I'm not going to be parted with him." The little dragon snorts a puff of smoke issuing from his nostrils as if he is in agreement with that point. "You promised you wouldn't tell anyone about the stone and you said you'd respect my decisions."

"That was before the stone became a dragon."

"It's the same thing." She strokes the little dragon's snout and the thing begins to purr. "Now please can you fetch some milk?"

I've been a fool. Letting those words slip from my mouth.

I'll do anything for you.

This girl is going to hold me to that.

Funny thing, I ponder as I head towards the door, *I don't think I care.*

"Oh, and it'll need to be warm," Briony calls after me.

"Right," I say, reaching for the door-handle.

"And we'll need something suitable to use to feed it to him. A teaspoon maybe or a syringe."

"Fine."

Halfway across campus, I doubt my decision to leave our thrall alone with a newborn dragon. It looked helpless and tiny. What if it's not? What if I return to find her badly burned or scorched alive?

I flex and fist my fingers.

I'm catastrophizing. The girl has already survived far worse. Beaufort described the scars on her back. Beaten to a pulp, were his words. If she withstood that, she can handle a dragon.

I hope.

Five minutes later I'm heating milk on the stove.

"You're back," Dray says, bounding into the kitchen in nothing but a pair of sleep pants. "What was it the little kitten wanted to show you?" He grins. "Was it her pussy?"

I stir the milk. What do I tell him? Dray is my bond brother. We haven't kept secrets from one another since the bond between us activated – the day Dray, the youngest of the three of us, turned eighteen.

But I promised Briony. I made a scared promise. I can't break it.

"Her room," I say. He isn't convinced.

"Her room. Right," Dray says, still grinning. "Sure she did, pal." He jumps up onto the counter, legs swinging and watches me stir the milk. "What the hell are you doing?"

"She wanted some warm milk." At least that isn't a lie.

"Oh man, I knew it. You are gone for this girl."

Tiny bubbles appear in the milk around the edges of the pan.

"Aren't you?" I say.

"Fuck, yeah, totally." He sweeps his hand through his long hair. "I didn't expect it to be this strong. Did you?"

I shake my head.

"Beaufort has to be right," he says, "even though ..." He

lifts up his arms and peers at his wrists. Then drops his hands back into his lap. "Do you think she feels it?"

I consider his question, switching off the heat and pouring the milk into a hip-flask.

"Yes," I say, "yes, I think she does."

"Man ..." he mutters, the grin on his face stretching even wider. "Maybe I'll come back to her room with you."

"No," I say abruptly, screwing on the top of the flask with more force than necessary.

"We're bond brothers. That means sharing, Thorne." He pouts like a kid who's had a toy snatched away.

"Does she want that?" I point out.

I've been told over and over again by Dray that we are every woman's walking fantasy. Three powerful shadow weavers bound together by our bond, forced by fate to share a mate. Every woman, according to Dray, wants to be that mate. But Dray talks nonsense. I'm not sure Briony would want that. She's only just coming round to the thrall idea.

"I spoke to her about it," his eyes twinkle, "you should have smelled how wet she got at the idea."

"Not tonight," I growl and stomp out of the kitchen, hoping he doesn't decide to follow me. You can never tell with Dray.

I find Briony lying on the bed, curled round the little dragon.

She presses her finger to her lips. "He's sleeping," she mouths.

I nod and place the flask of milk on the floor by the bed. Then I return to my spot by the door.

Briony strokes a forefinger over the dragon and my gaze flits from her to the little creature and back again.

I can't decide which is more fascinating. Dragons have

been extinct for hundreds of years. This may be the first dragon born in centuries, nestled in Briony's bed.

And yet, as fascinating, as crazy as that is, my eyes are drawn back to the girl.

She's even more fascinating. The way she curls around the dragon like a cat. The way the firelight dances in the golden strands of her hair, the way her body falls and rises in curves – nipped at the waist, rounded over her hips and her backside.

She's taken off her academy blazer now it's warm in the room and rolled up her sleeves and her skirt has risen up her thighs. Inches of bare skin, milky white turning pink with the fire.

Does she have any idea how much it's killing me, tearing me up inside, shredding me to pieces, that I can't touch her? It's all I want to do. All I can think about.

Just to rest my ungloved palm on the flesh of her thigh, to feel the heat of her skin, the softness of it.

I've cursed this stupid affliction before. Railed at fate and my inability to touch. But not like this. I've come to accept it over the years, to come to terms with my fate.

Only now it's so much harder.

She must feel something in my magic because she looks up from the dragon to me with curiosity and then she smiles.

A genuine, sweet smile, like she's happy in my company, content.

People smile at me. But it's not often. Not often at all.

When they do, it's with a greed in their eyes. They want something from me.

This smile is different.

"He's so cute, isn't he?" she whispers.

Fascinating maybe but I would not describe the bony scaly creature as cute.

Beaufort has wondered aloud over and over again why fate has picked this girl for us, what it can mean. He told me about the torture, about the scars that riddled her back. She clearly has no hidden powers. Yet, all along she had a firestone, a firestone that called her to it, a firestone which has now hatched into the first live dragon in centuries.

This must mean something. What did Beaufort see in that flash of a vision and what can it mean?

Briony's words stir the little thing and it mews and nips at her fingers.

"I think he's hungry," she says.

"The flask is right there," I tell her.

"Could you pass it to me please?"

"You know I can't."

"We can be careful," she says.

"I don't want to hurt you." I don't want to hurt you like I hurt them. I don't want to lose anyone else precious to me. I refuse to let it happen.

"You won't," she says. "I trust you."

The girl is incorrigible.

I walk back to the bed, pick up the flask and place it on the mattress. She's still smiling.

"See, the world didn't end."

"This isn't a joke," I say.

Her smile fades. "I know. I'm sorry."

She unscrews the lid and I squat to sit on the mattress in the small sliver of space beside the bed, watching as she takes a sip of the milk to check it's not too hot.

The little dragon sniffs at the air and mewls.

"You want some, huh?" she asks it, then directs her next question to me. "Did you bring a spoon?"

"No," I say, "I forgot."

"Hmm," she says, "never mind." She dips her little finger into the milk and holds it out to the dragon. It sniffs at her digit and does nothing.

"He doesn't know what to do," she says, gently guiding her finger between its beak. "Jeez, that's sharp."

The little dragon starts to suckle, when he stops, she dips her finger in again and repeats the process.

"How do you know how to do this?" I ask.

"Oh," she nudges her finger into the dragon's mouth. "I once found a kitten in the forest. I guess it had been abandoned. It was a matter of trial and error to get it to eat. This proved the best way." Her face darkens. "Then Muriel discovered her and ... well ..."

"Muriel?"

"My step-mom."

"She was the one who beat you." I say it as a statement. If the woman was cruel enough to harm a kitten, I bet she was cruel enough to harm her step-daughter.

Briony says nothing, fussing with the dragon.

"Would you like me to kill her?"

"What?" she says, alarmed. "Who?"

"Your step-mom."

She chews on her cheek and I can tell she's considering it. "No," she says finally.

I'm glad she doesn't make me promise, though. Because that is a promise I may not be able to keep.

Chapter Twenty-Six

B riony

Neither of us sleep much that night. The baby dragon wakes every few hours crying for milk and Thorne is forced to return to his tower in the early hours to restock.

"Jeez, for something so little, he has a big appetite," I say, wondering if my plan to keep him is going to work out.

As the little dragon suckles from my fingers, I voice my concerns to Thorne. "How am I going to keep him fed? How am I going to keep him hidden in my room? And don't say I should take him to the Headmaster. I can't give him up."

In the brief time we've spent together, I've realized for all his gruff, silent and brooding exterior, Thorne Cadieux is a big softie. Beaufort wouldn't let me keep this dragon. He'd be marching me over to the Headmaster's office right now. And Dray wouldn't be serious enough to help me. But

Thorne seems to be someone who would happily wrap himself around my little finger.

"I'll find him some food," he says. "And I can magic him up some kind of cage."

He looks over at the available space in the room.

"A cage?" I say, in disgust.

"It would be for his own safety," he says. "If you leave him to free roam, he could hurt himself."

"Or I could skip lessons and stay here to look after him."

"And draw attention to yourself. And the fact you are keeping a baby dragon in your room."

I want to stick my tongue out at him, because, of course, he is right.

Keeping the stone hidden was relatively easy. Keeping a dragon hidden will be much harder. So I decide for now to go with the cage idea and work something else out later.

"I still think it would be better to hand this dragon over. If the Empress were to find out you had a dragon and it hadn't been declared–"

"Please can you just magic up the cage? Only, make it a snuggly one. He's only little."

"We can use the extra blankets I conjured here last night to make it comfortable."

"Thank you," I say.

Thorne watches the dragon while I freshen up in the tower bathroom, then leaves right before dawn. I feed the dragon some more milk. He seems to be growing in strength with every meal. By the time the seven o'clock bell clangs, he's crawling about across my bed and beginning to uncurl his wings. Occasionally he'll let out a snort of smoke, but no real fire, and his steps are pretty unsteady.

"I guess, if you're planning on staying around, we ought to give you a name, huh?" I say to him as I stroke a finger down his knobbly spine. "Something ... dignified? George? Charles? Albert?"

The little dragon snorts at those suggestions and I take it he doesn't approve of those regal-sounding names.

"Something a little less formal perhaps? Hmmm ... Berty?"

The dragon shakes his head as if he understands, then lets out an almighty sneeze, that has him zooming backwards across the bed as a burst of fire shoots out of his nostrils.

"I got it!" I say, scooping him up and hugging him to my chest. "Blaze."

When Fly knocks for me, I tell him I'm skipping breakfast and don't place the baby dragon in the cage until the very last minute.

I've tried to make it as comfortable as best I can with the blankets and one of my old shirts.

I use the lid of the flask as a dish and leave him some milk.

"I have to go," I say sadly, feeling more guilty than I have ever been in my life. "I promise I'll be back. Just ... be good."

It feels totally surreal to be closing the door behind me and leaving a dragon in my bedroom. As I skip down the stairs, I debate whether I dreamed the whole thing up. Thorne, the fire, the dragon. Was that all just some crazy fantasy?

But my drooping eyelids, and inability to stop yawning, tell me it was real.

"Did those Princes keep you awake all night?" Fly says from nowhere, making me jump a mile.

"No," I say.

Fly! Did he hear anything strange last night? Should I tell him?

But I can't. Thorne implied I will be in trouble if it comes out I've been hiding a dragon and I don't want my friend implicated.

He studies my face, a wicked grin on his.

Is dragon written across my forehead?

He must be able to tell.

"I slept in my own bed last night," I tell him. Not adding that Thorne Cadieux was in my room.

"Stars," he says, "things are moving at a glacial pace."

"Don't you have your own love life to keep you entertained now?" I point out. "You no longer need to rely on mine for entertainment."

"But yours is so much more interesting."

"Clearly not," I mumble as he links his arm through mine and we head off toward Professor Tudor's classroom, my belly filling with a dread I can't understand.

A dread that is probably warranted because, as I shuffle into the classroom behind Fly, Fox's head snaps around and he glares at me, his nostrils flaring and his eyes glowing even more vividly than usual.

What the hell?

I feel those glowing eyes on me as I cross the classroom and take my usual seat on the bench in the middle row. He's still glaring at me once everyone else has taken their seats and the minutes tick by, the other students fidgeting uncomfortably on the benches.

Henrietta Smyte turns around in her seat to determine what exactly the professor is staring at. When she discovers it's me, she rolls her eyes.

"Professor, are you planning on starting the lesson?"

He frowns and drags his gaze away from me. For a

moment, he seems lost in his thoughts, then his shadows swim across to the blackboard and words appear as he begins a monologue about the responsibilities of safe magic.

"What the fuck did you do to upset him this time?" Fly whispers in my ear.

"Your guess is as good as mine," I whisper back. But unease is flooding through my veins.

This isn't good – I'm absolutely sure this isn't good.

A feeling that is only magnified when Professor Tudor's gaze flicks between me and the blackboard non-stop. He doesn't even pretend to make the lesson interactive or interesting. The monologue drones on and we're forced to copy down notes from the board. I'm already struggling to stay awake after my interrupted night and this lesson is not helping. The classroom may be cold but it's also dark and Professor Fox has a deep, rumble of a voice that lulls me towards sleep. Twice I jerk awake; thankfully only Fly notices, giving me a look that suggests he does not believe I spent my night alone.

However, the third time, Fox spots me.

"I'm sorry, Miss Storm, am I keeping you awake?"

Everyone in the classroom turns around to stare at me.

"Falling asleep in lessons, Professor Tudor," Henrietta chimes with obvious glee. "That definitely warrants punishment."

Her eyes positively gleam and I half expect her to offer to be the one to mete out said punishment.

"For once, Miss Smyte, we are in agreement. Stay behind after class Miss Storm."

"Seriously?" I can't help blurting out. I'm beginning to take this personally. Half the other students appear to be snoozing around me, but I'm the one having to stay behind. Professor Tudor has it in for me and I have no idea why.

"This is starting to become a habit," Fly mumbles under his breath.

I glare at Fox who simply glares right back.

When the bell clangs to signal the end of lessons, I'm more than annoyed. I'm furious.

He's the only teacher in the academy from a commoner background, who comes from Slate Quarter. You'd think he'd give us kids a break. He knows where we come from. What it's like. Instead, he wants to pick on me.

I stride to the front of the classroom, stopping a few paces from him, folding my arms across my chest and scowling at him. He's leaning against his desk, but even then, he's much taller than me and broader and stronger. I should be intimidated. For once, I'm not.

His arms are folded over his chest, and he's scowling right back, his cool magic sparking with annoyance in the air.

I wait until all the other students have filed out of the room, Henrietta clearly taking her time as if she'd like to hang about and watch my berating. However, eventually, with a glare from the professor, she leaves too.

I open my mouth to give the professor a piece of my mind, but he beats me to it.

"Why the hell do you smell like a lizard?" he grunts.

That ... that was not what I was expecting him to say.

And do I? Do I smell like a lizard? I hadn't noticed.

I lower my chin and give myself a subtle sniff. All I can smell is milk.

"I do not," I say.

"Miss Storm, I have an exceedingly good sense of smell, and you do. You reek of it." His top lip curls in disgust. "I could smell it as soon as you stepped inside my classroom."

If I wasn't so mad at him, I'd be peeing my pants. How

long before he works out the lizard he can supposedly smell is actually a dragon? But, luckily, I'm too angry to be scared.

"Is this the real reason you kept me behind? To tell me I stink?" I spit.

"Once again you are failing to appreciate how things work in this academy, Miss Storm. I am the teacher. You are the student. I ask the questions, not you. And you answer them." He pushes away from the desk and stands to his full, towering height. "So, tell me, why do you smell of lizard?"

"Oh I'm sorry. Do I not smell like flowers and fruit and all things feminine and delicate like I should? Well, as I'm sure you know, I have no freaking money. I can't afford soap or perfume or any of those luxuries. I have to make do with what the academy provides for us. And it's not my fault if that smells like," I lift my hands and make inverted commas with my fingers, "*lizard* to you."

"Miss Storm, no one else in this academy smells like a lizard."

"Maybe," I say sarcastically, "because I'm the poorest person in this academy and am the only one who can't afford my own soap." It's a lie but I'm sticking with it. Striking back at him may be my only means of defense.

"You're the Prince's thrall," he scoffs with such disgust; it's as if the words taste rank in his mouth.

"I am not."

His gaze rakes angrily over my face. "Are you telling me you're *not* sleeping with them?"

My mouth falls so far open I hear my jaw click. "Wh-wh-what? That is so far from inappropriate, it's untrue!"

"I'm just trying to unscramble my way through all your lies, Miss Storm."

"You're trying to gaslight me, that's what you're doing."

"Gaslighting?" He laughs. "You're the one telling me the reason you stink of lizard is because of the soap."

I lift my chin and glare at him.

"I don't like liars, Miss Storm," he whispers ominously, making me shiver despite all the burning anger in my veins.

"And I don't like bullies," I whisper back.

"Really? That's not what I saw," he says. "I saw you being pulled into the shadows to get up to who-the-fuck-knows-what with one of the worst bullies in the academy."

All the blood rises to my cheeks and they sizzle. What with the cracking stone and baby dragon, I'd completely forgotten about the ball and mine and Dray's run in with the professor.

I shouldn't feel shame or embarrassment about that. I wasn't the only one making out in the hall (okay it was more than that but the professor doesn't know that ... does he?).

I cringe.

"You're making me late for my next lesson," I mutter, hurrying to the door and praying with every bone in my body he doesn't stop me. "And it's with Madame Bardin!"

Chapter Twenty-Seven

B riony

I haven't spoken to the Madame since our altercation in the maze. She was at the ball but apart from that I haven't seen her around the academy the last few days.

Deep in my heart, I've been praying to all the stars that she'd left the academy, so ashamed by what happened, so frightened I'd report her, so bound by Thorne's magic, she'd scarpered. But even deeper down in my heart, I know I won't be that lucky.

When have any of the abusers in my life 'come to their senses' or voluntarily left my life? None. Exactly, none.

And so, as I approach her classroom and hear her sultry voice meandering down the hallway, I'm not surprised at all, although I am nervous. All that angry energy has burned away and now I'm just plain scared.

What if Madame smells lizard on me too? What if

Madame realizes it's not lizard, it's dragon? What if she isn't done with me? What if, like Thorne, she has no problem breaking the sacred promise?

I hover outside the classroom door, gripping the handle, and attempt to steady my nerves.

I just came from yelling at Professor Fox and theoretically he's a lot more scary than Madame.

Inhaling, I push down on the handle and step inside the classroom.

Madame's kohl-lined eyes snap to me, then away and she continues issuing instructions about a potion without acknowledging me at all.

I search for a spare seat and am somewhat relieved to find Dray's in the class as usual. I don't think Madame would try anything with him here.

I'm less pleased to find him signaling toward an empty chair he's saved next to his. This puts me right in the front row and right in Madame's firing line. However, there are no other seats so I don't have a choice but to take the one offered.

I tiptoe across the classroom as quietly as I can, even though everyone is watching me, and slide into my seat. Almost immediately, cauldrons, implements and ingredients appear on the desk in front of me.

Madame claps her hands.

"Begin," she says.

I look down helplessly at the collection of objects. I have no clue whatsoever what we're meant to be doing.

"And remember, anyone who fails to complete this task will be staying behind for detention."

Madame smiles, her red lips stretched wide and I'm sure that smile is aimed like a weapon at me. The last thing I want to do is spend a detention with Madame. Firstly, because I have a hungry baby dragon to feed. Secondly, she might kill me.

Dray bumps his elbow against me.

"We're turning lead into gold," he says.

"I thought that was illegal," I mutter.

"Is it?" he says with a wink. "You need to start by dousing your piece of lead in bat's piss."

"Ewww." I scrunch up my nose. "That is gross"

"It's actually a delicacy," he says, chewing his gum. His eyes flick down my form. "Just like someone else I know. You know your pussy should be considered the most precious delicacy–"

"Can we get back to the lead and the piss?" I say, peering over my shoulder at Madame who I am sure is listening in.

"The bat's piss smells pretty good, although freaking strong." Dray lifts up a stoppered bottle on his desk and holds it up to the light. He takes a deep inhale. "Yeah, it's nice."

I sniff too, but I don't have his wolfish olfactory skills and I can't smell a thing. However, I'm guessing the bat's piss is hiding any scent of dragon that may be lingering on my skin. A good thing. I don't need Dray interrogating me in front of the Madame.

"Mr. Eros," the Madame calls, from where she is rearranging her case of cigarettes as she perches on her desk, legs crossed, feet dangling and quite a bit of thigh showing. "I'm sure Miss Storm can do this without your help."

"Bet she can," he says, all smoldering eyes and good looks, "but I just can't stop myself from helping others," he rests his hand on his chest, "it's like an addiction."

"Then rein that addiction in. Students should be working alone," she says, a little more frostily.

"I wish I could," he says earnestly, "honestly, I really wish I could. But it's impossible. Plus she's our thrall," I frown, "so the compulsion is even stronger."

He smiles at Madame and to everyone else the smile probably seems perfectly sweet. I can see there's something sinister about it, though. A warning for Madame not to interfere.

The Deputy Head uncrosses and recrosses her legs. Then mutters, "Very well."

"Was that wise?" I whisper to him a few minutes later as he's helping me to boil my bat's piss with his magic. "Madame is in charge of the academy."

"Yeah, but not the fucking realm, Kitten." He laughs, like I'm being delightfully stupid.

I don't entirely understand his meaning. Dray doesn't know about Thorne helping me in the maze. He doesn't know Thorne stopped and restrained Madame Bardin. He also doesn't know it was Madame who attacked me.

As well as soaking the tiny piece of lead in bat's piss, we're also required to add a collection of equally delightful ingredients. Wild boar toenails, frog's intestines and rat balls. Each is more revolting than the last and nearly everyone is dry-heaving into their fists by the time we come to the final ingredient.

A pinch of sprite dust.

When we get to this point, Madame unlocks a well-secured cupboard at the back of the classroom, and then a heavy metal box. She extracts a small white marble pot, its lid fixed by a golden hinge. On the top of the lid is painted a tiny dancing creature.

Madame walks around the desks, adding a pinch of the sparkling pink dust into each potion as she does.

"Can't we do it ourselves?" the shadow weaver Ashleigh

asks from the front row, obviously expecting the Madame to submit to them.

"No," the Madame says sternly, "this pinch of powder is worth more than I'm sure most of the Slate students' families earn in a year." She smirks at me. "In fact, it's utterly priceless. The only people that own such dust are me – for teaching purposes of course – and the Empress herself."

Madame continues weaving her way around the desks; when she reaches the front row where the shadow weavers are sitting, she's more generous with her pinch. Except for me. She goes to pinch her fingers into the marble pot, lifting her hand and releasing her fingers over my potion. Nothing falls from her grip.

"That didn't work," I point out. She's already moved on to the next potion. Bet she did that deliberately. I'm certain of it. "Madame Bardin, nothing sprinkled into my potion."

"Don't be ridiculous," she dismisses. "Of course it did. Everyone saw me sprinkle dust into your potion. There's no need to be greedy, Miss Storm."

"I'm not," I insist. "Nothing fell into my pot."

"Surely, you could give her just a tad more," Dray says, with a characteristically charming smile, "just to be sure."

"Certainly not," Madame says, snapping shut the lid. "This dust is precious and can not be wasted just because some silly girl isn't observant enough."

A couple of the shadow weavers giggle, although they stop when Dray swings his dangerous gaze their way. He pushes his chair backwards and lumbers to his feet. Casually, he strolls towards Madame Bardin, blowing a bubble with his gum as he does. When he reaches her, the bubble pops with a bang.

She doesn't flinch. She doesn't look happy, but she also doesn't look intimidated.

"I will personally ensure that the additional sprite dust is replaced," he says, holding out his hand, palm side up.

"And how will you do that?" the Madame says, lips curling into a seductive smile.

"I will ask the Empress personally to replace it from her own collection."

A hush full of tension falls across the classroom.

The Empress? How the hell can Dray promise something like that?

The smile on the Madame's face twitches but she holds it there and places the pot into Dray's hand.

I watch, gobsmacked, as he strolls back to my desk, opens the pot and dumps a pinch of pink dust into my potion.

"There you go, Kitten," he says with a wink, before tossing the pot over his shoulder.

The classroom takes a collective gasp as the delicate pot sails high towards the ceiling, everyone half-expecting for the lip to flip open and sprite dust to spatter everywhere.

However, Madame Bardin moves with unexpected speed and grabs the pot in mid flight.

One boy in the back row claps but stops pretty abruptly when Madame snaps, "Back to work!"

Fifteen minutes later, we're draining the potion and fishing out the tiny pieces of lead resting at the bottom of our cauldrons.

I gasp when I hook my piece out. It's only the size of my thumbnail but, where moments ago, it was dull and gray, now it shines a golden color between my fingers.

"It worked!" I say, amazed. "It actually worked."

"Some magic doesn't require powers, Kitten," Dray says beside me, pocketing his own piece of gold – at least three times the size of mine. "Like orgasms for instance. Like the ability I have to wring a pretty awesome orgasm from your pussy with my tongue–"

But I'm not really listening to him. I'm too busy staring at my piece of gold with wonderment.

I did it. I actually did it.

As I swing my gaze around the room, I realize I'm the only commoner who has succeeded, which means Dray probably helped me out.

For once, I don't care. This means no detention with Madame Bardin.

Which, as well as being really freaking satisfying, is also a massive relief, because I have what I expect is one truly hungry baby dragon waiting for me in my room.

Chapter Twenty-Eight

B riony

"I need to head back to my room for a bit before I grab some lunch," I tell Fly as we walk away from Madame Bardin's classroom.

"I'll come with you. I need to fetch something from my room too," Fly says.

"You don't have to," I say, probably a little too quickly, because he eyes me with suspicion.

"You're acting really weirdly today," he says, "well, you're always weird, you're just being even more weird."

"Gee, thanks."

"It's a compliment, Cupcake." He shrugs. "I like weird. It makes things more interesting. I was just making an observation and pondering what could have caused this additional weirdness."

"Probably just tiredness," I half lie. "I didn't sleep well last night."

When we reach the top of our tower, we find Thorne waiting outside my room.

"Didn't sleep well, huh?" Fly mutters with a raised eyebrow.

I wait for him to disappear inside his room, muttering something about enjoying our lunch break. Then I turn to Thorne.

"I came to see how the little one is doing," he says.

I press my finger urgently to my lips and peer towards Fly's door. The outer walls in this tower may be formed from thick stone, but the inner ones are paper thin.

I signal to him to move to one side and open my door. As soon as I do something comes streaking towards me. I shriek and duck as it skims over my head, and soars up towards the ceiling.

"What the hell was that?" I mutter, peering up towards the rafters and the thatched roof.

"Shit," Thorne says behind me as the door clicks shut.

"What?" I say, dragging my gaze from the shape up above and down to my room. "Oh!"

My room is once again trashed. The cage Thorne created is smashed. My bedding is all messed up. And most disturbing, the entrails of something that was once alive are strewn across the floor.

"Blaze!" I cry, rushing forward.

Did someone find out about him? Did someone–

"Briony!" Thorne barks, pointing upwards.

I lift my gaze to find something hurtling towards me from above. I screech again, lifting my hands to cover my head.

"Briony!" Thorne repeats. "It's the dragon!"

I peek through my fingers to find Blaze hovering in the air in front of me, his little baby wings flapping like crazy. He gives me a toothless grin and zooms straight into my chest.

"*Oofff*," I grunt, catching him in my arms. He snuggles up against me and licks at my neck. I stare up at Thorne in disbelief. "He could barely crawl first thing this morning," I point out.

"Dragons must develop quickly." He goes to inspect the damage to the cage. "It looks like he burned right through the wooden bars." He turns to look at the dead thing on the floor, nudging it with the toe of his boot. "Rat."

"Did you catch a rat, Blaze?" I ask the little dragon, who growls when he sees Thorne inspecting his kill and flutters that way, grabbing a piece of intestine with his mouth and shaking it about.

Something I did not need to see right before my lunch.

"Blaze?" Thorne asks.

"Yes, I named him."

"But where did he catch a rat from?" Thorne asks.

"The roof's infested with them," I say, which makes Thorne frown. "But at least, I won't have to worry about what to feed him."

Thorne doesn't smile at my joke, instead he twitches his fingers and his shadow magic rushes around the room, tidying up and repairing the damage. Blaze growls at the shadows too and spurts a tiny flame at one that rushes close by. The flames merrily flicker through the shadows, doing nothing to stop them.

They are mesmerizing to watch, shimmering as they swirl and swim and slide in front of me. I'm so tempted to reach out and touch them, even if Thorne says they are dangerous. But I don't have permission and I can't help thinking it would be a violation. Just like with Thorne himself, I'll have to be resigned to looking and not touching.

"Thank you," I say, when the room is back to normal and his shadows are retreating. He nods. "I'd better hurry to the canteen before all the good food goes."

"You could ..." He looks at a point over my right shoulder, not meeting my gaze. "Come to the Shadow Weaver Dining Hall. Thralls are welcome."

"Other thralls, probably not me," I point out.

"What does that mean?" he asks, his dark eyes now flicking to mine.

"Oh, nothing."

"It wasn't nothing," he says, as Blaze somersaults in circles above our heads.

"Be careful," I warn the dragon. Then sigh, and address Thorne again. "I think you three, and possibly my friends, are the only people in the academy who believe I should be your thrall."

"That's not true."

"Erm, it is."

"Does it matter?"

"No, but I'd rather have lunch with my friends than a roomful of people who resent and hate me."

"They don't know you."

"You don't know me," I tell him, smiling. "We barely know each other."

"I know you, Briony Storm," he says.

●

"So Thorne Cadieux too, huh?" Fly says with a big grin, when I join him and Clare at the lunch table later.

"It's not like that," I say.

"He still doesn't like you?" Clare asks sympathetically.

"Oh he likes her," Fly says, "you should have seen the way he was looking at her out there on the landing. I bet her clothes were off within a microsecond of the bedroom door closing."

"Well, you suppose wrong," I snap, slicing a potato in two so aggressively one half skids across the table.

"Woah, okay," Fly says, raising his hands in surrender. "Why so touchy about it?"

"I'm not touchy," I say, chomping down hard on the same potato.

"Is it because you want to sleep with him but he doesn't want to sleep with you?" Clare says frankly, adjusting her glass.

"I don't want to ..." I begin, then trail off because who am I kidding? I do want to. Fly is right, the way that man looks at me is like fire. All this time I've been mistaking it for hatred. Now I see it for what it is – want, an unfulfilled want, a want he thinks can never be fulfilled. No wonder he's so freaking angry about it. I feel pretty angry about it myself. "It's complicated."

I poke at the remainder of my potato with a lot less force.

"It's always complicated with you and those Princes," Fly says. "If you ever turn around and tell me it's easy and simple, I'll drop dead of shock."

"Some of it is easy and simple," I muse. Fly snorts. "It is!" I insist. "I don't know, I've spent time with Thorne now and I kind of like him."

"But he doesn't feel the same," Clare says, nodding her head as if she's worked out a tricky puzzle.

"Erm, actually no." I drop my fork and slump back in

my chair, twisting a loose piece of hair back into my usual bun. "I think he does like me."

"So what's the problem, Cupcake?" Fly says. "You haven't exactly proved shy when it comes to these men so far." He leans in close. "You know there are rumors swirling about you and Dray at the ball."

"Tsk," Clare dismisses, "there are rumors swirling about everyone. Including you Fly."

Our usually overly confident friend shuts his mouth and peers around the canteen as if to check whether people are talking about him right now.

"Like I said," I sigh, staring down at my unfinished lunch, "it's complicated."

Clare removes her glasses and wipes the lenses with her sleeve. "A problem shared, is a problem halved."

I chew on my cheek. "He can't touch me," I whisper quietly. They both lean in closer.

"Does he have OCD?" Clare asks. "Or an aversion to sex or something?"

"It's his powers. He says if he touched me, he'd hurt me." I shake my head in frustration. "I don't really under-stand it."

"Ahhh," Fly says, "that explains the gloves. I thought that was a strange fashion choice."

"But he controls his powers. I don't see why it would be a problem," Clare muses.

"According to him it is."

"There must be more to it," Clare says.

"If there were, though," Fly says, "wouldn't he have told you?"

"I don't know," I say.

Thorne Cadieux isn't exactly the talkative type.

Chapter Twenty-Nine

B riony

When I return to my room after afternoon lessons, telling my friends I'm skipping dinner to catch an early night, I find it less trashed than lunchtime and Blaze curled up on top of my bed sleeping.

Several of my socks have been strewn across the floor, several of them ripped to pieces, and the cage has once again been scorched, but there are no half-eaten rats this time.

As I climb onto the bed beside him, I discover why. He lifts his head, yawns, attempts to lick my face, then shoots up into the roof, yanks a rat out of the rafters by its tail and swallows it whole.

"Yuck, Blaze, that is seriously gross!"

Although, I have to admit, it's better than rat remains all over the room.

He spins some somersaults in the air, letting out some

puffs of smoke, dive bombs one of my socks, then settles back into the bed beside me.

"I'm not sure I should be letting you sleep up here with me," I tell him, as he begins to purr, "I think it sets a bad precedent." I assume Blaze is going to grow pretty big. He's already grown on this first day. Eventually he'll be crushing the bed with me in it. But he's so damn sweet, little legs twitching as he falls asleep, that I can't help relenting.

"I'd be really grateful if you wouldn't wake me up throughout the night," I yawn, as I snuggle into him and drift asleep.

I wake to Blaze nudging my cheek with his beak before spreading his wings and whizzing about the room. A slice of dim gray light by the window tells me it's at least several hours before the seven o'clock bell.

I lie in bed watching the little dragon zooming about the rafters. This is surreal, totally surreal, and several times I pinch my thigh just to check I am awake.

It's also clear this dragon has way too much energy and confining him in this room is going to be difficult. When he hovers by the window, whining, I decide I need to let him out.

"Blaze," I say, and to my surprise he comes flying right towards me, landing on the mattress. "We can go outside, but you have to promise to stay hidden. No ..." I scrabble for the best word to describe the strange noises this fellow makes, "growling."

I am probably mad, but the way he stares at me with those golden eyes has me convinced he understands me. Of course, that's totally impossible and this plan I'm forming in my head very likely to go horribly wrong.

I dress quickly, then wrap myself in the winter coat Clare's given me and invite Blaze inside. He understands immediately, snuggling into my chest as I fasten the coat around us.

Okay, I look an unusual shape, but hopefully no one will be up this early. Even Thorne. I still take a deviating route out to the forest, avoiding the field just in case the shadow weaver is there early this morning. While I don't mind him seeing us (although I'm sure he won't approve of this plan), if he's out there, there'll be at least one or two of his oglers watching and I don't want them spotting me with my bundle.

I walk several feet into the forest until we're well hidden and then I peer down into my coat, finding Blaze peering back at me.

"I'm going to let you out for about an hour of play time." Talking to a dragon this way is ridiculous. He is not Barney, my old dog. Then again, it seems as good a way of talking to him as any other. "Do not fly above the tree-line, stay down in the canopy, okay?" He blinks up at me. "I'm serious, if you fly up high, you'll be spotted and then ..." He cocks his head as if waiting for my next words. "And then ... I don't know exactly, but I'm not sure it will be good for you or for me."

I unbutton my coat and immediately Blaze zigzags through the trees with so much speed and energy, it's hard to keep track of him. Alarm shoots through my gut. If he takes off now, I'll never be able to catch him, and I'll have no hope of finding him. Although, as I watch him swoop up into the branches and pluck a squirrel twice his size from the branches, I query whether he actually needs me. He can clearly take care of himself.

Should I let him go? Is it fair to keep him hidden away in my room?

The little dragon answers my question for me.

He comes hurtling back through the trees, dropping the now-deceased squirrel at my feet.

"Jeez, thanks?" I say.

The dragon turns somersaults, then shoots away again.

I stare down into the squirrel's vacant eyes. Is that meant to be a present or a death threat?

Before I make up my mind, the little guy is back again, this time stopping to lick my face three times before zooming back into the canopy.

I wipe my face with my sleeve. I am going to need to scrub myself extra hard under the shower in the morning, otherwise even those with the weakest olfactory skills will be able to smell dragon on me.

The next hour passes in much the same way: Blaze flying up into the branches, sniffing around dead piles of leaves and generally causing mischief, but returning every few minutes to check I haven't gone anywhere.

When the academy clock bell clangs seven, I call his name, and he comes fluttering in to land on my shoulder, this time taking issue with my bun, growling, pulling and biting at it.

"Hey, I've already lost patches of hair. I don't need to lose any more." I lift him off my shoulder and cradle him in my arms, stroking at his head. "I'm afraid it's time to go back," I say, with a yawn. The dragon whimpers as if he understands but doesn't struggle as I tuck him back into my coat and smuggle him back up to my room.

The next few days, Blaze and I fall into a routine. We rise early every morning and I sneak him out to the trees for an hour's fly-around. He spends the day in my room hunting rats, destroying my socks and napping on my bed. I sneak him out for a late night flight after dinner and then we snuggle up together in my bed. My friends are a little on the annoyed side, assuming I'm sneaking off to spend time with the Princes – but it's not like they can complain about that. Both of them encouraged the relationship.

I'm also extra careful to scrub in the shower and change my clothes after every snuggle with the little dragon, although I still have to endure another lesson with Fox scowling at me and scrunching up his nose. Dray makes one comment about me smelling strange right before history class but then I secure a seat at the back of the classroom away from him so that he can't spend the entire lesson sniffing at me.

By Saturday afternoon, I'm exhausted. The academy, with all its demands, is not exactly an easy ride as it is. Throw in a demanding baby dragon and I seriously need about two weeks' sleep. After yet another grueling circuit training – one I'm most definitely am not acing like last time – I collapse down on the grass and try to catch my breath. Clare collapses down beside me.

We're halfway through a serious bitching session about circuits and exercise in general, when a shadow falls over us both.

"Exercise is essential for a healthy body and a healthy mind," Beaufort Lincoln says, standing over us dressed in shorts that show off a pair of muscular thighs and a shirt that stretches over his impressive chest. I can't help but let my gaze meander over him. He definitely has a very healthy body.

"Perhaps," I tell him, "but it still sucks."

"If you ate more, it would suck less."

Clare snorts. Then covers her mouth with her hands

and looks up at Beaufort with alarm. "Sorry," she mutters meekly.

"What was so funny?" he asks with amusement.

"Briony eats plenty. She has a very big appetite." Beaufort cocks an eyebrow at me and I can guess how he's interpreting that comment. "In fact, I don't know how she does manage to eat so much. The food in the canteen is disgusting."

Beaufort looks at me for a minute, hands on his hips, beads of sweat racing down his neck in a way that shouldn't be as sexy as it is.

"Come to our tower at seven tonight. You can eat with us."

I raise my own eyebrow. "Hello, Briony," I say. "Do you have any plans for tonight? Would you like to have dinner with me?"

Clare swings a wide-eyed gaze from me to Beaufort, obviously alarmed I talk to the all-mighty Beaufort Lincoln with such sarcasm.

"You do have plans," he says, kicking at the grass, "with me."

"It would still be polite to ask."

He huffs and strides away.

"Sometimes I think you like to provoke him," Clare says. "Is it because it makes things hotter between the two of you?"

"No," I squeal, rolling on to my side and punching Clare on her arm.

She laughs. "Just saying. He invited you to dinner. That was a nice thing to do."

"Yeah," I say, rolling up to my feet. "But it was the *way* he asked."

"I wish someone would ask *me* to dinner," Clare says, peering across the field wistfully.

"Do you need to wait to be asked? Couldn't you ask someone yourself? (and by someone are we referring to the boy in your history class?)"

"Ask him?" she says, eyes wide behind her glasses.

"Yeah, why not? This isn't the sixteenth century."

"But what if he said no?"

"You'd be no worse off if he did. And we'll give him such evil looks for the rest of his time at the academy, he'll wish he was never born."

Clare giggles. "I'll think about it."

I offer out my hand and yank her to her feet. "Don't think about it, just do it. That's my motto ... which, come to think about, it may be why I end up in such shit."

"Come on," Clare says, "I think dinner with Beaufort Lincoln calls for a new outfit."

I sneak back to my room first to check in on Blaze. I promise him I'll be back in time for his evening fly-around, and then I meet Fly on the landing and we walk over to Clare's.

"You've been spending a lot of time in your room lately," Fly says casually as we weave around a group of students passing around a bottle of alcohol.

"Have I?"

"Yes. Are you sure you don't have a fourth Prince hidden away in your room, Cupcake? Or maybe you have your own thrall."

"Can commoners have thralls?" I ask, trying to divert the conversation as best I can.

"Sure they can. I mean it's not like it is here in the academy with collars and protection and shadow magic. But if two consenting adults want to establish that type of relation-ship ... of course," he adds, with a frown, "there are relation-ships where it isn't consensual and that is just plain abusive."

I think of how Muriel used me as her own personal servant, forcing me, a young kid, to do all the chores and jobs she hated the most. How she made me do them even when it didn't seem like they needed doing.

"And that's why I hate this stupid thrall thing. A rela-tionship is one thing – being a thrall quite another."

"So you're in a relationship with the Princes now?"

I stop walking. Am I? And am I happy about that? I didn't really have much choice about things in the begin-ning but lately I've been spending time with them – *doing* things with them – of my own free will.

It just sort of happened. I haven't stopped to consider if I'm happy about it.

If this mate thing is real, is this fate pulling us together?

"Don't tell me, Cupcake," Fly says, pulling on my arm. "It's complicated."

Clare's door stands ajar, one of her records playing softly in the background. We find her arranging potential outfits on the bed. Fly goes over to inspect them.

"I like the way you've matched this skirt with this sweater. Your taste is definitely improving," he comments. "It's down to my influence."

I pull Clare to one side as Fly rearranges clothes items. "Did you do it?"

Clare adjusts her glasses and nibbles on her lip. "Not yet, Briony. Give me a chance!"

"You need to do it before you build it up into this big thing and chicken out." She grimaces. "Would you like to have dinner with him?" She hesitates, then nods. "Then do it."

"Okay, okay," she says.

We agree on the skirt and sweater Clare picked out because, to quote Fly, "it shows off your legs and makes your chest look bigger than it is".

Then I kiss them both goodbye, guilty I'm leaving them for another evening, and hurry along to the Princes' tower. I could deviate quickly to check in again on Blaze, but the bell chimes seven. I pick up my pace and am knocking on the door a few minutes later.

I cringe at the realization that Beaufort has already trained me to be here on time.

Son of a bitch.

Chapter Thirty

Beaufort

I open the door to find our little thrall scowling up at me as usual. I assume I've done something to irritate her, but what the hell that is, I have no fucking idea.

Not that it bothers me. Those scowls are hotter than the sun. The sun in Onyx Quarter. Because here at the academy we hardly ever see it.

"Nice to see you too," I mutter, striding away down to the kitchen.

The front door shuts behind me and I hear her scurry to catch up. At the kitchen door, I pause and she comes to stand alongside me. She looks at me in puzzlement, then into the kitchen.

The table has been laid for two, with a tablecloth, the finest porcelain dishes and candlelight. More candles flicker all around the kitchen, and strings of burgundy flowers decorate the room, their fragrant aroma filling the space.

"Oh," she says, blinking at the spectacle.

"Come on." I take her hand and lead her inside.

The first course, scallops, lays waiting on the plates. I pull back her chair and wait for her to take her seat. Then pour her a glass of wine before taking the seat opposite.

"Is it only the two of us?" she asks.

"Yes," I say, lifting my wine glass to take a sip.

"Why?"

I lower my glass. Her question annoys me. She spent Wednesday evening with Thorne. She spent most of the ball with Dray. I've had fleeting glimpses of her attention and frankly I want more. Yeah, I know we're meant to share. Yeah, that's hot. But I also want her to myself. Her eyes on *me*, her mouth kissing *my* lips, her body entwined with *my* body.

I try to suppress my annoyance but it escapes in a pissy little sigh.

"It's the full moon." I point to the window where the large silver disc hovers, framed by the window.

"Is that meant to be an explanation or ..." she says fiddling with her cutlery.

"Dray is a shifter. The full moon sends him, and all his other little buddies, half-crazed. They'll be off rampaging through the forest, terrorizing squirrels most probably."

Dray was pissed he was missing this meal. Especially as we're leaving for the training assignment tomorrow. Extra pissed because usually he crashes after a full moon and takes a full twenty-four hours to recover. He'll be slinking in after the moon sets and we'll be out the door again in a matter of hours.

I twist my glass in my fingers. I haven't told her about the leaving bit yet.

"Is Thorne affected by the full moon too?" she says.

"No, Thorne's just fucking anti-social."

"He's not—" she starts to protest.

"You spend one evening with the dude and you think you know him better than me – his bond brother."

She takes a sip of wine. "I guess not."

I take a gulp of wine from myself. This isn't going how I want it to.

I gesture to the food on her plate. "It's scallops. I thought you might not have tried it before and I thought you might like it. Also," I say, picking up my cutlery, "it's good for you."

"Clare was exaggerating. The food in the canteen is perfectly fine." Although as she lifts a piece of scallop between her lips and starts to chew, I'm guessing the food in her mouth is a hell of a lot better than the food in the canteen. She actually swoons. "Oh my gosh, that is so good," she moans.

I smile to myself. "I thought you'd like it."

"If you're trying to seduce me with food—"

"I already tried that," I say. "I don't think it was particularly effective."

"You didn't feed me this before," she says, placing another piece in her mouth and making a face so reminiscent of how she looks when she comes, I'm stiffening in my pants.

"Actually," I say, "I am trying to butter you up. I have some news you aren't going to like." Or maybe she will like it. Who the fuck knows with this one.

"Oh," she says, with suspicion, chewing.

"We're going away from the academy for a short period of time."

A cacophony of expressions flicker over her face and it's impossible to read if she is or isn't pleased with this news. "All of you?"

"Yes."

"Why?"

"There's been an infraction through the usual protections out of the East," I say, playing down what I suspect has happened because I don't want her to worry. "They want to use it as a training exercise for some of the shadow weavers at the academy."

"Is it going to be dangerous?"

"No," I lie.

"And ... how long will you be gone for?"

"Most likely, four weeks."

She nods. "Okay."

That's it? Just an okay?

I'm disappointed. I wanted her to be a little more pained by the separation. Because I am. I don't want to leave her. Especially in this damn place.

"You could be a little more disappointed, sweetheart," I snipe.

"Why? You're coming back, aren't you?"

"Yes," I say, even though that's not guaranteed. Nothing is, after all. "But that doesn't mean I won't worry about you while we're away." *And miss you. Fuck, I'm going to miss you.*

"I can look after–"

"Yeah, I think we've established that you can't." She scowls at me, but doesn't argue. The evidence is stacked against her and she knows it. "Promise you won't do anything stupid while we're away."

"I didn't do anything stupid before. It's not my fault people want to kill me."

"Who wants to kill you?" I growl.

"It's just a figure of speech," she dismisses.

"Just ... don't go poking into stuff about your sister while we're not here."

"Why?" she says, eyes narrowing.

"Because it could be dangerous."

"And why, Beaufort Lincoln, would it be dangerous? Her death was an accident, remember?"

I look her right in the eye. "And if it wasn't, if you are right and someone deliberately killed your sister, then who's to say they won't come for you too."

Her mouth falls open and she stares back at me in disbelief. "You believe me."

"I'm saying it could be a possibility. One I will help you look into. *When* we return."

She smiles at me, her entire face brightening. It's been a long while since she last smiled at me. She looks so damn pretty when she smiles. I prefer it to the scowls.

"I can't promise you," she says. "If something comes up, I won't be able to help but–"

"How did I know you'd say that," I mutter, shaking my head. The girl is damn infuriating. Whenever I'm with her, it's like being inside a whirlwind, rattled and shaken so hard your brain bounces around inside your skull. I hold her gaze. "I guess *I* know you well."

She takes the final bite of scallop, licking her lips when she finishes it.

"Of course, I wouldn't have to worry about your safety, if you just wore this." I pull the golden collar from my pocket, lay it on the tabletop and slide it towards her.

She examines it with a mixture of disgust and interest.

"You know I'm never going to wear it."

"And you know I'll never understand why. It will protect you, Briony. Keep you safe."

She reaches out and strokes her finger along the fine silk.

"If it's the color," I say, "if it's too showy. If it's not showy enough–"

"It's what it represents." She turns it over in her hands. "Couldn't it be a bracelet or a belt or something?"

"It wouldn't be as visible. It wouldn't act as a deterrent."

"Deterrent?" She tosses the choker back on the table. "Do they even work?"

"Yes."

"Funny, because Odessa was wearing hers when I punched her in the throat."

I nearly choke on my food. "You what?"

"Punched her in the throat," she says, with more than a little bit of satisfaction. "She was bad-mouthing my friends."

"So you just walked up to her and punched her in the throat." I tut. "This is what I mean by taking risks."

This girl!

"No, I asked her very nicely to stop and in response she stabbed her knife into my hand. Then I punched her in the throat."

"What the fuck! She is going to wish she was never born!"

"You don't need to do anything. I already dealt with it. Despite her wearing that collar."

"The collar works," I say. "It will protect you."

"Odessa's didn't."

I stroke my chin. I shaved for her. The places I plan to kiss her tonight, I wanted to be smooth for her.

Why didn't Odessa's collar stop Briony from hurting her? It's strange. And I will be looking into it.

"It's just a necklace, Briony." She shakes her head. "Is it so bad if people know you belong to us?"

"I don't belong to anyone."

"Sweetheart, you're ours."

"You mean the mate thing." Her forehead crinkles.

Dray.

I'm going to fucking kill him.

"Who told you about that?"

"Dray keeps calling me that. Thorne said I'm your mate. But I don't know why you'd think that. If it's laughable that someone like me could be your thrall, it's the biggest joke in the realm that I could be your mate."

"It's not laughable. It's not a joke." I peer into her eyes. "Don't you feel it, Briony? This attraction between us? It's like a magnet pulling us together. It's fucking irresistible."

"That's just sex, Beaufort."

"No, it's not. You ever felt anything like this before?"

She hesitates, then shakes her head, biting at her lip. "But I haven't exactly had much experience."

"This is different. This is fate."

"But how do you—"

"I saw it."

"You saw it?" she says, looking even more confused.

I lean back in my chair and scrub my hands over my face. Time to come clean. Time to tell her the truth. It may be the only way to protect her. To keep her safe.

"I have visions, Briony. If you can call them that. More flashes of the future. Fleeting and vague." I frown. "But always correct. Always true." I pinch the bridge of my nose and close my eyes, trying to yank that vision back in front of my eyes. "I've had them for as long as I can remember. But only Dray and Thorne know."

"It's a secret?"

"Yes."

"But why?"

"I don't want anyone else to know. It could be ... dangerous."

She studies me, obviously unsettled by that answer.

"And you saw a vision about us?"

"Yes. And in that vision, the four of us were together. Bonded by fate."

"What does that mean 'bonded by fate'?"

"You are our fated mate, Briony Storm."

Chapter Thirty-One

B riony

"I'm not," I say, yanking up the sleeves of my cardigan. "See, no markings. I don't know what you saw in that vision, but either it was wrong or you misinterpreted it. Maybe the girl you saw wasn't me."

"I know what I saw. There was no mistaking it. You had the markings on your arms and we had matching ones on ours."

"And do you have those markings on your skin now?" I ask. He scowls at me. "Show me." I jerk my chin.

Reluctantly, he rolls back the cuffs of his shirt and turns his arms over, showing me the soft skin of his wrists. I can see the delicate bones that connect there, the green and blue veins that run through to his hands, but no markings. The skin is clear. Just like it's always been.

"Nothing," I say. A flatness transcends through my body, dragging my shoulders down. Disappointment.

What the hell?

I don't even want to be their thrall, let alone their fated mate. Tied to them until the end of our days. Sure, Beaufort is hot and he makes my body feel things it shouldn't, but half the time I don't know if I even like the guy.

Then there's the other half ...

He leans across the table and captures my hand in his, stroking his thumb over the tender inside of my wrist.

"In the vision, the marking is right here. And it's the most incredible, the most beautiful thing I ever saw."

I swallow. My emotions are all a tangle. I don't know whether to believe him. He could be lying. He could be lying to himself. The visions may be nothing but hallucinations.

Shadow magic is such an incredible thing – so peculiar, so strange. Pushing the boundaries of reality and sanity. I bet there are more than one shadow weavers who skirt close to madness.

Henrietta Smyte for starters.

Beaufort leans down even further and presses his mouth to my wrist next, kissing me there.

"Your pulse is racing," he murmurs.

"Unfortunately, you seem to have that effect on me."

"Unfortunately?" he says, grazing my wrist with his teeth next.

"Beaufort, do we even like each other?"

"I like you a lot," he growls. "But I'd like it even more if you sat on my face."

Desire shivers over my skin. Something I don't miss.

"Dray hasn't stopped talking about how good you taste, little thrall," he whispers. He licks my wrist, demonstrating just how skilled and enthusiastic he'd be with his tongue, sending a pulse beating between my legs. "I need to taste you."

"And what if I want to taste you?" I say, my voice trembling with desire.

He lifts his head, and his gaze, burning with fire, meets mine. "Fuck," he mutters, then smirks. "I think there's a way both of our wishes can come true."

The next thing I know, I'm being yanked to my feet and led upstairs.

I could complain. We never made it past the first course and the food was delicious. But, damn it, I'm way more hungry for this, especially when I know it's something I won't be able to consume for the next twenty-eight days.

Twenty-eight. That hadn't sounded so long when he said it earlier. Now it seems like an eternity.

Upstairs, he leads me inside his bedroom, shutting and locking the door behind us, before stalking towards me like I am prey and he is the hunter. I pace backwards until the back of my legs hit the bed, and then, he's pushing me down onto the mattress, his hungry mouth on mine.

I take a grip of his shirt and drag him down with me and then we're pulling at each other's clothes, only pausing in our kisses to lift my sweater over my head.

Then I'm in nothing but my bra and my panties. And for the first time ever, I peer down at them and cringe.

Linny, the bitch, even destroyed all my underwear in that rampage through my room. I'm stuck with a few pairs Clare gifted me as well as a bra that didn't fit her very well. I may be small and lean but Clare is even smaller with cute boobs. Which means everything is a little tight, my breasts pretty much spilling out of the bra.

This doesn't seem to be a problem for Beaufort though.

The silver of his eyes morph into the dark gray of storm clouds. He takes ahold of my wrists, gripping right where fated mate markings would be if I had any, and pins my arms over my head.

Then he takes the cup of my bra in his teeth and yanks it away, releasing my tit right into his mouth.

With his wet tongue, he circles the sensitive skin of my nipple and they crinkle and harden between his lips. He groans and sucks on them and oh stars, it feels divine. So divine, I can't help but lift my hips and grind against him.

"Needy little thing," he murmurs, nibbling at my nipple next, before turning his attention to my other breast. I squirm underneath him, attempting to pull my arms free so that I can wrap them around him. But he holds them down.

"I want to come," I moan.

"Well, you're going to have to wait," he says. He trails his kisses down from my breast, over my ribs and to my stomach. He halts here and peers up at me, smirk on his face.

I scowl right back at him.

"Fuck, you have no idea how hard those disapproving looks of yours make me, little one. You wanna come?"

I want to tell him to go fuck himself. But as I'd much rather he fucked me, I nod.

"Then be a good girl, for once."

Shadow magic races from his hands and coils around my wrists, holding them in place as he releases the grip of his hands.

He kisses lower, and my pulse races even faster, my breath coming in expectant pants.

When he reaches the top of my panties, he grips them in his teeth and slides his fingers under the hem, then slides them down, his mouth follows with them, kissing over my mound and my curls, down my thighs, over my knees and my calves, and right the way to my toes.

I'm getting wetter with every moment, the pulse between my legs becoming more urgent.

"Beaufort!" I protest, as he takes his time kissing the tip of every toe.

"You kept me waiting for this, remember, sweetheart. It's only fair I have my revenge."

"Kept you waiting how?"

"Three fucking weeks!" he says, before parting my thighs and staring right down at my pussy.

I should be squirming with embarrassment. I've seen my pussy in a hand mirror. It is not exactly a work of art – although I have no idea if other girl's look any better. Beaufort actually groans like someone's plunged a knife straight into his gut, like he's gazing down at something exquisite.

"Fuck, I love how pink and swollen and wet you are for me. Such a fucking good girl." He licks his lips. "And good girls get to come!"

"Too fucking right!" I mutter, which makes him chuckle.

He's still chuckling as he throws my legs over his shoulders and nestles his face into my pussy, kissing me passionately like he just kissed my mouth.

It's intense, my core tightening and my fingers clawing at the bed covers.

"Beaufort!" I cry out as he sucks my clit into his mouth and goes right on sucking. My core tightens even more, my legs shaking around his head, and shivers of something beginning to build in my body. I'm on the cusp of it, the feeling building and building towards its summit, my spine arching and then ...

He fucking stops!

"No!" I scream, rubbing my pussy unashamedly against his mouth, chasing that friction and that feeling. "No!" I scream, as I collapse back down on the mattress, unsatisfied and seriously pissed off. "Why did you stop?"

"It's called edging, sweetheart, and it's the best sort of torture there is!"

He plants an innocent peck of a kiss against my clit, that in itself enough to have me trembling again, and then he licks at me – slow, gentle licks at first, becoming faster and harder over time until he's flicking at me with force and all that tension crescendos again, lifting me right up to the end.

"Please don't stop," I beg him, "please don't stop this time!"

But Beaufort Lincoln is not one to take orders and so once again he leaves me hanging.

"No!" I screech, thrashing about on the bed, trying to release my hands to finish the job myself. "You're such an asshole."

"I always used to get in trouble for playing with my food," he says, absentmindedly, eyes fixed on my pussy, stroking his fingers over my thighs. "You're dripping now, sweetheart, so wet it's untrue. I've never seen a girl this wet before."

My hands may be restrained, but my legs aren't and I manage to kick him for that.

"Do not talk about other girls when your head is buried between my legs."

"How can I make it up to you? Like this?" He licks me again, like he did before. "Or this?" He kisses my clit, pressing it between his lips. "Or this?" He sucks me right up into his mouth.

"All of it!" I pant, my body covered in a fine sheen of

sweat and the sheet beneath me damp with my arousal and his spit.

This time he does as I say. He gives me everything, kisses and licks, flicks, and sucks, twirling around my clit one minute and fucking my pussy with his tongue the next. This time, when the pressure builds, he doesn't pull away, he lets it build and build and build until I'm crashing over the edge into ecstasy itself.

"Oh stars," I mutter, as I sail away somewhere heavenly, tingles racing across my body and my pussy contracting in waves. I hang there suspended for several long seconds and then my body jolts with the aftershocks.

The shadows at my wrists race away and Beaufort flops down on the bed beside me, wiping at the wetness on his face and licking his lips like he just gorged on chocolate mousse.

"Good?" he asks, tweaking at my nipple.

I'm still catching my breath. I have no words.

He massages my breast. "Ready to go again?"

"What?!" I cry, but he's already heading down south. This time he lies on his side and rocks me onto mine, lifting my leg so he can access my pussy.

The way he is curled around me, his crotch is positioned right in front of my face, his boxers bulging.

He gives me a lick, then peers down between us. "You going to return the favor this time, sweetheart?"

"You don't have to ..." I start, but never finish, because he's already licking me.

"Got to make up for all those lost days," he says like a man on a mission.

I lower his boxers and his cock springs eagerly out, hard and erect and already dribbling pre-come.

I lean in closer, licking his head like he is licking me.

It seems only fair to return some of the torture – or edging as he called it.

Except, I don't have as much self control as him. I never thought I'd like to do this. But I like the way he tastes, the way he smells, how big he feels in my hand. I want him in my mouth.

I wrap my lips around his head and suck, running my fist up and down his shaft as he circles my clit.

My brain struggles to know where to focus; on the dick in my mouth or the tongue in my pussy. It flits back and forth and I'm so turned on, I know I'll come again with little effort.

"Sweetheart," Beaufort groans, "don't stop."

I jolt, realizing that's exactly what I'd been doing, too lost in the sensations he's creating through my body, too in love with the way he's worshipping my pussy.

I concentrate with more focus on returning the pleasure. Swirling my tongue around his head one minute, then sucking him far back into my throat the next. He throbs against my tongue, hips jerking. He moans against my clit and I come a second time, sucking down hard on him and moaning myself as the pleasure ricochets around my body.

"Fuck, that's hot," he grunts, coming right into my mouth. I gulp him down and his cock jerks in my mouth and then he rolls away, his soft cock, slipping from my mouth with a pop.

"Shit," he says, lying on his back, hands combing through his long hair. "Shit!"

I scramble up onto my knees and peer down into his handsome face.

He smiles up at me and it's more genuine, than ever before. Even a little shy.

"Fuck, we are going to have a lot of fun tonight, sweetheart."

"We have," I agree.

He pushes up onto his elbows.

"*Have?*" he says.

"This was ..." I bite my lip. Hot? Dirty? Sexy? Better than anything I could ever have imagined? But I have a baby dragon waiting for me in my room. I can't stay any longer. I already feel like a bad person. Neglecting a baby for this.

I cringe.

"You saying you didn't enjoy it?" he scoffs with disbelief.

He is such an arrogant jerk and why is that so incredibly hot?

I need to leave before it becomes impossible to.

"I have to go."

"No you don't. You can stay the night." He reaches for my hand. "I want you to stay the night, little thrall. In my bed."

I shake my head. "I want to," I say. "I really do." I sigh as my gaze travels down his sinful body. "But I can't."

"Why?"

I reach for my discarded sweater and tug it over my head. "I can't tell you." I look at him earnestly because for once, I'd like it if our time together didn't descend into an argument. "But can you trust me for once and not push this." He doesn't look convinced. "Please Beaufort." I lean forward on my hands and knees and kiss his mouth. "Please."

"Okay," he says, although it's obvious he's not happy about it. "As long as it's nothing that's going to land you in trouble."

"Of course not," I say, looking away so he can't read the lie on my face.

He lies on his bed, watching as I hunt around the room for my remaining pieces of clothing.

"Kiss me again before you leave," he tells me, once I'm dressed.

I pad back to the bed and he sits up, embracing me in his arms and kissing me – this time slow and longingly like he wants to imprint the kiss in my memory.

"Be careful," he says, "and if anything happens–"

"It won't," I tell him.

But I guess he doesn't trust me completely, because when I'm back in my room, I find the collar tucked into the pocket of my skirt.

Chapter Thirty-Two

D^{ray}

I collapse onto my bed face down, arms spread wide. My body's covered in sweat and mud and grass. I smell like shit and every muscle in my body aches. My stomach growls with hunger and my cock is hard as steel. All those base animalistic instincts still roll through my body.

All I want to do is hunt and fuck, fuck and hunt.

But I'm also fucking exhausted. I've been running through the woods for eight hours straight, high on adrenaline and the full moon. My throat's sore from howling and there're bits of rabbit stuck between my teeth.

I wanna sleep. We move out in three hours.

I also wanna hunt and fuck.

More precisely, I want to hunt down my little kitten and fuck her.

I groan, thrusting my hips into the bed. I can smell her

in the tower. I can smell her fucking arousal. It makes my mouth water.

There's no way I'm sleeping. I roll onto my back. There's no way she's going to let me fuck her smelling and looking like this.

I stagger into the bathroom, ram on the shower and duck inside. The warm water races down my body, turning a rusty brown with mud and blood. It pools at my feet, and swirls down the drain.

When finally the water runs clear, I smack my fist against the button and step out, wrapping a towel around my waist. The thing tents around my cock. Still stiff. Still determined. Adrenaline and energy pulses through my veins, my heart beats in my chest.

Hunt, fuck, hunt, fuck.

I stagger to the sink, wipe the side of my hand across the condensation gathered on the mirror, and stare at my reflection as I comb my fingers through my tangled hair. I look all right. Still, I need to do something about those teeth. I brush them twice, spitting organic matter into the sink and even gargling with fucking mouthwash.

Then I grab a pair of sweatpants and start hunting.

She's no longer in our tower. I follow my nose from Beaufort's room, down the staircase towards the front door.

Standing right in front of that door, arms folded over his chest, gloves off, is Thorne.

"Hey buddy," I say, my voice low and threatening. "What you doing?"

He glares at me and the message is clear. He's blocking my exit.

"I need to see her," I growl.

"No!" he says.

I take a menacing step towards him. Nothing and no one is going to stop me from fucking that girl.

"Go back to bed, Dray," Beaufort says from behind me. "We're leaving in a couple of hours. Go get some sleep."

I growl at him too and bare my teeth.

Shadows flicker from his fingers in warning.

"It's too dangerous," Thorne says.

"I'm not going to eat her," I hiss. "I'm going to fuck her. I'm going to pump her full of my seed and she's going to breed my pups."

"Fuck," Beaufort mutters. "He's still fucking feral."

I growl at him again and snap my teeth. I'll give him fucking feral.

"It's too dangerous," Thorne repeats, shadows starting to weave from his bare hands. "You can't see her like this."

"She's my mate. I need to fuck my mate," I say, my own magic hissing in the air. "Pups conceived under a full moon are always the strongest."

It's instinct. It's the pull of the moon. It's in my blood. It's in my fucking balls. Dictating my actions. Demanding them.

"Fucking hell," Beaufort says, "you're not impregnating anyone. Least of all our mate."

"That's what mates are for," I growl at him. Then swing my gaze Thorne's way when I hear the floorboard beneath his feet creak.

I hold one hand out in Thorne's direction and one in Beaufort's. I swing my gaze between them as they creep towards me.

"You'll regret this," I snarl.

I'm the strongest wolf in the realm. I'll tear them to pieces if they stop me from seeing my kitten. My soft kitten who I want on her hands and knees, purring as I thrust into her from behind. My scent spikes.

"Shit, that stinks," Beaufort mutters. "He's worse than usual. I didn't think it would be that bad. Thank fuck she's not here." He takes a step towards me. "So much for a mate being a calming influence."

"Let me through!" I growl. And then it happens. They both jump me at once. I fire magic at them and it collides with theirs mid-air, sparking and splintering.

I swing my fist, punching Beaufort's cheek, feeling it crack. My knuckles crack too, but the adrenaline masks any pain.

I go to swing at him again, to sink my teeth into his shoulder, but then Thorne's magic whips around my torso. I howl in agony, all the fight in me fleeing in an instant.

I sink to my knees, struggling to breathe. The pain is so intense, I feel like my brain is going to explode in my skull. I screw my eyes shut, clamping my jaw together, whimpering.

Bile sloshes in my throat. I might vomit. Instead, I pass out.

◆

I wake to Beaufort shaking at my shoulder.

I blink open my lids and look up into his face. He has a bruise ringing his left eye.

"Did I do that?" I ask, yawning.

I look around. I'm in my bed, dressed in a pair of sweatpants. I've no idea how the hell I got here, or why the hell every part of my body hurts so much.

"Yeah," Beaufort says, touching his cheek. "You were fucking feral."

"I was?" I grin, rolling up to sit, which fucking hurts. "What I do?"

"Only threatening to go fuck a litter of pups into the belly of our thrall."

"Fuuuuuck," I say, running my hand through my hair, only for my fingers to be caught in a web of tangles. "That sounds hot."

"It's not. She could've been hurt."

"Maybe she would have liked it. Did we ask her?"

Beaufort scowls at me, which makes his cheek move. He winces.

"Why haven't you healed it?" I ask.

"I was getting some sleep! We gotta be out of here in half an hour."

"Oh, man!" I moan, yawning again.

Then I smack my hands either side of his face and blow my magic across his cheek, healing the broken blood vessels and removing the coalesced blood.

"Good as new," I say, flopping back on the bed. "Want to return the favor? I feel like shit."

"No, you were an asshole," Beaufort says. "Only seems fair you should suffer."

"It wasn't my fault," I whine. "It was the full moon."

Beaufort scoffs, and heads for the door. "Thirty minutes. We have to be ready to go in thirty minutes."

Thirty minutes? Does that give me long enough to race over to our little thrall's tower, pin her down and–

"Don't even think about it," Beaufort calls from the landing.

I laugh. My bond brother knows me well. The full moon's effects haven't dissipated yet. They're still shimmering in my blood.

Chapter Thirty-Three

F^{ox}

I watch, hidden around a corner, as the selected shadow weavers pile into the waiting trucks. No chauffeur-driven vehicles or top-range motors this morning. It's early and there are no crowds of admirers either. These students are being taken for 'training' – to face danger and death. There's nothing glamorous about it.

The last door slams shut and the trucks rumble into life, then chug off in single file out across the moorland until they're lost in the early morning mist.

Wrapping my cloak around me, I turn and walk away. Is it a relief that they are gone? Damn, yes, it is.

The jealousy has been churning around in my gut, eating me from the inside out, stirring me half mad. Now, with the Princes gone, it's not something I have to consider, not something my stupid brain has to imagine intrusively. For the time being at least, I can have some peace.

I trudge down into my classroom and watch the clock next, its hands ticking away the seconds, minutes and hours achingly slowly.

And then it's time.

Her scent catches my attention, long before I hear the first footsteps on the stairs or the first murmur of voices, and my gaze slides to the door.

She's last to enter – right at the rear of the line of students, tucked behind her tall friend, gaze fixed to the ground, shoulders hunched, those green eyes lost in thought. I attempt to read her features. Is she sad that they are gone? Happy? Relieved? I can't convince myself either way. She's sleeping with them – that much I know, that much I am tormented by. But I have no idea if she actually likes the three of them.

I watch her all the way to her seat, not giving a damn how obvious it must be, too desperate for this opportunity to soak her in to care. These moments are too fleeting after all. I will savor them for all they are worth.

Finally, when she's retrieved her pen and notepad from her bag and lifted her gaze to meet mine, I find the strength to drag my own gaze away and focus in on my class, all waiting expectantly.

"I see our numbers are depleted this morning." The obnoxiously large shadow weaver whose name I can never recall, his friend and one half of the set of twins for starters. I saw each of them climb into those trucks this morning.

"Do you know where they've gone, Professor?" one of the commoners asks me.

My gaze flicks immediately to Briony and I watch as she nibbles on her nails.

"Training assignment," I say. I can see the curiosity shining in the students' eyes. They want all the gruesome and gory details but even if I were sick enough to indulge in that, I am not at liberty to share the information. I ignore the question and begin the lesson instead, trying to teach what remains of my class how shadow magic can be amplified and strengthened with dedication and practice. It's a waste of time. The commoners have no powers anyway and the shadow weavers I've been left with are the weak sort that no amount of concentration or dedication could improve.

Towards the end of the lesson, I give them some exercises and stroll around the classroom, offering bits of advice and specific instructions.

I reach Briony and her friend last, they're slumped on the bench gossiping and not even attempting the exercise.

"This is becoming tiresome, Miss Storm. Could you not at least pretend to show me and my lesson the respect it deserves?"

She frowns at me, chin lifted in defiance as always. "There's no point. You know there isn't. It's stupid that they even make us attend these lessons. Most of us here don't have any powers."

"And you don't think it might be useful to understand how magic works?"

"Why? I'm never going to use it," she snaps back.

"But," I say my voice lowering into a growl, "you seem to be happy to get up and personal with a bit of magic."

Her friend's eyes, wide and alarmed, flick between me and her.

"What's that meant to mean?" she says, although I take it from the way her cheeks redden that she has a fair idea.

"You are a thrall, are you not? You are dating shadow

weavers? You don't think it would be to your advantage to understand how their magic works?"

She has nothing to say to that because she knows I'm right.

The bell clangs far away and around us the students begin to clear away their possessions and collect up their bags.

"I advise all of you to practice this," I call out to them. "I'll be testing you next lesson."

She rolls her eyes at me as the first students filter out of the room.

Her friend nudges her, but she doesn't move, she's still glaring up at me.

"Aren't they all powerful enough as it is?" she sneers at me. "Is it really necessary to make them even more powerful?"

"If we want to keep our realm safe, then yes."

Her friend fidgets on the bench attempting to push Briony along it in the direction of the door. She refuses to budge and with a resigned sigh, her friend slings his bag over his shoulder and heads for the door, leaving us alone, the door slamming shut behind him.

"Wouldn't your time be better spent helping the weavers to better control their powers?"

"What happened to your sister, Briony, was unfortunate but rare. Accidents happen."

"Accidents?" she scoffs. "Accidents shouldn't be happening at all." She stands. "And some shadow weavers are struggling – you're the teacher in charge of teaching shadow weaving. Why aren't you helping them?"

I consider her.

"Who exactly are we talking about here, Briony?" I ask, my voice lowering.

"No one in particular ... I've just seen ..." I raise an eyebrow. "Thorne Cadieux."

"Thorne Cadieux," I repeat, that jealousy sliding into life in my belly. I knew she was sleeping with Beaufort Lincoln, Dray Eros most probably too. But now Thorne Cadieux as well. I stroll towards my desk, straightening the pile of books on the surface, my back turned to her so I don't have to look at her face. "We will cover control. It will come later in the year."

"But he needs help now. You should be helping him."

"Me?" I say with incredulity. The boy has the one thing I want most in the world. The one thing I can't have. Her. Why the hell would I help him? "Thorne Cadieux is an incredibly gifted shadow weaver. He doesn't require my help. Which I'm sure he would tell you himself."

"He does need help," she insists. The spite and sarcasm in her voice has gone. Her tone is earnest. She really does want to help him. She really does care. "He's struggling. His powers are dangerous, lethal."

"Exactly. He is gifted, Miss Storm."

"Gifted? He can't even touch anyone!" she cries in despair. "He can't even touch me!"

I spin around.

There's more than friendly concern on her face. There's despair.

I huff out a bitter laugh.

"So this is why you want me to help him. So he can *touch* you?"

"N-n-n-no," she stutters, but all that color – all that blood – rushing to her cheeks tells me once again that I'm right.

I take a decided step towards her, closing the distance between us, her chin tipping back as she holds my gaze.

"And what about me?" I say, my jaw tight, my voice restricted in my throat.

Her brow crinkles. "You?"

"What if *I* want to touch you?" The words fall from my lips before I can stop them. I take another step closer, pulled there by the strength of her orbit. We're so close now, I can feel the warmth of her flesh and the tickle of her breath. "And what if I can't? Who is going to help me?"

Her mouth falls open, but that blood doesn't leave her cheeks, it settles beneath her delicate skin, and her eyes grow darker as the black of her pupils widen.

"Do you ... do you want to touch me?" she asks, her voice full of amazement and something else. Something just as dark as her gaze.

I screw shut my eyes, my hands bunching into tight fists, my toes curling inside my boots.

It's all I want. All I can think about. All I am dreaming about. It's consuming my every thought.

But just like Cadieux, it's something I can't have.

It's just as dangerous. Just as lethal.

"Get out of my classroom, Miss Storm," I whisper and when I open my eyes again, she's gone.

Chapter Thirty-Four

Beaufort

We reach the border town where the attack occurred just as the sun rolls towards the horizon, the sky as red as the blood that covers the paths, the doors, the walls. Blood. Everywhere we look.

There are bodies too. Mutilated and violated beyond recognition – strewn about the place, hanging from rooftops, impaled on spikes.

It's not the first time I've seen such a monstrosity. That doesn't make it any easier. For a moment, it still startles every bone in my body and all I want to do is climb straight back into that truck, drive back to the academy, wrap my arms around her, and bury my face in her soft sunshine hair.

I can't do that, though. I'm Beaufort Lincoln. I don't show weakness, fear, or compassion. So I steel my features, push the carnage from my mind and go with the others to meet the old general waiting for us. Her face is lined with the sun and old battle scars that couldn't be repaired. Across her left eye she wears a black patch and her uniform is gray with dust.

There's no welcome, she inspects us with her good eye, hands clutched behind her back.

She rolls her jaw and then she speaks.

"This attack occurred just over twelve hours ago. The demons broke through our defenses about thirty miles in that direction." She points out towards the horizon where the sky is still light. "Most of the damage had been done by the time our forces arrived and that was even with them traveling by displacement. The threat is yet to be eliminated. This is a much bigger intrusion than we've ever seen before. Our forces are out there tracking down and engaging with the demons still on the loose. We also have a team repairing and rebuilding the infiltrated defenses."

"And why are we here?" Dray asks, he slouches beside me giving off unbothered, unconcerned vibes, but I can feel in his magic that every single cell of his is tense and alert.

"I was just coming to that, Mr. Eros," the general says. "Our forces are engaged with the largest group of demons. But we believe there may be a smaller group heading out towards the East. We have some of our best tracking them now. You'll be helping to find and eliminate them."

"And how about this?" I say, sweeping my hand towards the direction of all the carnage and death, trying my best to avoid the vacant, glassy-eyed stares of all those dead people. Slate people – farmers tending crops out here in the only part of Slate Quarter where anything will actually grow.

"We have a team coming from elsewhere in Slate to clean this up," the general says.

I stare down at my feet. Yeah, leave it to the commoners from Slate to deal with all this mess.

"How about the crops?" one of Kratos's pals asks next. "Won't it be harvest time soon?"

I stare out towards the horizon again. He's right. I can see the silhouettes of the growing corn against the setting sun.

"Why?" Kratos snorts. "You volunteering, Nathan?"

His friends all chuckle like there's nothing funnier than the thought of a shadow weaver carrying out such manual, menial work. Maybe I'd have laughed too some months back. Now all I can think about is Briony.

"Not part of my job description," the general says, smiling too as if there isn't a massacre right behind her. "But I'm sure they'll move some workers here soon to deal with it." The general adjusts the cap on her head and squints through the growing darkness at us with her one eye. "Right, if you're ready, let's move out. The sooner we find these fuckers, the better."

Chapter Thirty-Five

B riony

With half of the shadow weavers gone, the atmosphere in the academy changes dramatically.

It's as if the tension hovering around the campus dissipates slightly. People walk with their heads held a little higher, their shoulders a little lighter. They're freer with their words and with their actions. Even the teachers seem a little more relaxed.

The academy plods along without them and we could almost fool ourselves into believing they were never here in the first place.

Except they were. And I catch myself looking for Dray in my lessons before I remember he's not there, or searching for Thorne out on the field. Several times I even find my feet carrying me towards their tower only to find it empty.

It's crazy how quickly three people can infiltrate your

life like that. How used you can become to having them around. The days seem a little grayer without them, a little longer. But the days keep coming, keep passing by. One day, two days, three days, a week ...

Luckily, I also have a lot more time on my hands. Time I can spend caring for Blaze, wondering what the hell that was with Fox, and reading through the books with Clare. Apart from that mention of the kid who was banished, we've found nothing else of interest or of help. It's frustrating and as the days drag on, I start to feel more and more irritable.

"Jeez, someone is miserable as fuck," Fly says over dinner, when I snap at him to pass the salt. "Those Princes can't return soon enough, Cupcake. Someone needs to get laid."

"It's not that," I say, shaking salt aggressively over my food. "We're not making any progress with my sister."

"Uh huh," Fly nods, "sure that's the reason."

Maybe I do miss them a little? After years of no one caring for me, touching me, loving me, perhaps I was starting to get used to it. Even greedy for it. Shit, a few heady orgasms and I'm as good as an addict.

"I'm reading as fast as I can," Clare protests.

"I know me too. It's just frustrating that we haven't found anything."

"We can spend tonight going through the books some more if you like," Clare says. "The next trial is a while away still and maybe if we combine what we've learned so far something might pop up."

"Thanks, Clare," I say, trying my best to smother my frustration. It's not my friend's fault we haven't got anywhere. If anything it's my own – what with the princes and now a baby dragon. But she's right, maybe a bit of brainstorming might help us. "I have to pop back to my room for a bit, but then I'll be over," I tell her, earning another suspicious look from Fly who can't understand my sudden willingness to want to spend time in my horrible room.

Maybe because I don't want to keep my friends waiting, but I hurry back from the forest after playtime with Blaze later that evening and must not take my usual care, because there waiting for me as I step off the field and onto the path is Odessa.

She's wearing a fur-lined coat with matching hat and muff. If I didn't know she was from Iron, I'd assume she was a shadow weaver. Okay, she doesn't have the magical aura about her but she most certainly has the clothes. I curl my toes inside my worn boots and hug Blaze more tightly to me inside Clare's old winter coat. I also pretend I haven't seen her. I don't want an altercation, or even a brief conversation right now. My friends are waiting for me and I'm not sure how long I can keep the dragon inside my coat from wriggling and giving me away.

However, Odessa is determined to catch my attention, stepping right into my path as I try to avoid her. My heartbeat starts to thump inside my chest. Odessa would be probably the worst person in the world to discover my secret. The absolute worse. Anyone else I might be able to reason with, or influence. Potentially even bribe. I won't be able to do any of those things with Odessa.

Maybe Blaze senses my apprehension, because he remains completely motionless as Odessa eyes me.

Please don't notice the odd-shaped nature of my coat! Please don't notice. Please just dismiss it as crappy Slate fashion!

"What are you doing sneaking around in the forest, Slate slut?"

I try my best to calm my nerves, glowering at her with my chin raised. If I come across all meek and passive now, she'll definitely know something's up.

"I wasn't sneaking around."

"You don't even have a light."

I narrow my eyes at her. "Neither do you. Are *you* sneaking about?"

She snorts. "As if! I'm on my way to have tea with some of the shadow weaver girls who didn't go off on the training expedition."

She swishes her hair like this is the greatest honor ever awarded anyone in the history of the realm. Like she's going for tea with the Empress in the actual palace.

"Sounds lovely," I say, with a ton of sarcasm and my biggest fake smile. Which is probably dumb considering I shouldn't be provoking her if I want this conversation to end quickly.

She ignores my tone, swishing her hair the other way. "Kratos and the boys were keen to see I was well looked after while they were away. They asked the girls to take care of me and I've made quite an impression."

"I bet you have."

"I notice you haven't been invited," she sneers with a smile

"I'm obviously devastated."

"Those Princes obviously don't care much for you." Her smile grows wider. "I wouldn't be surprised if they're planning on dumping you. Especially when they find out you've been sneaking off to the forest for a secret rendezvous. Is it that boy you're always with? Is that who you're fucking behind the Princes' back? I should have known – you're such a slut."

I glare at her. I know how this goes. I know what she's

planning. I can practically see the evil wheels spinning in her head. She's going to tell everyone who will listen that that is what she saw and before you can say fuck-a-doodle-doo it will be the gospel truth with ten more eyewitnesses.

"I think you're projecting," I tell her. "Just because you're sneaking around the pathways on the way to lick some shadow weaver pussy behind your protectors' backs, does not mean I am doing the same thing."

Horror overtakes her face before she schools it into something more neutral.

"Oh, little Slate scum," she says, pouting, "I know they didn't educate you properly back where you come from. I know all they did educate you on is how to lie on your back and open your legs. But tea is not the same thing as that."

I shrug. "That's what I heard."

I take a step towards her, for a moment forgetting what I have hidden inside my coat. "So just be assured, Odessa, if you go starting rumors about me, I'll be starting them about you."

"Yeah, but the difference is, no one will listen to you," she says smugly – which is true. Still, I'm guessing my threat might be deadly enough to stop her. The last thing she wants to do is lose her protectors and any sort of rumor of cheating is probably too much of a risk for her. My momentary thoughts of triumph vanish almost instantly though as her gaze drops to my chest and she frowns, observing the lump in the front of my coat. "What's that?" she asks.

But I've had enough. I'm not going to stand here and let her interrogate me.

"Nothing," I say quickly, stepping around her. "Good night, Odessa. Enjoy your *tea*."

Once I've returned to my room, I kick off my boots, flop

down on the mattress with a relieved sigh, then unbutton my coat and let Blaze out.

"You did so well, baby," I say, as he clambers over my face, licking my cheeks. "You were so well behaved."

Except he isn't that well behaved because I spend the next ten minutes trying to wrestle my left boot out of his mouth – he clearly doesn't like the idea of me leaving him.

"I don't want to go either, buddy," I tell him, shoving my foot back in the boot before he can snatch it from me again. "But I've neglected researching my sister long enough and it's important to me."

He stares at me with his golden eyes, before curling up right in the center of my bed. I leave him snoozing, and walk through the campus to Clare's room.

I'm more cautious stepping outside this time but it's a quiet evening, too bitterly cold for anyone to want to hang outside. Everyone's tucked up inside. I swing my head back and peer up at the stars up above. They're the same stars that filled the sky back at Slate. Unchanging, constant. For a moment, I let myself think about the Princes, wondering what they can be doing, where they might be. Are they staring up at the exact same stars? Something deep inside me pangs and I suspect I do miss them, but I push that thought aside. Tonight, I'm focused on Amelia.

Clare is sitting in the center of her room with the books all spread out around her. Fly is there too, laid out on her bed and flicking through a novel.

"You were ages," he murmurs as I enter.

"Yeah, the thing I had to do took longer than I thought."

"The thing?" he says, eyes narrowing.

"Yeah and I ran into Odessa."

Fly lifts his head from the pillow. "And yet you have all your body parts. How is this possible?"

"I have all my body parts, but don't be surprised if there are all sorts of gross rumors flying around about the two of us tomorrow."

"Ewww," Fly says, "do I even want to know?"

"Nope." I drop down on the floor next to Clare. "So anything in particular you think we should look into?" I ask her.

"Nothing solid," she says, flicking over a page and pushing her glasses up her nose. "But ..."

"But?" I say hopefully.

"I've been thinking–"

"Did it hurt?" Fly snorts.

"No." Clare blinks, confused.

I give Fly a warning look. "What were you thinking?" I prompt.

"Did they ever tell you the names of the shadow weavers who were responsible for your sister's death? It occurred to me that I never asked."

"No, they didn't."

Fly places his book down. "They never gave you any hints? The kids who came back from the academy never told you who it was?"

"No one really talked to me after Amelia died. It was weird." I peer down at my chewed fingernails. "Like my grief was an infectious disease nobody wanted to catch."

"It can be difficult for people to know what to say," Fly says softly.

"Maybe. But anyway, I don't know if it just never got spoken about or whether they weren't aware."

"There must have been rumors," Fly says. "Do the books say anything?"

"Not about that, but I've been making note of who I think may be the most likely suspects." Clare pushes her notepad towards me. Written in a neat list down the page are six names.

"Why them?" I ask.

"They seemed to be the most powerful shadow weavers at the academy at the time. The one with enough power to …"

"Kill?"

Clare nods. "Do you recognize any of those names? Did they ever come up at all?"

The six names hover in front of my eyes like six flickering flames and I stare at them so long, they crawl across the page, my vision blurring into a mass of ash. I rifle through my memory, straining for any half-overheard conversations, any whispered words. I find nothing.

Finally, I shake my head.

"Do you recognize any of the names?" I ask.

"No, but then I don't know so much about shadow weavers," Clare says.

"Give the names here," Fly says, holding out his hand and shaking it at us. Clare passes it over and his eyes flick down the list.

"I recognize three or four of the family names. They're well-known shadow weaver families. Powerful ones."

"So if they killed someone," I say, through gritted teeth, "it would be in their families' and the academy's best interests to cover it up."

"I don't know about that," Fly says warily. "And these are powerful people to go around accusing of murder, Cupcake."

"How can I find out more about them?" I ask them both.

Fly sniffs. "That's pretty obvious isn't it? The Princes."

Chapter Thirty-Six

D ray

I dive to the ground as a torrent of fire races above, hot, destructive and deadly. Then I'm on my feet, my shadows streaming from my hands and slamming into the demon that is sweeping my way. The thing squeals and hisses, its forked tongue slipping from its raw mouth, its crimson eyes luminous. It thrashes in my grip, and I grunt, straining to keep the freaky fucker contained.

Its claws rip through my shadows, tearing at them and the pain strikes right in my belly.

"Ahh no you don't," I spit. I squeeze all the harder and when it opens its mouth to scream, I let my shadows shoot down its throat and then the creature is exploding into a thousand million pieces, the blast sending me flying back down to the ground.

"What the hell are you doing down there?" Beaufort

calls out to me as he sprints past me towards another demon swooping our way.

"Killing fucking demons, what else did you think? Scrabble?" I mumble, jumping back up onto my feet.

Behind me, Henrietta has a demon by its tail and is swinging the creature around her head as she laughs hysterically, seemingly unconcerned with the blood rushing down her face. I shake my head. I'd offer her my help, but the girl is as insane as everyone suspected – this little expedition has made that clear – and she might take my offer of help as an insult and have me hanging by the balls.

Instead I look for my bond brothers. Beaufort, only a few feet away, is using his magic to shield himself from the fire a demon is shooting at his body and further away, is Thorne.

I should be helping, but for a few minutes I can't help but stand and admire the dude. He stands, both arms outstretched in opposite directions, his gaze intense, his jaw set, his face wet with perspiration. Shadows blast from his open palms and several demons are caught in the onslaught like fish in a net.

"Dray!" Beaufort snaps and I run to his side, blasting at the demon that has cornered him. "Fuck," he mutters, as the demons shrivels away into nothingness. "Thanks man," he slaps me on the shoulder, swiping sweat from his eyes.

But there ain't no time to sit about congratulating each other because two more demons come swarming towards us.

I've seen demons before. I've *fought* demons before. Not like these ones though. These are big, ugly, grumpy fuckers – powerful and relentless.

It makes this a lot more challenging and a hell of a lot more fun.

Fuck, this is nearly as much fun as licking out my little kitten.

Almost. Not quite. Let's face it, there isn't anything better in the whole entire realm, in the whole damn universe, that is as good as that. Except I suppose, licking at her pussy with my fingers in her ass. Hell, I'd love to sink my cock into that ass too. Would love to do it even more in my wolf form.

The shadows in my blood buzz and I flick between my forms, my head and my balls buzzing too.

Fuck me, it's been too long since I saw that little kitten. Two whole weeks. I can tell by the weight of my frustrated ball sack.

And while hunting demons is fun and all, it isn't like being with her. I can tell the others feel the same. Thorne is in such a black mood, no one will go within ten damn feet of him. And Beaufort has been snapping everyone's head off. I reckon his balls are aching just as much as mine.

Just thinking about my little kitten puts a huge smile on my face and I dispose of the next three demons without even thinking about it. My shadows all fucked up and high.

"You enjoying yourself?" Beau asks, spotting my expression.

I bounce on my toes and puff out air. "You bet I am. This is what we were born to do, right? Wanna try that thing next time round?"

"The thing is stupid."

"So's your face," I tell him, blowing him a kiss. "I could go ask Henrietta." We can both hear her manic laughter. I don't even want to know what she's up to now.

"I'll do the thing," he says reluctantly.

I wrap my arm around his neck, tug him towards me and land a kiss on his stubbled cheek. Then, as he tries to break free, I bend us both in half, avoiding the ball of fire that was coming for our heads.

"Ready," I whisper in his ears.

He rolls his eyes but nods. We let our shadows twist together creating one strong twist of rope and we go out fishing for another demon fucker.

Because the sooner we kill all these fuckers, the sooner I can be back in the paws of my precious little kitten.

Chapter Thirty-Seven

B^{riony}

Turns out it isn't only the sex I miss about the Princes.

I also realize that despite what I may have thought, the presence of those three shadow weavers must have been acting as some kind of protection. With them gone, a lot more people have accidentally barged into me, tripped me in the hallways or intentionally elbowed me over the last three weeks.

I go out of my way to avoid Odessa – even if she's seemed less murderous since I punched her in the throat – even if my threat to spread retaliatory rumors stopped her in her tracks – I'm not taking any chances. I also avoid Linette – the remaining Smyte twin. While she's never attacked me like her sister has, and while she seems a lot quieter without her sister around, I'm not taking any risks there either.

There are some people I can't avoid though – even if I wish I could.

Madame Bardin.

She seems fixated on finding reasons to give me detentions in every single one of her lessons. She doesn't attack or interrogate me in any of these, but she does sit, smoking her cigarettes and glaring at me as I'm made to wash out class equipment, scrub classroom floors or empty and dust all the cupboards.

"Your company really is tedious," she mutters, stubbing out her cigarette at the end of my fourth detention in a row. "And despite what others may say, you smell revolting, reptilian even." She curls her lips in disgust. "I'd also venture that you're not very bright. And you're obviously a weakling." She sighs. "I don't know why they go through the pretense of sending *Slate* children to the academy." She emphasizes the word, her violet eyes flashing. "We all know where you're going to end up."

This evening, she has me scrubbing the floorboards. Usually they are spotless and gleaming. Tonight, they're covered in mud and other questionable stains I'm pretty sure she added for effect.

I'm not used to scrubbing floors anymore, and it doesn't take long for my hands to sting from the scalding-hot water, that mysteriously never seems to cool.

It's clear the sacred promise is preventing her from torturing me outright like she'd like to. It's not stopping her completely though. She's finding other ways, testing the boundaries of that promise.

I stare down at my raw hands as I scrub the stained cloth over a patch of ingrained dirt.

Beaufort and the others believe this idea that I'm their fated mate.

Wouldn't that be my ticket out of Slate Quarter? Three shadow weavers as powerful as the Princes would want their fated mate with them – not languishing in the worst Quarter of the realm. It's not as if they'd lower themselves to visit me there. Does that mean I'll be coming to Onyx Quarter with them?

Inwardly, I laugh at my own naivety.

Of course not. This will all turn out to be a game. A way to raise my hopes, only for them to be crushed cruelly.

"I said," Madame says, strolling towards me and stopping right in front of me. I stare down at her boots. Polished, expensive leather. Her feet bent in an ugly angle to accommodate the three-inch heel. "We all know which Quarter you're heading back to, don't we Slate girl?"

I lift my head, my gaze skirting up her voluptuous body to her twisted face.

"I guess that will depend on my performance in the next few trials."

Madame glowers down at me. "I don't know who helped you in that maze or how," she hisses, "but you won't be so lucky next time. I'll be sure of that. You'll be on your own and we all know how that will go." She glances down at the floor. "Can't even remove a bit of mud from the floor. Pathetic."

She swings back her foot and kicks over the boiling hot bucket of water. I have to scurry backwards to ensure I'm not scalded.

"You can leave once it's all clean." She swings around and saunters towards the door. As she does, I wish with all my heart I had the power to make her slip in those stupid shoes and land on her ass on the wet floor.

As I'm thinking about it, I can hardly believe my eyes.

Her foot slides, her legs slip from underneath her, and she falls backwards, crashing with a thump on her backside.

Did ... did I do that?

I stare down at my hands.

Impossible.

It was just a coincidence.

Madame Bardin screeches, tugging off the offending boot and hurling it in my direction. I duck as it sails over my head and hits the far wall with force.

"You silly little bitch," she says, "can't you do anything right? It's a simple job and yet you ..."

But I don't hear the rest of her words, because I'm somewhere else entirely. Dark and cold.

But safe.

Safe.

Where no one can hurt me.

I don't know how long I stay there but when I jerk back to myself with a sudden inhale of air, I'm in the classroom alone, Madame and her boots gone and the water puddled on the floor stone cold.

How long was I out?

I shake myself, squinting at the window. It's pitch black outside. I've probably missed dinner and Blaze will be flapping around my room like a wild thing, desperate to get outside for his evening flight.

I groan. My body is stiff and cold. In fact, I'm shivering. Or am I shaking?

I rub my frigid hand down my face. It was her words – so similar to Muriel's as I kneeled before her. It was all too familiar and triggered something inside me, some response.

The Madame is right, after all. I am broken and it makes no sense that I would be the fated mate of the Princes. No sense that the stone – that Blaze – would call me like he did.

I'm damaged and messed up. Incapable even of avenging my sister's death.

I pick up the rag and, quickly as I can, scrub away the remaining patch of dirt and mop up the water, before hurrying back to my room.

At dinner the next day, I explain to Fly and Clare about what happened – leaving out the part where, for one ridiculous moment, I thought I'd been the one to make Madame fall.

"Sounds like you had a panic attack," Clare says, blinking behind her glasses. "Which isn't surprising. The Madame is pretty foreboding."

"A panic attack?"

"Uh huh," Clare says.

"Soldiers have them all the time back in Iron Quarter, Cupcake," Fly says, resting his hand on mine. "Of course, they don't call them that back home." He rolls his eyes. "It's usually because they've been through some traumatic event."

"Or just struggling to cope," Clare pipes up.

"I'm not struggling," I say, poking at the crust of my soggy pie.

"You lost your sister, though. That must have been traumatic," Fly says softly.

I nod. But I know that isn't the reason for what happened last night.

It was Muriel. It was what Muriel did to me.

Fly squeezes my hand. "Anyway, I have a feeling all the detentions will end once the Princes return."

"Yeah, although I don't like having to rely on them being

around not to fall apart."

"There's nothing wrong with relying on people," Fly says. "Or trusting them."

I nod. Deep inside, I know he's right. It's just hard to unlearn years and years of behavior that has kept me safe, if alone and unhappy.

Clare sighs and looks off toward the boy she's been mooning over. "I'd happily rely on them."

"Have you asked him yet?" I ask. It's been weeks and she still hasn't plucked up the courage, inventing new and ever ridiculous excuses not to every time I raise the topic.

Her gaze flicks to Fly, her cheeks redden, and she shakes her head.

Fly's eyes narrow. "Ask who what?"

Clare lays her forehead on the table and folds her arms over her head.

"She wants to ask that boy over there if he'd like to have dinner with her."

"So why doesn't she?"

"Too scared," Clare says, her voice muffled.

"Don't be dumb," Fly says, taking a hold of her hand and attempting to yank her to her feet. They spend a few minutes tussling. "Jeez, you're stronger than you look. Also, everyone is starting to look."

Immediately, Clare stops resisting and lets Fly pull her to her feet.

"Let's go talk to him," Fly suggests.

"I wouldn't know what to say."

"Don't worry, we'll think of something," Fly says, not releasing her arm and dragging her towards the boy's table.

I watch transfixed from the safety of our table, both cringing on Clare's behalf and willing her forward. Fly begins the conversation and at first Clare shuffles on her feet, her face the color of a tomato, saying very little. But the boy she likes smiles at her with genuine affection and soon she's speaking, in fact she's so engrossed in her conversation she doesn't notice Fly slip away.

He returns to the table with a triumphant little bow.

"Wowsers," I mutter, "that was quick work."

"I know," he says. "I'm blessed with the art of small talk. It's a talent."

"And yet you have so few friends," I tease.

"That's because my stupid Quarter doesn't appreciate talents like mine. Maybe I should embark on a career as a matchmaker or something."

"Is that a thing?"

"It should be. I could set up a little service here, offer up my skills – for a fee of course."

"I don't think you want to get yourself mixed up in the drama of other people's love lives."

"Oh, yes I do!"

"You're crazy!"

"Well, duh," he says. "Why else would I be friends with you?" I give him the finger and he blows me a kiss. "Now, are you scuttling off to your room again to be a loner or are you actually going to spend the evening with me and Clare for once?"

I motion towards our friend who is now sitting around the table with the boy in question – his friends all having made themselves scarce. "I don't think she's going to be hanging out with you tonight. Or ever again," I add, spotting some serious footsie business happening under the table.

"The girl is on the way to losing her V card," Fly says, then focuses back on me. "This makes it even more imperative that you hang out with me. I'm not spending my Saturday evening alone."

"I'm sure you could find that redhead–"

"Cupcake!" He looks at me earnestly. "I miss you."

"I miss you too. I'm not doing this to be a bitch."

"Then, why?" He pouts at me and I realize I have been a bitch. Fly deserves to know the truth. I also need to trust people more, didn't he just say that?

"Okay," I say, "I'll show what's been keeping me tied to my room–"

"Tied to your room, or tied up in your room?" he asks. The memory of Beaufort restraining me in his bed using his shadow magic floats right to the front of my mind, but I bat it away. Not helpful. "Just promise you won't freak out."

"Jeez, Cupcake," he says, intrigued, "what the hell is it?"

Chapter Thirty-Eight

B riony

"A dragon!" Fly shrieks, backing towards the door, with his hands flattened against either cheek. "But ... how? ... what? ... A dragon?"

"You said you wouldn't freak out," I say, trying my best to stop Blaze from dive bombing Fly and smothering him with kisses.

"Ahhh," Fly wails, spinning around in circles, "he's trying to eat me!"

"He's not trying to eat you! He's just trying to kiss you."

"With his sharp little mouth!"

"He likes you!" I clap my hands. "Seriously, Blaze, give him some space."

"Yes," Fly says, "give me some space, please."

Blaze goes for one last dive bomb, dragging his rough little tongue right down Fly's cheek and making him shriek again, then zooms off, landing on my bed, gaze flitting between me and my friend, tongue hanging from the side of his mouth and panting. He reminds me of a dog and in the few weeks I've had him he's grown to the size of a small one.

Fly rubs at his eyes and mumbles to himself, "I must be seeing things, hallucinating. Or maybe I'm dreaming. Dragons don't exist, do they? They died out like hundreds of years ago."

I shrug and sit down on the bed beside Blaze, letting him climb into my lap and tickling under his chin. "I don't know what to tell you."

From the other side of the room, Fly examines both of us, eyes narrowed. "He seems surprisingly tame. In fact, he looks like he likes you."

"He does," I say, then make a kissy face at Blaze. "You love me, don't you?" The dragon raises his head and licks my chin.

"What does he eat?"

"Woodland animals ... and ... erm ... rats and mice."

"Ew, gross." Fly places his fist over his mouth, then wipes at his face with the sleeve of his blazer. "Are you sure he's not dangerous?"

"No, he's lovely," I say beaming. If truth be told, maybe I've been a little bit desperate, waiting for an opportunity to show Blaze off. He's a hard secret to keep. A lot harder than a stone. "Come on, he won't bite." I pat the mattress beside me and cautiously Fly approaches, lowering himself down carefully onto the bed.

Blaze watches him but he's enjoying the chin tickles too much to attempt another love-bombing.

"I'm so confused," Fly says, "when the hell did you get a dragon?"

"He hatched about three and a half weeks ago."

"Hatched?" Fly says.

I tell him about finding the stone and keeping it hidden all this time. I explain about how the stone started to crack the day of the maze trial and how placing the stone by the fire caused it to hatch open completely.

"This is so weird," Fly says, shaking his head in bewilderment. "How did a dragon survive in that stone all that time? And why didn't he hatch sooner?"

"Your guess is as good as mine. Thorne thinks that–"

"Thorne? Thorne Cadieux?"

"Do we know any other Thornes?"

"You told Thorne about your secret dragon but not me. Do all the Princes know?"

"No, only Thorne, and now you, know. You're the only two people I've told."

"But you told Thorne before me," he points out. "What happened to hoes before bros, bestie?"

"He hatched the night I was meant to be at the Princes," I say, then quickly change the subject because I don't want to explain why I now trust Thorne Cadieux more than anyone else in this academy. "Fox may also suspect. He keeps complaining that I smell like lizard."

"Fox?" Fly lifts an eyebrow.

"Oh, Professor Tudor."

"On a first-name basis are we now?"

I chew on the inside of my cheek.

"Err, yeah, I guess." That weird interaction with the professor a few weeks ago is another thing I haven't told my friend about. Mainly because I'm still trying to unscramble the whole thing myself – half convinced I imagined most of it. Why would the professor want to touch me? Why does the idea of it have strange sensations stirring in my belly?

Fly leans in and sniffs me. "You smell the same as

always. I don't know what the hell the professor is going on about."

"Who does when it comes to the professor?" I mutter.

"I don't know, you seem to have a better understanding of him than most."

"What makes you say that?" I ask, with alarm.

"You're similar, maybe it's your shared background or something."

"I am nothing like the professor!"

"You are! Moody, mysterious, secretive." He points to the dragon in my lap. "You'd make a great couple." He laughs.

"He kissed me!" I blurt out. It seems once one secret has leaked out, it's hard to keep any others.

"He what?!" Fly shrieks his voice soaring several octaves higher than it was one second ago.

"Actually, he didn't kiss me." I shake my head vigorously.

Fly shakes his head too. "Huh?"

"He *nearly* kissed me. Or at least it felt like he was going to kiss me but then he stopped himself."

"You're sure?"

I pinch my friend on the thigh. "I may not have a heap of experience but I do know what it's like when someone is going to kiss you."

"Then why didn't he?"

"I'm his student!" I point out.

"Meh," Fly says. "Did you want him to kiss you? The man literally terrifies the pants off me. But if he tried to kiss me, I think I'd wilt like a violet in the heat. I'd be unable to resist all that dark, moody, broody, masculine energy."

"Yeah," I say, butterflies stirring in my belly just thinking about it. "But I'm meant to be with the Princes."

Fly rolls his eyes. "Just because you're with one person – or three – doesn't stop you from admiring other people, doesn't prevent you from developing little crushes."

"But I don't admire Professor Tudor and I don't have a crush," I say decisively and I'm not sure who I'm trying to convince myself or my friend.

"So what exactly is your plan with this dragon, Cupcake?" Fly asks, as Blaze curls up and starts to snore.

"I usually take him for an evening fly about around this time. You can come if you want–"

"No, I mean what's your plan in the long run, Cupcake?"

"I ... I don't exactly know yet."

"Don't dragons grow really big, like really really fucking big?"

"I suppose so," I say, peering down at Blaze.

"What does Thorne say?" Fly says a little bitterly.

"He thinks I should hand him in. He thinks I'm going to be in big trouble when they find out I have a dragon and haven't told them about it."

"Obviously." He gazes at the sleeping dragon. "I wonder what they'll do with him."

"I don't know," I stroke Blaze's head. "But I don't think it will be good," I say, thinking of my sister.

Chapter Thirty-Nine

T horne

The old general, her face weathered with age and too many battles to count, walks along the line, inspecting each one of us in turn.

She reaches me at the end and nods.

"You did good today, real good. Now go back, get cleaned up and heal yourselves. We'll be back out here again for night exercises. And then I think it's about time we got you back to the academy. You'll be starting the journey back the day after tomorrow." She salutes. "Dismissed."

I lift my bare hand to my forehead and salute in return, just like all the other shadow weavers from the academy lined up alongside me.

It's only with this movement, I feel the slight tremble in my arm.

Adrenaline, anger and fear pulsate through my body, my shadow magic roars in my ears and I'm dizzy and sick.

As the general walks away, I lower my arm and stare down at my hand, flexing and curling my fingers. Around me the others are talking excitedly about the prospect of returning to the academy.

I spit on the ground, then pull my gloves from my belt and slip them back over my hands.

At once that feeling of suffocation, of imprisonment, encases me. I close my eyes.

"Fuck me, we did more than good today, boys." I open my eyes to find Dray slapping the shoulder of my other bond brother. They are both waiting for me, standing a couple of meters away.

"Thorne, you were awesome," Dray continues, "the way you sliced the head off that demon's shoulders. Oh man, it was fucking incredible."

He may be impressed, smiling at me even, but he makes no attempt to move closer. He does not slap me on the shoulder. He's been more wary of me since the full moon. Keeping his distance, careful not to come too close.

And suddenly an intense weariness overtakes me.

It's nothing but destruction. Pain, violence, death.

No softness, no affection, no touch.

What I would give for one squeeze of my shoulder, one slap on my back, one hug.

It is so exhausting.

So lonely.

Is it worth it, this existence?

"What's wrong?" Beaufort says and I wonder if for once, I've betrayed my emotions on my face.

"Nothing," I say, "just tired."

I start trudging in the direction of the barracks. The

other two follow after me. I can hear Dray garbling on behind me, his excitable words carrying across the distance.

"Three days and we're back at the academy. Never thought I'd be in a hurry to return to that shithole, but fuck me, I can't wait to get my hands on that little thrall. I miss her scent, and her soaking wet pussy."

I pick up my pace. I don't need to hear this. I don't need to be reminded of all the things I'm missing. Of all the things I want and can't have.

Fate is cruel and twisted and sick.

Why give me the thing I want most? The thing I can never have? Why tease me with it?

I glower down at my hands – my damn hands, balling them into fists. The hem of my gloves ride up my wrists as I do and I spy it.

I halt dead in my tracks.

Behind me, my bond brothers stop too.

"What now, man?" Dray asks, bouncing on his toes.

"My wrists," I say, staring at them in disbelief. Am I imagining this? There's blood and mud splattered across my face. I can taste it. Black spots dance in front of my eyes. Are these the aftereffects of battle? Am I hallucinating?

I rub my gloved fingers over my wrists to see if the faint marks will rub away. They don't, although they fade a little as I pull the skin taut.

"Are you hurt?" Beaufort asks.

I drag my gaze from my wrist and to my two bond brothers, staring at them open-mouthed. Then I thrust my hands forward.

Dray leaps behind Beaufort. Then, seeing I'm not about to attack him, shakes his body out.

"Shit, man."

Beaufort studies my face and then my wrists. His silver eyes widen with wonderment.

"I was fucking right," he says, yanking back his own sleeves, examining the skin, rubbing his fingers against his flesh aggressively. "Nothing," he hisses. "What the fuck?"

"Dray?" I ask.

He rolls up his sleeve. "Nothing," he says with obvious disappointment. "In the vision," he asks Beaufort, "did we all have–"

"Yes," he snarls. "It was all of us. She belongs to us all."

I gaze down at my wrist. Then why me? Why would I be the first one to show the fated mate sign? The one fated mate who can not touch her.

I drop my hand back down to my side and trudge back to the barracks.

Dray is rambling on again.

"This means you were right."

"Of course, I'm fucking right," Beaufort says. "The visions have never been wrong. And I know what I saw. Did you actually doubt me?"

Dray chuckles. "Of course, I fucking doubted you, Beau. She's from Slate. She has no powers, no influence, no money and no friends. She isn't the girl I imagined would be our mate."

"*It is not for us to question the designs of fate,*" Beaufort says, quoting the old saying.

"Yeah, and anyway, the first time I fucking caught her scent, I knew you were right." I can hear him bouncing on his toes. "Maybe all fate wants for us is to make a hell of a lot of babies with her. Fuck," he shakes out his body again, "I want to pump her full of my seed."

"Seriously, this shit again?" Beaufort says. "The full moon was three and a half weeks ago."

"You don't find that hot?"

"What, diapers and screaming and sleepless nights? No, that is not fucking hot. Not at all."

Dray's silent after that and we're all lost in our thoughts.

I'm with Beaufort. Why would I want a kid I couldn't even hold in my arms?

Fate has other plans for us, I'm certain of that. The stone, the dragon, the girl. They must mean something.

Then again maybe fate is a fickle bitch who wants to make our lives as difficult as possible.

Because I can't imagine either Dray or Beaufort's families will welcome our mate with open arms.

Especially Beaufort's.

Chapter Forty

B riony

There's an eerie atmosphere about the academy the day before the missing shadow weavers are due to return. An anticipation mixed with fear.

People seem less talkative, less willing to raise their hand in class. They keep their heads down and hurry along the pathways, hugging their books tightly to them.

"Is it me?" I ask Fly, as we walk to history class, "or is everyone acting dead strange?"

"The next trial is in a couple of weeks. Probably nerves kicking in."

Except I don't remember everyone acting so strangely before the last trial. Then again, I was wrapped up in my own preparation and the stuff going on with the Princes. I wasn't at my most observant.

Today, I can't help but be. Is it my imagination or is

there more whispering than usual? Are more people glancing my way?

That could be down to the Princes returning tomorrow. I remain a key piece of gossip on campus even if nothing is actually going on in my life to warrant it – or nothing that they know of anyway.

I fidget on my seat. Am I wrong? Do people know about Blaze? Have I been careless? Is this what the whispering is about?

At dinner, I catch Odessa herself staring my way. When our eyes meet, she gives me a sinister smile. Despite myself, a shiver of fear transcends my spine. She did nearly kill me after all and stabbed me in the hand. The girl is psychotic. Has she started to spread that fake rumor after all?

She turns back to her friends. Automatically, I reach for the collar residing in my pocket. I haven't removed it and I finger it now. Then yank my hand out of my pocket. I am being ridiculous.

Although I can't shake this unsettling feeling or the idea that Odessa's smile was a message, a warning of some kind.

Even Blaze greeting me with enthusiasm and licking at my face can't dispel the feeling, and as I walk with him hidden in my coat out to the forest later that evening, I peer over my shoulder several times, just to check I'm not being followed.

Under the trees and far from campus, I relax a little, my heart full as I watch him zoom joyfully through the trees.

He's becoming a better and more proficient flier – faster and more precise. His hunting skills have improved too – he yanks roosting birds from the branches, rabbits from their burrows and even takes down an owl in mid-flight. On occasion, he's also spewing lungfuls of fire, shrieking through the trees like a bolt of lightning.

He comes swooping back to me now, dive bombing me three times to slurp his tongue up my cheeks before shooting off again.

"Thanks, Blaze," I laugh, "I love you too."

As I say the words, I realize how over-brimming my heart feels, how happy I am.

I thought coming to this academy would be hell itself – far worse than the abuse, torture and loneliness at home.

But I've been proved wrong. I have friends. Three men who want me. And a freaking pet dragon. The classes may be tough, the training brutal, the trials potentially life-threatening – but this is still the happiest I've been in years.

I search the debris by my feet and find a small stick.

"Hey, Blaze," I call, grabbing his attention. Then I throw the stick through the trees and the little dragon darts after it, making me laugh again.

It's as my laughter dies away and the little dragon wrestles the stick on the ground as if it were a wild cat, that I hear it.

Footsteps. Voices.

It's faint, but I spin around and peer through the trees.

Squinting in the darkness, I see the flash of a flashlight and movement. Movement that seems to be coming this way and quickly.

Then that same torch flashes up into my face, blinding me for a second.

"She's over here," a voice cries out.

What the hell?

I snap my gaze back to the little dragon and run his way, leaping over logs and ducking under branches.

When I reach him, he leaps up at my face to lick me and spins somersaults in front of my eyes, panting with excitement.

The footsteps are louder now, pounding the ground. Many of them running in my direction.

I have a split-second decision to make.

"Blaze," I say, "you need to fly away and hide." The little dragon stares at me with his big round golden eyes. "Blaze!" I say, with more urgency, "you need to go hide." I push at him but he doesn't move, just hovers in place. "Blaze!" I snap more aggressively, making him flinch away from me. "You need to go hide NOW! I'll come find you later I promise. GO!" I yell.

The little dragon dips his head and whines pathetically.

"It's for your own good," I tell him. I try to push at him again but all that achieves is the little dragon licking at my hands.

Real fear bubbles in my gut. I don't know if these people mean me harm – although I strongly suspect they do – but, regardless, if they find Blaze I don't know what will happen to him – except that he'll most definitely be snatched from my care.

"Please, Blaze," I beg, "please just go! Go hide!"

I point my hand out towards the forest.

He looks at me again with a big soggy, clueless grin on his face. Should I snatch him from the air and hide him in my coat?

But whoever is coming would find him before I'd even buttoned up my coat.

Desperately, I scrabble at my feet, finding a stick and two big stones.

"Blaze," I say, "I don't want you here. Go away! Go away now!"

I throw a stone in his direction. He dodges it, panting like this is the best game ever. But I throw the second one in quick succession and the stick right after. The second stone hits him smack in the chest and the stick whacks one of his wings.

He whimpers, then whines again, looking at me like he doesn't understand.

I pick up another handful of stones, lifting them to my shoulder in a threatening manner. "Go on, get!" I yell, in an aggressive voice.

He blinks at me, his eyes full of a sadness that makes my heart crack. Then, as the torch swings through the air and the ground beneath my feet seems to shake, Blaze spins in the air and darts off through the trees. I watch him go until he's out of sight, trying to memorize the direction, praying he'll stay hidden, praying even harder he knows that I love him, that I didn't mean to hurt him.

There's no time for me to run now, I reach for my pocket and the collar, but I'm not wearing my skirt. I don't have it with me.

I am going to have to stand my ground and face whoever is coming. And I'm going to have to do it alone.

I turn slowly around as the pounding footsteps slow and the torch burns right into my face.

I hold my hand up, trying to shield my eyes and see who is there, but it's no use. I'm blinded and they are hidden in the darkness.

"Who's there?" I call out, clutching the handful of stones – my only weapon. "And what do you want?"

"What we want, Slate scum," says a muffled voice, "is to teach you a lesson."

"Is that wise?" I say, trying to calm my voice and keep my face neutral. "The Princes have said that if anyone–"

I don't finish my words. Something large and heavy swings through the air. I catch sight of it too late, no time to duck or jump away or even throw my stones. It smacks me across the side of the skull and I tumble straight down onto the floor, the world spinning and my skull screaming with pain.

There's no time to catch my breath before the blows and the kicks start. The torch shines in my eyes, blinding me completely, and I have no warning of where they are coming from or when. All I can do is curl myself up into a ball, wrap my arms around my head, and attempt to protect myself from the worst of it.

I'm kicked in the stomach, punched in the ribs. Someone spits in my face and another stamps on my head.

The pain is sharp and brutal and I dissociate, removing myself from this world and this pain and accepting the darkness with open arms.

Chapter Forty-One

F ox

The waxing moon splatters light through the leafless branches of the trees, splinters of silver radiating down onto the forest floor.

I drag the back of my hand across my face, wiping the blood away and stepping into a curtain of moonlight. I tip back my face and let the light play out across my face. It's nothing like sunlight. There's no warmth or radiance to it but as I look up, I can see the dust swirling in the air, caught in the moonbeam, sparkling vibrantly.

Sparkling silver.

Not golden.

I close my eyes and groan.

Because my thoughts once again stroll to the golden-headed girl with the angry green eyes. Briony Storm. I can't stop thinking of her. Night and day. Day and night.

And even now, out here deep in the forest where even the night-time animals are too frightened to stir, I can smell that delicious scent of hers in my nose, making my stomach growl and my cold heart stir.

It's so vivid, so real, for a moment I can almost imagine she's here. Out in the woods too.

I snap open my eyes, and my head whips around.

I am not imagining that scent.

It is real.

It is here in the woods.

She is here in the forest.

I take a long inhale, deep into my lungs, letting her scent rush through my mouth and my nose and my throat.

And then I frown.

There's that other smell too. Lizard. The one she denies. The one I've continued to catch the faintest hints of since that first day I noticed it. Now strong and clear in the night's air.

I move quickly and silently through the forest, hugging the shadows and avoiding the moonbeams now.

I catch her voice on the wind. Hear something whip through the air. The sound of branches snapping.

I race through the trees chasing that scent, hunting it down.

I think I hear her laugh. I think I see the flash of fire in the distance.

Where is she?

I close the distance, but she's moving away, deeper into the trees.

There is no one with her. She is alone.

Anger spirals through my gut, burns in my chest.

Alone in the woods at night.

What is she thinking?

Doesn't she know there are monsters?

Doesn't she know there are monsters that wish to hunt her down?

I force myself to turn back the way I came. I retrace my steps. I stumble as far away from her as I can and then I freeze.

Blood. Fresh and potent, carrying on the wind.

Her blood.

Ice as frigid as the poles glides down my spine, my hands shake. But for once my empty stomach doesn't growl. It isn't want that grips me. It is fear.

I move, fast as lightning through the trees, pulled in the direction of that blood, praying to every star I am not too late, that too much of her precious, precious blood has not already been spilled.

I hear voices now and footsteps, but there is no time for revenge and punishment. There is only time for her.

I find her crumpled on the floor, resting in a pool of dark scarlet blood, a pool that grows and slides across the hard forest earth.

The voices are long gone, although their footprints, the trampled undergrowth, displays clearly where they have been.

"Briony!" I murmur, falling to my knees beside her.

For the briefest of moments, fear grips me in its icy embrace and I am frozen with indecision, too afraid to learn what I cannot learn, which I could not bear.

Then I force myself to break through its cage and rest my hands on her lifeless form.

Warm.

She's still warm.

And alive.

Her body shakes with the feeblest of breaths.

A sob of relief gargles in my throat and my magic comes hurtling from my veins swimming over her body, searching out the injuries, meaning to heal her, to stem the flow of her sweet, sticky blood.

There's too much of it, too many wounds. They cut too deep. Have done too much damage. They have broken her. Destroyed her.

The girl I considered indestructible.

Gently, I lift her into my arms, holding her close against my chest, against my useless heart.

"It's okay, sweetheart. I got you."

She doesn't stir. Her eyes are shut, her face frozen in that blank expression, her skin paler than the moonlight.

I run again, fast through the trees, across the field and back to the academy.

The blood keeps seeping from her body, the warmth too, her breaths becoming weaker and weaker.

I hurtle unseen along the pathways and crash right through the clinic doors, glass smashing around me.

"Help!" I boom. "Somebody help me!"

I swing my gaze around desperately. It's late. Is there anyone here?

I fall to my knees again, my magic swoops around her desperately, hopelessly; I bury my face against her ear.

"Please," I whisper, "please, no, Briony. I'll do anything. Anything!"

The blood comes less quickly. Her breath's barely audible. Her skin cold as mine.

It's too late.

I close my eyes. I beg the stars, promise them anything and everything. I will protect her. I will care for her. I will love her. Just keep her here ... don't force me to ...

And then there're voices, footsteps like there were in the forest.

Hands lift her from me. A palm rests on my shoulder. Anxious words echo around the sterile corridor but I can make no sense of them.

They whisk her away.

Silence again.

I'm left on my knees, her blood dripping from my hands and onto the white clinic floor.

Chapter Forty-Two

B eaufort

The journey back to the academy drags on for an age. The trucks rattle our bones and have us sliding into one another when we career around corners. The sooner we graduate and are allowed to displace, the fucking better.

Not that they'd want us to even if we were given permission. They like to keep a watchful eye on us. Don't want anyone deserting and shirking their responsibilities.

The journey is made even more painful by the fact Kratos is sitting opposite me with a shit-eating grin on his face, every now and again, turning to mutter something I can't hear over the rumble of the truck in one of his bond brother's ears.

I don't know what he's so happy about. It's clear Kratos's one desire in life is to see the three of us toppled from our position as the most powerful shadow weavers of our generation. He'd love for him and his brothers to steal that crown. But if these last four weeks are anything to go by, that is far from likely. Time and time again during this 'training' camp, we've shown our power and our dominance. Kratos and the others don't even come close. Not even Henny and her erratic but fierce magic is a threat to our superiority.

So I smile back at him, then close my eyes and try to sleep. It's impossible. The other thing that's making this journey a drag, is knowing what's waiting for me back at the academy.

Our thrall.

Not just our thrall. Our fated mate. Those marks on Thorne's wrists confirm it.

Not that I'd ever admit it to the others, but I'd begun to wonder myself if I was wrong this time. If the vision in my head was not a vision at all, but some warped creation of my mind, determined to sabotage every plan set for me by tying me to some weakling from Slate Quarter.

But I was right. Am I glad about it?

She's not weak. The scars on her back prove that. She's endured torture, grief, ridicule and yet she keeps her head held high and refuses to be cowed.

Fuck, I love that about her.

The truck hits a bump in the road, jolting us about violently on our seats. I open my eyes to find Kratos watching me. I close my eyes again, forgetting all about the other shadow weaver and imagining all the things I'm going to do to our little thrall once I have her in my bed again.

The hours pass, and then Dray's shaking me awake.

"We're nearly here," he says, pointing to the front of the truck. We're driving through heavy woodland but in the distance, over the canopy of the trees, are the tops of the academy towers.

My stomach spins with excitement. I feel like a little kid.

Another half an hour and we're weaving through those towers themselves and parking up in one of the courtyards. A small crowd has gathered to welcome us back, among them the thralls standing to one side together, each wearing a golden collar around their neck.

I scan their faces even though she won't be there. It's not her style. I should know that by now, and yet I can't avoid the inevitable disappointment.

"Thrall not here, Lincoln," Kratos says as we move down the truck and jump out onto the cobbled ground. "I wonder where she could possibly be ..."

He grins right in my face and I can see all the golden teeth crowded in his mouth. He strolls away, wrapping his arm around the neck of his thrall and bending down to kiss her mouth. When they break apart, his thrall peers over her shoulder and his arm, and catches my gaze. She smiles right at me too, curling her tongue behind her teeth.

My blood runs icy cold. Immediately, I understand.

"Briony," I say to the others, striding quickly away, breaking into a run as soon as we're out of sight of Kratos and the others.

"What's wrong?" Dray asks as he sprints behind me.

"Didn't you see the look on Kratos's face? On his thrall's face?"

"What? Those stupid dumbass looks? That's because they don't share a brain cell between them."

"No," I say, "it wasn't that."

I bolt up the staircase of her tower, two girls flattening themselves against the wall as I pass. At the summit, I hammer on her door, leaning against the frame as I catch my breath and then hammering again when it doesn't open.

"Are you looking for Briony?"

I spin around to find her two friends huddled in the doorway of the boy's room. I'm not liking the concerned expressions on their faces.

"Where is she?" I boom.

"We don't know," the boy says, voice trembling. "She wasn't in her room this morning. I thought maybe you got back early or something, but then she didn't turn up for breakfast or first periods."

"We've been looking for her," the girl adds. "Asking around."

"But people are being weird as shit."

I glance at my bond brothers. This isn't good. Kratos's smile seems more and more sinister to me with every passing second.

"When did you last see her?" Dray asks them both.

"Dinner time," the girl says.

"And then where did she go?" Dray asks. "Back to her room or ...?"

The boy glances at Thorne and then swallows. "She may have gone out to the forest."

"The forest?! Why the hell would she go to the forest at night?" Damn that girl. Didn't I tell her to be careful?

"Erm." His eyes flick to Thorne again. Is he worried my bond brother might unleash his deadly magic? "She's been going there every evening."

"Why?"

He shrugs but I can tell by the way he can't quite meet my eyes that he knows the reason. The reason isn't important right now though. That can wait. Right now, we need to find her. She could be in danger. Or hurt. Or ...

Bile rises in my throat and my heart stops beating.

Not that. Not that. I shake my head.

I'd know if it were that, wouldn't I? I'd feel it in my bones. In my heart.

"Did you hear her come home after her visit to the forest?" Thorne asks – and thank the stars someone is thinking straight.

"No," Fly says, "but I'm often asleep before she gets back."

Fly glances once again at Thorne which is really starting to piss me off.

"Why the fuck is she going into the forest?" Dray says. His face darkens and he growls. "To meet some other dude?" And I can't help it, but that thought has my hackles rising too.

"You'd be able to smell if she was with some other man," Thorne points out, my shoulders relaxing. "We can worry about questions later. Right now, we need to find her."

I rub at my chin, covered in a layer of thick stubble, the bristles sharp against my finger tips.

"We can split up," I suggest. "You two," I point to Briony's friends, "can go check the commoners' clinic again. Thorne, you can–"

"There's no need," Dray says, already striding towards the staircase. "If I can find her scent, I can track her down." He descends the first step. "What are you fuckers waiting for?" Thorne and I follow after him, the other two remain where they are. "And you, too," he snaps, making the boy and the girl scurry after us.

Out on the pathway, Dray sniffs the air, then turns back to Fly.

"You know whereabouts in the forest she goes?" Dray asks.

"Yep," Fly says.

"Then show us," Dray gives him a little push, "and pick up the pace."

We sprint along the pathways, the boy struggling to keep up with us and the girl left far behind. Out on the field, we wait for him to catch us up.

"Whereabouts?" Dray asks.

"She usually goes off that way, towards the east of the forest." The boy hunches over his knees, catching his breath. "It's more hidden from the academy in that direction."

Dray yanks off his sweater and toes of his sneakers, leaving them abandoned on the field. He starts sprinting out onwards the forest, his sweatpants ripping in half as his body morphs from human form to wolf, four solid paws soon hitting the ground.

In this form, he's a hell of a lot faster than me and Thorne, disappearing into the trees before we're halfway across the field. We chase after him and find him standing still under the trees, sniffing the air, then the ground, then the air again, then walking in a zigzag fashion, sniffing all the while before spinning in circles and retracing his steps. Then he halts. His tail flicks up straight and his ears flatten on his head. Nose to the ground he trots through the trees, his path direct at first, then once we're deep in the forest, it becomes more meandering. Then he stops, peers up at us and growls before his nose hits the ground again and he pads through the trees.

He stops again and immediately I can see why.

There was some kind of disturbance here. It's clear from the trampling of the dead leaves on the ground something rolled through them or kicked them about.

Dray growls again, only this time it's sinister and deadly – making my blood run cold.

Together Thorne and I step forward to examine whatever the wolf has found.

"Fuck!" I say, dropping down to crouch. Blood – splattered across the ground and over the leaves. I reach out and touch it with my fingers. It's not fresh, but it isn't old either.

"She was hurt," I say, peering up at Thorne. His eyes are fixed on the blood on my fingertips. "I can't see a trail of blood," I say, "which means she either patched herself up or someone moved her."

"Can you track her from here?" Thorne asks the wolf.

He sniffs, then snarls, his nose crinkling up in disgust.

I peer at Thorne. What the hell does that mean?

But then Dray is moving through the trees again and we're scrambling to keep up.

He leads us out of the forest, and across the field.

Her two friends are crouching on the ground, still catching their breath.

"Did you find anything?" the girl asks, adjusting her steamed-up glasses.

"Looks like it," I say, gesturing to the wolf and then running after him as he weaves along the pathways.

It causes an inevitable commotion. Some people scream when they see the wolf bounding along the pathway, others scatter and the rest stand and stare.

"Where the hell is he going?" Thorne hisses, as a group of clueless girls giggle as we race past them.

Dray takes us right through the heart of the academy and out the other side, to a modern building that squats to the north, hidden by one of the large towers. The shadow weaver clinic. I've had no need to visit the clinic since my arrival and its shiny and modern appearance surprises me.

What surprises me more is that someone brought Briony here. Don't get me wrong, it's where I would bring her myself. Where any of us would if she were too hurt for us to heal her ourselves. But she wouldn't be brave enough to come herself, and what other shadow weaver would bring her?

Dray transforms back into his human form. His long white hair is damp with sweat and so is his body. He's also completely fucking naked, not that he cares. He pushes against the door, steps inside and strides straight up to the reception desk, large cock swinging between his legs.

The eyes of the young receptionist on the other side of the desk nearly pop right out of their sockets.

Dray isn't in a flirting mood today, though. He leans over the desk and fixes the dude with a menacing glare.

"Briony Storm – is she here?"

"The girl that got hurt last night? She's in room three back there," he says, pointing over his shoulder. "But you can't–"

The three of us stroll right past the desk and towards the door of room three.

Dray pauses, hand on the door-handle.

"There were other scents out there," he says, "including Tudor's."

Chapter Forty-Three

B riony

Something is beeping incessantly. Right by my ear.

Beep. Beep. Beep.

I try to open my eyelids. But they won't. They are heavy and sore. Instead, I lift my arm to bat the noise away. But it is sore too. It doesn't move when I ask it to.

I panic. The memories come flooding back. Where am I?

But then the darkness returns.

The next time I wake, the noise is still there. Persistent like a small baby bird.

Blaze!

I roll up to sitting and pry open my eyes. This time my body obeys, but it's painful and sore.

Light hits my eyeballs – bright and stark and I groan and shield my eyes.

This isn't the forest. For a moment, I think I must have died and ended up some place else. Then the room comes slowly into focus and I understand where I am.

A clinic of some sort.

I'm lying in a raised bed under starched sheets and bright electric lights; lines run in and out of my arms and that beeping noise is a machine above my head.

Cautiously, I examine my surroundings. This isn't the clinic at the academy. I've been there. It's worn and old. Most of the machinery was broken and the whole place dirty.

This room gleams and the machinery positively sparkles. It's modern and sleek.

"Miss Storm, glad to see you are finally with us."

I jolt. I had no idea anyone else was in the room with me, but when I peer towards the end of the bed, I find Fox standing there, bathed in the only shadow in this room. Seriously, does he hunt them out?

But even in the shadow, I can see how disheveled he looks. He's missing his usual jacket and tie, his shirt is creased and splattered with blood. His usually neat hair flops into his eyes and his beard is tangled. Dark shadows ring his eyes that seem to glow with less intensity than usual.

"What happened to you?" I gasp.

He stares at me dumbfounded. Snorts. Shakes his head. Run his hands over his face. Then lets out a bark of laughter.

"Stars above, what happened to *me*?"

"No offense, Professor. But you look like shit."

"You're not looking so good yourself, Miss Storm. What happened to *you*?"

"Oh, you know, the usual. Someone decided to beat the crap out of me."

"Some*one*?" he asks, tension in his jaw.

"It was a group of people and before you ask, no I don't know who they were. It was dark, they were shining a torch in my face."

"You didn't recognize their voices?"

"They were muffled."

"Probably wearing masks. Spineless dickheads," he spits.

"Erm, where exactly am I? And how did I get here?"

"The shadow weaver clinic. And I brought you here. I ..." He swallows, brushing his hair away from his face. "For a moment, I thought you were dead."

"The number of kicks to the head, I should probably be," I say cheerfully. I glance down at all the wires trailing in and out of my arm. Are they pumping me full of drugs because I feel pretty good considering a gang of hooligans just beat the shit out of me? "But seems I'm not that easy to get rid of." I smile at Fox, which makes the poor professor actually flinch. Then run my tongue over my teeth checking I didn't lose any.

"What the hell were you doing out in the forest in the middle of the night?" he says. "Are you asking for trouble?"

"I like the forest," I say, considering my answer carefully. My answer needs to sound convincing. "I always have. I spend nearly all of my time out in the forest back in Slate Quarter." Anything to avoid Muriel.

"That's Slate Quarter. This is the academy. It's dangerous."

"Oh, those squirrels are truly deadly."

"Maybe not, but the shifters can be."

I sniff. Dray in wolf form is a big bouncing ball of fluff.

Not deadly at all. "So this is the shadow weaver clinic?" I ask.

He nods.

"But I'm not a–"

"Doesn't matter."

"Because of the whole thrall thing," I say bitterly, thinking of Clare's friend who has been stuck in the commoners' clinic for weeks now.

"No, because I brought you here," he says.

"Oh ... well ... thank you?" He glowers at me, leaning on the end of my bed. "But I feel okay. I think I can get back to my ..." Blaze is out there somewhere in the forest, all alone and thinking that I abandoned him. I go to tug the wires from my arm but Fox growls so fiercely, I jolt my hand away.

"You're staying right here until the doctor confirms you're well enough to leave."

"But I need to get back to ..." I trail off, chewing on my lip.

"You need to get back to ..."

"How long have I been in here exactly?"

"Twelve hours."

"Twelves hours!" I say, jerking up.

Blaze has been out in the forest on his own for twelve whole hours. He will most definitely think I've deserted him. Or he may come looking for me and then ...

"I really have to go."

"Briony!" Fox barks, so forcefully I drop back against the pillow. "The shadow weaver doctor spent five hours healing you. You were barely breathing. You had internal bleeding – including a bleed on the brain. You nearly died."

"It wouldn't be the first time," I mutter.

"The scars," he growls. "Want to tell me about those?"

"No," I say. "I don't."

He runs his hand down his face again as if trying to remove his annoyance. I really do wind him up. I'm surprised he didn't leave me in the forest to die. It would probably have made his life more bearable. "You need to stay here and rest until the doctor says you are well enough to leave."

"And how long will that be?" I ask with exasperation.

"As long as it takes." He shifts his weight from one foot to another. "Look, if there is something you need to do urgently, then I will do it for you. I will help."

"Seriously?" I ask, surprised. "Why?"

Does he mean the wanting-to-touch-me thing? I'm so confused. Most of the time I appear to irritate him and then there've been these other rare occurrences when he looks at me like he wants to kiss me. And he saved me – brought me here to make sure I got the treatment I needed.

"Because," he says, "contrary to what the world may think about me, I am not a bad person."

"I don't think you are a bad person."

He screws up his eyes as if I just punched him right in the gut. "Maybe you would if you knew," he whispers.

"What do you mean by that?"

"Nothing," he dismisses. "What do you need?"

I consider him. Do I trust him? I was tempted once before to tell him about the stone, to show it to him. But that was when I believed it was him who had rescued me from the maze. He did rescue me last night. But this was different. He's a teacher here at the academy. He holds a position of authority in the academy and the realm. Do I truly believe he wouldn't tell the necessary people about the dragon?

No, I don't.

"I'd really like to see my friend, Fly."

"That's it?" he says. "That's the urgent thing?"

"Yes, and it is urgent."

He strokes his fingers through his matted beard. He knows there's more. He knows I'm keeping secrets from him. But unlike Madame Bardin, he isn't going to torture me for them.

"All right," he says. "I'll fetch him for you," I smile, "right after the doctor has given permission for you to receive visitors." I frown.

"Are you not a visitor?"

"No, I'm your professor."

And, shit, these drugs they have me on must be really strong, because the way he says that makes me shiver.

But I don't get a chance to analyze that reaction because, suddenly, the clinic door flings open.

Chapter Forty-Four

F ox

The Princes.

It was inevitable they'd show up. Briony is their thrall. Eventually, they'd track her down, even if I've been careful not to tell anyone where she is here. They returned from training exercises today and of course they'd go looking for her. Of course they'd find her missing.

"Little Kitten," Dray Eros whines, pushing past me to hurry right to the side of her bed. He's as naked as a newborn baby, not that he seems aware of the fact. "What the fuck happened?"

"Yes," Beaufort Lincoln growls close to my ear, "what happened?"

I turn my head slowly like I have all the time in the world and meet his glower with my own.

"Are you implying something, Mr. Lincoln?" I ask through gritted teeth.

"I was attacked," Briony calls over to us, clearly aware of the tension in the room and wanting to defuse it. "I was jumped. Professor Tudor found me and brought me to the clinic." Beaufort's glare becomes more intense like he has several questions, but Briony is still talking. "But I'm fine now, completely healed. So maybe you could take me back to my room." She stares at Thorne Cadieux as if trying to impart some secret message with her eyes.

"She isn't completely healed," I say firmly. "The doctor has said she shouldn't be moved until she deems her well enough."

Beaufort and Thorne both nod.

"Who attacked her?" Thorne says. His magic is crackling beneath the surface and I can sense from the drawn nature of his brows, he's struggling to retain it.

"I don't know," I say. I glance her way. "And she claims she doesn't know either."

"I don't," she says. "Torch in my eyes, remember?"

"I have a fair idea," Dray whispers, stroking a piece of hair away from Briony's bruised face. He's perched on the side of her bed, his cock resting on his thigh.

"Can someone get him a fucking gown?" I snap.

But no one moves and Dray gazes over his shoulder and winks at me.

I grind my molars so hard together I'm surprised I don't crack a tooth.

"How did you find her exactly, Prof.?" Dray asks, suspicion flickering in his eyes.

Involuntarily, my gaze flicks to hers and then away. "I was out in the woods. I heard something."

"Heard her being attacked?" Beaufort asks, his magic

fierce in the air as well. "Didn't think to intervene to help her?"

"He saved me," Briony says. "Don't be a dick, Beaufort."

I smile to myself. So I'm not the only one she likes giving lip to then? I'm glad she isn't bowing and scraping and licking their boots.

"What were you doing out in the woods, man?" Dray says, eyes still searching.

Does he know?

Impossible.

Dray Eros is a wolf shifter. I'm surmising it is down to him they found Briony here so quickly. Followed our scents most probably. That doesn't mean he knows how obsessed I am with her.

Unless, of course, he's reading it right now in my damn eyes.

"That's a question I'd like Miss Storm to answer."

Briony ignores the question, instead, fidgeting with the tube in her arm.

"I really just want to get out of here. Would one of you please go find the doctor so we can make that happen?"

"Probably best the prof does it," Dray says.

"No," I say. "I'm staying here."

"There's no need. She's in good hands now," Beaufort says. "We'll take good care of her."

I can't help snorting at that.

"Something funny, Prof.?" Dray says, with his usual humorous tone, but I can see the threat hovering in his eyes.

"Yes." I shake my head. "Take good care of her? Because you've done such an awesome job. You know, she'd be dead if I hadn't found her when I did."

My words cause a silence to sweep across the room like a cold, bitter wind.

Dray springs up from the bed, but Briony grabs his hand before he can lunge forward and Beaufort raises his hand to tell him to be quiet.

"Yeah and we're very, very thankful for that Professor Tudor," Beaufort says with a tight smile. "But you can go now."

"No," I say. These boys might be used to getting their own way, to ordering people about. Probably including most of the academic staff. But that doesn't include me.

"No?" Beaufort smiles. "Why the fuck not? Don't you have lessons to teach?"

I ignore his insolence. "I'm not leaving until I know she is all right."

"I am all right," Briony mutters.

"Why?" Beaufort says, stepping forward.

Suddenly, her scent is even stronger in my nose, and her beating heart even louder in my ears. It's so obvious, so clear. I swear it must be carved across my forehead.

"We will look after her," Thorne says. I realize I've hardly ever heard the kid speak and when I have it's usually spitting with anger. Today, his words are softer. Fuck, even a little kind.

"Like protectors look after thralls?" I spit. I know how they take advantage of students weaker than they are, in return for a protection they barely provide.

"As if she were our fated mate," he says.

Dray gasps and Beaufort mutters an obscenity under his breath. "Shit, man, what are you doing ..."

But I barely hear his words. My eyes flick between him and Briony.

Fated mate? That can't be right. That can't be true.

"It is," he says and I realize I spoke those last two thoughts out loud. He pulls back his sleeve.

"What is that?" Briony asks.

He paces towards the bed and presents his arm to her. From the distance, I can make out the faintest of marks across his wrists.

Amazement swamps her features. She examines her own wrists but they're too covered in bruises to see anything even if she did have the markings.

I stagger backwards. "That can't be right," I mumble.

"Do you have them too?" she asks Dray and Beaufort, not hearing my comment.

"Nope," Dray says, "Thorne has beaten us to it."

She gazes up at Thorne and smiles – it's a little shy but damn is it pretty.

My stomach moans.

"She doesn't have the marks," I snark out, petulantly. "It must be some other girl."

Thorne shakes his head. "It's her."

"Briony?" I ask. Because she must know – she must feel – that it isn't him. That it isn't any of them.

But she's still lost in Thorne's gaze, oblivious to anything else around her.

"So you see," Beaufort Lincoln says, stepping in closer and resting his hand on my chest. "She's ours and we will protect her. You're no longer needed. You can go."

"No," I say again. "I'm not leaving."

"Why the fuck not?" Dray snaps with annoyance.

"Because she's my mate too."

Chapter Forty-Five

B riony

"What?" I say, blinking hard against the fiercely bright clinic lights. Did I catch that right? Did I hear what I think I heard?

Fox hangs back in the only shadow in the room and I can't read his face.

I push back the stupid blanket and scrabble over the bed.

"What did you just say?" I whisper, my body shaking.

I must have misheard. There is no other explanation for it. Because Fox Tudor could not have said what I think he just said.

"Are you on something, man?" Dray says to the professor. "Drink something a little psychedelic?"

"I'm perfectly sound of mind," he snarls.

"But you said–" I begin.

"You're not her mate," Beaufort says, stepping into the space between me and the professor. "That's bullshit. And I don't know why you think you can mess with our heads and her head, but–"

"Messing with *your* heads?" the professor snorts. "Why would I waste my time?"

"I don't know, you tell us."

"She's *my* mate" he says and I can't help gasping, my head reeling. Because he said it again and this time, there was no doubt about the words he uttered.

The room spins and I have to grip the blanket in my fists to stop from tumbling away.

"Not possible," Beaufort says.

"You think just because he has some fucking marks on his wrists – ones none of the rest of you have – ones she doesn't even have herself – that makes you her fated mates!"

"No, there's more," Dray says.

"Such as?" the professor says, not sounding in the least bit convinced.

Dray peers Beaufort's way and his bond brother shakes his head.

"What ..." I begin, my voice catching in my throat. For the first time I realize how raw and sore it is. "What makes you think I'm your mate, Fox?"

It seems like the craziest thing I've ever heard – and jeez I've heard and seen a lot of crazy things since arriving at the academy.

There's a long pause. Beaufort must be right. The professor is just messing with us. I don't know why but–

"Your scent."

"Huh?" Dray says, ears obviously pricking up. As a wolf, I suspect he considers anything smell-related to be his domain.

"My scent?"

"Yes," he groans, "it's the most delicious, delectable, damn-right hypnotizing scent I've ever smelled. I can't stop thinking about it. I can't stop wanting it." His voice hardens. "I'm addicted to it. I'm addicted to you."

My mouth falls open. All those times it felt like he wanted to kiss me, and I dismissed them, sure I was imagining things. All the times I felt this electricity in the air between us and dismissed them too, concluding it was simply his magic in the air.

How did I not see this?

"Dude," Dray chuckles, making the professor growl. "Her scent is fucking awesome – you can smell how wet her pussy is all of the time," the professor growls more fiercely and his cold magic crackles in the air, "but that doesn't mean she's your freaking fated mate."

"It does," he says. "For my kind."

Dray considers the professor, something flickering in his eyes. "So it's true what they say about you, Prof.," he says, licking his lips.

"I'd like to talk to the professor alone," I tell the Princes.

"Err, no," Dray says.

"It wasn't a request," I tell him.

"Still, no."

"Come on," Thorne tells the others. "We'll be right outside the door," he adds, and I'm not sure if those words are directed at me or Fox.

The three Princes walk out of the room and Dray glares at the professor before closing the door.

When it clicks shut, I round on Fox.

"What the hell?" He takes a shocked step backwards. What was he expecting? Me to run into his arms? "Is this some kind of joke or–"

"No, I'm deadly serious."

"You truly believe that I am your–"

"Fated mate and I am yours."

"But I'm the Princes' fated mate," I protest, rubbing at my bruised wrists. This is the most incredible conversation. It was hard enough to believe that much was true – but Thorne has the markings now. Whatever exactly Beaufort saw in that vision, it must have been right.

It isn't possible for me to be Fox's mate too.

"So they say," he mutters. "You really think you can trust them?"

"But I should trust you?" I flop back on the bed, folding my arms over my chest and shaking my head in disbelief.

"Why the hell would I lie, Briony?"

"I don't know. Just like I don't know why they lied about my sister."

"Just like you're lying about whatever has been taking you into the forest every night."

"You've been watching me."

"Seems like I'm not the only one," he scoffs.

"Fox," I say with exasperation, his name making his body taut and alert with concentration. "Do you even like me?"

"I'm obsessed with you, Miss Storm. I'm on the brink of losing my damn mind."

"That isn't the same thing."

And why do I feel disappointed? I bet those in the academy who aren't crushing all over the Princes, are probably crushing over the hot and broody professor. I bet he has even more admirers outside the academy too. After all, the professor counts Madame Bardin as a past lover.

He says he's obsessed with me, yet my warped logic and really fucked up heart would rather he said he liked me.

Why do I even care? It's not like I have feelings for him too ... do I?

"When I thought you were ..." His neck cords tighten and his voice trails off.

"And you think all this just because I smell nice?"

"It's more than that, Briony. It's a sign. A clear sign."

"For your kind?" I repeat his earlier words and he nods. "Shadow weavers? But then why–"

"No, Briony, not shadow weavers."

His eyes glow in the shadows and I shiver, the air suddenly cold.

"Then what?"

He takes a deep inhale and slams his fist against the light switch. The bright lights extinguish immediately, plunging the room into darkness.

And then he's right beside me, eyes shining in the darkness, the coldness of his magic brushing against my skin.

I'd recognized almost immediately that he was different from most other shadow weavers. His magic cold, where theirs was warm. His eyes glowing like they do. But then Madame Bardin's had been similar and so I'd never really questioned it.

But now, I understand. They are different from the other shadow weavers. Just like Dray and the other shifters are different too.

"What are you?" I whisper. Although, deep down in my heart I already know. I've always known.

"Something deplorable. Something that belongs in the shadows. Something you should be afraid of."

"Vampire," I whisper, not wanting to believe it.

Not Fox Tudor.

Not beautiful Fox Tudor – so full of life and exuberance. So damn beautiful.

"Yes," he whispers, and there's a lisp in his voice now and through the darkness, I see his fangs have lengthened, sharp and pointed and ivory white.

"But you weren't always," I say, my voice sounding far away.

He's right, I should be afraid of him. Terrified maybe. And yet, I'm not. I'm strangely calm. I always have been in his presence, even if I've always sensed the danger somewhere in the periphery of my mind.

"No," he says, shrinking a step away, his fangs retracting. "I wasn't always. Once I was just a boy from Slate Quarter."

Now I understand the change. The sunlight sucked from his skin; the life sucked from his body. Changed from something alive and vibrant to something immortal, flickering always on the line between life and death.

"Then how?" I ask.

"Another vampire," he says. "They fed from me."

"But that would kill you, wouldn't it?" Or is he more dead than I think?

"No," he says, "a vampire can choose how much they take. Just enough to whet their appetite, to suppress their hunger, or enough to kill." I shiver again and he takes another step back as if he knows his presence is chilling the air. "But that in itself is not enough to transform a human into a vampire. The vampire must allow the human to feed from them – to take in their blood."

"Oh my gosh!" I say, hands flying to my mouth. "That's how you obtained your powers! You took another vampire's blood."

"Yes," he says, nodding, and pacing across the room. "And it's my biggest fucking regret. But I was young and stupid. Swayed and seduced by power and immortality. By a different life."

"Regret it?" I say. "But you're a shadow weaver. A professor. You escaped Slate Quarter."

He spins round and fixes me with those glowing eyes. "You don't know what I'd give to return home – to go back to Slate, to go back to how things were."

"Because you've forgotten how awful it is, Professor," I spit.

"You think this existence is a good one?" He turns his palms towards me. "Confined to the shadows, never able to feel the sunlight fall across my face. Forced to feed on the weak, always hungry, never satisfied. No friends, no companions. No chance at a family or a life of my own."

"Feed on the weak?" I cry. He can't mean ...

"What do you think I was doing out in the forest last night, Miss Storm? Searching for my next feed." He must register the horror on my face and the way I shrink from him. "Not humans," he spits, "I'm not a monster."

"Then what?" I ask.

"Deer mostly," he says with disgust. "Rabbits and squirrels if I'm desperate."

I let out the breath I was holding.

If he wants my sympathy, I'm finding it hard to give it to him. Then again, I know what it's like to have no options, for others to dictate your decision.

"The vampire who forced you to–"

"Didn't force," he says firmly. "Fool that I am, I chose this existence, Briony."

Chapter Forty-Six

D ray

"That's it!" I say, slamming back the door. The lights are out and I click my fingers. They flick back on and the little kitten and the professor jolt in surprise. He's lurking by the bed, but scurries away back into the shadows, hissing as he does. "I don't know what freaky made-up shit, he's told you. But he is not your fated mate and there is no way in his twisted version of hell he's sinking his fangs into you."

"What?!" she says in alarm. Like the little thing hadn't considered that.

Isn't that every freaking girl's fantasy? To be pinned down and sucked off by a vampire? That or pinned down and taken by a fucking great wolf.

The professor slinks further into the shadows, shame sagging his shoulders, and if I was a properly functioning human being, I'd feel sorry for him.

But I'm not, she's ours.

"I need to think about this – all of it," she says next, rubbing at her forehead.

"There's nothing to think about," I snarl.

"I'm too tired to argue right now," she says, with a sigh of exasperation.

"You need to rest," Beaufort and the professor say at the same time, before glowering at one another.

This situation is fucked up.

"I agree," she says, and Beaufort looks shocked out of his skin. That must be the first time ever that she has. "So can you all just leave me in peace."

"We need to stay here and protect–" Beaufort starts, but that momentary snap of time where she was agreeing with him has ended.

"No, I need you all to leave me alone so I can think about all of this."

"We're not leaving the clinic," Beaufort says.

"Me neither," the professor says.

"Don't you have class to teach?" I say.

"Don't you have class to attend?"

"Fine, stay in the clinic if you want, just get out of this room," the little kitten snaps, her claws now out.

"Come on," Thorne tells us all, moving towards the door.

"I need to talk to you first," she says. I grin at the professor. His jaw tightens. "Just Thorne," she clarifies and now the professor is smirking right back at me.

Beaufort, the professor and I stroll slowly to the door, none of us want to be the first to pass through the doorway.

"After you, Prof.," I say, holding out my arm and bowing a little.

"You first," he growls.

The three of us tussle in the doorway and finally Thorne snaps.

"Get out!"

We file through the door; me first, then the professor and then Beaufort. The door slams behind us.

"Why does she want to talk to him and not us?" I whine.

"Probably because he isn't a shithead," the professor says. "And he's not walking around with his dick hanging out."

"I didn't have time to change. Besides, she likes my cock." I imitate his annoying smirk and anger flashes in his glowing eyes.

"Cut it out," Beaufort says, walking a little way down the corridor and flopping down onto a chair. "And he's right, put on some clothes."

"Where exactly–"

"Magic some up."

I chuckle and then I let my magic weave through the air, a pair of sweats landing with a thump on the floor. I pull them on and sink into a chair beside Beaufort. The professor remains on his feet and starts pacing up and down the corridor like a first-time dad waiting for the arrival of a baby.

I lean my forearms on my thighs, both legs bouncing up and down and whisper to Beaufort: "You think there's any truth to his shit?"

"You do know vampires have exceptional hearing," Beaufort says in his normal voice.

I snap my head his way. "Can you hear what Briony and Thorne are talking about?"

The professor pauses, then shakes his head. "Thorne's using a blocking spell."

"What the hell?" I say, peering at the closed door. Why

would he do that? There's meant to be no secrets between bond brothers.

"And I don't give a shit what you think, Eros, I'm telling the truth."

I jump up into a crouched position on the seat of the chair and spin around to face him, leaning my forearms on the back of the chair.

"Okay, so she smells good to you. How do you know that that isn't all it is? A bit of a crush." He grinds his teeth together in irritation. "Hey, no judgment, we all have them and she is fucking cute."

"Do you know how many girls pass through this academy every year? None, not a single one, has ever caught my attention like this. I've barely registered their scents, let alone become obsessed with it. Yet the moment she stepped into the Great Hall I noticed it among all the other scents. It stood out like a beacon. It pummeled straight to the core of my brain and lodged itself there."

"That doesn't mean—"

"It does. It's the sign for my kind." He runs both his hands through his hair. "You don't think I've researched the shit out of this? You don't think I've considered it's just lust or a crush? It's not. Briony is my fated mate."

"Well," Beaufort says, looking up from his chair, "she's ours too, so where the hell does that leave us?"

I jump off my seat, gathering my hair into my hands, twisting it into a knot behind my head. I stink of dog and the forest and the weird-ass chemicals of the clinic.

"You know what, I think we have bigger things to worry about right now."

"Like what?" Beaufort says.

"Those other scents that were out there in the forest." I rub at my nose. "You smell them too, Prof.?"

"What scents?"

"The scents of the cunts that attacked our little kitten."

The professor's eyes flash a blood red and his magic soars in the air. "You recognized the scents?"

"You didn't?"

He places his hands on his hips. The dude looks rough, something I only just noticed. "I don't have your sense of smell. Don't get me wrong, mine is good. But it's mostly just prey and blood I can smell ... and her. Most human scents all smell the same to me."

"Well," I say, rubbing my hands together, "I recognized some of them for sure. The question is, what are we going to do about it?"

Chapter Forty-Seven

B riony

I open my mouth to speak, but Thorne holds up his finger to his lips, then weaves his hands through the air.

When he's done, he says, "The professor has a very good sense of hearing."

"Oh," I say, considering this for a moment. All this new information has fried my brain. I need to sit with it, marinate in it, before I can work out what it all means.

But I don't have time for that just yet.

"Blaze," I say.

"Where is he?" Thorne asks.

"I was taking him out for his evening flight when I was attacked. I managed to get him to fly away before they got to me. I told him to hide, but I don't know if he understood or whether he's okay or whether he thinks I abandoned him or–"

"Briony," he says, "it's fine. I'll find him."

I chew on my lip. "But he might not come to you."

"He likes me."

"Hmm," I say; if he's scared, I'm not sure there'll be anyone but me he'll come to. And even then, after what happened, he might not come to me either. I imagine him out there alone in the cold, dark forest. I don't exactly have a choice. "Fly knows about Blaze now too."

"You told him," he says, his face emotionless.

"I needed some help and you weren't here." I chew my lip some more. "Have you told Beaufort and Dray?"

"No, you asked me not to." He gives me a look and for once I can tell what he's thinking – I'm not allowed to tell my best friends, but you get to tell yours.

"Good," I say, nibbling at my lip. The revelations this morning are enough for today. I don't want a barrage of questions about the small dragon on the loose. A scared little dragon who probably thinks I hate him. A sob bubbles up into my throat from nowhere. I'm not someone who usually cries and I sniffle and wipe at my face, puffy and sore from the beating, despite whatever they've been doing to me at this clinic.

"We'll find him, Briony. You don't need to worry."

"Thank you," I say. I lift my hand to take his and squeeze it, then remember that isn't possible. Instead, my hand hangs in mid-air between us and we both stare at it, aware of the invisible wall that hangs between us. One we can't break through. "I will find a way ..." I whisper.

"You don't think I've been trying, that I haven't tried?" he says, although not unkindly.

"Yes, but have you met me?" I smile at him, something he examines with as much intention as my hand. "I'm pretty determined and pretty stubborn."

"You also have other things to worry about."

"Yeah," I say, "a dragon and my sister's death."

"No, getting better. You must have taken one seriously big beating, Briony."

"I ... I honestly don't remember." He shakes his head as if he finds that hard to believe. "My mind sort of just floats away when the pain gets too much. It's ... it's like it's protecting me." I smile flatly. "And then there's unconsciousness which is also quite handy."

"I think they must have been trying to kill you," he says.

"It wouldn't be the first time."

"They will regret it," he says and for the first time I'm not sure that threat is an empty one – hyperbole from some jacked-up shadow weaver high on his own importance.

Thorne means it.

He leaves me in peace after that and although I know the other Princes plus the professor are lurking somewhere outside the room, their mumbled voices carrying through the door, I am alone.

Alone with my thoughts. Which are many and varied and tangled like Rapunzel's locks on a bad hair day.

I've never believed in fate or destiny, mystic powers or star-determined forces before. I thought I knew how the system worked even if everyone else insisted on walking around with the wool pulled over their eyes.

The powerful decide where we end up, which Quarter we serve, how our lives will pan out. Whether we'll live a life of luxury in Onyx, comfortably in Granite or in misery and poverty in Slate. Nothing to do with fate.

Now I'm doubting everything I believed.

It can't be a coincidence that the stone called me to it and that fate has deemed me the mate of the Princes and possibly also Fox.

Fox? Plucked from obscurity in Slate and given a life as a shadow weaver, given powers, given immortality.

My head spins again and I close my eyes and try my best to arrange my tumbling thoughts.

If this is fate, or destiny, or something written in the stars, then why me?

I open my eyes and stare down at my hands. Small and weak, my fingertips calloused, a scar slicing across my palm.

Unless ...

Unless for the first time in my miserable existence fate has decided to lend me a helping hand. I want to find out the truth about my sister and fate has given me four strong shadow weavers to aid me. Four strong shadow weavers and a dragon.

I can't exactly see how that's helpful right now but maybe I have to trust that it is.

Chapter Forty-Eight

Thorne

"You must really like her, huh?" Briony's best friend asks me as he scurries along by my side. We're making our way through the forest, returning to the area where Dray first picked up her scent.

I glance at him and then back to scanning the undergrowth.

"I mean, I bet you wouldn't normally go traipsing through woodland looking for a girl's lost pet. It doesn't really seem like your thing."

"Do you always talk so much?" I mutter.

"Only because you don't speak at all." I stop, searching the undergrowth for something I recognize. He stops beside me, hands on his hips and runs his gaze over me like I'm under inspection. "You just sort of grunt and glare a lot. Not the best of conversationalists, but you've been spending a lot of time together so I'm betting she finds that hot."

"I've been helping her with the dragon."

He sniggers, laughing even harder when I glare at him. "Is that what kids are calling it these days?"

"If it's code for something else, do you want to explain what you've been doing with her?" I growl.

He takes a little step away from me. "I've said this numerous times, it's actually becoming tedious, but she is not my type. And judging by the guys she is into, I am not hers either. Sheesh, you guys really need to rein in the possessive and obsessive vibes."

"Maybe she likes that too."

He smiles. "So he does have a sense of humor."

I snort. "Come on. We're wasting time."

"Have you seen how fast that thing can move?" he says, a few minutes later. "He could be anywhere."

"You're right," I say. I dip into the pocket of my jacket and pull out a small package wrapped in cloth.

"Stars above, what in the realm is that?" Fly says, pinching his nostrils with one hand and waving his other in front of his face.

"Blaze's favorite snack."

I unwind the cloth and hold the dead rat up by the end of its tail.

Fly gags into his hands, his nostrils still pinched. "Gross, that is actually so disgusting."

I wave the rat around in front of me, walking deeper into the forest. We're far from the academy now and soon we'll hit the hilly landscape of the highlands, with all its boulders, crevices and caves. The kind of landscape I suspect might attract a dragon.

"Blaze!" I call. "I got a ratty for you."

Fly cups his hands around his mouth and calls too. "Here, draggie waggie. Good draggie waggie."

I roll my eyes and keep calling the dragon's name, waving the rat about in all directions.

"This isn't working," Fly moans after a few more minutes.

"You don't have much patience," I observe.

"You sound just like my mother."

"Give it time. He has to catch the scent of the rat."

I keep calling while Fly leans against a tree and examines his nails.

After another fifteen minutes there's still no sign of the dragon.

"We should have brought Dray," I mutter. "He would have been able to follow the dragon's scent."

"Can't you use your magic or something?"

"Funnily enough, I don't know any spells for retrieving lost baby dragons."

"But do you know any for retrieving, you know, lost items in general?"

I frown. I hadn't thought of that. I run through the ones I know in my head. None are suitable for this specific task, but there is one I could try to adapt.

I let the shadows race from my fingers (Fly taking four decided steps away from me) and start whispering into the air.

It's a struggle. The shadows are raging hot, bent on destruction, retribution and revenge. They want to crush the people that hurt her. Annihilate them completely. But that will have to wait. Right now, I have a dragon to find.

I keep whispering, my voice rising, as I battle to control

my magic. It soars and sweeps around the trees, and I grit my teeth, battling to keep it under my will.

"Keep back!" I warn Fly as I grapple with it, the words flying from my mouth more quickly.

But it's no good. The shadows are too angry. They tried to kill our mate and revenge is all they want.

With a grunt and a heave, I force them back inside my body. Then I stand there panting and sweating, my breath loud in the suddenly silent forest.

"Wow," Fly says, "that was–"

"Hopeless," I mutter. "Come on. Let's keep searching."

"Do you think she's doing the right thing, not telling the teachers about this dragon?"

"No," I say, "and yes."

Fly bites at his nails. "But, I mean, someone tried to kill her last night. And this time, not just a push from a rope ladder or an electrocution by kite, they nearly beat her to death." He glances up at me with concern in his eyes. "And it sounds like if Professor Tudor hadn't found her, they would have succeeded."

"What electrocution by kite?" I say, dropping my hand down by my side.

"Oh, it's just, err, Iron figure of speech."

"If she wore the collar, she'd be safe."

"Yeah, I've told her that a million times, but she's really damn stubborn. Maybe this will change her mind."

We walk for a few minutes, the top of the first of the Highland hills visible over the tree-line.

"If the officialdom finds out she's been hiding a dragon, she'll be in serious trouble – the kind even Beaufort won't be able to help her escape," I say. Fly nods, and bites at his nail again. "But if she hands the dragon in, there'll be all sorts of questions about where she found the stone, how and why. I can't help feeling that might put her in even more danger."

"You sound like her," he observes. "Are her weird conspiracy theories rubbing off on you?"

"You mean her sister?" He nods. "I think it's strange."

"Hmmm," he says, then lets out a huff of frustration. "We've walked miles. I'm starting to get a blister."

"We need to find him," I say. I can't imagine returning to Briony with the news that we've failed.

"Yeah, I know." He peers at me and the dead rat and then towards the hills, then places a forefinger and a middle finger from each hand in his mouth and blows really hard. A high-pitched whistle sounds through the trees.

At first nothing happens, and I think, like every other attempt to find this dragon, it's going to come to nothing.

Then I hear a distant sound, like the rustle of branches.

"Hear that?" I ask.

"Uh huh," Fly says, standing on his tip toes and scanning the canopy.

The next thing we know a dragon the size of a dog comes swooping out of the trees and snatches the dead rat right from my grasp. He takes off into the canopy immediately afterwards and zooms away out of sight.

"Was that him?" I ask.

"Looked like it. And, do we truly think there could be other dragons out here?"

It's a good point, but I still say, moodily, "He's grown a lot."

"Well, at least we know he's alive," Fly says.

"Yes, but how are we going to convince him to come with us?"

"Got anymore rats in your pockets?"

"No."

"Then beats me."

I consider our options. "We know he's safe," I muse, "and keeping well hidden. I think we leave him until Briony's well enough to come fetch him."

"How long do you think that will be?" Fly says.

"I don't know," I say, thinking of her pale face and the whirring machines. "They nearly killed her."

Chapter Forty-Nine

Beaufort

"Who?" I whisper, my eyes boring into my bond brother's.

"The Hardies' thrall and her band of merry little friends," Dray answers.

"You're sure about that?" Professor Tudor asks, rubbing his fingers through his beard.

"Absolutely. The little bitch stinks of jealousy and envy. It's a real fucking distinct kind of flavor." He wrinkles his nose.

"Kratos put her up to it," I say.

"That's one hell of an accusation to make."

"Was it Kratos who manipulated the maze trial?" I ask the professor, glaring at him. Thorne said he knew who it was. Thorne said the professor would deal with it. Now I understand why he was so damn willing to help.

"No," the professor answers, "and that problem has been dealt with."

I shake my head. We seem to have fucking enemies in all directions.

"Kratos put his thrall up to this. You should have seen the way Kratos was sitting there in the truck on the way back to the academy," I say, "grinning at me like he'd just been named the next Emperor of the realm."

"That isn't exactly evidence."

"I don't give a shit. I'm still going to rip out his throat. Followed by his ball sack ... actually I'm going to go with his ball sack first, then his throat."

"And start a civil war?" the professor dismisses.

"You don't think he was attempting to start a civil war when he tried to get our thrall killed?"

"Something he will deny," the professor points out, "and you have no proof."

I grit my teeth. The professor is right. Not that I have to like it.

"So what you saying, Prof.?" Dray says in outrage, bouncing up on his toes, and getting all up in Tudor's face. "We let him get away with it?"

"No, I'm saying barging in with all your magic firing, instead of thinking about it first, will only lead to trouble. And," he says, clearly identifying our weak spot, "more danger for Briony."

"Shit," Dray says, backing away. Then his gaze flicks to mine. "We won't be able to stop Thorne."

"Does Thorne know who did this?" Tudor asks.

"No, not yet."

"Then I suggest you hold off telling him until we've worked out what to do about this."

"We have to strike back," I say, "if we don't, they'll only

try again and I won't have Briony used as some kind of pawn in their power games."

"We could kill their thrall," Dray says, "an eye for an eye and all that. It would only be fair."

"And you think they wouldn't retaliate in return?" the professor says. "You think that would keep Briony safe?"

Dray lands his hands on the professor's chest and pushes at him. "How about you stop criticizing all our ideas, and start coming up with some of your own suggestions then, brainiac?"

"We could take this through the official route."

I groan, scrubbing at the back of my neck. "Are you serious?"

"You don't think having their thrall expelled would piss the Hardies off?" he says with sarcasm.

"It doesn't exactly seem like a just punishment for what they did, though."

"How about if she were expelled and sent to Slate Quarter?"

Dray bursts out laughing. "Can you imagine the look on that little bitch's face?" He turns to me again. "Could you make it happen?"

"Fuck," I mutter.

Could I? Probably. If I say the right things, make the right promises. I'd also have to reveal information I'd rather keep to myself.

Then again, there doesn't seem to be an alternative. Not one that prevents a war between shadow weaver factions.

"Yeah," I say with very little enthusiasm. "Yeah, probably." I scrub at my face. "I'm still going to beat the shit out of Kratos though." The professor goes to argue with me. "I'll make sure he keeps his ball sack and his throat. But I am going to make him hurt for this."

"Hurting his fragile pride," Tudor says, "will always be more painful to Kratos than anything you can do with your fists."

Dray spends the next hour fidgeting like a toddler on a sugar high, climbing across furniture, raiding a vending machine and interrogating any passing member of staff. After a while I can't take it any longer and send him off on a mission to find out more information about last night, who was involved and how they were persuaded to take part.

He bounds off eagerly, leaving just me and the professor behind.

"He is ... a lot," the professor mutters, rubbing at his eye sockets.

"He's my bond brother," I growl.

"Congratulations," the professor says, showing his fangs off as he pulls a fake smile.

We sit in silence for another hour, both eyeing each other, until the doctor arrives accompanied by two nurses.

Immediately, we both spring to our feet.

"Is there a problem, doctor?" Tudor asks, beating me to it.

"No," she says. "I'm just going to check in on my patient and give her another dose of treatment."

"Will this heal her completely? Will she need more? Was there any permanent damage?" I word vomit.

"Beaufort Lincoln?" she says, staring at me with surprise.

"She's our thrall," I say, answering her obvious question: why the hell are you interested in this girl from Slate?

"How about I finish this treatment and then come back to update you?"

"I'd like to observe the treatment."

The doctor hesitates, obviously unsure whether she can refuse me.

"Come on, Lincoln," the professor says, slamming his cold hand on my shoulder. "Let's leave the doctor to do what she needs to do in peace."

I consider arguing the point but I want Briony healed – the sooner the better.

The doctor nods hesitantly and then ducks inside the room with the two nurses. I sit back in the chair, watching the minutes tick past on my wristwatch, wondering how long this could take.

Her injuries must be bad if it's taking this long, if they're keeping her in the clinic like this.

I rub at my cheeks with my hands and peer at the professor.

He's still here, unwilling to leave her side.

Is he telling the truth? Is she his mate as well as ours?

I remember my mother telling me never to trust a bloodsucker. Then again she made it clear I shouldn't trust anyone. Some days I wonder if I can even trust her.

And what if he is telling the truth? What the hell does that mean?

This girl from Slate Quarter – scars on her back from where she's been abused – has not just three powerful mates, she has four.

I strain to see that vision in my mind's eye. It had been so fucking fleeting and yet so vivid, so intense. I hadn't just seen it. I'd felt it in my bones, in my blood, in my marked soul. But had there been a fifth person in that vision? A fourth mate? Another man?

Perhaps there had been – a shadow, lurking in the background.

"What do you think it means?" I ask the professor.

"I think she was badly injured and the doctor needs time to heal her properly."

"No, I mean – us, her." I meet his glowing eyes. "Do you really think fate has brought the five of us together?"

"All I know is that it has brought me to her."

"I'll have to take your word for that."

"Yeah, and I'll have to take yours."

We stare at each other. The professor rubs his fingers against his bearded chin.

"I don't know why fate has brought us together. But I guess we'll find out."

"I don't like surprises," I say petulantly.

"Life is full of surprises. It's the one constant you can depend on."

Except I have the vision. Tiny insights into what's coming. If only I could have one that would answer this question.

"Have you told anyone?" he asks me. "About your situation with the girl."

"No, as far as anyone else knows she's just our thrall." I hold his gaze. "I'd like to keep it that way. And I'm assuming you won't be telling anyone about your situation, seeing as you're her teacher." I spit the last word and he draws his hands down his face.

"No, I won't be telling anyone." He drops his hands into his lap. "But before you ask, no, I won't be staying away from her either. I tried that, and it nearly got her killed. Twice."

"I'm sleeping with her," I say, not sure if I say it as a

boast or to provoke the dude. "It won't be long before Dray is too."

"She get a say in that?" he growls.

"She gets a very big say in that." I smirk.

"Real mature," he mutters.

I lean back in my chair. "Do you want to sleep with her, Professor?"

"I think that's her choice to make and none of your business."

"She's my girl. Of course, it's my business."

"She's my mate," he says, "it's inevitable."

I hold his gaze, jealousy erupting around my body, but I can't deny the truth of the statement. The attraction between mates is too strong. No matter how hard two people fight it – destiny and desire combined are two brutal forces.

"It seems to me we have two choices, Beaufort." He leans against the wall, folding his arms over his broad chest. "We can be rivals. We can fight for her attention and her affection. We can make each other's lives and hers hell. Or we can accept the situation as it is and work together to keep that girl safe. Because," he says, "whatever our fate, I suspect it has something special in store for her – I can't understand why it would have brought the three of you together, and then brought all of us to her otherwise."

I'm quiet for sometime, mulling over his words as voices murmur in the room behind and machinery somewhere deeper in the clinic whirs away.

"Okay," I say finally, "I think we should work together."

"Does that mean," he says, eyes locked on me, "that if she wants to be with me, you won't stand in our way?"

"Are you asking me if you can sleep with her?"

"It's not your choice." He hesitates. "But I'd like to know you were okay with it all the same?"

I scoff. "It's hard enough knowing I have to share her with two other men as it is — and they are my bond brothers–"

"I'm not exactly thrilled with the idea myself," he mumbles.

My hands are damp with perspiration and I rub them along my thighs.

"But then sometimes I think about what it would be like to share her ..."

I let that idea hang in the air and we're silent again.

"It's her choice," the professor repeats.

Chapter Fifty

B riony

I'm dozing when the door opens again and the doctor comes in accompanied by two nurses.

"Ahh, you're awake," she says, striding to the machines above my head and checking the readings. "How are you feeling?"

"Fine," I say, "very ready to leave."

"Are you?" She laughs. "Most of my patients appreciate the opportunity to rest and have a break from the academy."

"I'd rather get back to my friends."

"And we'll get you back to them as fast as we can." I nod eagerly. "But not until we're 100% satisfied that you're better."

"You know the treatment isn't quite so thorough over at the commoners' clinic."

"Yes," the doctor says, stiffly, "but this is the shadow

weaver clinic. You're very fortunate Professor Tudor brought you here. That the Princes are your protectors. I'm not sure they would have had the resources or the skills to have saved you over at the commoners' clinic."

"That hardly seems fair, does it?" I say, just as stiffly.

The doctor ignores my comment, taking my arm in her hand and feeling for my pulse. "Much stronger." She closes her eyes and I feel her magic penetrate under my skin and into my body. "The healing is working," she murmurs, "although there is still some damage to that ruptured spleen," one of the nurses scribbles down notes on a clip-board, "and some bleeding on that right kidney." She opens her eyes and looks at me. "They really gave you a thorough kicking."

"Uh huh," I say, despite all the healing the doctor has done, my body is still littered with bruises and cuts from the attack.

She closes her eyes again. "I'm going to work on healing these some more. It may feel a little uncomfortable." She mumbles something under her breath, her brow crinkling with concentration, and a peculiar sensation crawls under my skin.

I was unconscious for the previous healing by the medical staff and she is right, it isn't exactly pleasant. Not like when Beaufort has healed me. That was incredibly pleasant, bordering on seductive. This is not. I grit my teeth and try to think about something else.

The minutes tick by and a sheen of sweat appears on the doctor's brow as sweat trickles down my neck. I want to ask her to stop but she must already think I'm a complete pathetic weakling.

Finally, however, she does, releasing my hand with a loud exhale of air.

She wipes the back of her hand over her brow.

"There," she says, squeezing my shoulder. "The spleen is healed and the kidney has stopped bleeding. I may need to do some more work on that. I'll check again in a few hours." She smiles at me. "You did well."

"I did?" I say, surprised.

"Oh yeah," she says, "most grown men are begging me to stop after just a few minutes."

The nurses titter and they gather up their equipment and head to the door.

"We'll be back in another couple of hours to check on you. If you need anything in the meantime, just ring the buzzer."

"Thank you," I say. I hesitate. There's something else I want to ask the doctor, but I'm not sure if I'm brave enough.

She's almost through the door, following the nurses, when I make up my mind that I am. "Doctor?"

"Yes?" she says.

"Could I ... could I talk to you alone for a moment?"

She shuts the door behind her and walks back over to the bed. "How can I help?" she asks.

"Does doctor–patient confidentiality apply in this clinic?" I bet it does for the shadow weavers but do the same rules apply to me?

"Of course." She eyes me. "If you are at all concerned you may have been pregnant–"

"Pregnant?!" I screech. "No!"

"We ran a test just to make sure. It's surprisingly common."

"That ... that wasn't it." I shake my head. "We use protection." My cheeks sizzle.

She nods. "We can give you the shot if you're interested. It's more reliable."

"Thank you." Maybe that doesn't sound like such a bad idea. "That would be good. But that wasn't what I wanted to ask you about … although I guess it is sort of related."

She looks at me with puzzlement. "Are you worried about sexually transmitted diseases, because we checked for those too."

"Good to know," I say, with a half-smile. "Can you … do you know much about fated mates? I mean, scientifically or medically."

The book the library threw at me (literally) had a lot of information, but most of it read like myth and legend. There was nothing scientific about it.

She stares at me and then her eyes drift to the door. I don't know if she suspects I'm talking about me and the Princes – me, the Princes and the professor. But I bet if she did suspect that, she'd dismiss it pretty quickly. Then again, it would account for the fact they're all lurking about the hospital.

"It isn't my area of expertise, but I do know a little. What would you like to know?"

"If there's any truth in it. If it's all just mumbo jumbo."

"No more than any other type of magic," she says.

"It just sounds so incredible."

"I've brought patients back to life who were on the brink of death – including, Miss Storm, you. A lot of magic is incredible."

"But how does it–"

"Work?" She slides her hands into the pockets of her white coat and considers my question. "It is hard to explain when you aren't a shadow weaver yourself." She clicks her tongue, searching for a way of explaining. "The magic that exists in our veins is a part of us, is ours, but it also has a mind of its own." She scoffs. "That may sound ridiculous to someone who can't wield magic."

"It doesn't," I say, thinking of the way Thorne struggles to control his magic.

"I don't have a fated mate, but the way I've heard it explained is that sometimes our magic meets its match. Magic to which it has a connection." She jingles something in her pocket. "Of course, there are theories that all magic originated from one place – that it was split and given to shadow weavers. That each time a shadow weaver is born that magic is split a bit more. It's why some people believe our magic is weakening over time. And that with the phenomena of fated mates – it's just the magic recombining."

"Weakening?" I say. I've never heard that before.

The doctor blinks as if just realizing who she's talking to.

"It's just one theory," she mumbles.

"And how is that different from bond brothers?"

"Gosh, I don't know. A romantic would say because there's love involved. A cynic because there's a sexual attraction. Either way, I believe the connection between fated mates is even stronger than it is between bonded brothers – or sisters."

"But I don't have magic," I say, "so how could this apply to me?"

"To you?" She shakes her head. "I don't believe it's possible for a commoner – someone without magic – to have a fated mate."

I fall silent, considering the implication of her words.

"Was there anything else?"

"No, no, that was all. Thank you."

"Good, then try and rest. I'm hoping we'll have you out of here tomorrow."

She leaves and a few minutes later, there's a knock on the door.

"Come in," I murmur still lost in my thoughts.

The professor enters followed by Beaufort.

"Is Thorne back yet?" I ask.

"No," Beaufort says, "not yet." I nod my head. "The doctor says you're making good progress towards healing."

"Yeah," I say, wringing the blanket between my hands.

"What's wrong?" Fox asks. "If you're worried about things between all of us, we've talked it out."

I swing my gaze from Fox to Beaufort. "Talked what out exactly?" And is it my imagination or do both these hulking great men with boundless powers look down right sheepish?

"We are going to work together to protect you," Fox says.

"If you think I'm going to be *your* thrall–"

"You're my mate," he says.

"We won't stand in your way of that," Beaufort mumbles, not looking particularly happy. Is he suggesting ... I swallow.

"Do you ever feel like things are spiraling out of your control?" I whisper. "That nothing makes sense around you and you're struggling to hold all the pieces together at once – to understand what it can mean?"

Fox meets my gaze. "All the time."

"Yeah," I say. "But I feel like the answer is right there staring me in the face ... it's just out of my reach. Only, I can't quite grasp it, can't quite bring it into focus."

Chapter Fifty-One

D ray

I let myself into the Hardies' tower. No one is home and so I stroll through the first floor. Their tower isn't as luxurious as ours but the layout is similar. On this floor there is a kitchen and a lounge. I wander into the lounge, laugh at the fucking awful decor, then stride into the kitchen, pull out a chair and take a seat, swinging my booted feet up onto the table-top. I take my gum from my pocket, unwrap the silver foil and pop it into my mouth.

You see, if Beaufort was serious about me leaving Kratos and the others alone, he wouldn't have sent me off without a babysitter. He knows exactly where I'd go and exactly what I'd do. Heck, I bet he's counting on it.

I tap my fingers on the table, chewing on my gum, my toes tapping out a rhythm.

My magic vibrates in my veins, pushing at my fingertips and I swing my gaze around. I could take a leaf out of our little kitten's book and trash this room. Then again, trashing Kratos's face will be a lot more fun.

I don't consider the fact that there are three of them until the front door opens and I hear their voices.

They're fucking high as kites. And I know why. The anger in my veins roars.

"I'm in here, dickwads," I call out. This has already taken too long. I want to get to the bit where I make them beg for mercy.

The chattering stops and then the three of them are standing in the doorway. Kratos at the front. First there's shock on his face, but it's quickly replaced by a smirk when he sees it's just me.

I guess I am alone. Outnumbered, and Thorne is the one with the terrifying reputation.

That's the thing about me. People never see it coming. Because I smile and crack the odd joke. Because I have the face I have, they think I'm good. They don't see how bad I really am until it's too late.

"Hey fellas," I say. I blow a fuck-off big bubble with my gum and let it pop with a bang.

"Good to see you, Dray," Kratos says, cracking the knuckles of his right fist into his left palm.

I spit my gum onto the floor.

"Well, I'd like to say the feeling was mutual, but I'd be lying."

"Although, I'm a little surprised," Kratos says. "I thought you'd be by your thrall's bedside. Rumor has it she had a little accident."

I swing my boots lazily off the table and rise to my feet,

the tension in the room soaring dramatically. "Now, we all know it was no accident. And we all know who was behind it. Which means we all know why I'm here."

I grin at them all. They peer round one another with an obvious air of a group of men who believe they have the upper hand. They don't.

"You been sniffing too much grass, Eros." Kratos's second, Prentice, laughs. "'Cause you're talking bullshit."

The smile melts slowly from my face. "I'm not." I tap the side of my nose. "The thing about scents is they never lie – unlike people – so, you see, there's no doubt in mind who was responsible, and while you boys may not have been there, may not have thrown the punches or kicked her body," I say, my voice quiet and deadly, "I know you were behind it."

"You know fuck all," Kratos sneers.

I could transform straight into wolf form and tear these shadow weavers from limb to limb in a matter of seconds. It wouldn't be the first time. People believe Thorne is the most powerful and dangerous weaver in the academy but that's because they've never seen my wolf at his most deadly. But – despite what Beau and Tudor may believe – I've no interest in endangering our mate by starting a civil war. The wolf is out of the question – I don't know if I could prevent myself from going for the kill.

It'll have to be the old human form.

A form that can still do a hell of a lot of damage.

"You've got two choices here, boys," I tell them. "You can get down on your knees and beg for forgiveness, grovel your little hearts out and come up with some damned inventive ways to make it up to our thrall – including giving me the names of all those who were involved. Or ..." I grin because obviously I'm hoping they'll choose the latter option, "I can make you hurt real bad."

Kratos scoffs. "There are three of us, Eros, and one of you."

"Yeah," I say, "but you're a bunch of pathetic dickheads who can barely wield a fart, let alone a shadow."

It's all the reason they need, the three of them are charging me at once, their magic shooting across the kitchen.

I lift my arm and let it bounce off me as if their magic is nothing more than raindrops. Then with a yawn, I open my fist and let all the shadows that have been raging since I smelled her blood on the forest floor, blast towards them.

You see, that's what all these losers don't understand. They think it's about control and intellect. They think they can study hard, work out in the gym, train on the field, and one day they'll be as powerful as me. But shadow weaving isn't about that. It's about feeling and emotion. It's about your fucking soul. And right now my fucking feelings are vengeful, angry and destructive and nothing in the entire realm could stop them.

My shadows hit the three men with an explosion, sending all of them tumbling, groaning as they hit the ground.

I laugh.

"Ahhh, maybe I'm being unfair. You wanna do this the old-fashioned way?" I roll up my sleeves. "No magic?"

Kratos scrambles up onto his knees and fires magic my way; I swerve out of its path and stride towards him. The others are up on their feet too and together they send another flurry of blasts my way. I deflect some, dodge some others, but one hits my shoulder.

"Fuck." I laugh, as it singes through my shirt and burns my skin. "That feels good."

It's nothing like Thorne's magic. That was so freaking painful, such all-consuming agony, I'm still waking in the night bathed in sweat just dreaming about it.

Their magic is like foreplay in comparison. It's a pain that reminds me I'm alive. That in fact, I live for this shit. I'm a shifter after all – hunt and fuck – it's in my blood, imprinted in my brain.

A couple more strides and I'm right in front of them. I swing my fist, hitting Kratos's heavy jaw. It cracks and so do my knuckles, pain ricocheting through my wrist, up my arm and into my shoulder. He hits me back and someone else jabs me in the ribs as another attempts to coil their magic around my neck.

I may be in human form but I'm feral now. All wolf.

I snarl. I snap my jaws. I hit and kick. Blast them with fire, zap them with sparks, strangle one with cords of shadow.

They fight back and my dislocated shoulder and the burn on my chest aren't the only injuries, but I'm winning, I'm in charge.

Soon Prentice is out cold on the floor, and Nathan is so dazed he's stumbling around on his feet.

And Kratos, he's on his knees after all, my grazed knuckles wrapped around his throat as he struggles for air.

I spit out a mouthful of blood and grin at him.

"You see, Kratos, that's the thing about us wolves. We grow up in packs. Fighting three of you at once is a piece of piss."

Kratos face has turned an attractive shade of purple and the blood vessels in his eyes are popping like corn.

"This is your warning. You only get one. Next time you touch our thrall – next time you send someone else to touch her – will be the last thing you do. Because I will kill you."

I laugh again, little specks of blood showering Kratos's desperate face and then I release him, being sure to step on the unconscious dude's ball sack as I walk out of the room.

"Thanks for the entertainment," I call out as I step through the front door, leaving it hanging open on its hinges. "I'll be sure to come again."

Chapter Fifty-Two

B riony

The doctor releases me from the clinic the next day, instructing me to return in three days time for a follow up.

The Princes are waiting to escort me back, and to my utter surprise, they've come bearing gifts – a bunch of red roses and a very large box of chocolates.

"What are these for?" I ask with suspicion. Apart from the clothes Clare gifted me, the dress Fly made for me and the necklace I'm pretty sure Dray stole, it's been an exceedingly long time since anyone gave me a present.

Dray looks down at the bunch of flowers he has in his hand with confusion.

"Isn't this what you're meant to get people when they stay in hospital?" He glances at his friends. "Isn't this what girls like?"

"I didn't say I didn't like them," I say. "It's just ... you've never really given me gifts before." My gaze flits around them with embarrassment, trying not to let Odessa's words bug me.

"Huh?" Dray says. "Seem to remember gifting you several mind-blowing orgasms, Kitten."

"And a collar," Beaufort growls. I nibble my lip and he seems to soften. "You're our mate," Beaufort whispers. "And we want to buy you things. So if there's anything else you want ..."

"Err, thank you?" I say, gazing at the gifts, a warmth spreading through my chest.

"How are you feeling?" Thorne asks me from two paces away.

"I feel dandy as a daisy." I sigh. "However, apparently, I'm not 100% cured yet and once all the medication wears off later today, I'm going to feel the beating I underwent." I sigh even more dramatically. "And let me guess what we'll be doing this afternoon – circuits."

"I think it's another assault course," Dray says. "Want us to get you out of it?"

I shake my head. After that attack, it's even more clear to me how much everyone in this academy hates me. I don't want to give them yet another reason.

Despite the relatively early hour, students are already out on the pathways this morning, many gathered in groups and gossiping to one another. As usual, the appearance of me with the Princes has them halting mid-sentence and gaping at us open-mouthed. It's even more blatant today and I'm guessing that's because the vultures have been feasting on the news of my attack and my visit to the shadow weaver clinic.

The climb up the stairs to my room is not as easy as

usual. My legs feel weak and I'm forced to stop once when I wobble.

"I'm definitely getting you out of that assault course," Dray mumbles.

"I'll be fine by this afternoon." I'm going to need to be. The next trial is only two weeks away and I can't afford to miss out on training and learning.

These Princes may have convinced themselves that I am their fated mate – that they're going to whisk me away to Onyx Quarter no matter what the outcome of the trials. But I know differently. The doctor said it herself – commoners without magic cannot have fated mates. They're mistaken. And yet, a little optimism must have rubbed off on me from somewhere, because I seem to believe I can score some points in the next trial and make it out of Slate. At least, I think I can if I can walk without keeling over.

At the top of the stairs, we meet Fly who flings his arms around me and hugs me tight.

"Jeez," he mumbles in my ear, "were you always this tiny?"

"Apparently I lost quite a bit of blood."

"Not the best way to lose weight," he says, looking me over. "They're not seriously making her do classes today, are they? She looks hideous."

"Thanks," I say flatly.

"I said we could get her out of it, but you know Briony."

"Hmmm," Fly says, taking my hand and dragging me into my room, closing the door in the Princes' faces.

"Hey!" Dray protests.

"She needs to get changed into her uniform," Fly calls through the door.

"And you get to watch that happen and we don't *because...*"

"No one is watching me change," I call back, going to lie down on the bed and catch my breath. Fly flops down beside me, the biggest grin on his face that I've ever seen.

"Are you okay?" I ask him.

"Am I okay? I'm freaking ecstatic. This may be the best day of my life and that is something considering one time Caelan Manship took it upon himself to show me where my prostate–"

"Best day of your life?" I interrupt. "Because I'm back?"

"No! Well, that too but ..." He examines my face. "You don't know, do you?" He glances at the door and shakes his head. "They didn't tell you."

"Didn't tell me what?" I say, rolling up to sit. This doesn't sound good. "Is it about Blaze?"

"No!" He takes my hand in his, grinning even more widely than before – so wide I'm scared his cheeks may split. "Odessa."

"Odessa?"

"Odessa has been expelled from the academy."

I stare at him in absolute shock. Expelled? Odessa? "No ... that can't be ..."

"It is. I, along with most of the rest of the students and faculty, watched her being marched off the academy grounds last night. And," he says, doing a little dance of excitement on the bed, "that isn't even the best bit?"

"Really?" I say, because Fly is right, that news has made my day. Probably my year. "Guess where she was sent back to?"

"Iron Quarter. Isn't that where she's from?"

"Nope, Slate."

"Fuck the stars above! What did she do?"

"What did she do?! Oh Cupcake, did most of your brain cells get knocked out in that beating?"

"Quit the wisecracks and just tell me."

"She was behind the attack. She masterminded the whole thing – recruited some of the other students and then led them to attack you. And each of those students has been punished too. They've each lost one hundred points off their score."

"Oh."

"Oh? That's all you've got to say about this?"

"Are you nearly ready in there?" Dray calls through the door.

"Nearly," I yell back, going to fetch my uniform out of my closet.

"But Odessa's done loads of shitty things like that before – remember my nose," I point to my face, "remember how she pushed me off that cargo net?"

"Yes, but you never reported those things before. So she never got caught doing them."

"I didn't report this attack either," I point out.

"I think you have Beaufort to thank for that," Fly says, inclining his head towards the door. I motion for him to turn around, and start stripping out of the clothes the clinic lent me for the short walk back to my room. "And possibly Professor Tudor too – although I'm not entirely sure how he's involved in all this."

"He found me," I explain, threading my arms through my shirt and quickly fastening the buttons. "How about the Hardies?"

"What about the Hardies?"

"Their thrall just got herself expelled, aren't they going to be pissed about it? Won't they come for Beaufort?"

"Their thrall tried to kill you!" Fly points out. "I don't think they can exactly complain. Anyway," he shrugs, "I guess they'll just find another."

"Because we're that easily replaced," I deadpan.

"Nope," he says, waving his arms above his head. "You are irreplaceable, Cupcake." He peeks over his shoulder to find me dressed. "Which is why I'm so damn pleased you're okay and that psychopath is gone."

"Yeah," I say, letting out a long exhale. Funny, but I am relieved she's no longer here. One less person to watch for over my shoulder.

The Princes aren't happy about me breakfasting in the canteen with my friends, using a combination of threats, persuasion and offers of sexual favors to tempt me into coming with them to the shadow weaver dining hall. I resist, although I have serious second thoughts when it dawns on me that the events of the last forty-eight hours are like nothing the students have experienced so far. This gossip is so hot it's burning literal holes and as a starring role in the events, the interest in me will be quadrupled.

We grab the table in the far corner and I hunker down as best I can but people crane their heads to get a look at me and several invent reasons to walk past our table simply to stare.

"I need some sunglasses," I mutter, trying to shield my face with my arms, "and a wig. Jeez, why can't people stop staring?"

"Because you got Odessa Gunvald expelled, and she was hated by most people in the academy. You're a hero," Clare explains.

"Hated?" I sniff. "Odessa was worshipped and adored."

"Worshipped maybe, not adored," Fly says. "People

were scared of her and what she'd do – that's why they sucked up to her."

"Tell that to her best friend," I groan.

The girl with no teeth who broke my nose is glaring right at me with a hatred that's palatable.

"She's down to forty-three points. Plus, Adrianna has been in love with Odessa for like forever," Fly dismisses, "because Adrianna has even fewer brain cells than you now own."

"Did something happen to your brain cells?" Clare asks with concern.

"Doctor says she lost about half in that beating," Fly teases.

Clare gasps with horror.

"He's joking, Clare," I tell her, ripping a corner off my toast and chucking it at Fly's head. "My brain is fine – at least I think it is."

"Your brain was never fine, Cupcake."

"I assume neither was yours – that's how we became friends."

"Touché!" He turns to Clare. "In conclusion, I think her brain is working just fine."

I laugh, which has everyone in the canteen looking my way.

"Oh, jeez," I mutter, relieved when the bell clangs meaning it's time to head off for classes.

"Will you be here for lunch?" Clare asks, gripping my arm as we follow the crowd out of the canteen. "Considering you weren't gone that long, you missed out on loads. I have so much to tell you." She glances through the crowd toward the boy from her History class and I understand.

"I can't wait to hear all about it." I squeeze her hand. After all, I have quite a bit to tell my friends myself.

Chapter Fifty-Three

B riony

I stare out at the assault course in front of me with apprehension. The last time I tackled this course was right at the beginning of my time at the academy. It seems like an absolute lifetime ago. On that occasion, I'd nearly fallen to my death. Okay, the person responsible for my fall is no longer here, but having just survived another assassination attempt I'm not exactly feeling confident, especially as my legs have morphed into jello and the pain medication has most definitely worn off.

Then there's the way Adrianna – Odessa's best friend – is glaring at me like she'd like to reach down my throat and rip out my heart.

I swing up and down on my toes, trying to find some sort of enthusiasm, waiting for one of the troll twins to blow their whistle and signal our start.

When he does, I set off at a slow jog. I don't have it in my legs right now to run at my usual speed. I haven't run two meters, though, when Dray and Beaufort appear out of nowhere flanking either of my sides and Thorne positions himself behind me.

"Wh-wh-what are you doing?" I ask.

"Making sure you get through this course without any serious injury," Beaufort explains.

We reach the first obstacle. A series of tires fixed to the ground. Other students are already hopping through them.

"Right," Dray says, scooping me up into his arms and skipping through the field of tires with ease.

"Is this even allowed?" I squeal.

"Do I give a shit?" he says, placing me back on my feet when we reach the end, the others right there with us.

"I can do this myself," I point out. They all look at me like I really did lose all those brain cells. "Fine, okay," I mutter, setting off on that slow jog towards the next obstacle, wanting the ground to open up and swallow me as Beaufort lifts me up and over a short wall blocking our path, handing me to Dray on the other side, who lowers me down.

"This is fun," he says, giving my ass a playful slap as we set off.

"This is your idea of fun?"

"Yeah, this course is usually way too easy. This makes it more of a challenge."

Although, I'm not sure it makes it that much of a challenge. They lift me through, over and along each piece of apparatus with ease.

Then we reach the monkey bars.

"There's no way you can help with this one," I say, watching the student in front of us try and fail to swing to the other side, landing down in the mud.

"Huh," Beaufort snorts, lifting me again and going to wade straight through the mud.

"There are spikes in there!" I warn him.

Thorne lifts his hand and his shadow magic swoops through the mud and plucks out each of the spikes, clearing Beaufort's path for him.

"You underestimate us, sweetheart," Beaufort says, staring down into my face in a way that has my pulse rate fluttering.

"Perhaps, but you're trashing your sneakers."

We're nearing the end of the course, when I realize I'm actually enjoying this. Sure, that's partly because I'm doing none of the hard work. But I've never hung out with the Princes like this before and they make me smile. They make me laugh.

At the end of the course, Dray leans in to whisper in my ear as we jog along. "We're going to leave you now, Kitten. We have to make it look a bit believable."

I wave them off and a few minutes later I'm crossing the line.

Twin number one peers at his stopwatch.

"You managed that pretty quick."

"Yeah, I'm getting better at this stuff," I lie.

"You're hardly even sweating."

I shrug and go off to wait on the grass for Fly and Clare.

Fly's the first to arrive, panting and out of breath. He rests his hands on his knees, sweat dripping onto the ground.

"You look much better than you did," he observes. "There's color in your cheeks."

"Is there?" I say, innocently.

"You looked like," he winks at me, "you were having fun."

"I don't know what gave you that impression."

"No, because what's not to like about two seriously hot men carrying you around."

I stick my tongue out at him and he comes to sit beside me. Clare is one of the last to stumble over the line.

"Are you coming to the changing rooms?" she asks me. "No Odessa to worry about now."

"Nope, I'm not taking any risks." I nudge Fly.

We've agreed that Thorne and Fly will take me out to the forest to find Blaze.

We weave our way through the academy buildings and out onto the field. The sight of the forest has bile rising up my throat and I have to pause for a moment and force myself to breathe.

"Okay, Cupcake?" Fly asks.

"Yeah ... it's just." I shake my head. "The last time I was here ..."

"What's wrong?"

I turn around to find Thorne examining me with concern.

"Nothing," I say.

"Are you sure you can manage this? It's a fair distance and I can't carry you like the others."

"It's fine," I say. "Fly can."

"Err," Fly protests.

"Come on, let's find Blaze."

"You got one of those tasty snacks again, Thorne?" Fly asks him.

"What tasty snack?" I ask, but Thorne's already striding on ahead, seeming to have forgotten already that my legs don't have their usual strength.

Soon the sun's setting above us, the last of the day's rays racing across the sky and painting it maroon, the temperature dropping rapidly until my breath hangs in a fog of smoke around my face.

"This is where I was attacked," I murmur a few minutes later.

"Yes, we discovered the place," Thorne says. "Or Dray and his nose did."

"You're lucky Professor Tudor found you," Fly says as we carry on deeper into the forest, the color leeching from the sky as it darkens. "I feel really bad that I didn't realize you hadn't returned."

"Hmm," Thorne mumbles, clearly agreeing.

"It's not your fault a bunch of psychos decided to attack me," I say. I peer through the trees. Above the canopy the dark outline of the first of the Highland hills looms large. "I can't believe he came this far."

"It's not too much further." Thorne cups his hands and starts calling.

I follow suit and Fly places his fingers in his mouth and whistles really damn loud.

There's a ruffle in the trees beyond us and then Blaze comes shooting through the trees like a bow from an arrow. He hurtles right at me, landing on my shoulder and attacking my face with his tongue.

A sob of relief escapes my throat. I was so worried he'd hate me – that he wouldn't forgive me for sending him away like I did.

"Gross!" Fly says.

"He's happy to see me," I say, wrapping my arms around the little dragon and hugging him to me. "And I missed him too. Oh Blaze, I'm so glad you're okay!"

I litter his scaly head in kisses of my own. He's heavier than he was a few days ago and bigger. I roll him over onto his back, checking his body for any signs of injury.

He has a few minor scratches here and there but nothing major.

"Oh you poor baby," I say as he nuzzles his head under my chin. "Were you scared?"

"Have you seen the size of his round little tummy?" Fly says. "I bet he's been having the time of his life!"

"Unlikely. He was all alone, and he probably thought I'd abandoned him." I stroke my hand down his spine and he purrs. "I was just trying to keep you safe. I would never ever abandon you, Blaze. I promise."

"You shouldn't make promises you can't keep," Thorne says.

"Well, I intend to keep this one."

"Really?" Fly asks me, "even when he's grown to the size of our tower?"

"I'll find a way," I say stubbornly, even if I know they are both correct. This situation isn't sustainable. I can keep Blaze hidden in my room for now and fed on a diet of rats and mice but that won't last forever. He's going to get too big, too loud and too smelly. "Come on, let's go home."

He wriggles from my arms and for a while he's happy to flap alongside us as we walk back through the forest. Then he gets bored, buzzing off to chase squirrels or harass the night-time birds emerging from their nests. When we start to near the academy, where the forest begins to thin, he lands on a branch and refuses to go any further.

"Come on, Blaze. We've got to get back." I beckon him over but he doesn't move, quirking his head to one side and staring at me with his big golden eyes. I stride over to the tree he's occupying and reach up to pluck him from the branch, but he flutters out of my reach and goes to sit on the branch above.

"Blaze," I say, "this isn't funny. We can come back to the forest tomorrow."

He makes a little whining noise at the back of his throat.

"I think he wants to stay here, Cupcake."

"Well, he can't!" I stamp my foot. "Blaze, come here right now."

The dragon lowers his head and whines again.

"Fly, will you get him down?"

Fly doesn't look happy about it, but he walks towards the tree and reaches upwards. Immediately, Blaze jumps up and sends a blast of fire Fly's way.

Fly screeches and jumps back, but not quite in time, the flames singeing the very top of his hair. He swears, patting at his head.

"The little shit," he mumbles.

"Blaze," I say, wagging my finger at him, "that wasn't very nice."

"He could have melted my face off!" Fly protests.

"Maybe it's safer if he does stay out in the forest," Thorne says.

"But he's so little and all alone."

"He's not so little anymore, Briony. He's the size of a doberman. And he can clearly look after himself."

"I don't know," I say. The truth is, in the month we've spent together, I've enjoyed his company more than I could have imagined. I can't bear the thought of being parted with him.

"He seems happy out here, Cupcake. I'm not sure it's very fair to keep him locked up in your room."

"But someone might find him out here," I protest, despite knowing Fly makes a very fair point.

"No one comes this far out into the forest," Fly says.

"And you could come back and visit him every night,

check he's okay," Thorne suggests. "As long as you bring one of us with you."

"Not me!" Fly says glaring at the dragon.

"He didn't mean it," I mumble. "I don't think this is a good idea."

"You should tell Beaufort and Dray about him," Thorne says. "Then one of us can accompany you out here each night to see him."

"I don't know," I say, "what if someone found him? What if something happened to him?"

But Blaze doesn't give me any choice because in the next moment he's flying away.

Chapter Fifty-Four

Briony

With Blaze hanging out in the forest and not locked up in my room, there's no reason to hurry off after dinner, so I go with Fly and Clare back to her room to hang out.

"There's so much to talk about," Clare says as we drop down onto her floor and I rip open the box of chocolates the Princes gave me, staring down at them in disbelief.

"They're so beautiful," I say. "I think they may be too pretty to eat."

"Fuck that," Fly says, dipping his fingers into the box, plucking out one of the carefully decorated chocolates and plopping it straight into his waiting mouth. "Oh my goodness, forget magic, these would be enough to heal you!" He closes his eyes and groans.

Clare and I look at each other, then follow suit.

The chocolate melts across my tongue immediately and

Fly is right. It's one of the best things I've tasted in my entire life. Chocolate was a rarity back in Slate and the one time I got to try it, the chocolate was powdery and hardly very sweet. This is like a taste explosion – like a freaking orgasm – in my mouth.

"I think it may be worth nearly being beaten to death just to have a box of these," I say, rolling down to lie on the carpet and savor the flavors dancing around my mouth. "So," I glance up at Clare, "how's things going with Damian?"

"Okay ... I think."

"More than okay," Fly says, picking another chocolate from the box, "they spent yesterday evening sucking each other's faces off."

Clare's face turns bright red, but she also smiles shyly. "We did. It was the best." Her eyes go a little dreamy, then she snaps out of it. "I hope you don't think that was really bad of me when you were recovering in a hospital bed."

"I told her it was really truly awful," Fly says sarcastically, "that a true friend would have spent the night lighting candles and holding a vigil."

"Stop picking on Clare," I tell him, "or I won't let you eat any more of my chocolates."

"Clare," he says, fluttering his eyelashes, "I'm truly sorry."

"But maybe it was a bit insensitive of me."

"Nope, that makes me really happy to know things are happening between you."

"How much *exactly* is happening between you?" Fly asks, waggling his eyebrows.

"Just a bit of kissing so far. Although he did slide his hand up into my shirt."

"Erotic," Fly mumbles.

"Ignore him," I tell Clare. "He doesn't own a pair of tits so he has no idea how good that feels."

"It did feel good," she says, nibbling her lip. "We're going to spend Sunday hanging out together ... if the two of you don't mind."

"Briony's been ditching us regularly for the last few weeks. Of course she doesn't."

"Of course I don't." I hold the box of chocolates out to Clare and she takes another.

"I do have another piece of news that may make up for my poor behavior."

"Ooo," I say, rolling up and selecting another chocolate for myself. "What is it? Has Fly been sucking people's faces off too?"

"I wish!"

"Nope, it's about your sister. I think I found something of interest in the second yearbook. Have you asked the Princes about those names yet?"

I shake my head, then place the chocolate into my mouth and chomp through it with my teeth. "What did you find out?"

"It seems it wasn't Professor Tudor teaching the fundamentals of shadow weaving back then."

"Yeah, he said he wasn't here when she was. He must have joined the teaching staff afterwards." I wonder what that means – when did he become a vampire? Was it at the academy? Or afterwards?

I'm half tempted to return to the library and find his yearbooks just so I can discover every little piece of information about him too.

But Fox Tudor isn't what I should be focusing on right now – even if my head is still spinning with that revelation.

"Exactly. It was a teacher called Professor Turmeric.

And I think something must have happened in one of the lessons your sister had with him."

"What?" I ask, sitting up a little straighter. "What happened?"

"Ahhh," Clare says, "that's the thing. The information has been scrubbed out of the book."

"Scrubbed out how exactly?" Fly says.

Clare scrambles across the floor on her knees, then pulls the book from under her bed and flips to the right page. She turns the book around so I can read, and Fly peers over my shoulder.

12th March – Turmeric lesson. Students were instructed to search for shadow weaving magic in their veins. They were encouraged to let any such magic flow through to their fingertips. The existing identified shadow weavers performed this easily. The commoners were unsuccessful ...

Several sentences follow but they have been scrubbed out by dark black ink.

"I've tried the usual tricks – holding the paper up to the light, making an impression of the page. I can't work out what's written underneath. But ... maybe someone with magic could."

"I don't understand. These books hadn't been read for years – it was clear no one had been in that section of the library for years."

"Then they must have scrubbed this from the book almost as soon as it was written," Fly suggests. "I wonder what it said."

"I'm going to find out." I grip the page and rip it from the book.

Clare squeals, her hands rushing to her face. "I can't believe you just did that."

"It's easier than lugging that book around."

"But the library is going to hate you even more than she already does."

"What you just said made no sense at all!" Fly says.

I fold the page up and stuff it in my pocket. I have a good idea who can help me with this. I'm tempted to go see him right now, but I promised I'd hang out with my friends tonight.

"So," I say, passing around the chocolates again because I'm not sure how my friends are going to handle the next piece of news, "I have news of my own."

"More news?" Fly says, rolling his eyes. "Nearly being murdered and then getting the academy's worst bully expelled not enough for you?"

"I still can't believe they expelled her!" Clare says, shaking her head.

"Well, this might be even more shocking," I warn them. I inhale. Then exhale. "Professor Tudor is a vampire."

"Ahhh," Clare says, "that makes sense."

"It does?" I say, confused. That was ... not the reaction I was expecting.

"Yes," Clare says, "totally makes sense."

I turn to Fly who seems more interested in his next chocolate than this piece of news. "You're not shocked either?" I ask.

"He's a shadow weaver. They are all peculiar in their own way. And Clare's right – now you've said it, it's really damn obvious. Pale skin, glowing eyes, loves to hang out in the dark."

"I guess ... I didn't even know vampires existed."

"They aren't exactly the most well-loved of the different types of shadow weavers," Fly says.

"On account of their feeding habits." Clare licks at her

fingertips. "But they have been highly restricted and regulated for the last couple of centuries."

"What does that mean?"

"They can't go around draining people of their blood," Fly explains.

"There's more," I say. "I was right about Fox – I mean Professor Tudor not being born a shadow weaver–"

"But you just said."

"He was turned into a vampire by another vampire."

This news does seem to shock my friends – and I haven't even gotten to the truly shocking part yet.

"Shit ... I didn't know that was possible," Fly says, pushing a chocolate around his mouth – first one cheek bulging, then the other. "They kept that quiet."

"Understandable," Clare says, adjusting her glasses.

"Why?" I say.

"Because if there's a way to be turned into a shadow weaver, don't you think every commoner in this academy would take it?"

"Fox didn't seem so happy about his life choices."

"That's because he's chosen to be a teacher – and that has to suck," Fly says. "Especially when he could be living it up in Onyx Quarter."

"I'm not sure that's the reason," I say, remembering the bitterness in his voice.

"Did he say who turned him?" Clare asks.

I shake my head. That wasn't a question I thought about asking and yet now it seems obvious. Especially as he made it sound like he was seduced.

Jealousy prickles in my stomach and I peer down to stare at it.

I need to tell my friends the last piece of news. The

truly unreal piece. I've kept many secrets in my time. But this one is burning way too big a hole in my pocket.

"There's more."

Fly rubs his hands together. "Oh good, this keeps getting more and more juicy."

I lift my gaze.

"Professor Tudor says he has feelings for me."

Both my friends are speechless. In fact, Fly goes and chokes on the remainder of his chocolate. He coughs and splutters and Clare is forced to slap him on the back.

"I'm sorry," Fly says, blinking, tears sliding down his cheeks, "I thought you just said Professor Tudor has feelings for you."

"He does. At least, that's what he says."

"Feelings of annoyance or irritability?" Fly asks.

"Err, no," I say, my cheeks probably glowing as vividly as Clare's were earlier.

"Romantic feelings?" Clare says in awe.

I nod.

"Wow," Fly says silently, "just wow."

"Yeah, exactly," I say. "I told you he nearly kissed me," I point out to Fly.

"Yeah, but I didn't really believe you! Do you have feelings for him too?"

"She's dating the Princes," Clare points out, observing me from behind her glasses. "Oh my gosh! Do you?"

Fly swings his laser gaze my way.

"Maybe?" I say in a teeny tiny voice. "Not that I've told him."

"Shit!" Fly says. "But where does that leave you and the Princes?" Alarm rushes into his eyes. "Do they know about this?"

"I have feelings for the Princes too," I say, laying it all

out on the table. "Crazy, weird but very hot feelings for all of them. Which is just insanely right and seriously fucked up. I'm fucked up," I say pointing to myself.

"You're not fucked up, Cupcake." Fly rolls his eyes. "All those dudes are incredibly hot – including Professor Gloom and Doom. Any functioning human being in possession of their right mind would find them irresistible – especially if they were all professing undying love to you."

"They're not professing anything like that," I mutter, although telling me I'm their fated mate must count for something.

"Okay, maybe not love. But they all want to fling you over their incredibly broad shoulders and whisk you off to bed."

"Blimey," Clare sighs, "have they actually done that to you?"

"No," I say.

"Ahem," Fly jabs his finger at me, "I saw them carrying you around the assault course this afternoon."

"Yeah, but what am I going to do about it?"

"About four hot dudes wanting you. Hmm," Fly taps his finger against his mouth, "let me think."

"I'm serious. I need some advice guys."

"I'd start by talking to them about all this," Clare suggests.

"Boring!" Fly says.

"But practical." Clare slides her glasses up her nose and gives Fly a look that reminds me so much of a teacher I think I almost see a glimpse of Clare's future.

"Okay," I say, squaring my shoulders. "Talk to them. I can do that."

After all, how hard can it be?

Chapter Fifty-Five

F ox

Am I sure?

It's a question I've asked myself over and over again, countless, countless times.

Because she'd been sure, hadn't she? So very sure.

We were destined to be together. Bound together by fate.

It was written in our stars.

It's how she convinced me.

Then again, I didn't need that much convincing.

I was stupid back then – and vain and careless. Seduced by the idea of power and magic. Immortality and, yes, her.

What a fool!

Because it was all a lie. All an elaborate trick.

Am I surprised Briony is more cautious? Less eager to believe me?

I shouldn't be. She has more sense than I ever did.

I skim around the edges of the academy, my cloak swishing in the violent wind, wisps of snowflakes spinning in the air tonight, the clouds thick and suffocating, the night more black than usual.

Her face spins in my mind like the crystalized flakes. Had that been shock on her face? Or was it disgust?

Or worse, pity?

What the hell is she thinking?

I can't stand it! I have to know.

I have to see her – even if it's foolish and stupid.

I will not torture myself any longer.

I move quickly and silently through the academy and then I'm standing outside her room, pounding on her door. The scent of her is everywhere, sunken into the floorboards and buried in the walls. I have the urge to press my face up against it and inhale deep into my cold lungs.

The door opens. She's standing there in an oversized shirt that grazes her thighs; her legs and her feet bare despite the frigid temperature. A temperature that will drop lower in my presence.

"I thought you might come," she whispers, drawing back the door and disappearing inside.

Over the threshold of the doorway, the room glows with a dull fire – a doorway I cannot pass through without her permission.

She peers over her shoulder at me with her startling green eyes, her golden hair wound in a plait that falls nearly to her waist.

"Are you coming in?"

"Not unless you invite me," I whisper.

The air swirls thick with her scent. It's intoxicating. My lifeless blood seems to warm in my veins for the first time in years. When I'm with her, it's like being alive again, as if she breathes life back into my soul.

She spins around to face me.

"You can come in, Professor," she says.

Despite the invitation, despite everything in me pulling me that way – heck maybe even fate and destiny and the stars – I hesitate.

This is more than a doorway crossed, it's a boundary. Entering a student's room. They could fire me for it. Bardin would find a way to have me fired for it. Or worse. Even if she herself did it countless times.

"We need to talk," she says, and I step inside, closing the door behind me.

There's no going back now. Taking her to the clinic, waiting there all that time – that was risky, but I could have explained it away as concern for a student. I couldn't explain this away.

There's only a bed in the room and an old rickety closet. A cold wind sweeps through the roof as well as vermin.

It's a long time since I visited these rooms. They are worse than I remember. My room in the dungeons is opulent compared to this. Have I become spoiled by the shadow weaver luxuries after all?

The only place to sit is the bed and as that is loaded with connotations I can't let my mind consider; we remain on our feet.

"You must despise me," I say as she opens her mouth and says,

"I need your help with something."

We stare at one another.

"I ... don't think I despise you," she says, her forehead crinkling.

"It was not fair of me to burden you with my feelings –

especially when you were recovering from your injuries. It was wrong of me. I was thinking of myself and not of you." My words sound so formal and stiff and the distance between us so vast it is impassable.

"Your hand was forced." I frown. "By the others."

So much of her blood was spilled in that attack, but already it has regenerated. I hear it rushing through the vessels beneath her skin and that familiar thud of her heart is loud in the room, the drumbeat to my very existence. "But you can make it up to me, by helping me now."

I frown even harder. This wasn't how I was expecting things to go.

"Why do I suspect I'm not going to like this bargain?"

"Because you're a highly cynical and bitter old man."

"I'm thirty-three years old."

"I thought vampires were hundreds and hundreds of years old."

"Miss Storm, you knew me back in Slate Quarter."

She shrugs, then turns around and strolls to the closet. "Thirty-three years old is pretty ancient too."

"It's only twelve years older than you."

She retrieves something from the closet – is it the object she hid from me the night of the trial? – then spins on her toes and strides back to me.

It's a folded piece of paper. One I haven't seen before. She opens it up.

"Fox," she says, "are you lying to me? Do you truly believe I'm your fated mate?"

"I know you feel it too," I whisper.

She meets my eyes with her penetrating green ones and something passes between us in the silence, something that tells me she does.

"Then I can trust you?"

"I told you, you can't trust anyone."

"But that's shitty advice, Professor, because we have to trust in this life otherwise it's really freaking lonely."

"Yes," I say, "it is."

She huffs in annoyance. "I'm choosing to trust you. If you break that trust–"

"You'll send those three halfwits after me."

"No, I'll come for you myself."

I scoff at that. How many times has this girl nearly died?

As if reading my thoughts she says, "How many times have they tried to kill me, and I'm still here, Professor? How many times have you nearly died?"

"Only the once," I tell her. "And now I am immortal."

"There are ways to kill even vampires, I hear."

"Are you going to kill me, Miss Storm?" It's a very real possibility that she will break my stone-cold heart.

"Only if you betray me."

She hands me the piece of paper.

"What is it?" I ask, gaze racing over the handwritten prose.

"It's taken from a book that contains an account of the year my sister was at the academy. There are several books for every year. It details every thing that happened in miniscule detail, from what was served in the canteen to who was screwing who."

My gaze flicks up to hers.

"And how can I help?"

"There's an account on this page of a class my sister attended. The class you now teach. Only someone has scrubbed out the details." Just like they scrubbed out the details of her death from the other book.

I lower my hands.

"This is dangerous, Briony. If someone has tampered

with the records, it's because they don't want the truth to be known."

"Exactly."

I shake my head. There is no use arguing with her, and, if I'm honest, I understand. I'd feel the same way if it were someone I cared about.

"Then how can I help?"

"Can you remove the redaction? Can you see what was originally written underneath?"

I stare down at the redaction. Immediately, I can tell it is complex magic. Not something easily removed.

"I can try," I say. She smiles. "But I'm not promising anything. Whoever placed it here, did not want it removed. Did not want the text beneath read."

I fold up the piece of paper.

"Aren't you going to try?" she asks in frustration.

"It needs my full attention and some time."

"But you'll look into it – as a matter of urgency?"

"If that's what you really want."

"It is."

"Then I will."

"Thank you."

I hesitate, then go to move towards the door.

I don't know what I expected to happen coming here like this, but now I feel nothing but shame, defeat, and disappointment.

"Fox?"

"Yes?"

"Are you ... are you the reason Madame Bardin attacked me?"

My head drops forward. I stare down at the bare floorboards.

"Yes," I say. "She understood what you meant to me,

probably before I even understood it myself."

"But why–"

"Jealousy. It's a very strong emotion." And don't I know that more than anyone. Haven't I had to endure imagining her with them? Haven't I had to watch it?

"She wants you for her own." I nod. "But you don't want her back?"

"No, I want you," I say simply and watch transfixed as a shiver of a desire spirals through her body. "And I think you want me too."

She bites her lip. "That doesn't mean I can have you."

"No, it doesn't. It would break just about every academy rule going."

She shrugs. "I have a feeling I've broken quite a few of those already," she mutters.

"This one–"

"Might be worth breaking."

My eyes flash. My fingers twitch and the shadows in my veins ache to touch her.

I close the distance between us until I'm standing right in front of her, the warmth of her skin – of her body and her blood – palatable. She tips her head back to stare up into my eyes and hers are the color of the forest back in Slate. So green, so welcoming, like home.

"Aren't you afraid of me, little one?" I whisper to her, watching as the dark night of her pupils swallow up all that lush green and my fangs descend in my mouth.

"No," she says. "I'm not afraid."

She reaches out her hand and cups my face, running her palm over my cheek, stroking at my beard, and then, with a little caution, touch my fangs, sliding the pad of her thumb right down the enamel of my tooth to the sharp deadly point. She pricks her thumb against it and I have to breathe hard to stop myself from sinking that fang through her delicate skin.

"Sharp," she whispers. "Do you want to ... is that what you want?"

My stomach growls. Yes, I want that so fucking much, but there are other things I want just as much.

"No," I say, "this is what I want."

I curl my hand around the back of her skull and the other around her waist and drag her soft, warm body against mine and my mouth against hers.

I kiss her deep and slow and long like a girl ought to be kissed, like I haven't done in years and years and her hands form fists in my shirt, her mouth moves invitingly against mine and her body presses against me.

I moan into her mouth and slide my hand from her waist, over the curve of her hip and to the rump of her ass. I squeeze it through the material of her T-shirt and pull her even more firmly against me so she's hard against my stiff erection.

A little whimper bubbles in her throat and she rubs herself against me.

Fuck!

There's no turning back now, no stepping away from this. I'm in too deep. Nothing could tempt me to step away from her needy kiss and her inviting body.

I slip my hand under the hem of her shirt and brush my fingers against the gusset of her panties. Eros was right. Damp. She's already wet.

I groan.

My hand travels down to her thigh and I squeeze that too, lifting her leg to curl around me so I can grind against her. She follows my lead, rubbing herself against me, both of us finding pleasure in the friction, lost in the feel of each other's bodies. Mine hard and cold; hers soft and warm.

I move my hand from the back of her head, fingers stroking over her hair and then to her throat. I stroke along the artery that runs there, feeling her pulse dancing against my fingers.

"Shit," I mutter. She whimpers again and I can't help but grind myself into her core with more force and more urgency.

We're standing in the center of her room making out and dry humping like I haven't done since I was a kid back in Slate Quarter. It's so innocent, so raw, so different from everything that came later, from all the twisted stuff I did with her.

It's a relief. Like a rebirth. Like an absolution.

Her mouth falters against mine, her thigh shakes in my hand and her head falls backward.

She's close.

"Come on, little one, come for me. I've waited so fucking long for this."

I grind my hard cock right along where she needs me most and she falls apart, a long strangled cry rushing from her lips and blood racing to the surface of her skin in beautiful crimson waves.

I can't help myself, I slip my hand up her thigh, into her panties, and trace along the plush lips of her pussy. Her body shakes in my arms.

"Fox," she murmurs, right by my ear, her breath hot. "Please."

And how can I refuse her? I slide my finger right into her cunt. She's wet and warm and she squeezes around my finger in waves of convulsion. It's too much. I follow after her, grunting and orgasming like I haven't done in years.

Free of shame. Free of repulsion. Free of self-loathing.

I'm too lost in her to feel any of that.

My finger still buried in her pussy, I scoop her up with my other arm and carry her backwards to the narrow rickety bed, dropping her down onto the hard mattress and crawling between her legs.

"Think you can do that again, pretty girl?" I say, sliding my finger from her.

"Do what?" she says, lips swollen from my kisses, face flushed, hair coming loose from its braid. She looks like every fucking teacher's worst nightmare.

"Come," I growl and slide two fingers inside her this time, stretching her open a little more, testing her. Could she take me? Could this tight pussy fit my cock inside? I reach high inside her searching for that spot. I know when I find it because she squeals, hips rising from the bed. "Fuck, yes," I say, stroking at it until she's writhing and bucking on my fingers, her arousal trickling down my hand to my wrist.

"Fox," she pants.

"Professor," I remind her, because fuck, if we're doing this, we may as well do it properly.

She scowls at me but she still does as I say. "Professor."

"Yes, Miss Storm."

I brush my thumb against her clit as I massage that spot inside her and she loses her ability to speak. Her eyes roll back in their sockets and her eyelids flutter shut.

She's fucking beautiful and I lean into her, squeezing at her breast through her shirt and pressing my lips against that pounding pulse of hers, feeling her blood flowing right below the surface.

I kiss that spot, then lick my tongue up and down that vessel full of her sweet blood, all the time playing with her sensitive little nub and the spot inside her cunt.

"So pretty," I murmur and she likes that, her pulse racing even faster. I kiss her a little harder, scraping my fangs against the tender skin and she comes for me a second time. I feel her orgasm in her cunt – in the way it squeezes and milks my fingers. I feel it in her clit – the thing quivering against my touch. But most of all I feel it in her pulse – feel it fluttering against my lips and my tongue.

I screw up my eyes and drag myself away from her.

Because it would be so easy – so easy when she's drowsy and content with her orgasm – to sink my fangs into her neck and drink from her.

So easy.

But I won't do it. I am not a monster.

As I pull away, she opens her eyes and blinks up at me.

"Does it hurt?" she asks.

"Does what hurt, little one? Are you telling me you haven't–"

"No," she says, her brows knotting together. "What is it with you men and your obsession with virgin–"

"What did you mean?"

My fingers are still buried in her cunt and reluctantly I slide them out of her. She frowns a little harder.

I'm covered in her arousal and I want nothing more than to plunge my fingers into my mouth and suck them clean. But I'm hanging on by the barest of threads here and that could be the thing that snaps it.

Instead, I wipe my fingers on the bed sheets and wave my hand through the air, using my magic to clean myself up.

She props herself up on her elbows. Her shirt's pulled up around her waist. Her panties are yanked to one side. One of her legs dangles over my lap, the other rests behind me. She's exposed and I can't drag my eyes away from her pretty pussy.

I lick my lips. What I'd give to taste it. What I'd give to sink more than my fingers into her.

But I can't trust myself. There's only so much control a half-man half-monster can command.

"When you feed?" she says, her gaze fixed on my fangs. "Does it hurt the person you feed from?" She reaches up and touches the side of her neck. My attention there has left a mark.

I swallow. Hard.

"For the briefest of moments, yes. But there's something in my kind's saliva that is numbing and soothing."

For a moment I think she might offer up her throat to me. But to my relief the moment passes.

"I have to go," I say. "I've already stayed too long."

"When will I see you, Professor?"

"In class I imagine, Miss Storm." I hesitate. "You know we have to keep this a secret, don't you? For now."

"But if we truly are fated mates–"

"This situation is unusual," I tell her. A commoner a mate of someone like Beaufort Lincoln. It's unheard of. And then for her to be my mate too – a man not bonded to the others by fate. I've never heard of it before. "And that is dangerous for all of us."

She nods and I kiss her again.

As I'm descending the steps of her tower, listening and searching the shadows for who may be watching, I consider if my words were disingenuous.

This situation is most dangerous for me. I am playing with fire.

I halt on the stairs and lean against the wall, the image of her hand stroking down her throat vivid in my mind, stealing away the cold breath in my lungs.

I was disingenuous to her then as well.

The magic in a vampire's bite is more than just numbing, far more than soothing.

It's like an opioid. It has the victim swimming in ecstasy, begging for the feeder to feed from them again and again.

And that's why I will never feed from her.

I am not like the Princes.

I have no desire to make her my slave.

Chapter Fifty-Six

B riony

If I thought I was confused after all those revelations back at the clinic, I'm even more confused after that encounter with Fox in my room.

I'm not sure how I'm meant to feel about it.

Frightened?

This wasn't how my time in the academy was meant to go. I was meant to keep my head down and learn the truth about my sister. Instead, I'm not only tangling myself up with three of the academy's shadow weavers, I'm also messing around with one of the teachers.

Couple that with the dragon I have loose in the forest and I'm clearly asking for trouble.

Guilty?

Beaufort said he wouldn't stand in my way with Fox but

there's a niggle in my gut that won't go away. One that tells me I've been unfaithful or wronged them or something.

As I dress the next morning, I meet my reflection in the mirror. There's the faintest of bruises on my throat from where Fox sucked on my neck, his fingers inside me.

A little whimper bubbles out of my mouth.

I shake my head.

What the hell am I becoming?

Before I arrived at the academy, I'd slept with one man and one man only. Now I'm sleeping with four – or at least, I'd like to be. It's pretty damn confusing. Am I meant to feel this way? Or am I seriously screwed up?

I decide the only way to know is to talk to them about it like Clare suggested.

Yeah, who the hell am I? Because talking, sharing my feelings – that is not my usual go-to response. Are they changing me? Or is it this place?

I shut the wardrobe door and head off for my lessons. There won't be a chance to speak with the Princes until tonight.

After dinner, Thorne meets me behind the academy buildings and we walk out the back way to the forest, right into the heart of the trees until we find Blaze. On the way we talk about mundane stuff – today's lessons, if my injuries are still hurting, the upcoming trial. After I've spent an hour throwing sticks for Blaze, we walk back and I blurt out what I've been wanting to say the whole time.

"I need to talk to the three of you," I say. His gaze springs my way. "I need to talk to you about Fox."

"Professor Tudor?" he asks. I nod. "Okay."

We don't speak again until we reach the Princes' tower. He opens the door and instructs me to take a seat in the lounge while he goes to fetch the others.

I'm too nervous to sit though, choosing to pace around the room instead as I bite at the inside of my cheek.

"Hey Kitten," Dray says a couple of minutes later, bounding into the room. "This isn't a Wednesday or a Saturday. Do we get more regular visits now?"

He skips right up to me, hooks an arm around my waist and drags me in for a long hard kiss. There's pure delight and excitement sparking in his eyes when he pulls away. At least, there is until his eyes land on that bruise on my neck.

Oh crap!

"What's that?" he asks, frowning as the other two join us in the room.

"It's what I wanted to talk to you about." I wriggle out of his embrace and take a decided step away. I can't think straight pressed up against his hard body.

"What's what?" Beaufort asks, hands deep in his pockets.

"A hickey," Dray says, "on her neck. You responsible for that, Beau?"

"No," he says, frowning.

"It was F– Professor Tudor," I blurt out.

"Fuck," Beaufort says, taking a step towards me. "Did he try to bite you?"

"No!" I say. "But ..." I swallow, "we ... did make out."

I flick my gaze around their faces. Why do I care about how they are going to react to this news? Is it because I don't want to hurt them? Is it because – as hard as I've tried – I'm developing feelings for these men?

My gaze falls to the floor and my throat constricts.

Damn it, Briony!

It's just sex. That's all it is.

"Is that what you came here to tell us?" Beaufort asks.

His voice is neutral and I can tell by the tone he's struggling to keep it that way – none of the usual snark or annoyance.

I look back up at him. He's struggling to keep his face neutral too.

"Just made out?" My eyes flick to Dray. He's smirking at me with wickedness in his eyes. "I find it hard to believe that's all you did, knowing you, Kitten."

"It was a little more than kissing," I admit.

"Did you sleep with him?" Beaufort asks.

I shake my head.

"Did he touch you?" Dray asks, eyes glinting even more.

I hesitate, then I nod.

"Did he make you come?" Dray licks his lips.

I nod again. Dray grins like a maniac. Beaufort's face remains neutral.

With trepidation, and for the first time, I peek at Thorne.

For once, his face isn't neutral. His neck is corded, his jaw hard and his eyes ... his eyes are swimming with hurt.

The sight of this man – so strong, so stoic, so damn hard – with pain like that in his eyes, breaks me. Tears prickle behind my eyes.

"Oh Thorne," I gasp, reaching out towards him, then remembering and pulling my hands away. "Beaufort said ... I didn't mean ... I would never ..." My words fade away. I inhale and exhale, shame burning my cheeks. "I betrayed you."

"No, you didn't," Beaufort says softly. "You're his mate – just like you are ours. It's what fate wants and we can't stand in front of that – none of us can."

I shake my head. "Thorne disagrees," I mutter.

Beaufort and Dray turn to look at their friend.

The usually emotionless shadow weaver, screws shut

his eyes. His shoulders rise and fall, and then he opens them again.

"You haven't betrayed me, Briony," he says.

"Then why does it look like I broke your heart," I cry out.

He looks a little startled at my outburst. A sad smile flickers briefly over his face, then fades away, and it has those tears in my eyes rolling.

"It's not ..." He meets my eyes. "It's what I want. I want to kiss you, Briony. I want to touch you."

We gaze at each other over a distance. A distance that feels so vast. A distance that neither of us can close.

"I know," I whisper. "I want that too."

The pain spirals in his eyes again and then he's turning and walking away.

"Thorne," I cry, rushing forward, but Beaufort catches me in his arms.

"Don't Briony," he says gently, "you'll only make it worse. Just let him be."

"It isn't fair," I sob.

"Nothing is in this life," Beaufort says, holding me tight.

Beaufort lets me sob into his chest, wrapping his arms around me and gently shushing me as he glides his warm palms up and down my spine.

All the intimate things we've done together and none has felt as intimate as this. It makes me cry even harder because as I do, I realize I'm not just crying about Thorne, about this twisted situation, I'm crying about it all. The loss of my sister. The loss of my dad. All the cruel, nasty things

Muriel ever said or did to me. How alone I felt. How lonely I've been.

All of it comes rushing to the surface and I ugly cry against Beaufort, leaving a wet mark on his shirt.

When there are no more tears to cry, he guides me gently to a chair, lowers me into it and swipes all the wetness from my face with his thumbs.

"Better?" he asks, resting his forefinger under my chin and tipping it upwards so I'm looking up into his face.

"A bit," I confess.

"Want some ice cream? A hot chocolate?"

"Something with a bit more kick?" Dray asks, from where he's watching us from the other side of the room.

"Ice cream, please," I say. "I've never had one before."

Beaufort pinches my chin affectionately, then pads away and Dray comes to sit by my feet.

"You really wanna touch Thorne that much, huh?" he asks, his vibrant eyes dancing over what must be my messed-up face.

I can't help giggling. "It's just been a lot. Everything that's happened, I mean."

"But, you do want to touch him?" he asks me, tugging off my boots and taking my feet into his lap, beginning to massage the soles with his thumbs.

"Jeez, that feels good," I say, sinking further into the armchair.

"I'm exceedingly talented at making you feel good, Kitten," he purrs, and I can't help smiling again. "But, you didn't answer my question."

"Yes," I confess. "I want to touch him. I want to touch all of you. Does that make me messed up?"

I'm not entirely sure why I'm asking Dray Eros for an

assessment of what's messed up or not. The shifter definitely skirts the fine line of crazy.

"Nah," he says, bringing my foot up to his mouth and nipping my big toe. "I'd think you were more messed up if you didn't."

"Who's messed up?" Beaufort asks, walking into the room with a large bowl in his hands. He comes to sit on the arm of my chair, handing me the bowl and a spoon. In the bowl rests a ball of something brown colored. "Chocolate," he explains. I dig my spoon into the substance. It's harder than I expected. I scoop up a little and bring it to my mouth. "Be warned. It'll be cold."

But despite that warning, it still takes me by surprise, that and the delicious, sweet flavor.

"Briony thinks she's messed up because she wants to fuck all of us," Dray says, kneading my feet again.

"That isn't what I said."

"But it's what you were thinking." He winks. "Tell me, Kitten, how exactly did that blood-sucking professor touch you? I'm dying to hear the details."

I take a large scoop of the ice cream, shove it in my mouth and peer sideways at Beaufort.

"Ahh, don't worry about him," Dray says, "he may pretend he isn't into all of that stuff, but trust me, Kitten, he is. He wants to hear as much as I do."

I shake my head. "He doesn—"

"I do," Beaufort says, and when I turn again to look at him, I find his features have darkened. It makes me shiver.

I squirm on the chair a little, taking the excuse of another mouthful of ice cream to work out what the hell I'm going to tell them.

"Are you embarrassed, Kitten?" Dray asks. "Because

you didn't seem at all embarrassed when I had my tongue up your pussy."

"Jeez," I mumble.

"How did he make you come?" Beaufort asks me, his silver eyes so smoldering, it's enough to make a girl light-headed.

"The first time or the second?" I ask, finding a little flirtatious courage and licking my tongue around the spoon.

"The first," Beaufort says.

"He kissed me," I swallow, "and then he had his hands on my ass and he was grinding me against him, against his ..."

"Cock," Dray chimes in helpfully.

I bite my lip and nod, electricity flickering around my body at the memory of it.

"And that made you come?" Beaufort says, "just rubbing himself against you like that?"

"Yes," I breathe.

"So fucking sensitive," Dray growls, tickling my feet. "I love how sensitive you are."

"Now, tell us about the second time, little thrall," Beaufort instructs.

I lose myself in those silver eyes.

"He carried me over to my bed and then he slid his fingers inside me and made me come while he sucked on my throat."

"Fuck, yes," Dray mutters, stroking his hands up my calves. "You like reliving it, don't you, Kitten? You like telling your protectors all about it."

I hesitate, then nod.

"And I like it too," Dray says, "I'm so hard listening to you talk about it." He takes my hand and then he's dragging me off the chair and has me straddling his lap. I can discern just how hard he is. "You feel that, little Kitten? Can you feel how hard you've made me?"

"Yes," I say, rotating my hips and grinding against him.

"Fuck," Beaufort mutters from above us.

"You wanna ride that cock, Kitten?" Dray growls. "You wanna ride that cock while Beaufort watches?"

My breath hitches, and I glance behind me at Beaufort.

"Ride him," he commands.

My belly swoops low. I can't deny, I'm seriously turned on by the idea. But is it risky? Is this the kind of thing boys brag to their friends about? The kind of thing they do with you one night, only to kick you to the curb the next morning?

But once again, I'm feeling reckless. All that grief I just spewed from deep with in me and now I want to feel alive, I want to feel wanted, I want to feel so good I fall apart.

I reach up on my knees, allowing Dray to slide down the waistband of his sweats. His cock springs up and he grips it in the fist of his hand. I stare down at it, more heat stirring in my core.

Inks are scribbled over his groin all the way down to the base of his cock. It's fairer than Beaufort's, his foreskin still intact, though pulled back tight. He's a tad shorter than Beaufort, though thicker and the fuzz that covers his balls is slightly darker than the hair on his head.

I reach under my skirt to hook my panties to one side and lower myself, hovering right above the tip of Dray's cock.

"Protection," Beaufort snaps. Dray groans, clearly unhappy about that idea.

I shake my head. "We don't need it," I say. "They gave me a contraceptive shot at the clinic."

"Fuck, yes," Dray says, his eyes full of wickedness. "I'm

going to pump you full, Kitten." He takes a firm grip of my hips and drags me down onto his cock.

The sensation has the both of us groaning and actual stars crashing against my vision as I ride him all the way down his shaft. There I stay, attempting to catch my breath as he grins up at me. For a moment I'm lost in the colors of his eyes and the sensation of fullness between my thighs.

Then Beaufort growls behind us, "Move."

"Yeah, Kitten," Dray purrs with a wink. "Ride me."

I've never done it this way before – although since this thing with the Princes started, I've definitely been fanta-sizing about it. I've heard girls talk about how good it is. How it hits all the right places, and when I rotate my hips and grind him inside me, I find that is true.

Dray groans, a noise echoed by Beaufort.

I peer over my shoulder at him, as Dray's hold on me tightens, encouraging me to move faster, rising up his long shaft, and then slamming back down to the hilt.

"Good girl," Beaufort mutters, gaze locked with mine and everything in my core flutters in response.

I remember that power I felt the first time I fell to my knees and took Beaufort into my mouth. This is the same. Dray may be moving me on top of him, but it's me who has reduced this pair of powerful men, who has captured their attention, who dictates how far this will go.

"That is a mighty fine view, Kitten," Dray says, as I once again slam down onto him, crying out as I do. "You know what would make it even better?" I shake my head.

"If you took off your top," Beaufort says, his voice low and lustful.

"Yeah, I wanna see those tits bounce as you ride me."

I lean forward resting my hands on Dray's taut stomach and sinking my nails into his flesh.

"Only if you take yours off too."

"That sounds like a bargain," Dray says, rolling upwards so our bodies are flush together. Then he's reaching down for the hem of my shirt, dragging it up my body.

"Don't stop, little thrall," Beaufort says, and I grind against Dray as he snaps off my bra and yanks his own shirt over his head.

Immediately, I feel the warmth of his skin against mine. He buries his nose in the crook of my neck, and I trace my fingers over the inks on his back, my breasts pressed against him, my nipples rubbing over the muscular planes of his chest.

He nibbles at my throat, his fingers sinking into the cheeks of my ass and I follow the inks up his back to his shoulder, running the pads of my fingers over the gnarled scar of his shoulder.

He gasps.

"Does it hurt?" I ask.

"No, Kitten. It feels good."

He takes my face in his hands and kisses me, thrusting his tongue deep into my mouth, then he's reaching under my skirt, reaching between us to find my clit. He presses his thumb against it, magic humming, and I cry out again.

"Gonna come, now, Kitten. Gonna come for me," he nips at my ear, "and for him. Let's give him a fucking good show."

Then he's rolling back down and his magic vibrates against me.

I buck up and down on his cock, my breasts bouncing with me, his magic vibrating my clit and the pressure inside me builds.

"Ooooh," I moan, leaning back and resting my hands on

his strong thighs, thrusting my pussy forward, grinding against his thumb.

"Such a good girl," Beaufort groans.

"So fucking good," Dray says. He winks at me and then his magic sparks more violently against my clit. It's too much, I come in a rush of feeling, my head falling backwards, my vision whitening and a hundred million sensations of pleasure swimming through every part of my body.

Below me, Dray thrusts up into my convulsing pussy and then his cock twitches inside me and I feel the rush of something hot and liquid.

His own head falls back against the floor, and for a moment shadows sparkle in the air around his body. His mouth curls into a sedated grin and he groans.

"Fuck, yes," he mutters, holding me firmly in place as his cock twitches again and again, more liquid flooding my pussy.

Catching my breath, I peer over my shoulder, back towards Beaufort.

He's sitting in the center of the chair now, hands gripping the arms. There's no color left in his eyes.

"Come here, little thrall," he says.

Chapter Fifty-Seven

$\mathbf{B}$eaufort

Dray rolls up, Briony still straddling his lap like a damn queen, and slurps his tongue right up her throat.

"Go on," he says, tweaking her left nipple, "be a good little kitten for once and do what he says, huh?"

She gives him one of her bratty scowls but to my delight, scrambles up onto her knees and then stumbles up onto her feet. She's giddy from her orgasms and that fucking, her skin damp with sweat and her cheeks flushed a rosy red.

Dray flops back and tucks his hands behind his head, his now flaccid dick, resting against his thigh. My guess? With what I have planned for our little mate, he'll be hard again in a minute.

I hold out my hand and she pads towards me, wearing just her skirt and her panties.

When she reaches out for my hand, I pull her right in

close, so she's standing between my knees. I reach up and cup her face, tracing my thumb over her kiss-swollen lips.

"Fuck, you look wrecked, sweetheart. Fucking wrecked. Can I wreck you too?"

She leans down and kisses my mouth, combing her fingers through my hair. I reach up to unhook her skirt and slide down her panties.

I won't lie. There's something fucking erotic about sitting here fully clothed while she stands in front of me, completely naked. So often, I've felt out of control in her presence. Feelings I've never experienced before crashing around my body, dreams I've never wanted before swimming in my mind, desires I can't resist tempting me beyond belief. Tonight, I'm in control. I know what I want and I'm going to take it.

She pushes her tongue deeper into my mouth and I suck on it as my hands slip between her thighs, sticky with her arousal and Dray's come. Because he fucked her without protection, got to feel inside her with no barrier.

I want that too.

I glide two fingers inside her. He's already worked her loose and I reach all the way up, three-knuckles deep, brushing against the spot that has her legs shaking. I work at it until she's tugging at my hair, and moaning right into my mouth.

"Beaufort," she murmurs against my lips and I have never heard anything so beautiful before. Like the sweetest of melodies. Haunting and precious.

"Yeah, sweetheart," I whisper back. "I got you. I always got you."

I take ahold of her hip and thrust my fingers in and out of her, hitting that spot each time; the sound wet. Her pussy walls flutter around my fingers and she grips on to me.

"Come on, sweetheart," I whisper. "Come on."

She whimpers, her eyelids flutter shut and her pussy clenches tight around my fingers, and then she comes, those pussy walls sucking at me hungrily.

"Shit," Dray says from the floor. "You're so hot, little Kitten."

I break away from our kiss, and sweep back the loose strands of hair from her face.

"That's it, pretty mate. You're doing so well."

"You're not doing so badly yourself," she says with a satisfied smile.

"You know how I could be doing even better?"

"How?"

"If you climbed into my lap and rode me like you rode him." I jerk my chin in Dray's direction and squeeze her ass. "Think your pretty pussy could take being fucked like that again so soon after the last time?"

"Yes," she says.

"Are you serious? The kitten can multiple-orgasm like she's magic or something." Dray chuckles. "She was made for multiple fuckings and multiple mates."

I place my hands back on the arms of the chair.

"Okay then, sweetheart."

I smile at her wickedly and she understands.

First, she unbuttons my shirt, sliding her hot hands over the contours on my chest followed by her nails. The scrape on my skin has me groaning. She grins and trails a finger all the way down the center of my chest, over my stomach and down to the waist of my pants. The sensation makes me shiver.

She yanks at my belt, biting at her lip as she does, and threads down the zipper, then reaches inside my briefs to curl her fist around my cock.

"Like that?" I ask.

"Uh huh," she murmurs.

"Then come ride it, sweetheart."

"We've talked about this, Beaufort," she says, with a wicked smile that reminds me of my bond brother. "You need to ask nicely."

"Little thrall," I say with a grunt, thrusting my cock up into her fist, "please come sit on my lap, sink onto my damn cock and ride me like you rode him."

My cock still in her grip, she places one knee on the far side of my thigh and then the other knee on the opposite side. She hovers above me like a siren, the smell of her skin divine. I lean closer and suck her nipple into my mouth, swirling my tongue around the stiff point before nipping at it.

She whimpers and sinks straight down on my cock like I asked.

"Fuck," I hiss, because it's the first time we've done this without protection and I can feel so much more; the tight soft, sponge of her walls.

"Beaufort," she mutters like she did when my fingers were inside her.

"That feel good, Kitten?" Dray asks. "You like his cock inside you?"

"Yes," she says, and as if to prove just how much she likes it, she grinds her hips, getting herself off on the feel of my cock.

I'm not in control any more, she is, and I lay my head against the back of the chair and watch her. Her blonde hair's shaken loose and it falls over her shoulder. Her skin is golden in the firelight. Her breasts voluptuous, her nipples pert and pink. My gaze trails down her body to where we're combined, to where my cock disappears inside her. It looks so damn good.

She grips my shoulders, her nails pinching my skin again, and then she's lifting up and down my cock. Bouncing on me. It's making her wild. Her face contorts with the intensity and the noises that fly from her mouth are unconfined.

I like the way she's unconcerned, unselfconscious. She takes her pleasure with no shame, no performance, no limits.

We come together as Dray looks on. She milks my cock like she did my fingers as I fill her deep inside her cunt.

When it's over, she flops bonelessly into my arms and Dray comes to kneel before us, pressing kisses into the crook of her neck.

"See, this is how things are meant to be," I say. "Together."

"Sharing," Dray growls.

"Maybe you're right," she says. "But if you are, that means Thorne is meant to be a part of this too."

Chapter Fifty-Eight

T horne

I meet her after dinner every evening for the next few days and accompany her out to the forest to spend time with Blaze. After what happened to her, I'm taking no risks.

We don't talk about that evening or the evening she came to our tower and confessed about her dalliance with Tudor. In fact, Briony seems to understand my silence and stays away from the topic of my bond brothers, the professor and our relationship altogether. Instead, she chatters away about inconsequential things – like the food in the canteen, her lessons that day and bits of gossip she's picked up from her friends.

Talk like this would usually get under my skin and irritate me. But I don't mind listening to her talk. I like the sound of her voice. I like her presence. There's an intimate feel about this routine we're forming and as it's the closest

I'm going to come to intimacy with our thrall, I'll happily take it.

The little dragon – who is definitely no longer so little – soon understands and is there waiting for us under the trees. He's excessively excited to see Briony each time, flying circles around her head and licking at her face, and though he seems to know not to come so close to me, he does seem happy to see me too, flitting my way and yapping at me excitedly.

The days pass. I know she visits our tower but I stay away, locked in my room, trying my best not to think of what she's doing with my bond brothers and failing miserably.

The other students are more wary of me, Beaufort and Dray than usual. They know what happened to the Hardies' thrall. They know that was us. There are also rumors flying about Dray and an altercation with the Hardies in their tower. One Dray denies, although he does so with a wicked grin and an exaggerated wink. I assume there is truth in it because the Hardies are staying out of our way too – mine especially. Whatever power grabs they have in mind have been put on hold for now.

The mood in the academy shifts too. With the next trial only days away, people look more serious. There's less chatter in classrooms, the pathways are solemn and quiet and once or twice I even spot students visibly shaking.

And then it's the evening before the trial and I am unnaturally unnerved.

It isn't the mood at the academy infecting my mood. It's knowing that while any trial will prove straightforward, probably easy, for me, it will be anything of the sort for our mate.

"Briony," I say, interrupting her mid-flow as she ponders

whether Blaze's wings have grown again. She looks up at me abruptly. "I may not be able to help you in the trial this time. I've tried to gain some insight as to what they have in store for us, but I've failed." My jaw tightens. I don't like to fail. I especially don't like to fail her. "If there is the opportunity to help you I will, but there may not be that opportunity."

She stops walking and places her hands on her hips. "I don't want you to help me, Thorne. Even if there is the opportunity to do so. It's too risky."

I stare back at her and she reads absolutely in my countenance that I will ignore this order.

"Thorne, I'm serious." She lowers her voice. "You were lucky not to be caught last time. You might not be so lucky again and I won't be responsible for you being banished!" She flings her hands up into the air.

"I need to protect you. I need to keep you safe."

"You need to keep yourself safe, Thorne Cadieux," she says.

"You don't need to worry about me."

"Well," she says, shifting on her toes. "I do. Actually, I worry about you a lot. And it isn't just the guilt I'd have to endure that makes me say I don't want you to be banished," she smiles at me teasingly, "I don't want you banished because I'd miss you."

I can't help but snort at that. No one has ever missed me. There's no one left. Only my bond brothers. And they simply endure me.

"Thorne," she says, more softly and with no more teasing, "I'm serious. You're important to me. And I don't want to lose you."

I stare at her, wondering how exactly I am important to her. Because I'm useful? Strong? Powerful? Or could she possibly mean ... I shake my head.

"Briony, you already forced me to make one promise I'm unhappy about. I won't make another. If I can help you, I will and there is nothing you can say that will dissuade me."

She examines my hard features and then sighs.

"I'd better make sure I don't land myself in any trouble then, so that you won't have to help me." She starts walking again. "Do you have any idea what this trial could be?" I shake my head. "No, me neither. Clare's had us studying loads. Researching as much as we can but none of us has a hunch about this one. Still," she inhales and straightens her shoulders, "I feel prepared."

"Good," I say, although that unease still lingers in my gut.

Chapter Fifty-Nine

F^{ox}

The knock on my door is not unexpected. The question is, which of the Princes have come to see me?

"Enter," I say, watching as the door draws back and I find Beaufort Lincoln standing in the doorway.

He ducks inside, eyes scanning the darkened classroom, finding me, sitting at my desk.

"You're here to ask me if I will keep an eye on her," I say.

"It's your job to hook kids out of the trial if they're in danger."

"Last time, yes. This time, no."

He frowns. "Why?"

"That compensation is reserved for the early trials. To give the ... less able students a chance to gain their stride before things get more difficult."

"So there'll be no help this time?"

I shake my head.

"Fuck," he says, running his hands through his dark hair.

"Can't you get her to wear that damned collar?" I say, appreciating how hypocritical I'm being, because I, right from the start, have loathed the idea of her wearing one.

"What do you think?" he says, pacing. "Besides, I wonder how effective those things are anyway."

"What do you mean?"

"Just something Briony said," he mutters, "about hitting the Hardies' little bitch while she was wearing her collar."

"That shouldn't be possible."

"Yeah, maybe she misunderstood." He glances around the classroom, then back to me. "What do we do?" he says. "How do we keep her safe?"

"If you're worried about her being attacked again, I've dealt with that. It won't happen."

"I'm worried about her getting hurt in the trial," he says.

"She won't," I promise. "I'll be watching her."

"But you just said–"

"I'll keep her safe."

He examines my face. Somewhere in the depths of these dungeons water drips rhythmically and a door rattles.

"Last time, someone manipulated the trial," he says, "she was in that maze for two hours."

"I know."

"Were you watching over her then too?"

"I ... yes," I admit. "But this time is different. This time I'll be on the look out for things that aren't quite right. This time I'll be expecting an attack – even if I find it unlikely that individual will strike again."

Beaufort blows out air through his teeth.

"There isn't a way to get her out of doing the trial?"

I look him in the eye. His irises are a pale silver color that catches the light like lightning streaking across the sky. "You tell me."

He pauses. Then shakes his head. "No exceptions."

"Yeah," I say, "no exceptions."

When he's gone, I walk over to the shelves at the back of my classroom and lift down the small bottle I've hidden behind a set of books.

I hold the little bottle up to my face, peering through the glass at the contents. The concoction inside has been brewing for a week now, slowly changing from a clear liquid to a dark brown sludge.

I think it's ready.

I yank off the stopper and give it a sniff anyway. The acidic aroma catches in the back of my throat and I cough, push the stopper back into the neck and take it over to my desk.

The piece of paper Briony gave me lies flat on the surface. Although I've tried several ways to remove the black bars censoring the words, it remains as bold as ever, the words underneath still completely hidden.

However, tonight might be my lucky night. I hope so because I've scoured my books for other methods of removing the dark magic that marks this page and this is the only one left to try.

The potion itself took me an evening to combine – and that was after I'd spent two days gathering up the unusual ingredients. It's been brewing for a week.

I sit at my desk and arrange the implements I need

neatly alongside the piece of paper. A fine paint brush. A muslin cloth. A scalpel. Tweezers. Blotting paper.

I remove the stopper once again and the acidic smell swims into the air, a fine curl of dark mist rising from the bottle's neck. I dip the paint brush into the sludge and then carefully apply it to the dark mark on the page.

Almost immediately, there's a hissing sound as if the dark mark itself is hissing at me. The sound reminds me of her – fangs bared, eyes cruel – and for a moment, I wonder if she was the one who censored these passages. The hissing noise is accompanied by bright sparks and vibrant red smoke that shoots from the page.

I halt. Has it worked? Or have I messed this up? Damaged the paper, removing the hidden words forever?

I take the cloth and dab at the page. The hissing sound fades, the smoke dies away.

I squint at the page. A piece of black – no bigger than a full stop has vanished and under it the partial line of a letter.

It worked.

Dipping my paintbrush back into the bottle, I repeat the action – pausing when the hissing and sparks start again, blotting it.

I do this over and over again. Not willing to go too quickly in case I damage the fragile piece of paper. It's painstaking and dull. If I weren't so eager to learn what lies underneath, I'd push the paper to one side and resume again tomorrow. But gradually letters appear. One. Then another. And another. Then a word. Two. Three. Half a sentence. A complete one. Until finally, all the black markings are gone from the page, lifted as if they never existed at all and the writing beneath is revealed as it must once have been laid out across the page.

I stopper the bottle, placing it in my desk drawer. Then I wipe the paintbrush clean with the cloth and place those away too.

My gut is churning with curiosity and I run my hands over my face, rubbing at my tired eyes.

Then I lower my gaze to the passage and I read it.

Maybe I half-suspected what I find there.

Perhaps not. Perhaps it isn't what I expected at all.

Either way, I have some questions for Miss Storm.

I peer down at my wrist watch. It's late and tomorrow is the day of the next trial. Briony needs her sleep.

Those questions are going to have to wait.

Chapter Sixty

B riony

I wasn't entirely honest with Thorne. I may be better prepared for this trial than I was the last two – Clare's made sure of that with all the studying we've been doing – but I'm not one hundred percent recovered from that attack, even after all the healing. My legs are a little more unsteady than they were and my head is just a tad fuzzy. It's not the best way to be going into a potentially life-threatening trial.

I debate spending the entirety of the night tossing and turning, unable to sleep, but there's nothing tying me to my room now. No egg to guard, no baby dragon to tend to. Which means ...

The door to the Princes' tower stands wide open and he is waiting there in the doorway as if he was expecting me.

"Hey sweetheart," he says softly. "Couldn't sleep?" I shake my head. "Me neither."

He holds out his hand and I take it, marveling at how nice the simple act of having my hand wrapped in his feels. It's like a promise – I will take care of you, you are safe.

I stare down at our joined hands as we walk through the dark hallway, up the empty staircase and into his bedroom. His fingers are long. His fingernails are blunt. I can see the crisscross of veins beneath his fair skin. The tips of his fingers are not calloused but there's a strength in his grip and a magic that tingles against my skin.

"Where are the others?" I ask.

"Dray's out running somewhere with the other shifters. Thorne's already asleep."

"So it's just us?"

"Just us." He brushes a loose strand of hair away from my face and strokes his knuckles down my cheeks, sweeping them under my jaw and into my hair. He sweeps my braid over my shoulder and then he's untwining the band at the base and uncoiling my hair, shaking out the braid until my hair is loose.

"You know I'm going to ask you something." He runs his fingers through my hair.

"And you know the answer is going to be no."

"It would keep you safe." He cups my jaw, and this time runs the pad of his thumb against my throat, tracing the place a collar would sit. "And it would look so beautiful."

"I'll be okay," I say, even if I don't feel sure of that.

"I can't lose you, Briony," he whispers.

"You're not going to lose me." I take his hand in mine, lift it to my mouth and kiss the palm where the lines of fate traverse his skin.

"When I thought we had ... when I thought we'd lost you ..." He swallows hard. "I can't imagine my life without you in it, Briony."

"It would probably be a much more straightforward one," I tease. "Imagine, you could have had a thrall like Odessa – very obedient and more than willing to be your little pet."

He frowns. "I'm serious. I want you just the way you are."

"Even though I drive you crazy?"

"Especially because you drive me crazy. There's no one else I want, Briony. There's no one I'm ever going to want. Only you."

"Because fate has chosen me for you," I say, turning his hand over and peering down at his wrist.

"Because I love you."

I gaze up at him, utterly amazed by his words.

Love me? Beaufort Lincoln says he loves me?

A million thoughts crash through my mind. That he must be lying. That this must be a trick. That there is no way someone like him could love me. That this has always been about sex, hasn't it?

But as I stare up into his silver eyes, I can see he isn't lying. Sure, there's lust and longing in his gaze, but there is more there too. So much more.

"I ..." I mumble.

"You don't have to say it back," he says softly. He knows me well now. He understands these things are hard for me. "Not if you don't feel it."

"Beaufort," I say, "I'm falling for you. I think I could fall head over heels for you. But that feels so dangerous." Even more so than the trial tomorrow. Because where does that leave us? Fate wants us together. But there are forces even stronger than fate out there and will they pull us apart? "Loving is difficult when you risk losing the thing you care most about in the world. I've learned that the hard way."

"Which is why I'll never stop asking you to wear our collar."

I place my hands on his broad, reliable shoulders and kiss him. He hooks his arms around my waist and pulls me flush against his chest, kissing me back.

Somewhere in the room a watch ticks and the fire crackles. But all I hear is the thud of his heart.

I kiss him for what feels like an eternity. Softly, serenely, saying with the actions of my lips, the words I find so hard to say with my mouth. He scoops me up into his arms, carries me to the bed and lays me out gently on the mattress.

"You'll stay tonight?" he asks. "The whole night with me, Briony?"

"Yes," I say and then we're wriggling out of our clothes, and I'm in his arms again. His body is heavy and warm against mine and I open my thighs, allowing him to lie between them. He kisses me, cradling his arms around me, brushing his fingers over my cheeks again as if he wants to map the contours of my face. He nudges at my entrance and I open my thighs wider letting him sink into me; an action that has us both groaning.

"You're so beautiful," he tells me over and over again as he fucks me slowly, languidly, as if we have all the time in the world and tomorrow isn't looming over us like a thunderous cloud.

I trace my hand up and down his strong back, lift my hips to meet his tender thrusts, whisper nonsense words in his ears, kiss his cheeks as he kisses mine, hold him close like I don't want to let him go.

Because I don't.

I want to stay here in this perfect moment, with him buried inside me, with his weight pressing me into the mattress, with his mouth on my skin. I want to stay suspended in this paradise and never ever leave.

I wake early next morning with Beaufort's arms still wrapped around me.

"Hey," he says, yawning as I stir. "You okay?"

"Uh huh." I peer towards the murky light filtering around the gaps in the blinds and roll up to sitting, stretching my arms above my head. "It looks like it's time for me to go though."

"Urgh," he groans, "don't go." He pulls me back down and kisses my mouth. I sigh because this is bliss. But unfortunately I can't stay. I squirm out of his arms and sit up again.

"I really do have to go. There's no other choice."

"At least stay for breakfast."

I shake my head. "I promised I'd meet my friends. But I will take advantage of your warm shower."

"Ahhh so this is the real reason you stayed the night."

"Absolutely," I say, bending down to kiss him again before I dart towards the bathroom.

"Can I join you?" he calls after me.

"I think that would be a bad idea. You'd make me late."

"I can behave."

I peer over my shoulder at him, catching him in the middle of ogling my ass. "Can you really?"

He grins at me and flops back down on the mattress. "Nope."

I race into the bathroom, locking the door behind me – not that a locked door would stop Beaufort Lincoln if he wanted to come in – because I don't want to be late for my friends today of all days and Beaufort is too much of a distraction.

When I emerge ten minutes later (after a shower that was ten times longer than my usual freezing cold one), I find him sitting on the edge of his bed, dressed in a pair of boxers.

"I made you a coffee." He points at a steaming mug on the bedside table. "And found all your clothes."

"Coffee?" I say. Just like chocolate, coffee is prohibitively expensive. We never had any back in Slate and the commoners' canteen certainly doesn't serve it. The bitter aroma wafts across the room towards me and tickles my nose.

"Does it taste nice?" I ask wrinkling up my nose as I slide on my panties and hook on my bra.

"Don't tell me you never had it? I couldn't live without this stuff." He picks up the mug and carries it over to me. "Here, try."

I give it another sniff. "Ewww."

"Seriously, it's good stuff and it'll wake you up better than a bucket of cold water thrown over your head." I do feel sleepy after that warm shower – and because I spent half of the night fucking Beaufort – although it didn't feel like fucking last night. It felt much deeper than that. I may even understand why they now call it making love. My cheeks warm at the idea – it sounds so cheesy and yet so true.

He holds the mug to my lips and I take a sip. The taste is dark and bitter, but I like it. I like it a lot, especially the way it has my head buzzing almost immediately. Maybe my taste in hot beverages is not that different from my taste in men.

"Mmmm, actually that is good."

"Told you," he says, settling back down on the mattress and watching me dress.

When I'm dressed completely, I tip back the mug and swallow the last remaining dregs, then hand the cup back to Beaufort.

"I guess I'll see you after the trial."

He nods and we stare at each other. My heart suddenly feels heavy. What if I never see him again? But I push that thought aside. The Princes are the most powerful shadow weavers in the academy. They will breeze through this trial, whatever it may be.

"Take care of yourself, Briony Storm," he tells me.

"Likewise, Beaufort Lincoln," I tell him back.

Waiting for me in the hallway by the front door, I find Dray and Thorne.

"You're up early," I say, trying my best to sound bright and breezy, hoping if I fake it I'll eventually feel it.

"Didn't want to miss you, Kitten," Dray says, before stepping forward and wrapping me in one massive, tight hug, burying his nose in my neck and taking a deep inhale. "You be careful, okay?"

"I will," I say, hugging him back.

When he finally releases me, I peer up at Thorne. His features are blank and emotionless as always but he holds my gaze in his.

"Remember, what I said, Briony."

"You too," I whisper and then because I can't stand this anymore, I rush out of the door and walk quickly back to my tower. I don't like this sense of doom. It makes no sense. Do I just feel this way because I have more to lose this time round, more I hold dear?

I try not to think about it as I change into my gray tracksuit – repaired and patched up by Fly. Instead, I try my best to go over everything we've been learning and reading instead. Even before Thorne helped me in the maze, I was doing well. I had a plan. And though I arrived last at the academy in the very first trial, I was one of the few commoners who didn't receive a beating. I can do this. I'm sure I can.

Once I'm dressed, I go knock for Fly and we climb down the tower steps silently, my friend slipping his arm through mine as we walk across to the canteen.

Clare is waiting for us at our usual table, an untouched bowl of porridge laid out in front of her.

"How you doing, Clare Bear?" Fly asks her as he takes his seat.

"You know, nervous," she says, trying to smile as she pushes her glasses up her nose.

"Did you manage to sleep?" I ask her. "Or were you up all night studying?"

"Erm," she says, running her spoon through her porridge. "Well ..."

Fly leans forward onto his elbow. "Did something happen?"

My mild-mannered friend looks up at us both with a wide, exuberant grin full of joy.

"Jeez," I gasp, "what happened?"

"Damian and I spent the night together," she whispers. "We went all the way!"

"All the way to where?" Fly says, feigning ignorance.

"To heaven and back I'd surmise by the smile on her face," I say, punching Fly's arm. Then I reach over the table and grab Clare's hand. "I'm so happy for you. Was it good? Did you enjoy it? Are you like a thing now?"

"It was good," she pulls a face, "I mean it took a bit of trying to make it work." Fly sniggers and I kick him under the table. "And it wasn't like earth-shattering like they'd have you believe in the romance novels but it felt really special."

"It's your first time," I tell her. "It'll get better with practice – especially when you're so into each other."

"We are." I squeeze her hand, knowing exactly how she feels, and we both sit there caught in a bubble of loved-up bliss. That is until Fly goes and pops it.

"What do you mean you couldn't get it to work? Is his dick crooked or something?" He's eyes grow round in his head. "Or does he have a massive cock?!"

"I have no complaints," Clare tells him, returning to her now lumpy and cold porridge.

"I'm really pleased for you, Clare Bear," Fly says. "Especially as this means you won't have to die a virgin."

"Clare is not going to–"

"That's why we decided to do it. No point in waiting. Especially as we could both be dead by the end of today."

"No one is going to die!" I say, assuredly.

"Oh," Clare says, adjusting her glasses.

"What?" I say.

"Statistically, this is the trial you're most likely to die in. I looked at the numbers."

"Why would you do that?" Fly cries.

"Morbid fascination." Clare shrugs.

"No one is going to die," I repeat, hoping with all my heart, I am correct.

Chapter Sixty-One

B riony

The next trial is set up in much the same way as the last. We're told to gather on the field, once again penned into sections with students from our existing quarters. At least, us students from Slate, Granite and Iron are here. The area assigned for the shadow weavers remains completely empty. Except for one student, standing in the cold, eyes fixed ahead. Thorne.

Seeing him there makes my heart flutter, because I can't help thinking he's there for me. A feeling that's only confirmed when he glances my way, catching my gaze and giving me a determined nod I'm sure is meant to reassure me.

I wish it would. But not only do I have to worry about myself in this trial, I'm now also worrying about him. Somehow, I have to make it through without him having to resort to helping me.

Beyond where Thorne waits, the stands have once again been erected as well as the large fence blocking our view of whatever lies beyond.

While we wait, shivering in the cold, the day overcast and the odd snowflake swirling in the wind, the dignitaries and representatives from the different quarters start to arrive, filling up the stands.

From the very back of the group of Slate students, I watch them take their seats, some gazing our way, pointing out various people. There's no sign of the Empress yet or any of the teachers and I wonder how much longer they'll keep us waiting. It's all part of the game – ensuring we're all so nervous we can barely walk.

The snow begins to fall in clumps, catching in my eyelashes and in my hair and making me shiver even harder. I blow on my fingers and stamp my feet and try to concentrate on all the things Clare attempted to drill into my brain.

"Where's your collar, Storm?" I jolt. Stanley is standing right beside me. I was so lost in my thoughts, I hadn't even noticed him.

His voice is low and he stares straight ahead as if he doesn't want anyone to spot he's talking to me.

Is that because he still considers me scum and too lowly to be seen with? Or is it because at this moment the other shadow weavers come striding across the field to take their places in their area, the snow somehow failing to fall on their heads.

"Why?" I ask him. "Were you hoping to steal it? I don't think it would work for you."

He snorts. "Didn't you see how many points I earned in the last two trials, Storm? I'm on my way out of this," his lip curls as he motions at the other Slate students in front of us, "and am on my way to Iron."

"Congratulations," I say sarcastically. "I'm so happy for you."

"Shame you won't be joining me," he snarls.

"Shame? I thought you'd be rather happy about that."

He shrugs. "I don't know. We had some fun times, didn't we?"

He lands his hand on my shoulder, and his touch is so repulsive to me, I jolt on reflex. He snatches his hand away with a quiet hiss as if I burned him.

"You weren't always so jumpy," he whispers. "You used to like my hands on you."

I gaze up at him in absolute disbelief. He's been treating me like I'm some kind of diseased vermin ever since that glow up meant he could throw his weight around back in Slate. He's avoided me, barely spoken to me and when he has, more times than most, his words have been accompanied by his fists. But now, he's looking at the time we spent together – those brief few weeks where he was into me and I was into him – with ... what? Fondness?

Is that because I now belong to the Princes and in his eyes that means I'm worth something?

I scowl at him.

"That isn't exactly how I remember it."

"Yeah, you were pretty inexperienced back then. Not exactly the best lay." His hard gaze flicks down to meet mine and there is definitely no fondness in his eyes. They are vindictive and cruel. "I've heard that's changed now though. I've heard you've become quite the slut." He slides his tongue along his lower lip and his gaze down my body. "So if you ever find you want to hang out ..."

He lets his words hang unfinished in the cold air.

I don't bother to respond, I push through the crowd of students to the front of the group, away from him.

What the hell?! Where did he get that idea from? Is he just making assumptions based on the fact me and the Princes are now hanging out? Or have the Princes been talking about what we've been doing?

He wouldn't be wrong in his obvious assumptions but that doesn't mean I want people talking about me in that way. It doesn't mean I want the Princes discussing the intimacies of our time together with their friends. Bragging about it. The idea makes me sick.

My cheeks burn and my heart hammers. I peer back over to the shadow weaver section and spy Dray and Beaufort laughing and joking with a group of other boys. Are they talking about me now?

But I don't get a chance to finish those thoughts because the academy staff are now parading out to the field. Madame Bardin, dressed in a black fur-lined cloak, climbs up onto the raised platform as Fox takes his seat in the stands.

"Welcome students to the third Firestone trial. Your hardest yet. For in this trial you will face your greatest fear." Inwardly, I groan. That doesn't sound good. "As before," the Madame continues, "you will be called forward one at a time in the following order, and admitted to the trial site." She waves her hand and the list from before appears – only this time everyone's scores are included alongside their name. A big fat zero against mine.

There's some murmuring among the students and from behind me I hear Stanley gloating about the number of points he's earned. I ball my hands into fists. He didn't even complete the maze and I did.

Madame claps her hands and glares at us all, everyone falling silent.

"The same rules apply as before. You'll have an hour to complete the task. You are not permitted to take any equipment into the trial with you. And you are not to provide aid to others or accept help from another student." She glowers down at me with such ferocity, several students turn their heads to see who exactly she is glaring at. When they spot it's me, murmuring ripples across the groups and Madame Bardin seems perfectly happy to stand and wait for it to peter out this time.

When finally, there's silence again, she claps her hands. *"By trial and truth, your Quarter calls."*

"Where's the Empress?" I hear one of the Slate students beside me whisper to her friend.

"No idea. Maybe she doesn't turn up to every trial," her friend whispers back just as Thorne's name booms over the field.

I watch as he strides calmly towards the giant fence, everyone else watching him too. There is something about the shadow weaver that is mesmerizing. His entire body seems to crackle with energy and power. It radiates from him in pulverizing waves. Thorne Cadieux, the most powerful shadow weaver in the academy. Probably one of the most powerful shadow weavers in the realm.

Over the distance it's harder to see the burden that places on his shoulders. The burden that costs him daily. When I'm with him, it's all I see.

Beaufort and Dray follow soon afterwards and then all the other shadow weavers in quick succession.

The snow turns heavier, beginning to land on the ground and covering the field in a blanket of white.

My teeth rattle as the Iron Quarter kids step forward, then Granite and then us.

Stanley goes first, being sure to knock right into me as he pushes through our group.

And then it's just me again waiting for my turn.

I glance over at Fox but he's not watching me. His eyes are locked on the Madame, sitting in the Empress's chair at the front of the stand, laughing and flirting with the men sitting around her.

Disappointment gurgles in my stomach. I could have done with one last nod of reassurance, possibly even a thumbs up. Anything would do. But nothing comes my way from the professor and before I know it, my name is called and my legs move automatically towards the door in the giant fence.

Twin one is there waiting. Whistle swinging around his neck.

He opens the door, pushes me through and slams it behind me.

And I am no longer at the academy.

I am in Slate Quarter.

Chapter Sixty-Two

B riony

I blink.

My eyes are deceiving me. They must be. Because it's not possible to be at the academy one second and here in the yard of our house the next. I am not a shadow weaver. I cannot displace. This has to be an illusion. Except, it's so real, so vivid.

The wind blowing through the yard and into my face, the same bitterly cold wind that always blows through Slate, chilling me right through to the bone. And the smell, the smell is the same too. Rancid, the air full of that thick choking smoke that gets into your eyes and mouth, sticking to your tongue, the taste of decay.

I stare down at my feet and it's the frozen mud of our yard, covered in a fine dusting of dirty frost. I stamp my foot hard on the earth and it doesn't shatter into a thousand pieces, doesn't melt away into ash. It's solid ground.

In the distance, I can hear the chug of the factories, the creak of machinery, the battering of the mining drills. The same as always.

There is no doubt about it. Home.

And when I lift my gaze, who do I find waiting for me on the far side of the yard? My step-mother.

Muriel.

Muriel right there, apron tied around her waist, gray shapeless dress beneath, brown stockings pulled up to her knees, old ratty boots on her feet. Her graying hair hangs limply and unwashed on her shoulders and she's tied an old rag around her head, and there is dirt in the tired creases of her face.

She observes me with her cold blue eyes and the permanent scowl on her face grows more pronounced. She reaches for the old broom resting against the tatty fence and grips it with both hands like a weapon.

"You brat," she snarls, and her voice is so loud, so real, this can't be an illusion, some misfiring of my brain. I'm back home, back in the nightmare.

Or maybe I've awoken and everything else was a dream. Maybe there never were any Princes, no friends – no Beaufort or Dray, Thorne or Fox, Fly or Clare. Maybe I invented it all in my sad lonely brain.

Fear spirals down my spine, because I'm back here, where I belong, where every moment is painful and so very lonely.

"Where have you been?" she asks me. "I've been calling your name for hours!"

She shakes the broom violently in her hands and takes a menacing pace towards me.

I attempt to back away from her, but my legs are like jello. They won't move. I'm frozen as always, unable to defend myself against this woman who hates me with every bone in her body.

"I ... I ..." I mutter, clutching my hands in front of me and wringing them.

Where have I been? What have I been doing? What can I say that won't make her angry with me? What excuse can I make that won't provoke her into a rage?

But I've never known the answer to that. Every word I've ever uttered has displeased her.

"Forget it. I don't want to hear your pathetic excuses. Leaving me to do all the hard work, shirking your duties. Lazy little bitch. Think you're too good for this place, do you?"

She marches closer and I see the menace shining in her eyes. I see it in the cruel smile pinned to her face. This is all a game to her. One that's rigged in her favor. One I can never win no matter how hard I try, no matter how hard I work.

"What's wrong, Briony? Cat got your tongue?" She snorts. "Or are you deaf as well as stupid? Can't even string a simple sentence together. Now," she glares at me, broom gripped in her hands like a threat, "I asked you a question. Where have you been?"

I try to open my mouth and speak – to move my tongue and my lips but they're stuck like glue and no sound emits from my throat.

I don't need to stay here and take this, though. I don't need to bear it. I can run, run far far away. Except my legs are as useless as my mouth. They refuse to move, frozen in a terror that grips every cell of my body.

"Not even an apology? You're going to pay for your laziness and your disrespect. I'm going to make you pay."

My legs shake. I know what's coming. I know what she is going to do.

The same thing she's done to me over and over again.

I try to recall if it's always been like this. Was there ever a time when we were friends? When she cared for me like a stepmother should? Did she beat me that very first day my father brought her home, or was it something that came on gradually? First a slap, then a punch, then finally the broom. I don't even remember anymore.

I let my face fall blank and I gaze out over her head, into the distance. Our home stands behind her, the paint peeling from the rotting wood, the panes of glass in the windows so dirty they're black. This house is no more welcoming than the woman herself.

I will not cry. I will not beg.

I will float away to my place of safety, where she cannot reach me, where I won't feel the pain.

Except this time I can't. I can't find that sanctuary. My brain is alert, taking in every word and her words penetrate loud and clear. Her horrid face is vivid in front of me.

"Nobody wants you here, you silly little brat," she snarls. "We don't need another mouth to feed. You're a waste of food and you're a waste of space. You would have been better off dying with your worthless mother. Dying like your whore of a sister did."

I blink again.

Usually those words would stab me like a thousand knives right in my heart. My sister, my precious sister. The mother I never knew. Haven't I longed to join them so many, many times?

But today, those words don't hurt.

Today they make me angry.

Raging, full on, freaking angry.

This woman was meant to care for me, to look after me. A little kindness. That wasn't so much to ask for. Instead, she chose to abuse and mistreat me at every opportunity.

I didn't deserve that. It wasn't my fault. It wasn't ever my fault.

"My mother wasn't worthless," I hiss, my hands shaking too now because I've never spoken back to her. I've never found that courage. Not once. I've only ever wanted to please her so she wouldn't hurt me anymore. Not today. Today, I tell her exactly what I think. "And you're the whore, not my sister. A cruel, miserable whore who deserves to rot in hell. And I will put you there if you come one step nearer."

The smile falters on Muriel's face, but she doesn't heed my warning. She swings back her broom to hit me.

I try to jump back, to duck away. I'm too slow. The first swing catches my shoulder but I don't feel it, and I manage to dart away from her next swing.

"Hold still, you silly bitch," she grunts, her face red with rage, her piggy little eyes bulging in their sockets as she swings the broom about frantically and I dart from side to side. Most of the hits I avoid, but one more catches me on the shoulder and another around the face. "You worthless bitch. Nobody wants you. Nobody loves you."

I freeze. Because that isn't true. Not anymore. Beaufort Lincoln says he loves me. I have four fated mates who want me. I even have friends, actual friends. And all that was real. It wasn't an illusion, it wasn't a dream.

I raise my arm and catch the broom in my hand.

She tries to wrestle it from my grip and the two of us tussling over the old broom – its bristles bent and missing, the handle cracked – makes for such a ridiculous spectacle that I laugh. She looks at me in horror, like I've lost my mind. And for the very first time, I see her for what she is. Not the demon, the monster, the witch, I've always feared, but a bitter old woman with nobody and no one who loves her – who even likes her. Not even my father, who I doubt remembers her name on most days. A bitter old woman so desperate she married a drunk from the dirtiest, poorest part of the most worthless Quarter in the realm.

I grip the broom-handle with both my hands and push her backwards.

"I'm not afraid of you," I spit. "Not anymore."

And just like that, as if my words are potent magic, my stepmother dissipates into smoke, curling away on the breeze. I watch as she's carried up into the sky and far, far away.

Then the broom in my hand melts away too, along with the yard.

And I realize it *was* all an illusion.

Was it part of the trial then? And if so, is it over now? Did I complete it?

I spin around on the spot, expecting to find myself back on the academy field, expecting twin number two to start blowing his whistle in my face and sending me on my way.

But I'm not.

Chapter Sixty-Three

B riony

I'm somewhere else, somewhere I don't recognize. The ground is hard like home but it's warm beneath my feet and the landscape is barren. No trees, no flowers, no grass. Not even any houses. Just hard brown earth and the wind hot and full of sandy dust.

I raise my hand to my eyes, shielding them from the glare of the startling sun, and peer across the landscape.

"Hello?" I call out, my voice coming back to me in a hollow echo.

Is this part of the trial again? Another round, the next level.

Far away in the distance, silhouetted against the vast blue sky and only just visible to my eyes, a lone figure crouches down low at the horizon.

Is that my next challenge? I swing my gaze around, there is no one else here – nothing else here!

I cross the empty landscape and as I come closer, I see the man is cowering on his knees, his hands crossed over his head.

For a moment, I think he's praying, then I hear a cry of such anguish it permeates right through to my bones.

I squint, trying to make out what's wrong. Is he hurt?

Then a crack of wings like thunder catches my attention. I tip back my head and look up into the bright dazzling sky.

The dark silhouettes of sinister shapes loom above. They circle like vultures and then, with vicious shrieks, dive at the man as he trembles in terror.

Dragons?

But I know they are not. They are more human than reptilian and there is something unsettling about their form. They aren't solid, as if their bodies are made from air and not flesh. They are long and thin and bony, their large scaly wings fanned out behind them, twisted horns crowning their heads.

These dark shapes slash at the man's head with pointed beaks and sharp talons, tearing through his flesh and ripping his skin to shreds.

The noise they make is hellish too, halfway between high-pitched wails and unbearable shrieks. I cover my ears, pain reverberating around my skull. But even still the sound of the injured man reaches me.

"No! No!" the man sobs. "I didn't mean to. Please, I didn't mean to hurt them. I was trying to save them. I didn't want that to happen."

I freeze on the spot.

Because I know that voice. I know it well.

The voice is Thorne's.

I squint my eyes.

Is it him? Is it really him? Or is this just another illusion? Like before, will he dissolve away into dust?

But like before, it's real, so vivid and once again a terror grips my body.

The monsters swoop down, attacking him with no mercy and no pause.

He doesn't fight back, doesn't try to brush them away, doesn't try to shield himself. Thorne just trembles and cowers on the ground. He doesn't even try to defend himself.

I don't understand. What's wrong? Why isn't he fighting? Why doesn't he blast them away with his powers?

"Thorne!" I yell over the distance, running towards him before I've even registered what I'm doing. Because what am I doing? This might not even be real. And what exactly can I do to help? I'm weak, powerless. I might be able to stand up to an old woman with a broom, but five, six, seven monsters? There is nothing I can do.

That doesn't stop me. I run as fast as my legs will carry me, my feet pounding the hard earth, calling his name as I do, begging him to get up and fight.

The monsters lift their heads, peer towards me but they take no notice, too busy with their prey, their jaws and their claws covered in Thorne's blood. It's pouring from his body, pooling on the ground around him. Scarlet against the dull brown earth.

"Leave him alone!" I shriek. "Leave him alone!"

But the monsters take no notice.

The distance closes. I keep running. I can see I will be too late. He's no longer crying out. No longer moving at all.

His body is lifeless. His head flops from side to side as the monsters slice at his flesh.

Thick bile lines my throat and the terror I feel is so vast it may drown me completely. Because I can't lose him. Not Thorne. Not beautiful, wonderful, tortured Thorne.

"No!" I sob, my feet slowing. "No! Thorne! Get up! Get the hell up. Get up and fight."

It's no use. They're going to kill him and I will have to stand here and watch and do nothing.

"NO!!" I scream with all my might.

No, I won't let that happen. I will not lose another person who I love.

And I do. I love him. I know it now deep in my soul. It's why he has the marks. It's because I love him and I can't lose him.

I charge towards the monsters feeding on my protector, lifting my hands as I do.

Anger and fear crash through my body, and all the pain, all the damn, damn pain, careens along my veins, shoots down into my fingertips, and then it's there streaking towards the monsters. A light so bright it dazzles my eyes. More radiant than the sun.

It hits the dark forms of the monsters and blasts them away from Thorne.

They squeal in pain, flames erupting across their large, outstretched wings.

"NO!" I scream again, the light shooting from my hands with a force I can't control. That I don't want to control. The flames race along the monsters' wings, curling into their bodies, burning them alive until soon they are completely consumed by fire. They twist and screech in the air, clawing at their burning bodies. The flames eat and eat at them. And then they are nothing but ash, fluttering to the ground like gray snowflakes.

The light races back into my hands, hitting my body with a force that leaves me gasping. I peer at my hands.

Did I do that?

Was that me?

Thorne!

I rush closer to him, falling to my knees by his side. He's a bloody mess, his skin ripped to shreds, and I can't tell if he's alive or dead.

I reach out my hand to touch him and his eyes flick open.

Horror registers over his face as he takes me in.

"Briony, don't touch me!" he croaks, his voice broken, hardly more audible than a whisper. "Please don't touch me."

"Thorne," I whimper. He's alive but barely. And for how long?

I flip back my head, curl my hands around my mouth and yell up into the wide sky. "Help us! Please somebody help us!"

The world swirls away again, Thorne and the blood-stained earth melting away before my eyes.

And then I'm kneeling in the snow. The forest of the academy right before me. The sky dark with the approaching dusk.

A hand lands on my shoulder.

"Come with me. Quickly!"

Chapter Sixty-Four

F^{ox}

I yank her up onto her feet, curling my arm around her waist, pulling my cloak around her shoulders and dragging her towards the academy.

Her frame trembles uncontrollably and when she looks up into my face, hers is as pale as the snow.

She yanks back at me weakly, trying to resist my effort to drag her away.

"No," she shakes her head in desperation. "No, Thorne. He's hurt. Dying. I've got to go back. I've got to help him. We've got to help him."

There are tears on her face, running down her cheeks. Her green eyes are wild and full of fear. I grip her shoulders and shake her.

"Briony, he's going to be okay," I reassure her. Then I

wrap my arm around her again and pull her along, searching the darkness for whoever may be lurking in the shadows.

Did she see? Does she know?

"Fox," she cries, stumbling in the snow, "he was dying!"

"Briony," I say sternly, "the others have him. He will be okay. You, on the other hand ..."

"Me?" she says in obvious shock, her wide eyes finding mine.

"Come on," I growl.

I lead her the back way, avoiding others as I best I can, relief flooding my chest when we reach the staircase and I pull her down to the dungeon.

Once we're inside my room, I lock the door with the strongest spells I know, then guide her to the chair before my desk, setting the flames roaring in the fireplace and striding over to the shelves at the back of the classroom. I retrieve a bottle of whisky hidden behind the books and two tumblers. Then I return to where she is sitting, shaking and sobbing.

I pour a stiff drink for her and one for me.

"Here," I say, holding it out to her as I knock back my own.

She peers down into the amber liquid, back up at me and attempts to stand, but her legs give way under her and I'm forced to catch her by the elbow.

I push her straight back down into her seat.

"I need to know he's all right."

"He is all right. I already told you. His bond brothers have him." I hold out the glass. "Now drink this. It will calm your nerves."

She tries to take it from my hand, but her arm trembles so much the liquid sloshes over the rim and I take it back in my hand and lift it to her lips, tipping the alcohol between them. She sips, her wet eyes watching me. When the glass is empty, I wipe the tears from her cheeks with the pad of my thumb. She's shaking a little less now but her face is still full of fear.

"W-w-w-what happened?" she says. "I don't understand what happened."

"You tell me," I say, pouring myself another drink.

She pulls my cloak tight around her body. There is blood on her knees but other than that she looks unharmed. Not a scratch on her. Completely different to how she looked after that last trial.

She rubs at her head, as her teeth chatter together.

"It's all right, sweetheart," I tell her. "You're safe now. You're safe with me."

She shudders, then seems to find the resilience to answer me. "I stepped through the fence and I was back there – in Slate."

I nod. "And what was there with you?"

"Who," she corrects, swallowing. "Muriel, my stepmother."

"The trial was set up for you to face your greatest fear," I explain. "Is she ... did she ..."

"She used to beat me," she says, motioning to the glass. I fill it up, then lift it to her mouth again and she takes another swig.

"The scars," I say.

"Yes."

I frown, my eyes scanning her form once again. Did I miss something? Is she hurt and I didn't realize? "Did she beat you?" I ask gently.

"No, she tried to, but I stopped her." She yanks my cloak tight around her. "I found I wasn't afraid of her anymore."

A smile hovers on my lips. That's my girl. Brave. Determined.

But then I remember.

"And what happened next?"

"I thought that would be the end of the trial."

"It should have been," I growl.

"But then I was somewhere else – somewhere I didn't recognize. And Thorne was there on his knees. And these *things*," horror radiates across her face, "these monsters were attacking him, killing him – and he wasn't fighting back, he wasn't trying to get away." Her eyes, far away one moment as she relives it, connect with mine. "What did it mean?"

"I don't know." I take a deep breath in. "Briony, what happened next?"

She looks at me with incredulity. "I ... I ..." Her body starts to shake again. "I don't know. I don't know. It never happened before. I don't understand how it happened. I ..." She closes her eyes and I wait for the moment to pass. Gradually, the shaking of her body ceases.

Sighing, I walk over to my desk, open the drawer and pull out the piece of paper from the book. I lift it up so she can see the page, the firelight dancing over the text.

"I removed the censorship."

"You did?" She hesitates, then stands and hobbles towards me, holding out a trembling hand to take the paper from me. "What does it say?"

I move closer to her, grip her chin and tip back her head so she's looking right into my eyes, so she can't look away when she answers me.

"I think you know what it says, Briony. I think you've always known."

I expect her to deny it, feign surprise, at least attempt to deflect.

She doesn't. She holds my gaze, something steely in hers. The fear dissipated.

"I don't know for sure. But I have my suspicions."

"And what do you suspect?" I ask, my eyes searching hers, my fingers stroking along her jaw.

She swallows.

"I suspect, Professor, that in that lesson," she pauses, "they discovered that my sister was special."

It's what she told me right from the start. It's what she's always said. And yet I never questioned it, never asked what she meant by that. Just dismissed her words far too easily. Because the people closest to us are always special to us, aren't they?

But maybe that isn't how she meant it.

"Special, how?"

"My sister could shadow weave."

I hold her gaze, losing myself in the deep green of her eyes.

"You already knew," I say.

She nods her head. "She showed me." Briony closes her eyes as if she's remembering it. "My sister could make the faintest of shadows dance across the palm of her hand. That's all, but it meant so much to us. It was like this beacon of hope. It was our secret. We never told a soul. Not even our dad. It was going to be our ticket out of Slate – together. She planned to show them what she could do when she arrived at the academy. She believed they'd teach her how to harness her powers and then she'd be whisked away to Onyx – and she'd take me with her." She opens her eyes and the green of her irises is so dazzling for a moment, I'm breathless. "That's what she believed would happen. What did the book say?"

"Exactly that. During the lesson, your sister was able to

weave shadows. A girl from Slate who shouldn't have any powers at all."

"But she did and that's why they killed her."

"Perhaps," I say, and she jolts a little as if she was expecting me to argue with her.

But how can I? The trial was manipulated yet again. Once could be dismissed as a mistake. Twice a coincidence? I don't believe in those. It looks like someone is trying to hurt Briony – and not just petty jealous students. Someone powerful. Someone like Veronica. I assumed she attacked Briony last time because she is no better than the students. Just as jealous. Just as spiteful. But now I know there is more to this story.

A lot more.

"And you?"

Her body starts to shake like before. Her words come out in a desperate rush.

"It never happened before ... I didn't know I had the power ... never suspected that I could shadow weave."

I peer towards the door. There is no one there and yet even walls can have ears.

Was I the only one who saw? Am I the only one who knows?

And if I wasn't – if someone else saw – if Veronica saw – is Briony right? Will they come for her like they did her sister?

I lean closer, my mouth brushing against her left ear and making her shiver.

"That wasn't shadow weaving, Miss Storm," I tell her, my voice barely a whisper, "that was something else."

***** End of Book 2 *****

. . .

Briony's story will continue in book 3 of the Firestone Academy series, ***Taste of Thorns***.

If you can't wait that long, you can find a bonus scene on my website — it's where you'll find all my bonus content as well as **special editions** of these books!

Want somewhere to discuss this story and chat with other readers? Come join my exclusive reader Facebook group.

If you enjoyed this story, please consider leaving a rating or review — it's a huge help to indie authors like me!

Also by Hannah Haze

All available on Amazon and Kindle Unlimited.

Paranormal RH romance
The Firestone Academy
Storm of Shadows
Spark of Sorcery
Taste of Thorns

The Arrow Hart Academy
Fractured Fates
Twisted Ties
Shattered Stars
Burdened Bonds
Destined Dawn

Contemporary RH omegaverse
The Rockview Omegaverse
Pack Rivals Part I
Pack Rivals Part II
Pack Choice

About the Author

A recovering cynic, Hannah grew up swearing she would never marry. Then in 2001, she met her husband and has been a card-carrying romantic ever since. Despite being an avid writer and reader, Hannah decided to do the sensible thing and study science at university, putting authoring ideas to one side.This all changed when she discovered the joys of a good romance book and came to the realisation that love stories are always the best ones.

She now uses her knowledge of chemical bonds and reactions to ensure her books are full of sparks. In fact the electricity between her characters is sure to set your pulse racing and your heart fluttering.

Hannah loves reading to her three children, including doing all the silly voices, and going for long walks in the countryside (the muddier the better). Her head is always full of new story ideas and you are most likely to find her avoiding the demands of her very naughty cat as she attempts to write them all down.

Sign up to my newsletter:
www.hannahhaze.com/about

Join my reader groups:

https://www.facebook.com/groups/hannahhazehotro
mancereads

https://www.facebook.com/groups/softandsteamy
omegaverse

Visit my website:
www.hannahhaze.com

Catch me on TikTok:
www.tiktok.com/@hannahhaze_author

Acknowledgments

As always I have lots of people to thank who have helped me along the way...

Firstly, a massive thank you to my readers for all the love book one received and for sticking with me on this journey into book 2. It's just getting interesting, huh?

Another massive thank you to my amazing beta reader team who help me to make my stories so much better. Thank you Kiki, Courtney, Sara, Aimee, Donna, Jenna, Jessie, Brandy, Leandri, Tara, Leslie and Melissa.

Thank you to Christian for another gorgeous cover, to James for finding all the typos and my PA team at Dragonfire for all their support.

And finally, thank you to Mr. D, Stephy, my children and the rest of my family. Love you all x